Milly Johnson was born, rais South Yorkshire. A *Sunday* the Top 10 Female Fiction au millions of copies of her boo writing highlights the importa.... ...community spirit and the magic of kindness. Her books inspire and uplift but she packs a punch and never shies away from the hard realities of life and the complexities of relationships in her stories. Her books champion women, their strength and resilience, and celebrate love, friendship and the possibility and joy of second chances and renaissances.

Find out more at www.millyjohnson.co.uk or follow her on X @millyjohnson or Instagram @themillyjohnson.

Milly Johnson

The *Mother* of all Christmases

SIMON &
SCHUSTER

London · New York · Sydney · Toronto · New Delhi

First published in Great Britain by Simon & Schuster UK Ltd, 2018
This paperback edition published 2024

Copyright © Millytheink Limited, 2018

The right of Milly Johnson to be identified as author
of this work has been asserted in accordance with the
Copyright, Designs and Patents Act, 1988.

1 3 5 7 9 10 8 6 4 2

Simon & Schuster UK Ltd
1st Floor
222 Gray's Inn Road
London WC1X 8HB

Simon & Schuster: Celebrating 100 Years of Publishing in 2024

Simon & Schuster Australia, Sydney
Simon & Schuster India, New Delhi

www.simonandschuster.co.uk
www.simonandschuster.com.au
www.simonandschuster.co.in

A CIP catalogue record for this book
is available from the British Library

Paperback ISBN: 978-1-3985-3514-5
eBook ISBN: 978-1-4711-6192-6
Audio ISBN: 978-1-4711-6317-3

Typeset in the UK by M Rules
Printed and Bound in the UK using 100% Renewable
Electricity at CPI Group (UK) Ltd

MIX
Paper | Supporting
responsible forestry
FSC
www.fsc.org FSC® C171272

The *Mother* of all Christmases

Paul's Gift

On 6 April 2018, my friend Clair's much loved husband Paul King died suddenly of an undetected brain tumour. Paul left behind a young daughter, Sammy aged twelve, and an even younger son, Bob aged nine.

Paul King gave people more precious gifts than Santa, because – in the actual words of his wife – 'He was an organ donor (the silly arse signed up twice!) He saved four lives the day after he died. The kids are referring to him as a hero – they are very proud.'

From the official letter sent to Clair from the NHS Blood and Transplant Authority:

> 'A gentleman in his late twenties who had been on the transplant waiting list for almost eleven years has received a kidney transplant. The other kidney has helped a gentleman in his mid-thirties who had been on the waiting list for around two months.

A gentleman in his late sixties was able to receive pancreas islets which are the cells that help the body to produce insulin, this will undoubtedly improve this gentleman's quality of life.

A lady in her early thirties was able to receive a liver transplant thanks to Paul's generous donation.

You and your family also kindly agreed to tissue donation which means that Paul was able to donate his heart tissue and eye tissue. Unlike organs, tissues are stored for a period of time before being matched and allocated to suitable recipients. As a result of this we are unable to provide you with any further information about those that will benefit from Paul's gift at this point in time. However, further information may be available in the future.

I hope that this brings you some comfort and that you feel proud of the difference Paul has made to others through the gift of organ donation.

Thank you once again and please know that Paul's gift can never be underestimated.'

It has been a great comfort to Sammy and Bob that their dad lives on in others and not just in them.

Be a hero like Paul King.
1971–2018

At the moment when a child is born,
a mother is born also.

ANON

THE FIRST
TRIMESTER

The *Daily Trumpet* would like to apologise to the Reverend Derren Cannon of St Thomas the Doubtful church, Rothsthorpe and his wife Mary. In the article 'At Home with the Cannons' on Thursday there was a grammatical error. It should have read, 'Mary Cannon sits with her feet on the comfortable old pouffe. Her husband, Derren Cannon, rests in his armchair', and not 'Mary Cannon sits with her feet on the comfortable old pouffe her husband. Derren Cannon rests in his armchair.' We apologise unreservedly to Revenant and Mrs Cannon.

Chapter 1

'Crackers, that's what this business is,' cackled Gill Johnson. A joke she had made every week since she had joined them; a joke she never tired of and which the others still laughed at because it had gone beyond corny to be reborn as 'kitsch'. The owners of The Crackers Yard, Joe and Annie Pandoro, groaned every time it was said, but they'd miss it when they didn't hear it anymore. Gill was counting down the days to her retirement, when she would be leaving them to live in sunny Spain.

'Oh shut up and get stuffing,' snapped Iris Caswell, the eldest of the workforce at eighty-five. She made a selection of 'oof' and 'eeh' sounds whenever she rose from a chair, and every joint she possessed creaked like an old ship, but if the rest of her were as fit and nimble as her fingers, she'd have been running the Grand National every April.

'I've forgotten what I was saying,' said Annie, eyebrows dipped in deliberation.

'How the menopause is robbing you of your memory,' Iris reminded her, tying a ribbon into an expert bow around the end of a cracker. 'You just got on with it in our day. You didn't go broadcasting you were sweating like a fat lad in a cake shop. You mopped your brow and carried on pegging out the washing.'

'Someone was on the telly saying women should wear badges with the letter M on them to highlight to the known universe that you were going through the change.' Gill's wry burst of laughter made it plain what she thought of that idea. 'What next? "I" badges for incontinence so you don't have to wait in toilet queues?'

'I'd have one of those,' said Iris. 'These days, when my bladder shouts, "Jump", I have to shout back, "How high?"'

'Well I'm not wearing a badge,' decided Annie, packing all the crackers her ladies had completed into a box. 'Even if I did, it would need to be P for perimenopausal.'

Her husband Joe poked his head out of his office. He was a man who loved to banter with women, but sometimes he felt the need to exit certain conversations and go and make some tea. Women's talk often terrified him and he was incredibly grateful to have been born a man.

'What on earth is perimenopausal?' he asked.

'It's when you're so worried you're menopausal, you have to open up a bottle of Babycham,' chuckled Gill, queen of the terrible jokes. Joe's head disappeared back into the sanctuary of his office, not understanding the punchline at all. Some things didn't translate properly into his native Italian.

The Crackers Yard was on a small industrial estate between the villages of Higher Hoppleton and Maltstone. There were also some offices there, a paint and wallpaper shop, a wholesaler for stationery products, a pet store and Bren's Butties, a sandwich shop that served them all and did a roaring trade. Their own unit was mid-sized with a ground floor and a mezzanine above. The front half of the lower floor housed the huge, expensive cracker machine that glued in the snap then rolled and closed the crackers for the very large orders and the guillotine for cutting the paper and card. There was an area reserved for storing the boxes of crackers that were ready to be shipped out and shelves of all the beautiful sheets of paper that came from Switzerland. At the back there was a small kitchen, the toilet and an office for those times when some privacy was needed, or when Joe needed to escape the conversation if it became too much even for his banter-hardened Neapolitan ears. There were two tables for hand-rolling the more expensive crackers, shelves full of snaps and novelties, hats, mottos and ribbons and a long central table where Gill and Iris sat stuffing, constructing and ribbon-tying. The mezzanine floor was used as a showroom for all their past commissions. If any clients preferred to come to the factory rather than for Joe go to them, this was where they'd talk shop and make deals. For such a tall, impersonal building it was surprisingly cosy, but then the products made there and the people who made them oozed good feeling and fun, which made a huge contribution to the buoyant atmosphere.

Fifteen years ago, Joe Pandoro had been a business consultant and Annie an accounts manager, both unhappy in their jobs, both wishing they could plough their energies into working for themselves, and had gone searching for a concern they could buy off the peg. They bought 'Cracker Jackie', as it was then, as a company run aground. They hadn't known a thing about the cracker industry and Jackie hadn't been helpful. They made a loss for two years, broke even on the third and made a bigger than expected profit in year four. Since then, they'd had an impressive year-on-year growth. Workers had come and gone but with the steady crew of Iris and Gill on board, somehow everything had fallen into place. The business had flourished to the extent that the Pandoros had orders coming out of their ears and they needed to take on more staff, not lose them to the charms of the Costa del Sol.

'My body is all over the place. Just when I think I've had my last period and I throw all my *things* out, along comes another one,' Annie sighed, putting a lid on a full box of crackers and taping down the edges.

'So don't throw them out,' said Gill. 'Sod's law you'll stop having periods if you've got a year's supply of sanitary towels clogging up your cupboards.'

'I hadn't had one since the middle of last year,' said Annie. 'Then a fortnight ago . . . bingo.'

'I used to be ever so heavy in that department,' said Iris, shaking her head as a less than savoury memory visited her. 'Those belts we had to wear. And rubber slips.'

Gill nodded. 'The curse of a woman. My mother threw a pad at me one day and said, "Do you know what this is, Gillian?" I hadn't a clue. Then she told me that for one week of the month I couldn't have a bath, couldn't wash my hair, couldn't stir eggs, couldn't do this, couldn't do that. I was bloody terrified.' She visibly shuddered. 'Best thing that ever happened to me, the menopause. I wasn't sorry to say good-bye to my monthlies. I'd had my kids and . . .'

Her voice withered and she wished she could have rewound time by a few seconds and not said those words, because she might have done her duty by Mother Nature and produced another generation – and so had Iris – but Annie hadn't been so blessed. And the end of her periods signified a goodbye to her ever-dwindling hope of being able to do so. Her window of opportunity had closed and the bolt on it was about to drop.

Iris noticed the awkward lull in the conversation and came flying to the rescue.

'And a fond farewell to a sex drive,' she said. 'Dennis and I settled into a nice pattern of a game of Scrabble and a hot chocolate before bedtime instead. Kiss on the cheek and we were asleep in five minutes. It's overrated, sex. It's for the young ones.'

Annie didn't comment on that. She and Joe might not have been at it like the rabbits they once were but they were still pretty much in tune with each other in that department. Their lovemaking had been particularly tender recently, as if they realised they were entering another phase of their lives and wanted to give and take comfort from each other as recompense. Last night, for instance. A goodnight kiss had blossomed into a very long snog and then hands had started to wander. They'd both had a better sleep afterwards than any game of Scrabble and a cup of Galaxy's Frothy Top might have induced.

Chapter 2

Eve Glace looked out of the office window at all the noisy activity going on. A few years ago this vista was merely a flat piece of boring landscape with a lot of spruce and fir trees growing at one end of it. Now it was a theme park devoted to Christmas. Winterworld had been her mad great-aunt's concept. Evelyn Douglas had been an old lady with a penchant for cats and Mr Kipling cakes, but only when they were on special offer. No one knew that she'd been a genius on the stock market and bought a plot of land from a desperate landowner that she planned to turn into her own personal North Pole. 'A theme park in Barnsley?' far too many had scoffed. But once upon a time, Alton Towers had been a mere hunting lodge with a big garden, so the scoffers could carry on scoffing because Winterworld was built, up and running and fantastically popular. Visitors had started to come from abroad now and the feedback received was terrific. Every year the park shut for a few months so that work could be carried out that would make it even bigger and better than before. They were in close-down at the moment, slogging madly behind the public scenes to make Winterworld ever more magical and special. There were more than enough places to eat in it now: lovely cafés and an ice-cream parlour with the most amazing flavours. There was an enchanted woodland where hidden machines made sure it could snow every day of the year. There was Santapark, packed with rides for the little ones and an ice rink and a small animal enclosure full of reindeer and llamas, white ponies and rescued Snowy owls and a hop-on, hop-off train that had a mind of its own and refused to bow to any engineering tweaks. The big concept for this year was for a bathing lagoon. It was a two-year project that Eve had pushed to finish in one – utter lunacy. The builders had found a natural spring near the Christmas tree plantation and it seemed the perfect place to put the lagoon that her aunt had outlined in her original plans. As soon as her site manager Effin Williams had agreed it could be done, Eve had given him the go-ahead to start it. As her Aunt Evelyn would have said, *there's no excitement in a comfort zone* and she should know. She'd found fun in turning eccentricity into an art form, but sadly her corset-busting freedom had come too late to see her ideas through to completion. The attraction was to be called after her: Lady Evelyn's Lake. Eve wanted it to appear as bewitching as if it had been a feature of a fairy forest.

Eve had been expecting her aunt to leave her something like a locket in her will, not the onus to build a fantasy world, in conjunction with a crazy half-French stranger whose name translated to 'Jack the Ice-cream'; a twerp of the highest order who kept his phone in a SpongeBob SquarePants sock. A ridiculous, insane, little-boy-trapped-inside-a-grown-up whom she'd hated on sight. Then a spell had been cast upon her, allowing her to see beyond the bouncy puppy image he projected and deep down to the heart of the man which was solid and brave and beat in time to her own. She had fallen in love with him and he had married her, as he had promised he would on their very first meeting.

She could see Jacques out of the window, matching Effin for dramatic gesticulations. Eve had thought Effin a strange one in the beginning. Brilliant at his job, he ruled his workforce with a rod of iron, a wand of fairness and a lot of Welsh profanities. His half-Welsh, half-Polish team all took him in their stride and, in time, Eve had come to realise that they wouldn't have wanted to work for anyone else.

She watched Effin and Jacques now playing out a regular scenario: Effin screaming that his workload was too much and he was going to walk out and Jacques telling him that he'd help him pack up all his tools. It had happened at least once a week this year, but she'd started to worry that Effin might actually carry out his threat because of her ridiculous expectations. There was a new film out in June called, coincidentally, *Winterworld*, starring a drop-dead gorgeous A-list actor by the name of Franco Mezzaluna. Eve had joked to Jacques about the possibility of inviting him to open their new attraction and just when they'd decided their chances lay between none and sod all, Franco's PR office had rung up and volunteered his services without having to be asked. Aunt Evelyn had engineered that from above, they were all convinced of it. And if Aunt Evelyn had a hand in it, then everything was going to work out fine.

Eve saw Effin's murderous expression cave in to laughter at something Jacques had said. Her husband could charm the robins out of the Christmas trees. There wasn't anyone that Jacques couldn't get on with: he could talk sensibly with banks, he could bargain with suppliers, he was patience itself with the elderly, eloquent and friendly with the press and a second Doctor Dolittle with the animals they had in the park. But he was really on his level with kids. Eve's goddaughter Phoebe adored him, probably because he was such a big kid himself. He had a Basil Brush alarm clock, a Superman dressing gown and the ringtone on his phone was the *Scooby Doo* theme tune. Bonkers – wonderfully bonkers. Children thought he was Santa with a modern-day makeover. Even little babies stared at him from their prams as if he were a creature not of this world.

With that in her mind, Eve went over to pour herself a cup of coffee from the percolator at the back of the office, an area guarded by a huge stuffed elk called Gabriel that had once belonged to Aunt Evelyn.

'What's he like, my husband, Gabriel?' Eve asked the bauble-wearing elk. She often talked to him when they were alone. He didn't answer back but his expression was always one that suggested he was contemplating. 'What's he like with kids?'

He should have his own, said a voice rushing at her from left field with such force that she felt it knock her sideways. It was a sentiment she agreed with because Jacques would make a wonderful father. But when? They were too busy for children, the park took up all their energies. Still, she wasn't yet forty and people were having their families later and later these days; so not now, but one day. When they had some time.

Wait for some time and it might never come said that same voice, and she couldn't be sure because it was so fleeting, but it didn't half sound like it belonged to an old lady.

Chapter 3

Palma Collins paused before alerting the inhabitants of number 15, Ladybower Gardens to her presence, because she could hear the argument going on within the walls from the bottom of the path. She loitered outside for a few moments, allowing time for the heat to leave the words; which she hoped would happen quickly, so she could do what she had to do and then get on her way.

Tabitha Stephenson had just called her husband a 'first-class prick'. Christian batted back with a 'condescending cow'. At least neither of them could be prosecuted under the Trade Descriptions Act.

The button for the doorbell was directly under the aspirations-of-grandeur 'Stephen's Hall' nameplate. Okay, so it might be one of the larger detached houses on the estate but it was hardly Downton Abbey. Tabitha had given her a guided tour on their first meeting in the early part of the new year to show her the grade of house the child would grow up in. Like a proud estate agent she had introduced Palma to her two reception rooms, study, country house-style dining room with egg-and-dart Lincrusta border, not to mention the eighteen-foot-long pergola and the stunning Arctic cabin in the garden. Now, that really had made Palma's jaw drop to the floor. You could keep the octagonal conservatory, the hot tub and the his and hers en-suites, each with a bidet, but the Arctic cabin – *oh my*. One day she hoped she would be rich enough to afford one of those, though it was highly unlikely. What she soon would be – with any luck – was getting paid a lump sum that would change everything, even though it wouldn't be anything like the amount needed to give her the indulgent lifestyle the Stephensons enjoyed. It would, however, get her away from the gutter, and that would do for now.

Stephen's Hall was magazine perfect and full of shine: shiny chrome kitchen units, shiny cupboard fronts, shiny glass tables and shiny wooden floors. Palma wondered how Tabitha would cope with sticky baby fingerprints dulling all the surfaces. Not very well, she concluded, but that was hardly her problem. Once the baby was born, Palma wouldn't think of it or the Stephensons again. Duty done, wish them all her best, and forget.

She'd hoped she would have been pregnant by now because the sooner it happened, the sooner those nine months would be over and the sooner she could get on with her life, but her last two periods had come along as regular as clock-work. *Third time lucky*, she said to herself as she extended her hand towards the bell, but held back from contact because the argument was still raging on.

The top part of the front window was slightly ajar, something the couple inside had obviously failed to notice. 'She'll be here in a minute, Christian, so shut the fuck up,' Palma heard from within. 'You shut the fuck up,' Christian returned.

Silence reigned for a count of three and Palma took that as a cue to finally announce her arrival. The doorbell released the grand tones of Big Ben's chime whilst she arranged her facial features into her best 'just-got-here' expression, one that was smiling in greeting and had absolutely no prior knowledge that seconds ago the Stephensons had been ripping into each other like savage dogs.

Tabitha opened the door looking glam as always, even in jeggings and jumper. One of those baggy tops that make thin women look fabulous and fat women look like a bombed sofa.

'Ah, Palma, come, come,' Tabitha said, shiny white teeth on full display, ushering her in. 'Here we are again.'

'Yep,' said Palma. *Here we are again.*

'You are still taking the folic acid aren't you? No tea and coffee. Plenty of water and seven-a-day fruit and vegetables.'

'Yes, Mrs Stephenson,' said Palma. Same question, same answer, same lie. She was taking the folic acid but though she had cut down on tea and coffee, she wasn't cutting them out altogether. It was bad enough not having alcohol. As for seven fruit and veg per day . . . dream on, love.

'Christian,' Tabitha shouted to her husband. 'Palma's here.'

As usual she pronounced it Pal-ma. 'It's *Palma*, as in the capital of Majorca,' she'd once said, but Tabitha persisted. She was one of those women who pretended to listen to you when there was actually cling film over her ears, Palma had rapidly come to realise that.

Christian appeared in the doorway wearing Armani jeans and a T-shirt with the Lacoste name and a super-size crocodile emblazoned across the front so one was in no doubt it was designer gear. He dressed down better than anyone she knew dressed up. 'Hello, Palma.' At least he pronounced it correctly.

'Hello, Mr Stephenson,' she returned. It was all very genial and normal until you knew that within five minutes Christian would be wanking into a jug, sucking it up into a meat baster and then she would be squirting it up her flue before lying back, pelvis tilted, legs up against the Graham and Brown wallpaper in their spare room, whilst sperm swam around inside her trying their best to locate an egg. All for five thousand pounds, which had sounded a small fortune when it had first been offered. She'd only get three of that, of course, the rest she'd have to hand over to Clint. He'd already got two hundred for brokering the deal. They'd get five hundred each upon confirmation of pregnancy and the rest nine months later, on handover day.

'Up you go,' said Tabitha, nodding towards the stairs. 'You know the drill.'

Yes, she knew the drill all right. Shoes off and up the cream carpet, thirteen steps, down the landing towards the small bedroom at the end. Drawers off and wait patiently until Mr Stephenson had knocked one out and could hand over the tube of baby juice.

She heard Christian enter the room next to hers. The master bedroom: it had a small plaque saying so screwed onto the door. She tried not to think about what he was doing when it all fell quiet. Palma didn't like him for a reason she couldn't put her finger on. He was polite and very handsome but his smile was oily, his gaze too intense and the first time she'd met him he'd hung on to her hand a beat too long when they'd been introduced. Hardly enough to damn him to hell, but, still, he put her on edge.

It didn't take more than a moment or two for Christian to collect the sperm. She expected him to hand it over quickly as usual and then retreat to let her get on with her side of things, but today he slipped inside the room, pushing the door softly shut behind him.

'Tabitha is getting impatient,' he said quietly, then held his finger up against his lip to shush what she had been about to say to that. 'I know these things can't be rushed, but we can always do it a more traditional way and lower the odds.'

It took Palma a few seconds to understand what he meant. It was only when he added, 'I'd see to it that you had a good time,' that the penny dropped.

'We can't do that,' she said with a horrified gasp. 'You're married.' Her instincts had been right; he was a lech.

Christian gave her his best expression of outrage.

'Palma, we wouldn't be making love, it would merely be a more . . . direct way of doing the job. Cutting out the middle man' – he held up the baster – 'the way nature intended these things to happen.'

Palma didn't care if Mother Nature was onside with it or not, it was wrong with a big fat capital W.

'No,' she said firmly and snatched the baster from his hand. But he didn't move.

'Well, I do hope it works this time,' he said. 'If it doesn't we may have to re-think the strategy. Tabitha agrees, in case you're wondering.'

She didn't ask what he meant, though a picture of Tabitha kneeling on the bed whilst Palma rested her head in her lap like Offred in *The Handmaid's Tale* drifted across her hippocampus.

'I should warn you that Tabitha is not the most patient of people, whatever impression she's given you. She's desperate – and desperate people do desperate things, Palma.'

She knew that. That's why she was here.

'I hear you,' she said. 'I'm doing my best.'

Then he did leave to let her get on with what she had to do.

If he had meant to make her feel expendable by telling her that, he'd succeeded. Christian knew she wanted this money badly. She'd made the mistake of telling them the first time they met how much she needed the cash in an effort to assure them that she would not back out of the deal, and in doing so had given a chunk of her power away.

Clint – the broker of this deal – had told her that Tabitha yearned for the child she couldn't carry herself, though she hadn't cried when Palma had twice rung to tell her that her period had come. Her tone had been more one of annoyance and frustration as they booked the next insemination date in their diaries. Then again, Tabitha wasn't the type to cry and wail. Maybe she was keeping the cork tightly in the bottle of her despair and was so at the end of her tether that it was only a matter of time before she pimped out her husband to 'do it as Mother Nature intended', turning a blind eye – and a deaf ear – to the spare room ceiling as it creaked with a fast-increasing rhythm.

As Palma inserted the hard tube inside her, she wondered how much extra she would accept to have sex with Christian if it was offered. Desperate people did desperate things, as he so rightly said. And if she was desperate enough to rent out her body for nine months, it might only take a few dollars more to open up that road.

Chapter 4

'Crackers, that's what this business is,' said Gill, chuckling cheerfully as she stuffed a dodgy-looking pink whistle into the open end of a sparkly cracker.

'What's crackers is you leaving us for a pipe dream,' said Iris, sitting across the table from her and scowling.

'Jealously will get you nowhere, Iris.'

'I'll not be jealous when you're home this time next year crying that you're missing your home comforts. And you're sick to death of the heat.'

Gill snorted with laughter. 'I'm going to live in Fuengirola, Iris, not in the middle of the Gobi Desert. There's not much you can get over here that you can't get over there.'

Iris thought for a minute, but the best counter-argument she could come up with was:

'Snow.'

'I hate the stuff,' said Gill. 'Get me on that veranda with a Pina Colada in my hand in the middle of December and I'll be laughing.'

'You'll soon get bored.'

'Trust me, I won't.'

'You'll miss your Viv and your Sal. You won't be able to nip off and go shopping to Meadowhall with them like you do now having one of your fancy Prosecco lunches,' tried Iris.

'They'll be coming over for holidays. Plus our Sal's moving to Cornwall in August. It'd take me longer to get to her if I stayed here than if I moved to the Med.'

'You're too old, for a start,' said Iris. 'What if you get taken ill?'

'They've got hospitals, Iris. And they're good ones. Are you trying to put me off going, because if you are, you've no chance.'

Iris got up from the table with a loud *oof*. 'I'm going to the toilet,' she announced in a gruff voice as if she was being forced to empty her bladder under duress. When she was safely out of earshot, Annie said, 'She'll miss you, Gill.'

'And I'll miss her,' Gill replied with a small sigh, 'We've been friends for a long time, but Ted and I don't want to leave it any longer. His arthritis doesn't bother him half as much there as it does here. We'll be able to FaceTime each other though. Our Sally bought Ted an iPad for his birthday and he's taken to it like a duck to water. Well, I say that but he very nearly did a Facebook live of himself sat on the toilet last week when he was fiddling about trying to find a bit of Dean Martin on YouTube. The whole world almost saw the struggle he was having with his motions.'

Joe smiled and lifted Gill's cup up from the table. He was on drinks duty that day. In fact, he was on drinks duty every day.

'And we will miss you too, Gill,' he said. He'd come over to Leeds from Naples to study at the university when he was eighteen and fallen in love with Yorkshire and two years later with Annie. His English was fluent after all these years but his Italian accent was still very thick. Gill always thought he sounded like Rossano Brazzi, her favourite film star. It had taken her five months to fall in love with Ted when they first started courting. If he'd had an Italian accent like Joe Pandoro, he'd have had her at '*Ciao*.'

'You all right today, Annie, love? You're very pale,' said Gill, studying her boss who was cutting up sheets of corny jokes to roll up with the hats.

'See,' said Joe, turning to his wife. 'She noticed it too.' Then he addressed Gill. 'I told her she looked pale but she doesn't listen to me.'

'I'm fine, really I am. Really,' said Annie, but there was a weariness to her voice that belied her insistence.

'You're working too hard.' Gill declared, deciding that was the cause of her pallor. 'Haven't you got a replacement for me yet?'

'We haven't had anyone show any interest at the job agency,' said Annie.

'Apart from those who've applied to show they're looking for work in order to keep their benefits, but don't want the job at all,' added Joe, waving his hand with a flourish. 'I don't want someone like that.'

'Well you'd better look for two people because Annie looks as if she's ready for dropping,' said Gill.

'I'm not sleeping properly,' Annie admitted to her.

'It's your age. I was terrible when I hit fifty,' said Gill.

'Oy, I'm forty-eight, cheeky,' Annie threw back with a laugh.

'The menopause is a bugger. Hit me like one of those big balls they knock down buildings with.'

'I'm going in the kitchen,' said Joe. 'I don't want to listen to all the lady talk.'

'Coward,' shouted Gill and didn't believe him at all. Mention the word tampon to Ted and he'd cough, blush and then announce he needed something from the shed, but Joe knew as much about herself and Iris as their doctors did. She would miss the Pandoros. Though she'd only known them a few years, it felt as if it were forever; but in a good way. And this job – constructing crackers on little more than a basic wage – might not have looked much on paper, but the banter was first class, the day flew, the kettle was always on and both Joe and Annie were kindness itself.

'There's a bug going round, you know, Annie,' she said. 'Iris's daughter had it. Knocked her stupid for a whole fortnight.'

Iris appeared, waddling back to the table rubbing her hip.

'I say, Iris, your Linda's had a bug hasn't she? I'm just telling Annie.'

'A bug and a half,' said Iris. 'Sick as a dog and white as a sheet she was. She lost half a stone in weight in the first week alone.' She sniffed and cast a sneer at Gill. 'You'd better get used to that weight loss with the water over there in the Costa del Diarrhoea.'

'Oh shut up, Iris, you're talking tripe.' Gill suddenly

remembered the story she had to tell. 'Eh, I tell you what'll take your mind off me flitting off to paradise. Have you heard about Brenda Lee?'

'The singer?' asked Annie.

'No, Brenda Lee from Canal Street,' said Gill. 'Brenda Lee with the funny eye. Iris'll know who I mean.'

Iris thought for a minute. 'Doug Lee's wife?'

'Well, widow if you're going to be factful. She's marrying a Turkish barman with one of them big beards called Mehmet. Her family are trying to get her sectioned.'

'Why has he called his beard Mehmet?' asked Joe, bringing in a tray of mugs and winking at Iris.

'He's called Mehmet, not his beard, you pillock. And he's half her age and a bit extra.'

'People in Yorkshire are *pazzo*. Crazy.' Joe was grinning and Gill thought he looked like a film star when his lovely teeth were on display. Even better than Rossano Brazzi.

'She said she's never had as much sex.'

Iris made a choked sound.

'It's true,' went on Gill. 'Up against the wall, in the back of the car ...'

'You sound like Doreen Turbot,' said Iris, referring to their mutual friend who had eventually married the love of her life forty-plus years after they'd split up. 'When she first got back with Vernon, she'd have made Christian Grey blush.'

'Mehmet chucks her round the bedroom by all accounts. He's a bricklayer by trade.'

'Give over, Gill Johnson. Geoff Capes couldn't chuck Brenda Lee around the bedroom. She must be forty stone.'

Annie was laughing so much she was almost crying now. Together Iris and Gill were the funniest double act she'd ever come across. The laughs would be thinner on the ground when Gill moved to the Costa del Sol. And she'd badly needed some laughter these past months as the door on her biggest dream was slamming shut in her face.

'Mind you, I like Turkish food,' said Gill, who would never have moved to a place with unfavourable cuisine. 'We like a nice kebab. Chilli sauce and salad,' and her tongue snaked out and licked her lips.

Iris shuddered. 'You don't know what's in those things. Pigeons, dead dogs . . .'

'Oh, Iris, stop,' said Annie, revulsion bleeding into her laughter.

'It's true. Me and our Linda watched a programme. They put all sorts in. Eyeballs, connective tissue, ground-up—'

Annie's hand clamped over her mouth as the contents of her stomach rose up inside her like a freak wave. She set off running to the staff toilet at a pace that would have had Flo-Jo trailing in her wake.

'You mark my words, Joe. It's that bug that's going around,' said Gill to Joe.

Joe nodded. He hadn't told Gill and Iris that Annie had thrown up quite a lot over the past couple of weeks and had totally lost her appetite. He didn't tell them that he was very worried about her because that's how it started with his mother and she too refused to go to a doctor because she was scared of what he would find. And when she eventually did go, it was the worst of news.

Chapter 5

Eve and Jacques were stealing some rare time to have a coffee in their office together, and Eve needed all the coffee she could get at the moment. They barely saw each other during the day at work because Jacques liked to be hands-on outside, especially now that the reopening of the park with its swanky new attraction was less than ten weeks away. Everyone was working ridiculously hard and stupidly long hours to get it all ready. It had been madness trying both to build the lagoon and extend Santapark in one single season, but they couldn't stop now. Eve didn't even want to think how much they were going to end up paying their staff in overtime.

Jacques, Eve joked, was seeing far more of Davy MacDuff than he was her. Davy was an old friend whom he'd set on, forcing Effin to accept him into his workforce, which hadn't gone down too well. Davy had been in Jacques' military unit but he'd had difficulty adjusting to civilian life and had been through a rough couple of years. He'd needed a job and that's where Jacques had been able to help. Davy was there with them now, summoned by Jacques, to check that he was settling in.

'Are your digs okay?' asked Eve, nudging a plate of biscuits over to him.

'The digs are great, Eve, thank you,' replied Davy, reaching for a Kit Kat. 'Very comfortable. I'm grateful to you both for this, you know.'

He said it every time he met with them. Jacques waved his words away. 'You'd have done it for me if the situation had been reversed.'

'Don't kid yoursel', pal. I wouldna have forced Effin on my worst enemy,' said the big Scot, biting down on his biscuit. 'He calls me "the haggis" and thinks I don't know about it.'

Eve hooted, but then Davy made her laugh a lot. She thought he was quite damaged when he'd arrived here a couple of months ago and he hadn't smiled much or cracked any jokes back then, but the park had worked its magic on him already.

'Effin's bark is worse than his bite, trust me,' said Eve. 'He's an absolute softie really.'

'I'm not quite sure that he's my greatest fan, but I'll win him round with my Scottish charm in time,' replied Davy, with an accompanying expression that implied he doubted his own words.

'Maybe it's a rugby thing,' Eve suggested.

Jacques added to that. 'Effin is rather passionate about his rugby. One of his sons used to play for Llanelli.' He'd picked up on the tension between the two men from day one, admittedly more from Effin towards Davy than the other way; but they were both good people and he figured they'd come to realise that from working together.

'His niece is a striking-looking girl,' said Davy after a slurp on his coffee.

Jacques raised his eyebrows. 'Now you are treading on thin ice. You might think you've been in a war zone, my friend, but that'd be nothing compared to what would happen if you made a move on one of Effin's own.'

Cariad ran the ice-cream parlour. She was twenty-two with long black hair, big brown eyes, a figure to die for and the sweetest nature. Effin guarded her like a giant Rottweiler.

Davy threw back his head and laughed. 'I might ask her out. I wouldn't have to do anything to kill Effin if I did. I could stand back and watch his head grow purple and blow clean off his shoulders.'

Eve was only half-joking when she wagged her finger and warned Davy to steer clear. She liked Davy but he'd eat Cariad alive. He was as worldly as she was innocent.

'I think I've got under Uncle Effin's skin a wee bit. I'm putting him off his game,' said Davy. 'I did hear that he seems to have been making quite a few mistakes since I turned up. I think he's noticed the timing too and blames me for all the mishaps.'

'Never. Effin Williams does not make mistakes,' Eve argued. She wouldn't have believed that.

Davy held up his hands in a pacifying gesture. 'Only what I heard on the Welsh-Polish grapevine. Don't shoot the messenger, *Missus.*'

'Oh, not you as well,' groaned Eve. She'd been saddled

with that nickname since the very early days of working with Effin's men. They called Jacques 'The Captain' and she got 'The Missus'. It was grossly unfair. 'Anyway, what mistakes?' She flashed a look at Jacques who was doing a terrible job of feigning innocence. 'Jacques?'

'Er ... the S fell off the Santapark sign after Effin was supposed to have secured it.'

Eve's eyebrows shot up her forehead. 'You don't mean the massive S on the Santapark sign? The enormous heavy one that could have killed someone if it dropped from that height?'

'Yes ... that's the one.'

Eve made a strangled noise of horror. 'Jacques, why didn't you tell me?'

'Because I'm trying to save you from worrying about something that I've dealt with,' Jacques answered her. 'It fell, it didn't hit anyone—'

'Thankfully,' Eve exclaimed.

'Yes, thankfully, but all is calm, all is bright now,' he carolled.

'So what else has Effin been doing?'

'Nothing really.'

Eve wasn't taken in. 'The word "really" totally cancels out that "nothing", Jacques.'

Davy jumped in. 'It wasn't anything much, Eve. He'd filled up his spare fuel can with petrol instead of diesel. Nearly poured it in his car. Silly mistake. Happens to lots of people.'

'Not to Effin it doesn't,' said Eve.

She needed another coffee and they were out of milk. For the past few days she had been so tired she wondered if she'd been bitten in the night by some strange bug that had delivered a dose of sleeping sickness and taken away all her energy. She'd drunk coffee after coffee in an effort to prop herself up but it hadn't worked. Their quietly efficient assistant Myfanwy, in the office next door to the left, would have some spare. Effin had the office next door to the right but she wasn't sure she wanted to see him at the moment.

'Going to get some milk, I'll be back in a few minutes,' Eve announced.

After Eve had closed the door behind her, Davy continued to stare at it as if he could still see her through it.

'Sorry about the Effin thing. I shouldn't have brought it up and caused that slight domestic.'

Jacques shook his head. 'Don't worry about it. I shouldn't have kept it from her.'

'Eve looks tired,' Davy went on.

'I've told her, though I didn't quite use those exact words because I'd like to keep my genitals intact,' Jacques said to that. 'But she won't take any time off. I tell you, Davy, I'll be glad when the lagoon is finished. It would have been easier to build a pyramid. The more natural you want something to look, the harder work it is.'

Davy laughed softly. 'She's a great girl and you are so good together. I need a good woman, Jacques. I want some of what you've got. I'll pass on managing the theme park but I'd like a place to call home and it's *braw* around here. I'd quite happily settle and put some roots down, make a few children and hope the boys inherit my stunningly handsome looks.'

Jacques smiled. 'That's the news I was hoping for. And its warmer than Glasgow.'

They chinked their mugs together in a celebratory toast.

'So when are you and your good lady going to start producing little copies?' asked Davy.

'Oh, I don't know,' said Jacques. 'One day. When Eve's ready. I'd have them tomorrow but it's not me that will have to carry them, is it?'

'I might start sooner rather than later,' said Davy, stretching the cracks out of his back. 'Cariad MacDuff. Rolls off the tongue, doesn't it?' and he narrowed his eyes mischievously.

Chapter 6

Déjà vu. That's what they called it when you felt you'd been here before but hadn't really, Palma mused as she stood on the doorstep of Stephen's Hall, finger on the doorbell and about to depress. Except she had been here before, listening to the heated interlude between the Stephensons escaping through the front top window that didn't close flush. The only difference was that the names were getting nastier. Tabitha and Christian were trading 'c' words this month, as well as 'f' ones. She could have rung the bell and cut it off but it amused her to listen for a while, to aurally witness the dynamics of their relationship. Then she wished she hadn't, because this didn't sound like a loving couple ready to accept a baby into their lives. Then again it could be argued that not having a baby was putting an undue strain on their marriage and as soon as she put one into their waiting arms, all their troubles would disappear. Her first thought had a louder voice though and she didn't like that one bit.

She pressed down on the button and the doorbell sounded, instantly freezing the battle within. Tabitha appeared at the door seconds later with her perfect swishy honey-blonde hair and trim fatless figure, welcoming smile pinned in place on her face but there were bags under her eyes that her thick layer of Clarins foundation and her Touche Éclat couldn't disguise.

'Ah, Pal-ma. Do come in. Fourth time lucky, I hope.'

Same routine. No 'would you like a coffee', only shoes off, up the stairs and into the end bedroom, knickers off and wait whilst trying not to think about Christian jacking off to a dirty mag in the master bedroom with the ornately carved four-poster. She wondered what sort of publication would best work for him: one full of boobs, she guessed. Not hers, which were a respectable B cup, but huge ones like Tabitha's. They were false, Palma knew, because she'd seen Tabitha in a vest top with no bra underneath and her knockers stuck out like twin zeppelins. They were far too big for her tiny frame, hard and unnatural-looking. Palma wondered how she'd convince people she could breastfeed with them, then stopped wondering because – again – not her problem.

The familiar knock at the door. And in walked Christian with his baster.

'Here you go,' he said. 'All nice and warm for you.' He closed the door slightly to give them privacy. 'I saved it up this time so there'd be plenty.'

Palma tried not to retch.

'Tabitha bought a kit from a witch on the internet,' he whispered. 'I reckon this is the batch that will do it.' He pointed the baster at her like a magic wand distributing a spell. Which it would be, if it worked.

'Thanks,' said Palma, reaching out for it but he withdrew his hand.

'If this doesn't do it, we really will have to rethink the situation,' he said, his voice low, faux-concern weighing down his groomed eyebrows. 'Maybe if you want your money you should consider what I said. We can meet in private. Or your place. I'm only telling you this because she said that she might ask your man to find us another surrogate.'

Palma's heart kicked in her chest. She needed that money. She needed the baby in order to get that money. And she needed his sperm inside her to get that baby.

Christian sighed in an almost apologetic way. 'Look, would it be so bad if we gave her what she wanted so that you could get what you wanted?' He waited for her response and when one was not forthcoming, his tone tightened slightly. 'She's already told me she doesn't mind how it happens. Clichéd as it might sound, I really am thinking about you two more than I am myself in all this.'

Did he really believe himself, thought Palma, trying not to react. He was so full of shit it had given him a false tan.

'Let me get on with it,' said Palma, wondering how he couldn't hear her heartbeat because it sounded like a set of Def Leppard's drums in her ears. He smiled, just out of one corner of his mouth, a smug, I-know-I'm-going-to-have-my-own-way-on-this smile that made her feel even more nauseous than the contents of the baster did. He knew that there was only one person stinking of desperation in this three-way agreement and it wasn't him or his wife.

*

Palma felt different on the way home. She couldn't put her finger on why; she even considered that it was mere wishful thinking, but she dismissed that because she *did* feel different. Sitting with her hips tilted and her feet resting on the Stephensons' expensively textured wallpaper, she willed those little tadpoles to search out her patiently waiting egg and start the ball rolling. She needed this pregnancy to happen *now*. She needed her periods to stop, for her to start getting fat, for her to wait out the nine months and then puff, scream and expel the cargo so she could get on with her life and not look backwards. There would be no tears or sentiment when she gave up the baby. Kids didn't feature in Palma's plans.

They shouldn't have featured in her mother's either. She didn't see Emma Collins: they had no relationship, they'd never had one really. Palma had been born showing signs of drug withdrawal, that's how much her mother had cared. Premature, jaundiced, needing a blood transfusion, Palma's first days had been dramatic; she had to fight and at times it felt as if she'd been fighting ever since. Emma had two more children, both of whom were immediately given up for adoption – they'd been the lucky ones. It had taken social services until she was fourteen to remove Palma and place her into care and that was the last time she and her mother had seen each other. Neither of them had protested about it, and if that had taught Palma anything, it was that she wouldn't have kids unless she were married to a kind man and living in a big house and able to afford nice things, which was unlikely but not impossible. The odds were weighted towards girls like Palma being trapped in a shit life; but those odds could be beaten. Nowhere was it set in stone that she had to end up as one of those who wore pyjamas 24/7 and existed between benefit payments. Taking advantage of a dodgy opportunity like this would at least allow her to leave the sink estate where she'd been raised before it was too late. The end would more than justify the means: she'd repeated that like a mantra to herself over the past few months.

It was peeing down with rain. Christian had offered to give her a lift and she'd refused it because she felt that being trapped in a car with him was a recipe for trouble; but it was falling like stair-rods now and she was soaked by the time the bus arrived. Once in the town centre, she had to catch the bus that dropped her off at the top of Edgefoot Hill because there was over half an hour wait for the Ketherwood Circular. She'd have to cut through the park, dark as it was, but she just wanted to get home the quickest way possible. If she stuck to the path where it was lit, she reckoned she'd be okay because it wasn't exactly the weather for muggers.

To be on the safe side, she positioned the keys in her hand so that the short one was sticking out from between her knuckles and would make a mess of an eyeball if someone decided to have a go at her. Not that there was anything worth nicking in her handbag, which was a secondhand leather one from the charity shop. Some bags cost as much as mansions; she'd read about it in a magazine in the dentist's waiting room. Hers cost a fiver but was attractively fat from its contents: a purse containing a cash card and about twenty quid in it, a lipstick, plasters, comb, tissues, ibuprofen, a few sachets of salt and pepper, a carrier bag, notebook and pen, sewing kit and a metal nail file. She liked to be organised and prepared for all eventualities.

As soon as she was home, she'd shut the curtains and watch the TV with the light off and pretend not to be in if Clint came round. He was getting impatient for his slice of the cake. He had suggested that he have sex with her to make it happen, in case Christian was a jaffa. God forbid that she'd bring an offspring of his into the world. Then again, six stupid bints already had.

There was a couple ahead of her hurriedly walking a tall, slim dog with long legs and at the sight of them her defences could take a rest from their high alert status. The dog was wearing a smart belted raincoat – it was better dressed than she'd been as a kid. One of her earliest memories was arriving at school in a sopping wet cardigan and one of the teachers going home at lunchtime to fetch her an old coat belonging to her own daughter. Yes, it was possible to feel shame at primary school. The couple took the right fork in the path that led up to the back gates whereas she needed to keep to the left. The path was well lit but there were a lot of thick bushes flanking it; her hand tightened around her key, her pace quickened.

She didn't hear the man approach until he was almost upon her. Alarmed by the sudden sound of fast footsteps she turned and saw a figure running towards her, black hood obscuring his face. Her instinct kicked in, she stepped quickly to the right and so did he. They collided and, even though he wasn't a large man, he hit her like a speed train, sending her careening to the ground.

'Jesus, sorry,' he said.

'Take it,' said Palma, kicking her bag towards him.
'There's nothing in it, so take it and piss off.'

'Eh?' said the man. 'I'm out running love, I'm not a bleeding mugger. You barged into me, I was trying to skirt round
you. Here, let me help you up.'

'I can get up myself,' said Palma, batting his hand away.
Her shoe felt loose when she stood up and put it back on
her foot properly. The cheap plastic had split down the side.
'Oh bloody great. I've broke my shoe.' Her beige coat wasn't
looking good either. She couldn't tell in this light if it was
scuffed or only dirty. 'Flipping marvellous.'

'Palma?' The man asked.

Palma's eyes flicked up to his face. She didn't recognise
him, though when he pushed his hood backwards off his
head, there was something vaguely familiar about his eyes,
as if they linked up with a very old dusty memory.

'It is Palma, isn't it? Palma Collins – it is you.'

'Yeah,' she said, warily. 'Who are you?'

'Tommy Tanner. We were in the same school. St
John's High.'

She knew the name instantly, not that it was a good sign.
The Tommy Tanner who'd been in the same group for
maths, English and science had left at the beginning of year
nine to go to a youth detention centre.

'Do you remember me?' he asked.

'Sort of,' she said, still wary.

'How are you?' he said, grin now turning up the corners
of his mouth.

'Piss wet through with a knee throbbing like a bastard and with a broken shoe, if you're asking,' said Palma, cross at that grin. How dare he grin.

'I am so sorry,' he said. 'I tried to get round you as fast and wide as I could because I didn't want you to feel threatened.' He pronounced it as 'frettened'.

'Well you did a great job,' said Palma, brushing her coat with her hand. Luckily it didn't look damaged and the muck would sponge off.

'I'm a boxer now. British welterweight champion. I'm in training for my first defence which is why I'm out running at this time of night, if you're asking.'

'I wasn't,' came the dry reply.

He laughed. 'You're funny.'

Palma took a step and the pain shot through her knee. She swallowed the blasphemy.

'What are you doing walking through the park at this time of night. It's not safe,' said Tommy Tanner.

'You're telling me,' said Palma. 'I'm trying to get home via a shortcut.'

'That's really daft,' said Tommy. 'They do drug deals behind those bushes. I thought everyone knew that.'

Palma did. Quite a lot of them were done by Clint, or *your man* as Christian called him. He wasn't her man, she wanted to say to that, and never would be. She took another step and winced.

'Do you want to lean on me?' said Tommy. 'I'll see you home. Where do you live?'

'Tollin Road,' lied Palma. She lived a few streets away

from it but she wasn't going to give him her precise address. 'And no, thanks, I'll be okay in a minute or two.' She flexed her leg, didn't put a lot of pressure on it when she took her next steps. Tiny, cautious pin steps. It would take her months to get home at this rate.

'Look, grab hold,' said Tommy, holding out his crooked arm. When she didn't he wiggled it and insisted. 'Go on, I won't bite.' She expected him to add the old chestnut, *unless you ask nicely* and was pleasantly surprised when he didn't.

Reluctantly Palma took it and Tommy started to walk at a pace conducive to her temporary disability.

'That's better, in't it?' he said. Then he looked at her and laughed, shaking his head. 'Palma Collins. I used to fancy you like mad at school.'

Palma's eyebrows made a small upward movement of disbelief.

'Yeah, course you did.'

'I did,' Tommy persisted. 'But you fancied Steven Bagshaw. I felt gutted when I heard that.'

Steven Bagshaw. She was suddenly back at her desk and mentally fist-pumping when Mrs Potter moved the class seats around and she found herself sitting next to him in tutorial. Cartoon hearts had pumped out of her eyes. She remembered smiling at him and seeing his eyes drag up and down her with disdain.

'You remember some stuff, don't you?' said Palma.

'I do. He's dead, you know. Alkie and druggie. Died two years ago. I went to his funeral.'

'Steven Bagshaw?' Surely not. He was one of the posher

kids. They lived in a big house and were stinking rich but his dad was a socialist and wouldn't pay out for a private school, that much she could recall. Steven Bagshaw was on course to be a doctor or a vet. His dad used to hit him when he didn't get As in exams, she also pulled that out of the memory bag.

They turned the corner into Tollin Road.

'Which one is yours, then?' Tommy asked.

'It's okay, I can see myself home from here.' She removed her arm from his. 'Thanks.' Then she huffed a little as the word bounced around in her brain with a sarcastic echo. *Thanks for what? Thanks for scaring the living daylights out of me and displacing my kneecap?*

'All right,' said Tommy. 'Well, it's nice to see you again. After all these years, crazy that. I recognised your hair before anything else. It was always a bit mad. Looks nice pink, though.'

She had naturally pale blonde hair, like watered-down sunshine Grace Beresford had once said, and she'd always worn it short and punky. Four years ago she'd shaved it off, apart from a mid-strip that she'd dyed black during a short-lived Mohican stage. She hadn't liked herself very much then. She was lost and alone and that's when Clint O'Gowan had wormed his way into her drawers.

'You can leave me now, I'm okay from here on. Nice to see you again, too.'

'You don't sound too convinced.' Tommy chuckled and she was visited by a fleeting picture of him as a teenager: twinkly eyes, smile constantly on display. The face of a cheeky pixie.

'See you.' Palma turned and walked slowly away from him towards the last house on Tollin Road, trying to keep the limp out of her steps. When she turned to see if he was still loitering, he was. 'I'm going in the back door,' she called and turned the corner, then set off at a fast hobble to her first-floor flat in Beckett Street.

The last thing she needed was another bad boy in her life. Especially one who had known her before Grace Beresford worked her magic.

An hour later, she was getting undressed for bed when the doorbell went and there was only one person who rang it like that: an insistent, impatient pulse that could be translated as *why am I ringing at all? This door should be open to me.* Palma let out a long breath, by which time there had been more buzzing, like an extremely pissed-off wasp. She considered pretending she wasn't in, but he'd only come back again so it was better to get it over and done with. She looked out of the window to see him staring up at her, arms outstretched, mouthing expletives at her for keeping him waiting.

She quickly slipped her jeans back on and fastened them up before pressing the door-entry button. She heard him crashing up the stairs two at a time. He burst in through the door because he was incapable of movements that weren't jerky or exaggerated since he'd taken too much of the stuff he was supposed to peddle. The smell of weed pumped out of his skin, riding on his sweat.

'What's happening, then?' he said, crossing to the fridge in the corner of the room and helping himself to a Vanilla Coke.

'Well, *it's* just happened and now I have to wait and see.'

'Taking a bit of a time, isn't it?' he said, sniffing. His long skinny nose was destroyed inside and he sniffed constantly. A lot of people knew him better as Sniffer O'Gowan than Clint.

'Well you can't push nature,' said Palma. 'I'm doing my best.'

'You fertile now?'

She knew where this was going.

'Fingers crossed I'm already pregnant.'

'If not, you can get your knickers off and I'll make sure you are.'

He was only half-joking. If she'd as much as smiled at that, he would have taken it as a green light. She felt sick at the thought. She'd slept with him once and it had been the biggest mistake of her life because he figured that now the door had been opened, it wasn't allowed to shut. It had taken a lot to fob him off, although she'd been helped by his being a guest at her Majesty's pleasure for a year. Give Clint an inch and he didn't just take a mile, but the road and the traffic lights as well.

'Christian Stephenson has got a rare blood group and the baby will have the same, which they'll find out when it's born.' It was a lie she'd thought of to use in case Clint suggested he act as surrogate for the father, just as she was acting surrogate for the mother. He'd swallowed it easily enough and wouldn't have thought to check.

Clint pulled a thin spliff out of his pocket and lit it. She hated the smell of weed but she was too wary of him to tell him to put it out.

'Well he can fuck off if he wants his money back if you're not up the duff,' said Clint.

He sat down heavily on the sofa and Palma sighed inwardly. She wanted him out of the house, not settling in.

'Clint, do you mind, I'm going to bed early. I've got a headache.'

'Fuck's sake,' he growled under his breath and pushed himself to his feet.

'It's a good sign though. You get headaches when you're in the very first stages of pregnancy, when your body starts to change.'

She was lying again. She hated lying and more or less everything that had come out of her mouth since Clint walked in had been a lie, but his brain was too destroyed even to question if symptoms could manifest themselves within hours of fertilisation.

He crossed to the door then returned to her. He came so far up to her face that she had to take a step back. His breath smelled of smoke, weed and unbrushed teeth. 'When you do a test, ring me. I want to know either way.'

'I will,' she said. 'You know I will. Straight after.'

More lies.

His footsteps on the stairs made a heavy noise for someone so light, Palma thought. The outer door crashed shut and only when she saw him strolling away down the street did she feel her shoulders relax and realise how much tension she had been carrying in them.

Chapter 7

Eve was having a crafty catnap when she was rudely awoken by a loud rap on the office door.

'Come in,' she said, quickly composing herself and instinctively reaching for what she thought was her still fresh, hot coffee – but it had gone cold, indicating how long she'd been out of it for. This level of tiredness that was felling her in the early afternoons couldn't be normal. In walked Effin, his mouth puckered into a disgruntled moue and his eyebrows low over his eyes. In short, he wasn't happy about something.

'Got a moment, Missus?'

'Yes, of course, Effin. Everything all right?' Though clearly it wasn't.

Effin sat down in the chair in front of her desk and opened his mouth to talk but it seemed that he was having difficulty finding a starting point.

'Can I be frank?' he said eventually.

Eve had never known him be any other way, so she was surprised he'd even ask. She nodded.

'It's the hag—' Effin stopped, coughed, began again, considering each word that he put down after the other this time. 'It's about Mr MacDuff. I wondered . . . how well do you really know him?'

'Well, I personally don't know him all that well,' said Eve, 'but Jacques does, and he speaks very highly of him. Is there something . . . specific you needed to know? Do you have a complaint about his work?'

'Oh no,' said Effin quickly. 'Not about his work.'

Eve would have bet her life savings that his complaint featured something to do with his niece, Cariad. She and Davy got along like a house on fire and Uncle Rottweiler didn't like it at all. But there was little Eve could do about it, if that's what this was about.

'Then . . . what is it, Effin?'

Effin took a deep breath before continuing. 'You're a woman, Missus.'

'I am,' agreed Eve, trying to hang on to a straight face.

'And you know how . . . women can be attracted to the wrong sort of fellow. The ones that have looks and charm and are a bit gung-ho. Ones that are a bit older than them and more . . . experienced, some might even say dangerous.'

'I do, I do indeed, Effin.'

Yep, she'd called it right. This was about Davy and Cariad.

'Whereas nice girls should go out with nice boys.'

'In an ideal world, yes, Effin. But you can't force a heart where it doesn't want to go,' said Eve, realising immediately that she'd said the wrong thing from the look on Effin's face. He hadn't found an understanding ear, that expression said. He stood up and made as if to leave. 'I think I've said too much. I'm sorry I've taken up your time.'

'Effin, sit down,' insisted Eve. 'I think I know what you're saying. You're rightly protective over Cariad and you're worried that she's attracted to Davy, am I right?'

Effin lowered his head. 'I am very worried,' he said. 'And I know she's an adult but I don't want her to get hurt. I want her to be with a nice lad. Like Dylan.'

Dylan Evans was one of the new boys who had joined them this season. Tall, handsome, young and Welsh.

'Dylan's a good boy, Missus. His dad Brynn and I were best friends when we were younger,' said Effin, who'd been only too happy to take the lad on when he'd rung and asked him for a job. 'Why can't she fancy him?'

Eve knew only too well how scary the power of attraction could be. It had been love at first sight when she met her first fiancé Jonathan and he'd left a relationship to be with her. It had caused all sorts of trouble. Cupid could be a total twat at times.

'You know, when I was going to propose to my Angharad, I asked her dad for permission, like a gentleman should. I'd always got on with Alun Hughes and so I wasn't expecting him to pick me up by the throat and slam me into the wall. He stared me in the eye and he said, *"Effin Williams, brifa Angharad fi, a wnai rwygo dy lyged allan a'u iwso nhw fel bolycs sbâr."* What do you think about that then, Missus?' He sat back in the chair and waited for Eve to respond.

'You might need to translate it, Effin, before I give my opinion,' Eve suggested.

'Oh, sorry. He said, "You hurt my Angharad and I'll tear your eyes out and use them as spare bollocks".'

'Wow,' said Eve. 'That's a threat and a half.'

'I promised I never would hurt her and I hope I never have. I could never understand why he said that to me. And then I had my own boys and Cariad came along and, of course, her dad died and I became her substitute father and I got it then. I understood why Alun would have cut off my bits if I'd messed his girl around.' He rubbed his head as if there was a pain sitting on his skull that he needed to soothe. 'Angharad would tell me that I should keep my nose out, but I'm worried, I am. I don't want my niece getting her heart broke.'

'You can't live her life for her, Effin,' said Eve gently. 'She's a grown-up. And, for what it's worth, Davy is a good man. I'm not saying anything is going on between them, before you think I am ...' Eve held her hands up '... but it's not something I can interfere in, if that's why you're here.'

'I don't know what I'm asking, that's the truth,' said Effin, getting to his feet a second time. He sighed heavily, then continued: 'My dad used to say that the curse of a parent was that your job was to prepare a child for leaving you and making their own way in the world. To have to let go of something you've raised with all your love is the hardest part of all. I know they have to trip up and fall in order to learn but it's hard to watch. Thank you for listening, Missus.'

Eve stared at the door long after Effin had gone and thought that if you did parenthood how it should be – and not as her lackadaisical mother had – it sounded terrifying, stressful, fraught with anxiety. Maybe she'd leave it a little bit longer before thinking about having children. If at all.

Chapter 8

'Oh Joe, you're going to have to get her to a doctor, lad,' said Iris, in her best quietest voice so Annie, in the staff toilet, wouldn't have a chance of hearing them. 'She's really not right.'

Annie hadn't been herself for nearly a month now, way past the point of this being a bug, and she refused to take any time off because they were far too busy. If they didn't know better, Iris and Gill would have been urging her to take a pregnancy test because her symptoms were textbook: constant queasiness, headaches, crippling fatigue, but Annie was forty-eight and that particular ship hadn't sailed because it had never even left the harbour. Pregnancy hadn't happened naturally despite tests showing there was nothing medically wrong with either of them. 'Just relax. Stress won't help,' they'd been told as they were sent away to let nature take its course, except nature hadn't bothered. Four rounds of IVF had failed and they had been refused the adoption route. Whatever Annie had now was cruelly mimicking what happened after conception, something nasty intent on sticking its boot right in.

'I have been trying to get her to the doctor's, but she won't go,' said Joe, a helpless tone in his loud whisper. 'She is frightened. And to be honest, I am frightened too.'

Annie came out of the toilet to face three pairs of concerned eyes.

'You'd better go and get checked, you know,' said Iris with a soft smile. 'It'll probably be the menopause, it takes all sorts of forms.'

'I know,' said Annie. But she didn't think it was and that's why she was scared.

After work, they drove home and Joe decided he would cook. Annie could tell that he was in full-on healing mode because Joe thought of food as medicine; he was trying to make her better with pasta and garlic and minced beef and pork. She couldn't match him in the kitchen: he was a superb cook, thanks to his Italian parents, who'd owned a restaurant outside Naples and knew all the little tricks that made food taste as if it had been shipped over especially from there rather than made in a kitchen in South Yorkshire. She volunteered to go and buy a dessert from the supermarket and the teabags for the office that she'd forgotten to pick up last week because as much as she loved him, she needed an hour's breathing space away from him. The air in the house was thick with his concern and that made her all too aware it was because he thought there was something horribly wrong with her.

She kept it light, told him she'd be back as soon as possible and left him happily grating parmesan and singing along to

Pavarotti. She drove to Morrisons in the centre of town, only to soon wish she'd driven past it and gone to Tesco instead, because if she was stressed out before she went, she was buckled under with the weight of it by the time she came back.

She only narrowly missed the man who stepped out in front of her Audi in the supermarket car park as she was turning into a spot. He flipped her the bird and strolled on, a scruffy long-haired blonde trailing in his wake, whilst Annie sat frozen, hands gripping the steering wheel so fiercely her fingernails were almost embedded in the leather. Her nerves were jangling, not because of the near miss but because of whom it was that she'd almost rammed into. She'd have recognised him anywhere: the gaunt face with the razor-sharp cheekbones, snake-dull eyes sunk back in their sockets, mean line of mouth, the baggy tracksuit bottoms hanging from the stick-like frame, baseball cap, a similar garb to what he was wearing the last time she saw him. In court. It could only be Clint O'Gowan.

About three years ago, she'd read in the local paper that he'd been sent to prison. Obviously not for long enough because if she'd been the judge, she'd have stuck him in there and thrown away the key, hoping he suffered, the way he'd made her suffer. And Joe – especially Joe.

She felt her stomach stir, but with a different sort of nausea to the one she'd been experiencing for the past weeks. This time it was agitated by long memories and hatred. And she really did hate the man now approaching the entrance of the supermarket. There were people on the planet that Annie disliked. Her incompetent local MP for one, who had been about as much use as a chocolate kettle when she had begged him for help. And the prosecuting counsel who had made Joe sound like a vicious thug to Clint O'Gowan's defenceless victim, but did she hate them? No. But Clint O'Gowan made her more than capable of the emotion.

Her legs were shaky when she got out of the car with her empty carrier bags. She could see him hovering by the entrance, pacing up and down, arguing with the security guard who had come out from behind his desk to refuse him admittance. Annie thought it best she wait until he had cleared off, but another − stronger − part of herself wanted to cross his path, look him in the eye, smash her fist into that bent, skinny nose and feel it splinter against her knuckles. She despised him further for making her even entertain such thoughts because it wasn't *her*. Annie abhorred violence, but he took her way past the boundaries of her moral code, forced her into ripping up her own rule book and tempted her to concede to the primal urges that were buried deep in her DNA. And it wasn't as if the police could do anything that would really wound her. Not in comparison to how she'd been hurt before.

She walked slowly towards the store. The security guard's arms were wide like those of an aggressive goose, a clear gesture that Clint O'Gowan would not be allowed past him. Another man rolled up behind the guard in a shirt and tie. O'Gowan appeared to give up the ghost then, threw up his hands in defeat and doubled-back out.

He started heading her way. Annie felt her jaw tighten, her head prickle as adrenaline pumped through her body and her hand took a firm grip on the bag slung across her body. Close up she could see he hadn't changed much in six years. He'd looked like a wizened older man then, when he was in his early twenties, but his cheeks were even more sunken now and there were horrible angry-looking sores on his forehead. As they passed each other, his eyes jumped sideways but there was no flicker of recognition. He might not have altered much, but she had. Her hair had been much shorter then and artificially lightened, plus she'd been three stone heavier. She'd lost the weight – and much more – from the stress of having the court case dangling over their heads like the sword of Damocles and never gained it all back. What hadn't changed about her was her anger at and disgust for that despicable low-life. If anything it had grown stronger as the years had passed.

Annie walked around Morrisons buying things she didn't need because she knew she would have to calm right down before she went home to Joe. She could talk to Joe about anything but not Clint O'Gowan – he was subject *non grata*. She'd plaster a smile on her face and eat the dinner Joe would put in front of her, even though she wasn't hungry at all, because she wouldn't have that piece of scum ruining another moment for the man she loved.

She realised later, when she had parked up outside the house, that once again she'd forgotten to buy the teabags.

Chapter 9

Palma had been devastated when her period came, because she'd been so sure that, three and a half weeks ago when she was last in the Stephensons' spare bedroom, *it* had worked. The arrival of that period meant that she'd have to go through the whole Christian charade again, if they'd let her. She decided that she'd call his bluff if he insisted that Tabitha would allow them to sleep together, because she'd thought about it and reckoned it wasn't the case at all. She'd ask Tabitha to her face, if necessary, and if she said that she didn't mind, then Palma would leave immediately. As much as she needed the money, she had to be able to live with herself and the prospect of Christian's hands all over her was almost as bad as the memory of Clint O'Gowan's. If she asked Tabitha and found Christian had been lying, then there would be no recovery from that anyway. She'd walk out and leave them to call each other as many f, b and c words as they could muster.

Then her period had stopped as soon as it had started and after waiting a few days she decided to do a test. Her fingers trembled with anticipation as she read the leaflet that came with the pregnancy test to make sure she understood what to do. As the instructions indicated, she urinated on the stick part then placed it on a flat surface, set the timer on her phone and walked around the small bedsit not daring to look at it whilst it was developing. They were possibly the longest few minutes of her life.

Two strong pink lines, no doubt about it. She was pregnant. She was ecstatic.

But Palma's head did not immediately swim with pictures of soft white towels and the scent of baby powder, but with packing-boxes full of her stuff. This result indicated the beginning of the rest of her life. She would leave this shit-tip and move to a much nicer area. And once she was out of here and away from scumbags like Clint she would never look back. She'd be forever grateful to the baby for allowing her to do that, but any gratitude wouldn't become love, she couldn't afford for that to happen. They'd part as friends and each go on to a better stage without the other: baby to a pair of upwardly mobile parents with lots of disposable income to shower on it and she to a job which gave her steady money and satisfaction and somewhere small and cosy to live where she could rest her head at night and not think about what was happening in the rooms below and above her. She didn't dare to dream any bigger than that.

Palma felt exhilarated by what those two pink lines meant. She'd play her part and bring the baby into the world after growing it the best she could. She would stay a long way from any cigarette smoke, not drink a drop of alcohol and make sure she ate well: plenty of fresh fruit and veg, pulses, seeds, fish; she'd look up what would be the most beneficial diet.

She wondered if she should leave it a few more days before telling the Stephensons. She should do another test to make sure. Then again, the sooner she told them, the sooner she'd get the first lump of money. They really should have insisted on paying her when she was twelve weeks gone and the baby was well bedded in because so many were lost in the first couple of months, so she'd read; but it hadn't been mentioned and she hadn't volunteered the information. She was still pondering what to do when the doorbell went – *press press press*. It had to be Clint. Could he smell that pregnancy test? She nudged her curtain out of the way so she could see below and though it was a man, it wasn't Clint. He had a different build: shorter with broader shoulders and though he had tracksuit bottoms on, they weren't horrible, hacky ones that hung from his non-existent backside and had never seen a washing machine since he first put them on.

The figure looked up, giving her a clear view of his face and she was too slow to move back before he spotted her. Tommy Tanner. What the hell did he want? And how had he found her after she told him she lived on Tollin Road?

She hid the test in the dishcloth drawer then went to the bottom of the stairs and opened the door. In the light his face looked the same as it had at school: boyish and cheeky. In fact, give or take a couple of crinkly lines around his eyes, he hardly seemed to have aged at all from then.

'I thought I'd come and find you and scrounge a coffee,' he said. 'I went to that house you said you lived at first.'

'I lied,' said Palma.

'I know,' he replied. 'They told me to try here. House with the green door, they said.'

Palma tutted absently. How the hell did they know where she lived, nosey bleeders?

'Well?' asked Tommy. 'Are you going to leave me out here to dehydrate? I've just been doing hill runs. Can I come in?'

'S'pose so,' said Palma, seeing as she couldn't think of a valid excuse why not.

He followed her up the dingy stairs with the worn lino and embarrassing fake-wooden panelling on the walls.

'I was going to look you up before but I've been warm weather training. In Tenerife,' he said.

'Lucky you.'

'Not really. It wasn't a holiday. It was hard work.'

'You do look a bit brown,' said Palma, giving him the once-over when they were at the top.

'I managed to get a few rays in,' Tommy replied as Palma opened the door to the room. 'Wow, this is nice.'

'It's not, it's a shithole,' she corrected him, crossing to the kettle.

'Well the building is, but you've done your place out all right,' he counteracted.

She gave a small sarcastic laugh, but then wondered how the bedsit would appear through his eyes. It was clean and tidy and everything was colour-co-ordinated: red, cream and darkest grey. Her furniture was cheap but thoughtfully picked. She couldn't do anything about the awful multi-coloured carpet on the floor, but some red rugs she'd picked up in a closing-down sale drew the eye towards them instead. The height of luxury would be picking her own carpet to put on a floor. Carpets like Tabitha and Christian had that were as spongey as trampolines.

'I thought we could have a natter,' said Tommy. 'We must have plenty to talk about.'

Well, you might but there's nothing I want to dredge up, thought Palma. Once she moved out of this place and handed over the baby, that's when she'd start having a life full of details that she might want to share. She'd take few things forward from the past and most of those were her memories of Grace Beresford. She wouldn't be here if it wasn't for Grace. She'd be in a prison at best, a box at worst.

'Tea, coffee? How do you take it?'

'Coffee, white,' replied Tommy. 'Cappuccino if you've got one.'

'I've only got instant.'

'I was joking,' said Tommy, sitting on the sofa.

It must be great being so constantly cheerful, Palma thought as she carried a mug over to the sofa for him and set it down on the sturdy square table she'd found in the Heart Foundation charity shop. She'd sandpapered the stained wooden top in her tiny bathroom until it was super smooth, then varnished it. It looked brand new when she'd finished it.

'So who's starting with the chat?' asked Tommy when Palma had sat down on the armchair. It wasn't a true match with the sofa but it looked as if it could have been. She'd searched for ages to find one that was like it.

'You'd better, seeing as I don't have much to contribute.'

'I'm sure that's not true,' said Tommy. 'But I will anyway. I'll start with the bad stuff. As you know I fell off the rails and ended up in Forestgate. I was a pillock back then.'

'What did you go there for?'

'Persistently being a pillock,' said Tommy. 'Smashing car windows, setting off alarms, robbing a warehouse, fighting. I was an arsehole. I was coked off my brain when I got arrested for the last time. It wasn't good.'

Palma wondered why the hell she had let him up here. He was making Clint sound like Mary Poppins.

'I fell to bits after me mam ran off. Didn't know how to handle it. It's not an excuse. My dad couldn't look after himself, never mind me. So I ended up with the bad lads.'

Palma had a sudden recollection of him and one of the O'Gowans having a major scrap in the school lunch break. Not Clint, because he was seven years older, but one of the cousins in the year above, a flabby wardrobe of a kid who thought he was hard as nails. A re-enactment of David and Goliath with the same outcome. Palma could see him now, blood pouring out of his nose and the bulky games master Mr Fowler dragging Tommy off him. No one tangled with the O'Gowans was the general rule, but Tommy Tanner hadn't been scared of anyone.

'It was my brother that sorted me out. My older brother that I'd never met before, from dad's first wife. He ran a boxing gym. Told me that if I wanted to fight so much to do it properly and make some money out of it. God knows where I'd have been if he hadn't got hold of me. He gave me a home, discipline and focus. And he's my trainer now.'

'He sounds a good bloke,' said Palma.

'He's the dad I should have had,' said Tommy. 'Then he got leukaemia the year before last and I thought we were going to lose him. I've got my title because of our Neil. That's why I won the belt. I did it for him. If I defend it successfully three times, I'll get to keep it and I'll be giving it to him.'

Emotion was present in his voice now, that chirpy smile had faded.

'He's okay now, he got through it. He drives me hard because I've got a defender coming up just before Christmas. You should come and watch me. I'll get you a ticket.'

'I might,' said Palma, though she had no intention of watching two grown-ups trying to smash each other's faces in. It was a common occurrence in Ketherwood, which she could watch from the comfort of her lounge window if she was into that sort of stuff.

'Other than that, I've been labouring: Silkstone Buildings, you heard of them? Really good bloke, my boss. Gives me work around my training time. I bought one of his houses. Nice little estate of twelve. You got a job, Palma?'

'I did have until a month ago. Nothing fancy,' she replied. She wasn't going to tell him that she managed the Ketherwood Fried Chicken shop. 'Fast food outlet. Boss was really nice but he sold up, the new owner put his daughter in charge and I got the boot.' Despite all those employment laws supposedly in place, they'd got rid of her easily enough and the new owners weren't the sort you argued with. 'I've applied for some positions but I've had two rejections so far and I haven't had replies from the others, which is annoying because I'm bored rigid, I need a job.' And now she'd found out she was pregnant, it was going to make it even harder to find one.

'You were brainy at school. I thought you'd have gone to uni or something,' said Tommy. Palma laughed at that.

'You're mixing me up with someone else.'

'I'm not. I remember you reading out a poem you'd written in class. It was a long funny one about a cat and a bird being friends. Didn't the cat have wings or something?'

His memory prodded something wrapped in cobwebs in her brain. That poem had been put forward for a county award and she'd won a runners-up pen.

'Blimey, you've got a good memory. I'd forgotten all about that.'

'I hadn't. I thought you'd be a writer or an English teacher or something one day.'

'Not me,' said Palma. 'I wasn't that good. I haven't found my talent yet. Maybe I don't have one.'

Grace used to say that everyone was good at something, that she could be anything she wanted to be and that her background was no obstacle to her future. What would Grace have said to her present situation, she wondered.

'So what about you, Palma? Fill me in on the missing years. Coffee's grand, exactly how I like it – nice and strong. I might come here again.' He winked at her.

She didn't acknowledge the self-invite. 'Nothing to tell. I went into care at fourteen. Ended up with a lovely foster mother but she died when I was eighteen and then I was on my own. That's all of it right there in a nutshell.' She didn't tell him she'd had a period of such blackness after Grace had gone that she'd considered ending it all. She didn't tell him that it had taken finding herself in bed with Clint O'Gowan and no idea how she got there to make her wake up and smell some very strong coffee of her own.

'You single?' asked Tommy. 'I am. If you are, maybe we could go out for a meal sometime. Fancy that? What do you like? Chinese? Italian? Thai? Then we can have a proper catch-up, can't we?'

Palma's eyebrows raised at the long string of questions. Which to answer first.

'Yes, I'm single,' she replied. 'And I like it that way.'

'Okay, well, as friends. I have to watch my diet. Two months before a fight and I'm on a really strict regime, but I can have the odd day off at the moment if I need to.'

The last time she'd been out for a meal had been with Grace. Grace had taught her that the plate on her left was her side plate and that she used her cutlery from the outside in. It had been a lovely posh restaurant where the waitress unfolded her serviette and placed it in her lap for her. She'd had a steak and it had come with potatoes that were piped into stars and 'flat peas' and Grace had laughed and told her they were called mangetout.

'Yeah, why not,' said Palma. A change of scenery would be nice. She'd become used to being lonely and she knew that wasn't good.

Tommy smiled. 'Great stuff. Friday night? You got a preference?'

'Surprise me,' said Palma.

'Okay, I will,' said Tommy, draining his cup, which he then carried to the sink and swilled.

'Actually, I like Chinese best,' said Palma.

'So do I. I'll pick you up at seven. Friday, yeah?'

'Okay,' said Palma, as he opened the door. The fat smelly woman who lived in the flat above was coming down the stairs. An unattractive mix of yeast and urine hovered around her like a rancid aura. She saw Tommy's nose twitch slightly.

'I'm moving from here,' said Palma quickly. 'Soon as I can.' She didn't know why she felt the need to make the point to him, but she did.

'You should,' said Tommy before he too went down the stairs. 'You were always better than this.'

Chapter 10

Eve had made a Sunday lunch with more trimmings than her Auntie Susan put on the Christmas dinner, which equated to a veritable overload. She and Jacques hadn't taken a day off in ages, and she'd done a really daft thing by suggesting she cook because she had almost dropped off to sleep whilst stirring the gravy. They had only six weeks until the lagoon opened and then they could take their foot off the pedal, but she had no idea how she was going to last the pace.

If she told Jacques how tired she felt, he would insist she stay at home and that's why she wouldn't. She'd pushed for the extension to Santapark and the lagoon and when Franco Mezzaluna had offered to open the new attraction, Eve's plans had spun like candy floss around a stick, getting even bigger and grander; and so there was absolutely no way she was going to dump them all onto someone else to fulfil.

'Where's this lunch, wench?' Jacques shouted from the dining room. 'And would you like a glass of red or white with it?'

'Neither, I'm having a glass of sparkling water,' said Eve. She couldn't drink alcohol during the day at the best of times without it closing her brain down, and she didn't want to waste her afternoon off snoozing on the sofa. She lifted up the plates and carried them through. Jacques was looking a lot more enthusiastic than she was at the sight of the feast she'd prepared. She'd spent the morning peeling and whisking, basting and boiling and she didn't want a single mouthful of it.

She forced down as much of it as she could, aware that she was pushing it around her plate as she used to do with her horrible school dinners.

'That was superb, so why haven't you eaten much?' Jacques asked, placing his cutlery on his empty plate which he had cleared in record time. 'You okay?'

'Fine, just tired,' Eve replied, rolling out that excuse yet again.

He humphed. 'I told you we should have eaten out. It was mad—'

'I wanted to do the wife thing,' Eve interrupted him. 'I wanted us to be at home eating a meal cooked from fresh for a change.' She stood up and reached to pick up his plate and Jacques gently slapped her hand away.

'I'll do the washing up. You choose a film and we'll settle down, put our feet up and relax.'

'Sounds great,' said Eve, stifling a yawn.

'I'll bring in a big bowl of ice-cream to share. Any particular flavour?'

'Ooh, you choose.'

But by the time Jacques had finished loading up the dish-washer, Eve was snoozing on the sofa looking absolutely dead to the world, although the snoring told him she was still very much alive. Jacques put a fleecy throw over her and slotted a cushion under her head, then ate all the ice-cream himself and put on a shouty action film as a consolation prize for the lack of company.

*

Palma decided to set off to the Stephensons' house at four. She knew more or less for certain that they'd be in because Tabitha had once told her that their Sunday nights at home were sacrosanct. It was odd that they hadn't contacted her first, she thought as she emptied her change pot for the bus fare. Tabitha had Palma's expected period dates in her diary and had usually called her two days after one was due to start to find out if she'd had it and, if yes, then to coordinate the next 'session'. Palma had done the second test from the packet that afternoon and the result was the same, as she knew it would be because she felt inexplicably pregnant. She put both tests in her bag as proof for payment and headed to the bus stop hoping that she didn't bump into Clint. A visit from him was impending and she shuddered slightly thinking about it. She couldn't wait to get her cash and start looking around for a better place. It didn't have to be big or fancy, just away from this area and preferably with a nice bath that she could lounge in. She'd read somewhere that unborn babies liked it when their mums lounged in water, so long as it wasn't too hot.

Mum.

The word hit her like a tractor from left field. She shouldn't think of herself as a mum – that was dangerous – because she wasn't its mum. She was a vehicle, a carrier, a temporary life support machine, whatever you wanted to call it but not *mum*. She didn't like it that the word had even entered her head. Tabitha would be the baby's mum.

The bus arrived on time and then she had only five minutes to wait in the main station to catch the connecting bus out to Maltstone. It was lovely there. Only four miles away from the town centre, Maltstone boasted lots of surrounding countryside and a garden centre café that she'd always wanted to try. Maybe, if she found a house in nearby Dodley, where the property prices were much cheaper, she might do that because it was only a few bus stops away.

Ladybower Gardens was just a short walk when she got off the bus. Up a slight hill, past the sort of houses that she herself would never live in. Houses with front lawns like bowling greens and remote control gates. People on this estate didn't catch buses into town, they chose between jumping in their little Audi TTs or their big Range Rovers. Palma could drive; she'd paid for her own lessons from her wages, but buying a car was a different matter. She didn't fancy an old banger that was going to cost her a fortune in garage fees and so, until she could afford something decent, she'd wait.

She hadn't wanted to phone and reveal this great moment to the Stephensons in advance. She wanted to be there to deliver the news in person and see Tabitha's delighted face and watch Christian reach for the cash out of his safe. His car wasn't on the drive but Tabitha's was and Palma just caught a glimpse of her passing the front window, so it wouldn't be a wasted trip. She walked up the path and for once didn't hear any domestic going on within the walls. The house was silent. No TV, no music, no anything.

She pressed the doorbell and Big Ben with his echoey bell-tails rang out then Tabitha's shape appeared in the frosted glass. When she opened the door, Palma's smile faded because Tabitha was barely recognisable without her usual inch of make-up on, plus her hair looked like unbrushed straw and as far from its usual honeyed sleekness as it was possible to get. She seemed slightly disorientated too, almost as if she didn't recognise Palma at first. Palma was about to ask if she was okay, when Tabitha clicked back into herself and apologised for being vague and invited her in. The group of couple-y photos in frames that had always stood on the hall table was no longer there, but on the floor were pieces of glass and broken wood; the photos were torn up into tiny pieces like confetti. The table itself was lying on its side at the bottom of the stairs as if it had been thrown.

'Oh my goodness, what's happened? Have you been burgled?' Palma drew the most obvious conclusion.

'Burgled?' Tabitha's brow creased, then the penny dropped and she gave a short laugh; a hard sound. 'In a way,' she replied. 'I've been stolen from, yes, Palma. Robbed fucking blind.'

Palma stood awkwardly whilst Tabitha bent and picked up a long dagger of glass, looked at it, and then flung it over her shoulder.

'Would you like a drink?' asked Tabitha. 'Tea, gin, vodka, red red wine. Apparently it makes you feel so fucking fine, but it doesn't, trust me, because I've tried it.' Palma noticed the slur in her voice now. She hadn't been disorientated at the door: she was pissed.

'Er, no thanks.'

'So, what can I do for you? Is it isen … insemer … *insemination* day again? My, how time flies.'

She turned too quickly towards the lounge door and would have fallen if she hadn't bounced into the jamb; she'd obviously been drinking plenty of that red red wine today.

'No I came to—'

'Because I have to tell you, Palma my dear, the deal is off. I won't be requiring your services and neither will he. My hus-band.' Tabitha pronounced the word with pantomime exaggeration of her lips, like an actor performing speech exercises backstage.

'What?' said Palma.

'Christian. He's been banging a little girl in his office.' Tabitha smiled nastily.

She was joking, surely? Palma felt as if she'd just been an unwitting victim of the ice bucket challenge because a shower of coldness claimed her from the skull down. This was not adhering to the script that she'd imagined would play out.

'You're kidding?'

'Do I look as if I'm fucking kidding?' Tabitha screamed at her then toned it down. 'I'm sorry, Pal-ma. I shouldn't have shouted. This is not your fault. You are not the one he's been . . .' She paused, considered, squinted. 'You haven't been, have you? Have you been fucking my husband as well?'

'No, I haven't,' Palma returned immediately. 'I haven't seen him outside our . . . arrangement.'

'She's twenty,' said Tabitha, her eyes travelling down the whole of Palma's length and back up again to her face. 'He likes them young and blonde and pliant. I replaced his first wife who was ten years older than me and now I've been replaced by someone ten years younger than me. Some might say that's karma. I almost feel sorry for her. She'll soon find out that her knight in shining armour is just a twat in tinfoil. As I did.'

'Surely it's . . . mendable,' said Palma, her heart rate increasing. 'Have you . . . have you spoken . . .'

'It's been going on for a year and he wasn't in a rush to choose between us so the bitch decided to force his hand by telling me herself. A whole. Fucking. Year. I didn't even smell a whisker of the rat, never mind the rat itself.'

A year. But that didn't make any sense.

'Why would he have agreed to this . . . surrogacy if he's been having an affair for a year?'

'Because he thinks with his dick and not his brain,' snarled Tabitha, wobbling as she prodded her head hard with her index finger. 'Maybe he thought it would make it easier for me to cope with his adultery if I had a baby. A consolation prize. Or maybe he thought I'd forgive him more easily if he crawled back with his tiny tail between his legs. Who knows. Who even cares. Thank God his sperm was as useless as the rest of him. At least we don't have that mess to sort out.'

Panic gripped Palma's throat with sharp, bony fingers. 'Tabitha, I am pregnant.' Her hands were barely in her control as she pulled out the two pregnancy tests from her bag. 'That's what I came to tell you.'

Time froze for a couple of seconds, though it felt like much longer. The only movement was Tabitha's jaw opening by degrees; then she made a grab for the wands, stared at them disbelievingly, and coolly handed them back.

'Pal-ma, do you honestly expect me to take on a child that has nothing to do with me and everything to do with the slimy shit who put it in you?'

Palma swallowed. 'Now hang on a minute. We had a deal. I—'

'Where's the binding contract, sweetheart? Where's the evidence of this so-called deal – show me? I suggest you do what I've done and get rid of every trace of him.'

Palma's panic segued quickly into anger. 'I'm having it for you, because you can't have bloody kids.'

Tabitha's hand came to her tiny waist. 'Who said I can't have them?'

Palma's face scrunched into a mask of confusion. 'What do you mean?'

'I *chose* not to. I don't want all those ... stretchmarks and things.'

Clint had definitely told her that Tabitha couldn't have kids. It was what had made her agree to this in the first place. As much as she needed the money, she would not have carried a child for someone who just couldn't be arsed doing it herself. Palma put both her hands on her stomach. 'This is yours, Tabitha, not mine. I am carrying this for you.'

Tabitha chuckled. 'Well I certainly don't want it. Buy yourself some gin and run yourself a hot bath, dear.'

Unable to contain herself, Palma leapt to a threat. 'I want my money. And if Clint doesn't get his money it won't be only photo frames that you're clearing up.'

Tabitha's mouth gathered into a tight little knot at the name. She opened a drawer in the tall unit behind her and pulled out a business card. 'Here,' she said. '*His* mobile number is on there. Get *him* to pay you. Tell him you're going to keep it and take him to the fucking cleaners with maintenance payments if he tries to fob you off, that should get you what you want. He's got plenty, he can afford to pay for the mess he's got you into. He's certainly going to have to spend lots to get rid of me. But my advice would be to trot off to the doctor's, darling. You can do it with pills if it's early enough: trust me, I know. Easy peasy, doesn't even hurt. Get your money first and then tell him you lost it.' She gave a little laugh. 'Looking at it now, it was hardly the most well thought-out deal was it?'

'You wanted this baby so much. Neither of us were going to back out!' Palma's voice had twisted to alarm again. She'd never foreseen this. There wasn't any paperwork because they didn't need it; Christian didn't want a paper trail and no one would cross Clint. People who made deals with him tended to stick to them and some snowflake like Christian wouldn't have dared mess with him.

'It's really not my problem, it's *his*,' said Tabitha. 'And now I'd like you to go. We don't have anything further to say to each other.'

Palma's eyes were filling with tears now – tears of distress, frustration and anger. 'This baby is yours, not mine, Tabitha.'

'No, it's yours and *his* and we have no connection. Not now.'

'He might be back. You can sort this . . .'

Tabitha turned on her then. 'Excuse me, miss, who the hell are you to give me marriage guidance? I do not want that duplicitous dickhead back. And I most certainly do not want his . . . his . . .' she stabbed her finger in the direction of Palma's stomach, then strode to the front door and opened it. 'Go, please,' she said. 'Ring that number on the card and speak to him and do what you have to, but don't come here again. I'll call the police next time.'

Palma couldn't move.

'Get out,' screamed Tabitha, which did galvanise her into leaving.

Palma's heart was beating so fast she thought it might explode by the time she reached the bench near the bus stop. Her fingers were trembling so much she could barely press the numbers on her phone to ring Christian on the number printed on the business card. Not surprisingly, he didn't answer.

Last week, we reported that Tommy 'TENT' Tanner would be fighting Londoner Frank Arse at the O2 arena in London on 23 December in the first defence of his title. There was an unfortunate spelling error and it should have read *Frank Harsh*.

Chapter 11

At eight o'clock the next morning, Annie was already queue-ing outside the doctor's. The surgery was over-subscribed and if she'd rung for an appointment, she might not have got one for a fortnight so this was her only option if she wanted to be seen quickly. Five people came after her but she secured the first free appointment, which wasn't for an hour so she waited, reading a magazine, but didn't take any of it in because her brain was rolling with worrying thoughts she couldn't bat away. It was a relief when they called her name and told her to take the first door on the left. And then, as Joe would have put it, everything went *pazzo*.

Dr Gilhooley, son of the Dr Gilhooley who had recently retired, looked exactly like his father had at that age. He even sounded exactly like the man who had diagnosed Annie with chicken pox in her early teens, his voice smooth as Guinness, with an inherent Terry Wogan-esque twinkle adding cadence to certain phrases. It messed with her head. Just as the words he was saying to her now were doing, too.

She could easily have believed that she was not in this room but in a mad dream, one that she'd had so many times before only to wake up and find her rocket of hope pulled down by the weight of disappointment.

'I'm sorry, what did you say?' she asked. The words had entered her ear but they couldn't find a home in any part of her brain that would accept them. Every door to them was closed, since they were universally acknowledged as deceivers of the cruellest kind.

'You are pregnant, Mrs Pandoro. There's no doubt about it. When was your last period?'

'I . . . I don't know. They've been all over the place. I didn't have one for nearly a year and then I did and . . .' Stupid – why didn't she have her diary in her handbag. She always carried a diary in her handbag but her brain was cabbaged at the moment. She'd marked all her irregular period dates down there. She dropped her head into her hand hoping the dark might pull the answer forward. 'Let me think.' She'd had to buy tampons because she'd thrown them all out months ago, when was that? She should remember; something about the date was memorable.

It came to her. 'St Patrick's Day. My last period was on St Patrick's Day.' She'd had tampons and Guinness in her shopping basket. She'd bought a four-pack for them to drink as a traditional touch.

'And presumably you've had sex since then?'

Annie nodded, feeling a small heat blossom in her cheeks.

'Ah, so you'll be expecting a Christmas baby in that case,' said Dr Gilhooley with a smile. He pulled out an

A5-size cardboard chart from his drawer. 'December the twenty-second, although your dating scan will firm that up. Congratulations, Mrs Pandoro. I understand you've been trying for some time.'

This wasn't real. This was *not* real. The receptionist had called her name, she'd taken the first door on the left and there the doctor had greeted her with the usual opening question: *What seems to be the problem, Mrs Pandoro?* She'd told him all her symptoms, he'd sent her off to do a urine sample in the toilet next door to give to the nurse whilst he saw another patient, and then she'd returned to his consulting room expecting him to tell her that he was referring her to the hospital.

'I can't be pregnant. I really can't. We've been trying for so long, years ... nothing ...' She reached up to scratch an itch on her cheek and found a teardrop. More followed.

'I can assure you that you are. Unless you've swapped urine samples with someone,' came the reply from the doctor. 'Any other symptoms, like sore breasts, food cravings or aversions, mood swings, headaches, constipation?'

'Oh my, all of those.' Annie was laughing and crying at the same time. She'd blamed her tender nipples on a new bra, constipation on lack of fibre in her diet, those headaches on needing new reading glasses. She fished in her handbag for a tissue. Dr Gilhooley put the chart back in his drawer and took out a tri-fold pamphlet which he handed to her along with a pack of booklets in a plastic sleeve.

'I'm trying out a new initiative and I hope you'd like to be part of it. It's for mothers with babies due either side of

December. It's a club where you can meet and talk through what might be worrying you, get a drink and a bun, learn about nutrition and smash some of those old wives' tales around pregnancy, for there are many. Rather than have parentcraft classes right at the end, this allows you to mix with other mums for longer, build up a support network. I've called it the Christmas Pudding Club.' He grinned, rather pleased with himself. 'If it works, I'm thinking about having a Summer Pudding Club.'

He could see that Annie was only half-absorbing all this.

'Read the pamphlet at home, Mrs Pandoro. You'd really be helping me and, more importantly, yourself if you decide to participate.'

'Thank you, thank you, I will.'

'There's a lot of information in there too about what to expect and your rights and all sorts of useful stuff. The midwife will talk through anything you don't understand at your first ante-natal appointment.'

Ante-natal. Her ante-natal appointment.

'Thank you, Doctor.'

'I expect you'll want to ring the father straightaway.'

'I'm not sure my fingers will stop shaking long enough to press the numbers on my phone.'

Dr Gilhooley laughed.

'I'm delighted for you, Mrs Pandoro, I really am. Why don't you sit in the waiting room for a few minutes until you feel calm? Are you driving?'

'Yes.' Annie stood to go, surprised that her legs could carry her. 'I'll be fine.'

'Congratulations, Mrs Pandoro. You take it easy now.'

Annie walked to the car and sat there for a few minutes before pulling her phone out of her bag. Then she put it straight back. No, she wouldn't ring Joe because she wanted to see his face. She wanted to stare him in the eye and make a memory by telling her husband that she, Annie Pandoro, was in the Christmas Pudding Club.

Chapter 12

'What the heck's the matter, Annie love? You're as grey as my mother-in-law's whites,' said Gill, as Annie walked into the factory just as she and Iris were waiting for Joe to serve up their morning brew.

Joe came rushing out of the small kitchen. His jaw fell open on seeing the ashen colour of his wife's face; Gill wasn't exaggerating.

'I thought you were going to ring me when you came out of the surgery,' he said.

Annie looked at the three faces with their concerned expressions, the worried set of their eyebrows and she wanted to laugh. Laugh like she never had before.

'I'm pregnant,' she blurted out because the words were too big to keep in. It wasn't what she meant to say, which was *Joe, can I have a private word with you,* but somehow the delivered words raced past the intended ones queueing in her voice box.

Joe didn't ask if she was joking because it wasn't something she would have lied about. The only thing he managed to say was, 'How?'

'Well, if you don't know by now, lad, you never will,' said Iris, rising out of her chair. Her arms opened wide. 'Come here, love.' And Annie walked into them, all the time staring at Joe over the old lady's shoulder. Iris passed Annie over to Gill who hugged her then said:

'Well if ever there was some good news to fly off to on Friday, this is it. I want regular updates. I want to see you swell up like a barrage balloon, ripe and plump as a peach.' Gill pushed Annie towards her husband. The pair of them stood in front of each other, stock-still. Then Joe grabbed her, squeezed her tight and when he pulled away, tears were thick in his eyes and in his throat. Tears of joy, good tears.

'I'm due at Christmas, Joe.'

'I thought something serious was wrong with you.'

'*I* thought something serious was wrong with me. But something serious is right with me, Joe.'

'Okay, okay,' said Joe, going into planning mode. 'You have to stop work immediately and stay at home. We can't risk—'

'Whoa, hold that thought, Joe Pandoro, because if I stop working, one: I'll go stark raving bonkers and two: we'll go under.'

Iris gave a haughty sniff in Gill's direction. 'You've picked a right time to swan off to Spain, you. You should be ashamed of yourself. You an ex-nurse an' all. Deserting someone in their hour of need.'

'Oh aye, heap all the blame you can on me. Here, let me find a spade for you so you can add a bit more,' Gill threw back.

'We'll manage, we'll cope,' said Annie. 'If this is possible, anything is possible.'

And it was. Stresses about how they were going to fulfil all the orders on their books with Gill leaving them weren't even on the radar today. The little Pandoro baby growing inside Annie was all that mattered.

*

Clint did come in handy for something, thought Palma, as she waited outside Tesco scanning for Christian's flash sports car. He hadn't picked up the phone to any of the calls she had made to him yesterday after she'd walked away from Ladybower Gardens, or replied to the voicemails she'd left or texts she'd sent, which hadn't surprised her but had begun to really annoy her. Well, he gave her no option but to roll out the big guns, she thought as she lay in bed, so the first thing she did that morning was to text again to say she needed to talk to him immediately or she'd make sure that Clint was at his workplace at eleven o'clock. She didn't think he'd like Clint turning up at his swanky Cheshire Holdings office in Leeds and embarrassing him in front of the thousand-plus workforce. Funnily enough Christian had rung her back within ten minutes. He said that he couldn't talk now but he would pick her up outside Tesco that evening at eight – only her, not Clint.

And so here she was with her pregnancy tests in her bag as proof and some pepper spray and a paring knife as insurance. She didn't think that Christian was the murdering kind, but in this day and age it didn't do any harm to cover your back.

Especially as she was probably the worst news possible in his life at the moment.

And here he comes, she said to herself as she saw the brag-red car turn right towards her and brake sharply when it drew level. She opened the door; he was staring straight forward. She got in and barely had a chance to click herself in before he sped off. She was thrown so far forward that she almost banged her head on the windscreen. He didn't apologise.

'Where are we going?' she asked.

'They're building a car showroom a couple of miles away. It'll be deserted. I thought we could talk there.'

'Well don't try anything funny,' she warned him, 'because Clint's following to make sure I'm okay.'

'What do you mean "okay"?' he said, flicking his eyes up to his rear-view mirror and then out to the wing mirrors. 'What does he think I'm going to do?' He sounded insulted by that and ever so slightly panicked, but she didn't care.

'Clint presumes everyone thinks like he does is all I'm saying,' she said, not even sure if she knew what she meant by that. It sounded like a real threat, though and that would do.

Christian muttered something under his breath, and though she couldn't work out exactly what he said, she could hazard a guess at it not being complimentary. She also bet that he could have made the *Guinness Book of World Records* for the number of annoyed sighs per linear mile. Or eyes darting to the mirrors looking for his 'tail'. No one looked at their mirrors as much as that once they'd passed their test, she thought.

They didn't speak again until he parked up. To Palma's relief, the area was well lit and he hadn't sought out a dark corner near the overgrown bushes. He unclipped his belt, rubbed his forehead, turned half towards her and said, 'So.'

Palma took that as a cue to get out one of the pregnancy tests. 'I did two to be certain. They're both positive. I'm definitely pregnant.'

'I suppose *she* gave you my mobile number,' Christian said, his head jerking slightly in the direction where it thought *she* might be.

'Yep. I went to deliver my good news to you both yesterday only to find her delivering bad news to me,' replied Palma. 'I've fulfilled my side of the bargain.'

Christian's head dropped and he gave a small laugh out of one side of his mouth. A laugh that had anything but humour in it.

'She told you that she threw me out, I presume,' he said.

'Well . . . I figured.'

'And what did she say about . . .' he pointed to her stomach.

'That she wanted nothing to do with it, and to see you.'

Again he swore under his breath; she heard the 'f' and 'x' sounds clearly enough to know that he wasn't overjoyed.

He thought for a moment and then said, 'How do I know you're telling the truth?'

Palma felt her jaw tighten. 'Because I am,' she said. 'Because that's what you are paying me to do for you.'

'That could be anyone's,' he said, nodding at the test wand.

'It's mine. Drive me back to Tesco and I'll do another in front of you if you want,' snapped Palma.

'I mean anyone's child.'

That stung. The cheeky bastard.

'It always could. This was a trust arrangement. I know you'd have had a DNA test done when the baby was born to prove it was yours anyway. I'm not thick and I'm not a liar. It's not my fault you ...' *got caught with your trousers down and your wife chucked you out* '... broke the deal. I never would have.'

Palma could imagine the cogs whirring in his head. Very shortly, he would tell her to go and get rid of it. Just like her mother had done with an inconvenient goldfish once. She was right.

'You'll get rid of it now, obviously,' he said.

'What, and not get paid the five grand you owe us?'

His eyes narrowed. 'Don't be stupid. Why would you want to go through with it?'

'I don't particularly,' said Palma. 'But I do want the five grand. A deal is a deal.'

He reached down to his side and produced an envelope which he held out to her.

'There's a thousand pounds in there. Take it and do what you have to.'

When Palma's hands didn't budge from her lap he poked the package into her arm as if to further bring it to her attention.

'And the rest?' she asked.

'No more. Why would there be?'

Was he joking? 'Because all the way through this, you've expected that if anyone would break the deal it would be me. But it wasn't. I kept my side of the bargain and that bargain was five thousand pounds.'

Christian dropped the package into her lap, a gesture of disdain. 'Here, take it. It's yours. Five thousand if you carried it to term, which you won't now, will you? Have a nice convenient abortion on the National Health and we'll never have to think about this again. Now be a good girl and take the money.' He reached over his shoulder for the seat belt. It was done as far as he was concerned.

No no no. It wasn't money he was cheating her out of but a new life. She had her foot firmly on the first step of a ladder now and there was no way she was about to take it off again and sink back into the rancid waters of dreadful familiarity.

She played her trump card.

'Clint wants the full money.'

'Oh for ...' Christian's fist thumped the steering wheel hard. 'It's not difficult to understand. I don't want the bloody baby. She doesn't want the bloody baby. No one wants the ... fucking thing.'

Palma stayed calm, but her hand crept into her bag, curled around the canister of pepper spray in readiness.

'You owe us four thousand eight hundred.'

'Tell Clint O'Gowan to ...' Christian pulled up his words before they found their way into the air and couldn't be unsaid. His stupid wife had rushed in and arranged all this and he'd gone along with it. Tabitha was desperate for a baby and had worn him down with her persistence. Now he couldn't understand why the hell he had agreed to it, but then, he'd been preoccupied with other things. Twenty-year-old other things with massive knockers.

'Let me put it this way,' said Palma. 'If you don't give

me the full five, then I'll have the baby and come after you for child maintenance. I haven't slept with anyone for over two years. There's only one person who could have fathered what's in me so that will be an expensive option for you. I bet even Tabitha would back me up if needs be. She certainly looked mad enough to yesterday.'

She watched the mottling pattern form on Christian's neck as quickly as if it was powered by a halogen bulb inside him. 'You really are a fucking little bitch, aren't you,' he said nastily, more angry with himself than her – and that really was saying something.

Palma's lips shrank away from her teeth, the gloves were fully off now. 'No, *you* fucking bitch. This is your fault it all went sour, not mine. I was prepared to give you what you wanted for a fair price. If you want to play unfair, then I will as well. And I'll be much better at it than you because I've got Clint watching my back.'

Christian thudded the heel of his hand into his forehead but no amount of bruising to the skull would get him out of this one. He was a lone king on a chessboard surrounded by threatening pieces of the opposite colour. He was unsteady, rocking on his square but not check-mated yet and he'd not go down until he was.

'You do know blackmail is a criminal offence?' he tried.

'So is buying children,' Palma parried. 'Newspapers love stories like that. But the bottom line, Mr Stephenson, is that if you decide to call my bluff then it would be a big mistake, because this *is* your baby and Clint *will* beat the crap out of you. And he'll keep doing it until you give him what he is due. And I'll bleed you dry for the rest of your life. And I'll go to the papers.'

Christian felt himself toppling. 'Shit. Shit. Shit,' he said, not under his breath.

'Seven grand,' Palma suddenly said, the two words surprising herself as much as him.

'What?'

Yes, sod it. Go for it. An extra two for having to put up with this crap.

'I want seven grand and I'll sign a legal form to say that I won't come after you ever for any child maintenance,' she said, astounded at how calm she sounded. 'Full and final settlement.' She remembered the expression from a drama about a divorce which she'd been watching on the telly and hoped it was the right one to use here.

'You can't keep it.'

'I can if I want. It's half mine.'

'Why would you? Oh . . .' The question swung to enlightenment. 'Benefits.'

That's how he sees me, Palma thought with an inner growl. Well, let him, she'd make it work for her. She'd swallow all pride if it meant she could get away from the Ketherwood estate.

'Got it in one,' she spat. 'So we'll both get what we want then, won't we? Or rather all three of us will, because if Clint isn't happy, then none of us are. You want to think yourself lucky you're getting me so cheap, because I could cost you a lot more.'

'You're cheap all right,' said Christian, with a sneer. If he'd punched her it would have hurt less than his tone did.

Christian turned the key in the ignition and the way he drove back mirrored his annoyance because she'd cornered him and men like Christian hated that. They wanted to be the ones calling the shots.

He pulled up so fast in front of Tesco that his brakes squealed horribly and drew the attention of several people.

'Give me two days. I'll be here on Wednesday at the same time,' he said, not looking at her.

'I'll see you then,' and she put the envelope in her handbag. 'I'll take this as the interim payment.' She got out of the car in a smooth, calm movement that belied the nerves jangling inside her. She'd disliked him before but she hated him now, trying to dispense with her as though she was rubbish. But what pulled rare tears to her eyes as she set off for the bus home was the feeling that she hated herself a little as well, for having to act like the Palma Collins too many people had thought she would grow into.

Everyone except Grace Beresford.

Chapter 13

Eve was sitting in the office trying to remember the important thing she needed to do but hadn't written down in her diary because she was sure she'd remember it when there was a timid knock on the door. She called 'Come in' and Effin entered. Or at least she thought it was Effin, because he usually strutted in like a stroppy peacock but this Effin wavered in as though he wasn't quite sure if he had meant to be here or not.

'You all right, Effin?' asked Eve.

'Er ... yes, yes,' he nodded, his tone contradicting his words. 'Missus, do you know anything about computers?'

'Well, it's a pretty wide subject, Effin. Can you be more specific?'

'Wages,' said Effin. 'I am absolutely sure that I recorded all the wages and saved the document but I can't find it anywhere. And I wouldn't know where to find it if it wasn't in the normal place. Will you come and have a look?'

As Eve prided herself on being pretty confident with technology she followed him next door to his site office and stood behind him as he sat at his computer and typed in the password slowly, with one finger so Eve saw that he had spelled out ANGHARAD, which wouldn't have been hard to guess at anyway.

'I saved it to the wages file. But it's not there. And I don't know what I've done with the sheet of paper with everything written down. It's a right pain this. The document's called MAYWAGE.'

Effin moved out of his chair so Eve could sit. She navigated through all the places where she thought it might be, including the trash bin, which was completely empty.

'Have you dumped it in here and then deleted everything recently?' Eve asked.

'I wouldn't know how to empty a trash bin,' said Effin. 'I didn't even know I had one. I thought that when you got rid of documents that they disappeared for good.'

'No, they go into there when you delete them which is a kind of purgatory for them,' Eve explained. 'Then when you really want to get rid of them, you empty your trash.'

'I've never emptied it,' Effin insisted. 'Ever.'

'Well, it looks as if someone has,' said Eve, checking again, but there was no MAYWAGE on Effin's computer.

'But I'm the only one who uses this . . . bloody machine,' said Effin, his voice raising with despair. 'No one knows my password or anything.'

'Did you save them to a memory stick?'

'What's one of those?' replied Effin.

'No other record at all?'

'Only the sheet I writ, but that's disappeared. It should

have been in my drawer. I always keep the sheets there, but it's not. I'm always so careful with the wages. I've never mucked them up in my life before. I can't understand it at all.' He rubbed his head as if it were a lamp and a genie might come out of it to rescue him. He looked at Eve and read her pained expression and his whole body sagged as if it were a punctured bag.

'They've gone for good, haven't they?'

'You definitely put them on a spreadsheet?'

'Yes. It's the only thing I use.'

Eve looked again. There was a FEBWAGE, MARCHWAGE, APRILWAGE but nothing else in Excel.

'Sorry, Effin, I have no idea where it is, but it isn't on here.'

'Oh f . . . lipping hell.' Effin looked gutted. 'I'll just have to ask everyone their hours again. If they can remember. The bastards are bound to rip me off.'

'Effin, I can show you how to use a memory stick at least.'

'No, no,' he shook his head. 'It sounds complicated. I'll stick to pen and paper in future. It never went wrong that way. Anyway, thank you, Missus, for trying to help.'

'I wish I could have found it for you,' said Eve, feeling his pain.

She was about to shut the door behind her when he called her back.

'That Davy MacDuff is a bit of a computer wizard isn't he, Missus?'

'He is. Do you want me to ask him to come over and see you?'

'No I do not,' said Effin firmly. 'I wouldn't be surprised—'

He cut off the words and shook his head. 'No, as I say, I'll do it the old way. I know where I am then. Thank you again, Missus.'

Eve went back to her own office and hoped Effin was all right. She had never known him to be anything but on the ball but recently he hadn't seemed like the same man they all knew. There was the incident with the Santapark lettering falling and that fuel mix-up and now this. And probably more that Jacques wasn't telling her. She wondered if it was catching, because her own memory was shocking at the moment too.

Tickets have gone on sale for £5 at Winterworld for the grand opening of the new lagoon attraction in June which will be opened officially by Franco Mozzarella, star of a new Hollywood film of the same name. All proceeds will go to the Yorkshire Fund for Disabled Servicemen. Site Manager F***ing Williams told the *Daily Trumpet* that the lagoon's official name would be 'Lady Evelyn's Lake' called after the original owner of the park, Emily Douglas.

Chapter 14

'Sign here,' said Christian, handing a pen to Palma with a small movement that managed to convey both hatred and revulsion.

She reached up to put on the in-car light because she couldn't read it properly. At the head of the document was the name of a firm of solicitors in loud black letters that stood slightly proud from the page and at the foot was a lot of incredibly small print. Everything in between was deliberately confusing legal jargon. Her brain cut straight through the crap and winkled out the nitty-gritty. Basically it said that he had handed over seven thousand pounds on the understanding that it was a full and final settlement (so that phrase had been spot on then) and she could not seek any child maintenance from him, ever. Palma wasn't even sure if it would stand up in court but it didn't matter anyway, because despite what he thought, she wasn't the type to hold him to prolonged ransom. He hadn't called her bluff, which she'd expected, so he must have believed her which helped her to claw back some pride, albeit a very tiny amount.

She signed it. He handed over a bulky envelope and she opened the flap and peered inside.

'Don't tell me you need to count it,' he said.

'No, it's fine,' she replied. Ironically she didn't think he would go to the trouble of cheating her. Plus she wanted to be out of this car and home as soon as possible. It didn't sit well with her what she was doing.

'I'm going to live abroad. You won't be able to find me,' he said. 'I don't want any news about . . .' he gave a single nod towards her stomach. 'So don't bother to tell me.'

Palma didn't know if it was true; probably not, but he didn't have to worry. She didn't want to see him ever again either.

'I wasn't going to,' said Palma. 'Full and final. I'll keep my word. As I have done all the way through this process. It wasn't me who moved the goalposts.'

'My mobile number will be defunct in the next couple of days. Don't ring me.'

'What would I need to ring you for?'

'Nothing, that's my point.'

'I won't. I want this done and dusted as much as you do.'

He put his seat belt back on, turned the key in the ignition and slipped into first gear.

'Can you drop me off at home instead, please? I don't want to be walking around with this cash in my bag,' she asked.

He gave a small jerk of his head that she took to be a yes

but at the lights he swung a left instead of going straight ahead and pulled up at the exact spot in the Tesco car park from where he had picked her up.

'Now fuck off,' he said.

*

Contrary to what might have been assumed from magazines or films, women did not want a man behind them making soothing noises when they were throwing up. Annie was quite happy to vomit alone and wipe her own face with a cold cloth. Besides, this wasn't just any sort of vomit, this was wonderful, fabulous morning sickness.

Joe knocked on the bathroom door.

'Annie, are you okay? Can I get you something to drink?'

'Joe, go away and leave me in peace, darling. I know you care, I know you want to help, but please let me throw up without you listening to me.'

'Okay, I go,' he said. She knew he hadn't because there was a creaky floorboard outside the toilet door.

'Joe. Bugger off.'

'Okay, okay.'

Now he was gone. He was going to be an absolute pain until Christmas, thought Annie fondly. But then that was Joe and she wouldn't have him any other way. And she couldn't have been happier that she was giving him the child they had been so desperate for.

She'd bought a Miriam Stoppard book from eBay and paid for next-day delivery; she hadn't put it down since it arrived. Annie had worked out that she was nearly nine weeks pregnant now, which meant that she had approximately three weeks of throwing up left, all being well.

She flushed the toilet and stood sideways on in front of the cheval mirror in the bathroom, lifting up her sweatshirt to check if she had acquired any trace of a baby bump since the last time she'd looked – three hours ago. *Not yet*, but it would come soon enough. She had her first antenatal appointment tomorrow in thirteen hours and forty-five minutes' time; a sample bottle stood on top of the loo in readiness for the morning.

It still didn't seem real. She'd already had a dream that there had been a faulty batch of pregnancy tests released to the public and she wasn't pregnant at all, but the aching boobs, the tiredness and this never-ending nausea gloriously said otherwise.

Chapter 15

'Well this is nice,' said Angharad Williams, pouring out tea for her husband, her niece and their guest. Young Dylan Evans handed the plate of roast potatoes to Cariad on his left, who accepted them with a smile, even if she was feeling less like smiling and more like spitting. She thought she was up here to have tea with her auntie, who had come up for a few days from Wales, and her uncle only and hadn't expected Dylan to be here. Her uncle was matchmaking when she had expressly told him not to on a number of occasions. They were speaking English because Dylan struggled with Welsh. His dad hadn't spoken much of it in the house, he told them, which surprised Effin. 'A Welsh oasis on the outskirts of the Pennines,' Angharad went on. 'Lovely.'

'Yes, isn't it,' Cariad replied, with more than a hint of sarcasm in her voice. 'Thank you for inviting me, Auntie Angharad.'

'It was your Uncle Effin's idea,' came the reply.

'Oh, I'll bet it was.' Cariad glared at her uncle, who coughed and lowered his eyes because he'd been caught bang to rights.

'He said, why don't we have Cariad and Dylan over and you cook your famous *Cig Oen a Mel*, and so here we are,' smiled Angharad, who had obviously no idea of the machinations behind a simple supper.

Angharad loved to come up to Yorkshire when Effin was working here and couldn't get home at weekends. He'd bought a cottage to stay in just outside Penistone. At work he shouted a lot; at home he preferred peace and quiet. He and Angharad liked nothing better than a walk and a pub lunch or sometimes they sat quietly on their terrace, which overlooked the moors and whilst Angharad read books at the side of the fire pit, Effin indulged in a spot of ornithology through his binoculars as this spot was a haven for kestrels and buzzards, tawny and barn owls. Bird-watching was balm for his soul and it had been since he was a small boy.

'How's your dad then, Dylan?' asked Effin, passing around the bowl of buttered carrots.

'As right as he can be,' said Dylan, with a little sigh. 'He doesn't complain.'

'Has he not found himself a nice woman then?'

'Well, there's not a lot of choice in the village and he'll never move,' replied Dylan.

'You should get Uncle Effin to match him up with someone. He reckons he's quite good at it,' said Cariad, narrowing her eyes at her uncle.

'Haven't you got any single friends for Brynn, Angharad?' asked Effin.

Angharad didn't answer but picked up the gravy boat and handed it to her guest. 'Tuck in, Dylan, there's plenty of food.'

'Thank you, Mrs Williams.' Dylan speared a piece of the honeyed lamb and lifted it to his lips, declaring it divine. 'You don't get food like this in the digs we're staying in.'

Angharad beamed. 'Effin and my boys have always enjoyed their food so I put plenty on the table. Mind you, young Cariad there could put away two potatoes more than a pig even when she was little.'

'You can't tell,' said Dylan, turning to her. 'What with your lovely figure.'

'I used to burn it all off dancing,' said Cariad. 'Not anymore though. I'll be twenty stone in a couple of years.' There, that should put him off.

There was a lull in the conversation whilst they ate, the only sound being cutlery on plate with the occasional 'mmm' of approval, then Angharad asked, 'So, are you all ready in the park for Mr Mezzaluna's visit?'

'Please, not whilst I'm eating,' said Effin, wrinkling up his nose with disdain. 'I don't want to talk about that *coc oen*.'

Dylan spluttered. That expression he did understand.

'Don't you dare call him a lamb's cock, Effin Williams,' said Angharad. Her look of reproach melted into a broad smile. 'He's absolutely gorgeous.' She turned to her niece. 'You might even get to meet him, Cariad.'

Cariad dismissed that with a shake of her head.

'He'll be far too busy. They'll have him on a tight schedule.'

'He won't be able to fart without a corresponding entry in his diary, with any luck,' sniffed Effin before Angharad smacked his hand with a serving spoon and glared at him before addressing Dylan.

'I think you could give Franco Mezzaluna a run for his money, Dylan. I bet you've got all the girls after you. What are you? You must be six foot two.'

'Six four,' Dylan answered.

'Big strapping lad,' said Effin, giving his niece a wink.

Right, thought Cariad, if he wants to play dirty, she'd wipe that smile off his face.

'Seen the *Daily Trumpet* today, Uncle Effin?'

As expected, his cheerful face morphed instantly to a glower.

'Yes, I bloody did, the stupid—'

Angharad clapped her hands together. 'Oh, I love to read the *Trumpet* when I come up here. They get everything wrong, don't they?'

'Today's entry is a cracker,' said Cariad; her turn to wink at her uncle now. 'They didn't get his name quite right. Thought Effin was a euphemism.'

'Oh, I'll have to look at that,' chuckled Angharad.

'And you should see what they called your perfect Mr Film Star,' Effin grunted. 'They called him after a cheese. He was on the telly last night. He's got a horrible twangy New York American accent. I'd soon get fed up of listening to that.'

'Oh, I don't know, Effin,' said Angharad, jumping to Franco Mezzaluna's defence. 'I've been thinking of sending you for elocution lessons so you can talk like him. It would be like someone pouring a melted Galaxy in your ear.'

'Give me a good deep Welsh voice any time,' huffed Effin.

'I must admit though, I do like to hear a Scottish lilt

too,' mused Angharad, which was definitely not the right thing to say.

'Oh, so do I,' put in Cariad with gusto. 'We've got a man at work with the loveliest accent, Auntie. Guttural and manly.'

'You talking about Davy?' asked Dylan.

'Yes, *old* Davy. *Sai'n trysto fe, sai'n licio'i lyged e.*' Effin slipped unconsciously into Welsh.

'What do you mean, you don't trust him and you don't like his eyes? He's got lovely eyes,' Cariad returned.

'He's too old for you,' said Effin, quickly.

'Auntie Angharad would leave you for *old* Tom Jones,' Cariad grinned. She was enjoying herself now, seeing her uncle squirm.

'I most definitely would.' Angharad nodded with a sigh. 'Those snakey hips. Those dulcet tones.'

Not to be outdone, Effin took that as a cue to wend the conversation back to Dylan's attributes. 'You've got a beautiful voice, Dylan. Deep and crisp and—'

'Even?' volunteered Cariad. 'Like Good King Wenceslas's pizza?'

Effin ignored her, determined to execute his mission. 'Talking of actors and films, there's a lovely little cinema in Penistone, if you fancied going to watch something. Have you been, Dylan, Cariad?'

If looks could have killed, Uncle Effin would have been slaughtered in his chair.

'I love the cinema,' said Dylan. 'Maybe we could go, Cariad, if you fancied it one night?'

'Oh go on,' encouraged Effin. 'You'd have a great time.

Two gorgeous young things like you.' He smiled trium-
phantly at his niece.

'That . . . that would be really nice,' Cariad said, stretching
her lips into the sort of smile that looked genuine to anyone
who didn't know her too well; but those who did – they'd
see more of an intent to murder.

Job done. Now Effin could relax and enjoy his lamb. He
was absolutely certain that Dylan Evans, son of his one-time
best friend, and his beloved niece were a match made in
heaven, just as he and his Angharad were.

After the meal Dylan offered to give Cariad a lift, something
that delighted her uncle even more.

'Isn't that nice of Dylan to see you home safely,' said a
euphoric Effin, talking to her as if she were six.

'Fantastic,' said Cariad with a bite in her voice, making
herself a promise that the next time he came in for an ice-
cream, she'd cover it in salt.

Dylan opened his car door for Cariad, something else
which set Effin off twittering with pleasure, like one of the
birds he watched finding a worm. Cariad couldn't wait to get
home. And that was telling, considering she shared her house
with flatmates who were the biggest bitches on the planet.

'They're lovely, your uncle and auntie,' said Dylan, waving
at Effin and Angharad.

Cariad made a non-committal sound and then said, 'My
auntie is a proper sweetie.' She wasn't going to say what she
thought about Effin.

'Not very subtle though, are they?' Dylan said.

'Oh, spotted that did you?' Cariad huffed.

'Look, Cariad, I'll be happy to take you to the pictures but I don't want you to have been forced into it,' said Dylan. 'We could go as friends. I'm not that bothered about any romance. I had my heart broke not so long ago and I'm in no rush to repeat the experience.'

Cariad sighed and two lungfuls of built-up pressure found their way to the outside world.

'Thank you for that, Dylan, because I don't want any romance either. It's the last thing on my mind.'

'Good, then we are in agreement,' he said.

'Thank you, Dylan.' Cariad gave him a genuine smile. At least her Uncle Effin was right about one thing – Dylan Evans really was a very nice young man.

Chapter 16

The next morning, Palma rang Clint. He was round within the half-hour. She put her coat on as soon as he rang the doorbell and said he couldn't stay long because she had to go out for a check-up at the doctor's. Clint was delighted that he'd got all his money up front. She was treated to the sight of his yellow grin and wondered how she could ever have ended up in bed with him four years ago. It was within months of Grace dying, the floor had fallen out of her world and she was living in a foul bedsit no bigger than a postage stamp. She'd felt out of her depth, alone, unanchored and without hope. Add alcohol to a period of depression – though she had never touched drugs – and the result was all sorts of stupid mistakes. Clint was, at least, the low point that galvanised her into making some key decisions and to start getting her shit together.

'How come the posh wanker paid the whole lot?'

'Because they split up and neither of them wants it,' she replied.

Clint laughed at that then spread the twenty-pound notes

into a fan and kissed it. He grinned again and Palma wished
he would stop because his smile was more sinister than his
resting psycho face. He stank as well, of weed and stale sweat.
He could stain the air where he stood.

'Well, that was easy.' He didn't ask Palma what she
intended to do about the baby. It wasn't any of his business;
besides he was too excited about going off to do some spending. Investing, as he called it. Drugs, obviously. Even if he
had asked, she couldn't have given him an answer. She was
trying not to think about the predicament she was now in
until her brain had some decent space for it.

For once, Clint couldn't wait to be off and as soon as he
had gone, Palma set her laptop on the table. It was so old now
it took a full five minutes to power up and it badly needed a
service but it was reliable enough because she looked after her
things. She searched for rented accommodation in Pogley,
Maltstone (fat chance), Dodley. Somewhere quiet, preferably
on the edge of the countryside. She didn't need a garden or
more than one bedroom, just a front door that she didn't
share with anyone else and a bath to lounge in and read.

There was a house in Dodley Bottom, which was a new
listing because it hadn't been there when she last searched and
there was no photo yet. Rainbow Lane. She looked on a map
and saw that it was off the High Street. Two up, two down,
small garden and the rent was doable. On paper it was perfect. She was searching for a pen when her doorbell buzzed.
A single long sound, not Clint then. She looked through the
window and saw the top of a bleached-blonde head, roots
showing. It hadn't taken long for the news to filter out that

she might have some spare money. It had been months since she last saw Nicole, her one-time best friend at school. The prettiest in the year, if not the brainiest. Predicted – unofficially – by their teachers to be the girl most likely to break free of her background. They'd been so wrong; Nicole was a skank. Like one of those little fish that hung around big sharks, that was what Nicole had become – Clint's bitch. What Palma could have been had she not woken up next to him that morning and realised she'd reached a never-to-be-repeated nadir.

Periodically Nicole showed up at the bedsit, thinner and scruffier than the time before, with a once-stunning smile now ruined by chapped lips and discoloured teeth. She'd make small talk for a while before asking for a couple of quid, a fiver, a tenner – anything – to tide her over. She'd pay it back, promise. She never did. And somehow, between walking in and walking out, she'd manage to nick something. A new tube of toothpaste once, a cheap bracelet another time, a toilet roll, a lipstick.

Palma moved away from the window and rang the estate agent, ignoring the repeated sound of the buzzer. Yes, she was available for a viewing that day. It wasn't soon enough.

Chapter 17

The *Daily Trumpet* would like to apologise to Mrs Freda Falworth of Wath for the report in last week's Gardening Special supplement. She was pictured with her prize Azaleas on show and not *Areolas*, as per the wording underneath. The *Daily Trumpet* has made a donation to the Wath Lady Garden Luncheon Club which Mrs Falworth attends.

Eve giggled. Surely that should be Lady Gardeners Luncheon Club, she thought. Another apology would have to be issued. The last garden supplement featured a woman who'd had her 'private bush' shaped into a crocodile and not her privet bush. The apology had appeared in record time, leading Eve to think she must have been quite influential. She took a glug from her coffee and made a face. Firms were always messing around with recipes and formulas when they'd got them perfect. There was an acrid taste to the brew that wasn't usually present. A dodgy bean harvest this year?

She turned the page and saw that Dr Gilhooley's son had started up a club for newly pregnant women and was calling it the Christmas Pudding Club. How would it feel, she wondered, to have a baby growing inside her. She couldn't imagine. Her friend Alison said that it was beyond weird when they started moving but it was what she'd missed most after Phoebe was born.

She and Jonathan were going to have children, which is why they'd bought a monster of a house to renovate over the years. He was on her mind a lot recently for reasons she couldn't fathom. He'd have made a good dad: strict but fair, but he wouldn't have crawled on the grass wearing camouflage make-up whilst hunting for dinosaurs the way Jacques would.

It was no good though, she could read no more. She'd hoped that two ibuprofen would have knocked this migraine on the head but she'd had four tablets in as many hours and it was still throbbing like a tireless tom tom in her temple. She hadn't had a migraine this severe for years. Not since Jonathan died; she'd had a chain of them then.

She closed her eyes and rested her head on her hands. There were over five hours until the end of her working day. If she was employed by someone else, she'd have picked up her keys and said she had to go home and lie down, but she was a hard taskmaster to herself. She'd made herself a chart, ticking off the days until the massive midsummer 'Half Christmas' relaunch event – forty days of full-on stress to go. Stress was a horrible thing. It wasn't only making her tired and giving her headaches but she felt on the edge of tears all the time. Stress was like an agricultural machine ploughing through her brain, disturbing all sorts of bad memories that she'd thought were calm in their beds: Jonathan's horrible parents, the crippling loneliness that isolated her from the rest of the world after he'd gone; and even further back to growing up with a mother who was to maternal care what King Herod was to running a nursery. Stress that starved her of sleep at night yet threw bucketloads of it at her during the day. Stress that toyed with her appetite and turned up the volume on her sense of smell to max.

It never occurred to Eve that all these symptoms had less to do with tensions about a bathing lake and more to do with the fact that, with so much on her mind, she'd been rather careless with her birth control pills over the past few months.

*

The midwife chuckled as Annie apologised for twittering like a sparrow on speed. The woman had only asked her how her general health was and instead received a full run-down of Annie's previous attempts to have children and why they'd all failed. She stopped short of talking about the adoption attempt.

'I'm sorry. I'm babbling. I'm not a natural babbler but . . .'

'It's fine,' said the midwife, who had introduced herself as Chloe Donovan. 'It's lovely to see.'

'I thought I was either going through the menopause or dying,' said Annie. 'It's a miracle for us. There's no chance there could be a mistake is there? I've had these dreams and—'

Chloe the midwife cut her off. 'Oh, the dreams. I had

some beauties when I was pregnant with my twins. Ugly baby dreams are quite common and are very disturbing. You're pregnant, there's no mistaking, Mrs Pandoro, so get ready for the ride of your life. Have you joined the Christmas Pudding Club?'

'Yes, I shall be going to the meetings. It'll be nice to meet other mums, though I expect they'll be a lot younger than I am.'

'It doesn't matter. You've all got quite a lot in common.' Chloe started rolling up Annie's sleeve so she could take her blood pressure. 'I'll be running them along with Sharon, the midwife at Dr Gilhooley's other practice, and we're really looking forward to it. I happen to think it's a great idea. You're Dr Gilhooley's guinea pigs, did he tell you? If it works, he's going to have a Summer Pudding Club and then lord knows where it will end. Rice Pudding Club, knowing him. He's keen, I'll give him that. Have you been taking folic acid?'

'Yes. Well, multivitamins with folic acid added.'

'Blood pressure is good,' said Chloe, sliding the collar from Annie's arm. 'Any morning sickness? Which came at every time of the day but the morning for me.'

'Awful sickness,' said Annie. 'But now I know what it is, I don't mind it as much, if that doesn't sound daft.'

'I get it,' said Chloe. 'It makes it all the more real.'

'In a nutshell.'

'You eating properly? It's important to keep up your liquids.'

'Yes and yes. Totally lost the taste for coffee, which can only be a good thing, I suppose,' said Annie.

'You'll get it back,' said Chloe. 'Had any spotting? It's usual to lose a bit of blood in the beginning.'

'None,' said Annie.

'Lots of pregnant ladies don't realise how many symptoms there might be. You might think your brain has been swapped for a turnip for instance. Some lucky beggars hardly get anything.'

'I think I've signed up for the lot,' said Annie. 'I haven't been able to retain a thing in my brain recently. I've had to become the queen of list-making so I don't forget things.'

'Let's take your height and weight.'

Chloe recorded Annie's height at five foot six, which was an inch shorter than she thought she was. Was she at the age to start shrinking already? Her weight was out too because she was half a stone lighter than she'd guessed at, which was a nice little bonus. Not that it would last. And not that she cared either. She wanted to be gloriously fat and full of baby.

'Now I'm writing all this information in your notebook and its very important you remember to bring it with you to all your appointments with me, with the doctor, when you go for your scan, everything,' said Chloe. 'If in doubt, bring it.'

'Message received and understood,' said Annie, watching Chloe put the A4 green book into a blue zipper bag. She felt a fizz inside her at the thought that she – Annie Pandoro – had pregnancy notes.

'You'll get an appointment for your first scan through the post,' said Chloe at the end of the session. 'If your dates are right, your baby is the size of a cherry, in case you're interested,' she went on. 'You'll probably start to show in the next couple of weeks. It's about the only time in her life that a woman enjoys parading a bulging stomach.'

Annie left the doctor's, her feet almost floating above the ground with happiness and, before going back to the car, headed off to the nearby Co-op supermarket.

She had a sudden and urgent craving for cherries and needed them *now*.

*

Palma's head was spinning. She'd known as soon as the owner invited her over the threshold into the little house on Rainbow Lane that she wanted to live there. It was tiny but cosy and on a quiet street with a square of garden at the back and – joy of joys – a bath. She'd paid the two-hundred-pound bond and the month's rent in advance there and then and spun the owner a yarn that she'd only recently set up in business as a copyeditor and didn't have three years' books to show as proof of employment. The landlady said it was fine, not to worry and Palma had felt immediately guilty for lying. She had once read that confidence tricksters were so successful because most people were predisposed to believe that others were telling the truth. She wasn't intending to rip anyone off but it didn't sit well with her that she could fool someone so easily; nor that she'd be living in this house because lies and blackmail had made it possible.

She arranged to move in on Saturday because there was no point in hanging about. The sooner she was out of Ketherwood, the sooner she could sort her life out. She went straight from the house to the local doctor's up the road to register herself as a patient.

The receptionist made her an appointment for Wednesday afternoon. That gave her nearly a week to sort out what to do about her 'passenger'; the life she had made happen, the mass of cells that was developing at a rate of knots inside her. Whatever that decision turned out to be, she'd need to make it quick – and final.

Chapter 18

The next day signalled Gill's last day at work and Joe cracked open a bottle of champagne instead of filling up a teapot. Luckily neither Iris nor Gill were driving home because they were plastered by three o'clock. Not a lot of cracker stuffing got done that afternoon. But a lot of baby talk was covered. And it wasn't the good stuff.

Gill slipped into a warm pool of reminiscence. 'I remember having our Viv. Contractions, they told me, build up slowly – well these buggers didn't. I felt like a bloke with hob-nailed boots on was kicking me in the back for ten hours.'

'Our Linda got stuck. They had to cut me a smile underneath,' Iris laughed fondly, determined not to be outdone. 'I couldn't sit down properly for weeks. A rubber ring was my best friend. My Dennis used to cut holes in the cushions for me. His thoughtfulness rekindled our relationship because, I tell you, I wasn't going to have him near me in the bedroom ever again. And we loved sex.' She threw another half glass of champagne down her neck and then made a long 'eeee' sound. 'He threw me around the bedroom so much on our wedding night they could only identify me by my dental records the next morning.'

Joe was bent double, laughing so much that his stomach hurt.

'It's all right you scoffing, Joe Pandoro,' Iris went on, 'but it's not you men that have to try and get a camel through the eye of a bloody needle. Linda was a huge baby. We've had smaller turkeys for Christmas dinner.'

Up for a competition, Gill launched in with details of her second daughter's birth.

'Oh, and they said to me that if you've had a difficult birth the first time, the next one will be like shelling peas. They were wrong about that an' all. She was worse. Breech. They had to shove her back up and, pull her out the right way round.'

'Never,' said Joe, enthralled, thinking Stephen King should be listening to this. He could make a book out of such gore and horror.

'Joe Pandoro, would I lie to you? And I did it all on a puff of gas and air and our Ted's hand to chew on. These days they cut them open for a laugh. And give them a tummy tuck at the same time. Some of those "too push to posh" celebrities must have more scar tissue than skin,' replied Gill, who hiccupped then giggled. Those two glasses of champagne had zoomed to her head.

'I'm still trying to get rid of my baby weight,' said Iris, jiggling her none-too-small stomach. 'Mind you, so is our Linda. She was probably at her thinnest when she was nine months pregnant. Now when she gave birth to my son Handy, I mean her grand— . . . MY grandson Andy, she had to have an emergency *slezarian*. It was like an explosion in a butcher's shop.'

Annie made a strange gurgle in her throat and when the others turned to her, they found that her face looked slapped with terror.

'Oh, Annie, lass, however bad it is, however much pain you're in, when they put that little baby in your arms, you forget it all,' Iris said with a wide soppy smile. 'It's a moment that stays with you forever. When they said "Mrs Caswell, you've got a daughter", I thought my heart was going to burst with joy. And I'd have been the same with a son. I just wanted it out and healthy – nothing else mattered. And she was: ten pound foursworth of healthy.'

'*Santo cielo*, I bet she was walking before you were, Iris,' said Joe, crying now. His laughter infected them all and they couldn't stop even though their cheeks ached from it.

'Oh, I'm going to miss you all so much,' said Gill, wiping away the tears leaking out of her eyes. Tears of mirth and sadness, all intermingled.

''Ere, have some cake, that'll stop you weeping,' said Iris, picking up the plate full of sponge.

Gill selected a slice. 'It's lovely this,' she said. 'I'll remember today all my life. I've had some wonderful years here. Wonderful.'

'Let's wrap it up for today,' said Joe. 'Two of my workforce are drunk and I'm going to take the third out for an early-bird special at the Royal. It's Chinese night on Fridays.'

'Ooh, a perfect end to a perfect day,' grinned Annie.

'But first . . .'

Joe dropped a gift bag down on the table in front of Gill as she was polishing off the last mouthful of cake. 'This is from all of us with our love,' he said.

'It's a little something for you to open,' said Annie.

'Oh, you shouldn't have, you really shouldn't.'

'It was my suggestion,' said Iris, proudly. 'Someone had one done for our Linda and Dino's pearl wedding anniversary and I thought what a smashing idea it was.'

Gill carefully opened the bag as if a jack-in-the-box was about to leap out of it, then she peered inside before lifting out a box.

'Go on then,' urged Iris, when Gill took an age before she removed the lid. 'we haven't got all day.'

Inside the box was a square glass block bearing an etching of all four of them, arms crossed, auld-lang-syne style, holding the ends of crackers. It was from a photo that they'd had done for the local paper a year ago. Gill's hand flew up to her mouth to stifle the cry.

'Oh, it's something I'll treasure forever,' she said. 'Look at us all. Crackers, the lot of us.'

'There's something else in the bag, Gill, don't throw it away,' said Annie.

'Is there?' Gill looked and brought out an envelope full of money.

'We thought that you and Ted could have a nice meal out on us.'

'Nay, we can't spend all that on a meal,' Gill protested.

There was a thousand pounds in the envelope. They knew that money was the best thing they could give her, since their place in Spain was fully furnished. They'd seen plenty of photos of it over the last year.

'At least spend some of it on that to celebrate your new life. Promise us,' said Joe.

'Oh, we will,' said Gill, tears streaming down her face. 'We will.'

Chapter 19

Palma spent most of that Friday packing after going to the local shops and cadging some empty boxes from them. Then she rang a number she'd found on the internet: 'A Man with a Van' as he advertised himself. Someone from out of the area because she didn't want anyone knowing where she had moved to.

She really could have done with not going out that night with Tommy but she had no way of getting in touch with him. Then again, maybe it would be better going out instead of sitting in this dump of a place any longer than she had to.

Palma didn't have a lot of clothes, but what she did have was the best quality she could afford. A capsule wardrobe, the magazines called it. Separates that could be put together to make it look as if she had loads of different outfits. She'd always been good at picking clothes that flattered her slender shape and colouring: black drained the life out of her, bold colours worked for her and made the blue of her eyes pop. She had no idea how posh the restaurant would be but she had a summer cerise-spotted dress and a jacket that looked smart but not over the top as if she were going to the races. Perfect for a warm May evening.

Tommy turned up, exactly on time. He waved up at the window after ringing the doorbell. He was wearing jeans, white shirt and a black leather jacket and looked really smart too and so she was glad she'd dressed up rather than down.

'All right,' he greeted her, opening the passenger door of his car for her, a dark blue Fiesta ST, brand new as well. She hoped he didn't drive it like a boy racer.

'Nice car,' she commented.

'Ta,' he said. Inside was as sparkling as the outside and smelled lovely: Jelly Belly Blueberry, she recognised it because she had the same air freshener hanging up next to her bed.

'I thought we'd go to the Royal. Have you been? It's Chinese night on Fridays.'

'No, I haven't,' said Palma, although she'd read a complimentary review of it in the *Chronicle*.

Tommy set off, smoothly pulling away from the kerb, thank goodness. He didn't try and impress her with fast acceleration.

'You got a car?' he asked.

'No, but I can drive. I'd like one. Nothing flash. Just something reliable to get me from A to B. Or work, when I eventually find something, because it hampers your chances not having one.'

'No luck?'

'Not yet.' She didn't like having to admit that she wasn't

working. She didn't want to be lumped in with those who were content to sit on their backsides and draw benefits and she hoped he realised she was with those who were keen to earn a wage and support themselves. She felt the sudden need to tell him that she wasn't stuck in a dead-end rut.

'I'm moving from my flat.'

'Are you? To go where?'

'I've found a house to rent in Dodley Bottom.'

She saw the grin spread across his lips. 'I'm at Dodley Top.'

'You live in Dodley? So what were you doing running round Edgefoot park the other night?'

'I run up the rocks at the back. Good stamina training. We'll be neighbours more or less. I don't know, one date and you're moving to live near me.'

He was obviously joking, or at least she hoped he was. And 'one date'? Is that what she was on now? She wouldn't have said yes if she'd known that. She'd have to make it very clear that she didn't see this as a date at all. She didn't want to lead him on.

She ignored the date reference when she carried on talking. 'It's a really nice house. Small, but a million times better than the bedsit.'

'Even by Ketherwood standards those . . .' Tommy stopped in mid-sentence and made an embarrassed face. 'I mean . . . well . . .'

'You're right what you were going to say,' said Palma. He wasn't telling her anything she didn't already realise. 'Even by Ketherwood standards that block of bedsits are shitholes. But it was all I could afford at nineteen and the area wasn't as bad three years ago as it is now. It's gone right downhill in a short time.'

She'd managed to put away some money every month; her cash-in-hand overtime payments from the takeaway had mounted up. She'd hated having to break into her savings when she'd lost her job. That five grand she'd taken from Christian might not have been a fortune, but it felt like one to her.

'I'm sorry. It must have been hard on you not having any family to back you up.'

'Well, you just get on with it, don't you?' said Palma. 'Living in a crappy bedsit and having a job dishing up chicken and chips wasn't exactly what I had in mind when the career officer asked me in year eleven where I saw myself in five years' time; but you have to start somewhere.'

'Where did you see yourself, Palma?' Tommy asked.

'No idea, but doing something I could get my teeth into and build up. I've never been scared of hard work and I hate being unemployed and having to sign on. I do have some pride. I want to earn my own money.'

Or get it by blackmail, said a voice in her head that she didn't like.

'I can tell that,' said Tommy. 'The way you dress.'

'What do you mean?'

'You having pride. You take care of yourself. You've got style.'

Palma half-wanted to laugh. Style was a word that had never been applied to her before, that she knew of anyway. But it was a sweet compliment and she accepted it and gave him a bashful, 'Thanks.'

He'd booked a table because it was a popular place, especially at the weekends, he said. He opened the front door for her and the smell of Chinese food rushed at them and her stomach responded with a discreet growl. She hadn't eaten all day, hadn't even felt peckish really, but suddenly she was hungry.

'What do you want to drink?' he asked.

'A Britvic 55, please.'

'Don't you want a wine or a gin and tonic? They do nice cocktails here.'

'No, I'm happy with a softie.'

He ordered a diet cola for himself. He didn't drink anything when he was driving, he said. He didn't drink much anyway these days. His body was a temple, he said, with his trademark grin.

'TNT. All right, mate?' someone across the bar shouted and gave him the thumbs up and Tommy responded with a modest 'Cheers.'

'Friend of yours?' asked Palma.

'Never seen him before in my life. It happens a lot though, it's nice, I like it.'

'Why TNT?' asked Palma when they were shown to their table.

'Tommy Neil Tanner,' he explained. 'Neil isn't my real name, it's my brother's. But I adopted it. Tommy "TNT" Tanner. That's how they announce me in the ring.'

He pronounced it 'bruvver'. On anyone else it might have been annoying, on him it was totally endearing.

Palma tilted her head and studied him, seeing him

through the awestruck eyes of the man at the bar for a second. 'Done well for yourself, haven't you, if you're the British champion?'

'Not bad,' he smiled and tapped the menu that she'd been given. 'Stop talking and pick. I'm starving. Let's get loads of dishes.'

Palma picked three, Tommy picked nine. He couldn't decide, he told the waitress who took their order, so he was having plenty for choice.

'So,' began Tommy. 'Fill me in on what's been happening to you since we were at school.'

Palma chuckled. 'I already did that. Bugger all.'

'Add some detail. Or make something up,' he pressed, and she thought what twinkly eyes he had. Laughter was dancing in those eyes and she hoped it wasn't because he fancied her. His timing was off if he did.

Palma shrugged her shoulders. 'Really, there's nothing.'

'I seem to remember your mum wasn't well,' he said. A memory came swimming back to him. 'Didn't she turn up at school . . .' Then that memory tuned into sharp focus and he waved it away. 'No, it wasn't you. Forget that.' But he hadn't got it wrong, they both knew.

'Yes she did, you remembered it perfectly,' said Palma. 'She turned up pissed as a fart. She'd decided to have a shot at being a proper mother and pick me up from school, two hours early and eight years too late.' Palma's cheeks began to heat as the old shame revisited her. 'She had a fight with the supply teacher and ended up scratching her face, you'll have remembered that as well.'

'I'm sorry. I didn't mean to drag all that back for you.'

'It's okay.'

'I feel really bad.'

'It doesn't matter.' Palma never cried, but she had that day, completely overwhelmed with humiliation. 'She did me a favour really, because it led to social services being called in again and started the ball rolling to get me away from her. I went into care after that.'

'What was it like?' Tommy was interested, leaning forward to hear more.

'It was okay, actually. I got fed proper meals and they were really good people who ran the home, then I got shifted to live with a foster mother. I think you'd ... you'd left by then,' she said.

The food arrived and took up all of the table. It both looked and smelled fantastic.

'Dig in,' said Tommy. 'Anything you want. Anyway, you were saying ... foster mother. And yes, I'd probably been sent away. I went just before Christmas.'

'I went into care in January and moved in with her in March,' said Palma. She had a sudden vision of herself being driven to Grace's. The snow was settling on the road and the car was skidding everywhere. It was dark and freezing and as they drew up in front of the house, there was a warm, golden light shining out of the front window. 'I was okay in the kids' home, I didn't really want to go and live with anyone, but five minutes after I walked across her threshold, I was sitting at a table with a big plate of homemade spaghetti Bolognese. I don't think I've ever tasted anything as wonderful in my life. Somehow I fitted into that house as if I'd been specially made for it.'

'That's nice,' said Tommy, after he had cleared his mouth of a prawn cracker. 'How long did you stay there? Four years, did you say?'

He'd remembered. She was impressed. 'More or less. Grace had a massive heart attack the fortnight before my A-levels. No wonder I failed them all.' Palma's voice cracked and she changed the subject quickly. 'Anyway, what about you?'

Tommy gesticulated at her to wait because he had just chomped down on a spring roll. He loved his food, that was clear. 'Sorry about that. You know, I felt for you that day your mum came to school because I couldn't ever remember seeing my mum sober before she left us. Dad was useless and I ran riot. I got sent to Forestgate, Dad died whilst I was in there and at the funeral I met this Neil bloke who introduced himself to me as my older brother. I didn't even know my dad had been married before. He kept in touch with me and, when I came out, he took me in, him and his missus, Jackie; they've been great.'

'And did you say he was your trainer?'

She'd remembered. He was impressed. 'I still had a lot of anger issues when I left Forestgate,' Tommy admitted sheepishly. 'He dragged me off to his gym and told me to take it out on a punchbag, make my aggression work for me. Channel it, he said.'

'And so you did?'

'I did. I love boxing. It's all I was ever interested in, it's the only thing I really understand, Palma. And it's the only thing I'm good at.'

'I bet that's not true,' she said.

'It is,' he came back at her with gusto. 'My life was a mess but somehow everything made sense as soon as I stepped in a ring. I'm not one of those natural fighters, I've had to work hard at it, but I do. I study my opponents beforehand so I know their patterns. I used to do it as a kid, play videos over and over again, study and study and study fighters so much that I could almost get into their heads and if I could do that, then I knew what their next moves would be. Take Frank Harsh, for instance –' he shuffled forwards slightly in his seat and Palma stifled the smile that bloomed in response to the passion in his voice – 'He's a brilliant fighter, heavy puncher, fast, slick, longer reach than me but I'll pulverise him because he's not an inside boxer. Close up, tight to him, I know I can beat him, and that's where I'll be in December, closer than his wife gets. I can't wai—' He stopped abruptly. 'Sorry. I get carried away talking about it. Boring you to death, aren't I?'

'You aren't at all,' replied Palma, smiling freely at him now to show that she was being genuine and not merely polite. 'I love your appetite for it.'

'Talking of appetite, have you tried that chicken and mushroom yet? It's fabulous.' Tommy scooped half the dish onto his plate and offered the other half to Palma. 'So where's your mum now?'

'No idea,' said Palma. 'I'm not bothered.'

'Same as me,' said Tommy. 'I've got all the family I want. At least for now. I'd love kids. I'd do it properly an' all. I'd look after 'em. They'd never see me drunk and I'd never hit 'em. I'd tell 'em I was proud of 'em. I always wanted someone to say to me that they were proud of me, so I'll make sure they hear it a lot.'

He said that so tenderly that Palma had a sudden vision of him play-boxing with a little boy. Totally ridiculous, she knew.

'Some people just churn kids out, don't they?' Tommy went on.

'Yep,' she said, spearing a mushroom and putting it into her mouth, whilst breaking eye contact.

'My life is a straight line at the moment, no complications, nothing in the way of my boxing because it's a young man's game, you can't overstay your welcome in that ring, but I definitely want them in the future. Do you think you'll have kids one day?' he asked.

Oh, that was too close. She could wreck this evening by saying, *Well, funny you should say that . . .*

'Not sure,' she said instead. 'I'm not very maternal.' She didn't want to think about her present situation until after the weekend. Top of the list was moving house, then what to do about her pregnancy, then she needed a job to allow her to continue living in the house. She changed the subject. 'So when's your next fight?'

'December the twenty-third.'

'Your first defence.'

'Yep. Can't wait. Here, try this, Palma. Duck. I don't usually like duck but that sauce . . . oh . . . *mmm*.' He kissed the circle that a finger and his thumb made and Palma smiled, delighting in his delight.

Talk flowed easily between them and yet later, when Palma would try and recall what they could have filled two and a half hours with, she couldn't remember it all. News about what some of the kids whom they both knew were doing now. The O'Gowans were mentioned. Tommy had heard that Leslie, son of the notorious Bull O'Gowan, was doing a long stretch for attempted murder. He told her that he'd come up against Leslie's cousin Clint last year for trying to deal 'roids outside the gym. He'd have killed the druggie scrote if Neil hadn't held him back from chasing after him. He took scum to a new level, he said. Palma didn't comment on that, but asked him if he'd heard about Bull's youngest Ryan, because he'd bucked the O'Gowan fate and was at university doing English. He'd been taken in by the woman who employed him in her café at weekends. Tommy already knew that because Ryan had done an inspirational talk for some of the kids he worked with – kids having troubles in the mainstream education environment – about how your past shouldn't nobble your future. Tommy was proof of that, too. There were lots of anecdotes from his time in Forestgate; not so many from Palma, but she did fill him in on the list of the jobs she'd done, beginning at Sheila's sandwich shop and ending with Ketherwood Fried Chicken. Next stop, head of ICI, she joked.

When Tommy dropped her off later, she thanked him for a lovely evening. And she meant it. He thanked her for her company but he didn't ask to see her again, which was probably just as well; though she thought that if he'd given her the option, she would have said yes. Instead he leaned over and gave her a friendly peck on the cheek. He said he'd wait until he saw a light going on in her bedsit so he could be sure she was safely inside. She switched the light on, then waved at him from the window and he drove off. That, as far as Palma was aware, was that.

Chapter 20

As Joe swung into the car park at the side of The Crackers Yard on the following Wednesday the new replacement for Gill Johnson was waiting outside. She was the fourth person the agency had sent them and, with any luck, the first one that would fit straight in. They'd hoped there would be a crossover period in which Gill could train them up but it hadn't happened; mind you, the job wasn't complicated and anyone with half a brain could pick it up in no time. That was the problem though, because so far the agency hadn't sent anyone with an ounce of gumption.

'Well, there's a good sign,' said Iris from the back seat of the Audi. 'She's on time. What's her name?'

'Mahogany,' said Annie with a little sigh. Some people didn't think about what they called their children too carefully, especially as Mahogany was as pale and blonde as if she'd been bleached. She couldn't think of a less likely name for someone. Iris was of the same mind.

'Looks more like limed oak than mahogany,' she said, then she gave an audible gasp. 'Mahogany what? Not Clamp.'

'Yes, why?'

Iris put her hand on her forehead.

'Well don't reckon on having any stock left at the end of the day. And check her bag before she goes home. I thought I knew the name. Our cleaner Hilda has had some right run-ins with the Clamp family. They've all got *Jeremy Kyle* names: Nepal, Velvet, Chartreuse, Chenille, Crimplene, Bri-Nylon. I wish I'd known, I'd have warned you.'

Still, Joe wasn't the type to pre-judge the young woman and greeted her warmly. He introduced her to Annie who shook her hand and Iris who gave her a begrudging nod.

Mahogany sat in Gill's old seat, opposite Iris and whilst Joe made the coffees, Annie set her on cutting up some sheets of jokes. It was usually such a jolly atmosphere but Gill's merry presence was missed. Gill liked to read the jokes out loud and, as terrible as they were, she had them all in stitches with her delivery. 'Crackers, these jokes are,' she'd say and they'd groan and smile at the same time.

'I've seen more life in a dead frog. The light might be on, but someone's definitely been playing with the dimmer switch,' Iris commented when Mahogany had gone to the toilet. 'At least you're safe from theft because I don't think she could be bothered lifting anything up to stuff in her bag.'

'Iris, shhh,' said Annie.

'Hilda's grandson took an overdose because of Nepal Clamp. And someone Hilda works for, her ex-fella went off with one of the other Clamps and she spent all his money. He won a load of cash on a scratchcard. In fact, she's like you.'

'Oh, thanks, Iris,' said Annie.

'Not the Clamp lass, Hilda's boss. She couldn't get pregnant, then married a policeman and she took on straightaway.'

Some of Iris's stories were so complicated, they had to be unpicked slowly.

'The one who owns a Van Gogh,' Iris went on. 'Oh, you'll have read about her.'

Annie gave up. She hadn't a clue what Iris was talking about. There were too many names with too many connections. She wished she'd told her that Mahogany's surname was Smith.

Joe's jaw was open with incomprehension. He hadn't heard any of the conversation after the Hilda's grandson part. 'Nepal Clamp? Someone with the surname Clamp has called their child *Nepal*?'

That had translated into Italian.

'Yep. And what's buggerlugs doing in there?' asked Iris, jutting her head in the direction of the toilet. 'She's been ages. I'm not even in there that long and I've got a retentive bowel.'

She had been a long time, thought Annie, glancing up at the clock. She crept over to listen for signs of life and heard one side of a whispered conversation. Mahogany was obviously on the phone. Any concern segued to annoyance.

'Everything all right in there,' Annie said, after giving the door a gentle knock.

'Er, yeah, just er ... just coming,' came the answer, immediately followed by a flush and then the judder that the hot tap made.

'Thought you'd disappeared into another world there,' said

Iris stiffly, as Mahogany returned to the table and hung her large bag over the back of her chair.

'Felt a bit sick,' said Mahogany. 'New job nerves.'

'No need to be nervous of us,' said Annie, not adding, *Well, maybe not Joe and me but Iris is a different kettle of fish.*

'Where did you work last?' asked Iris, wearing one of her best false smiles.

'Bar,' said Mahogany with a sniff.

'Barrister, or selling alcohol?' said Iris, with that terrifying smile still in place. Her comment went right over Mahogany's head. Not surprisingly.

'What?'

'I think Iris means, which bar,' clarified Annie.

'Just a few hours here and there,' came the reply, which didn't answer the question at all.

Iris watched Mahogany pick up the scissors and wondered if she was in fact part of a parallel universe where everything moved in slow motion. She worked out that Mahogany had done a twentieth of what Gill could have done so far. And it didn't exactly need a learned skill set to cut up a few sheets of paper. Her great-grandson Freddie could have done them faster with both hands tied behind his back – and he was at primary school.

The only time that Mahogany shifted with any speed was when they broke for lunch and she sprang from her seat and said that she was going to get a sandwich from Bren's Butties on the corner. She didn't ask if anyone else wanted one and an hour later, she hadn't returned. In fact she didn't come back at all. And when Annie went into the toilet it was to discover that the four loo rolls she'd put out that morning had vanished.

Chapter 21

It hadn't taken Palma that long to unpack when the Man with a Van – well men, seeing as there were two of them – had shifted all her worldly belongings into Rainbow Lane last Saturday. They kindly gave her a lift as well, away from the shithole that was Flat B, 33, Beckett Street. Posting the key through the letterbox of the empty bedsit felt wonderful even if she'd had to pay rent until the end of the month. She'd left it clean for the next person who would probably have moved in that same night because her landlord was a greedy bastard and, surprisingly, there was a waiting list for properties like hers full of people who wouldn't have cared that she'd polished the sink tap until it shone or bleached the toilet and Mr Muscled the grotty shower.

By Wednesday she had settled in so much that it felt as if she had been living there for months. The hot water tank was enormous, so she could fill the bath to the top and lounge in it for an hour reading a book; and she did a few loads of washing in the mini machine that sat on top of the work-surface in the kitchen, which the previous occupant had left.

But the biggest thrill of all was knowing that her path would never again cross with Clint O'Gowan's. Their 'business' was finished with, so why should it? Now all she had to do was find a way of being able to earn enough money to keep living there. And she would, because there was no way she was sinking back into the sewer.

She had started to get her affairs organised: there were address changes to be made, a budgeting sheet to be completed and she bought a new phone with a new number. Palma liked lists, she craved order. She'd never had a lot of money but even when she had been totally skint she hadn't gone overdrawn or had to rely on credit. She remembered when she'd lived in Hanson Street with her mother, hiding behind the sofa, pretending they weren't in whilst debt collectors hammered on the front door. Once they'd busted the door down and Palma had stood terrified in the corner whilst two men pulled out drawers, overturned furniture, looking for money or something to replace the value of whatever Emma owed them. Even now, Palma's heart skipped an unpleasant beat when anyone she wasn't expecting knocked on her door, because it sent her straight back to when she'd been a helpless child, not knowing what was going to happen when whoever was at the other side of it came in.

The elephant in the room was the baby problem and it was starting to feel big enough to consume all the air in the house. She'd Googled 'unwanted pregnancy' and ended up on the National Unplanned Pregnancy Advisory Service website which was ironic, seeing as this baby had been very planned. But there was no NDFAS (National Dickhead

Father Advisory Service) telling her what to do when a surrogate dad had been kicked out by his wife. She was about to click on Live Chat but didn't, because she already knew what her options were. There was no way she could get rid of a life that she had deliberately started and there was no way she could keep it when it was born. How could she? She had nothing to offer it.

Idealists raged on about love but love by itself was never enough. Love collapsed when it wasn't supported by other pillars, which left one option in her eyes: give the baby up for adoption. Let someone like Grace Beresford who couldn't have her own take care of it, but not some selfish cow like Tabitha Stephenson. She'd make sure that the baby was well-matched to a couple who'd not only love it but make sure it went to school clean and had wonderful Christmas presents delivered by Santa. Palma had never been given the chance to buy into the myth, because she'd been given an Argos catalogue every November to choose things from for as long as she could remember. It was the best decision to let the baby go to a good home. It was the only decision.

She didn't tell the doctor that when they met though. Dr Gilhooley was a young and personable woman who told Palma that she was just back at work from maternity leave and her pregnancy had given her husband – also a doctor – the idea of setting up a service for mothers-to-be who were all due to give birth either side of December. Would Palma consider being a member of the Christmas Pudding Club? Palma said she'd like that.

Pregnancy, of course, meant that Palma's job prospects would be next to nothing but she was determined to find something. Even if she was giving up the baby, she didn't want to make a truth of Christian's judgement that she was only in it to claim benefits. And it was good news that Tommy Tanner hadn't contacted her since their meal because she wouldn't have that complication to deal with. Then again, he wouldn't know how to contact her because he hadn't got her number or her new address; he hadn't asked for them and she hadn't given them up to him. It was meant to be.

Except it wasn't because, after walking back from the surgery, there she found him knocking on her front door, holding a vase of flowers.

'Nice of you to let me know you'd moved,' he said, with faux disgruntlement.

'I told you I was moving,' Palma replied.

'I didn't realise you meant so soon.'

No one had ever bought her flowers before. She'd bought plenty of bunches for Grace Beresford though and freesias, like these, had been her favourite because they used to perfume her whole front room. The scent of them always reminded Palma of those cosy, safe days.

'I didn't know if you'd got a vase so I thought I better bring one. They're *happy new home* flowers. Hurry up and let me in, then.'

Palma slotted the key into the door. 'How did you find me?'

'I had a look on the net,' he replied. 'There was only this and one of the big four-bedroomed houses on the McLarens estate listed for rent with a banner over them saying recently let. I went there first.'

'Very funny.' She walked in and he followed.

'Oh this is much nicer than your last place, Palma.'

'It's lovely, isn't it.'

'The house on Rainbow Lane. It sounds like Little House on the Prairie.'

Palma thought again what a genuine smile he had. Nice even white teeth. People who looked after their teeth looked after the rest of themselves, she always reckoned.

'Is here okay?' He asked permission before setting the vase down on top of her small dining table.

'Yes, thank you.'

'Unpacked your kettle yet?'

'That was a gentle hint. Not.'

'We should have swapped numbers, then I wouldn't have had to cold call. Have you got your phone handy? Here, give it to me and I'll type in my number so I can ring my phone from yours and we'll be connected up.'

She handed her mobile to him. 'I'll save it under Tommy Tanner, just in case there are a load of other Tommys in your phonebook,' he went on.

'There are. Hundreds.'

His own phone bleeped, the latest iPhone which had recently come onto the market and made her new phone look like a relic. He stored her number whilst he carried on talking. 'Do you like going to the pictures, Palms? When you've had time to settle in with all us Dodlians, we could go and watch a film. I don't mind what sort; I'll even do a romcom if you want. Think about it. Let me know. No pressure. But I'd like to see you again. I didn't say it on Friday because I presumed you realised that anyway but I didn't want to put you on the spot. And then you went blooming AWOL.'

He'd called her Palms at school, she remembered. She heard his voice, higher pitched, a loud whisper from the desk behind hers. *Oy, Palms, lend us your ruler.*

'Well?'

'Give me a chance to answer,' she snapped good-humouredly. 'Yes, I like the pictures.' *We'll never go, but it's nice to be asked.* 'Do you want a drink?'

'No, I'm not stopping. I only wanted to say hello and bring you those.' He cocked his head towards the flowers.

'Thank you. They're lovely,' she said.

'I thought you'd be the sort that might like flowers. A lady.'

She gave a hoot of laughter. 'Yeah, course.' Despite batting the compliment back, it felt like a small warm explosion inside her.

He walked towards the door and smiled at her from there. 'I've got a busy few days but I'll be in touch, promise. I'm going camping with the Personal Development Centre kids I work with, I think I told you about them, the ones who need some direction in their lives, bit of straightening out because they're struggling. Like I was. Paying it back, or is it forwards.'

'Both, probably. That's a nice thing to do.'

'We go fishing and bowling and play footie and do some boxing training, learn 'em some discipline. I try and show them that there's a better way forwards than what they're doing now, try and get 'em to find the right path and that with a bit of hard work and determination they can make something of themselves because if they don't get help, they'll end up inside. Some of them have had shit lives. No kid should have a shit life, should they, Palms?'

'No,' she replied. Her own baby would have the best life. It wouldn't be one of those kids.

'Some of them have had childhoods that make ours look sparkling. It's amazing what a difference you can make with a bit of time and patience. And we've had some great success stories. One lad could only write his name when he was fourteen and he's an apprentice plumber now.' He grinned proudly, as if it was his own son he was talking about. 'They're great kids, lads and lasses, and I can show them – not just tell them – that they've got choices.'

'Sounds brilliant.'

'It is. See you soon.' And with that he was gone.

Palma didn't realise she was smiling too until the small mirror at the side of the door, left there by the previous occupant, showed her that she was.

Chapter 22

The following week, Eve and her cousin Violet were out shopping in Manchester for the day. A rare day off for Eve, but Jacques had insisted she take some time out. She was exhausted and not her usual self and he persuaded her that a girly day out would perk her up. Violet was only too happy to oblige.

Eve knew she wasn't pregnant even though the thought kept drifting across her mind that she might be. She was on the pill, for goodness sake. Okay, so sometimes she missed one and took two the next day but she'd been doing that since she started taking it in her twenties. She was tired out because she was working ridiculous hours, hence the headaches and that stupid anxious feeling that something wasn't right; which a spot of Mindfulness would probably sort out if *one*, she had time and *two*, she had a clue what Mindfulness actually was. If she was pregnant, she'd have been throwing up and she hadn't, not once. She tried to put the silly notion out of her mind and concentrate on sniffing out some bargains.

They'd had a lovely morning, but then something happened to make Violet wonder if her cousin had been kidnapped and replaced by a doppelganger because one minute they were chatting happily, the next Eve had fallen quiet. As quiet as a woman who looked as if she'd been dropped from an alien spaceship and hadn't a clue either where she was or how to speak Earth lingo.

'You okay?' asked Violet.

'Yeah, I'm fine,' replied Eve.

Violet didn't buy it. For a start Eve was as white as a pot of emulsion. 'Let's go and have a coffee and a sit-down,' she suggested. Eve didn't resist.

Violet brought two Americanos over to the table and asked again because something was definitely wrong. Eve might have said again that nothing was but she was doing the rapid eye blinking thing she did when her brain was buzzing; it was a total giveaway.

'Okay,' Eve conceded eventually. 'I saw someone in the street and it was a bit of a shock.'

'Who?'

'Marie.'

'Oh.'

Violet knew that there was only one 'Marie' in Eve's life. A ghost that had haunted her for years. The Marie whom Jonathan had dumped for Eve. The Marie whom Jonathan's parents loved like a daughter and they'd never forgiven Eve for 'luring' their son to her like a Siren. They hated her so much they'd blamed her for his death and for a long time she'd believed they had been right in their accusations. Their viciousness had cast a long shadow and it had been Jacques who had dragged her from its prison into the sunshine. Except one stubborn little part of her refused to believe she deserved to be truly happy. Violet didn't want to see Eve drifting back to the darkness again.

'She was wearing a wedding ring,' Eve went on. 'She was with a man and she was pushing a pram.'

'Well, that's good, isn't it? She's moved on. People do move on. Look at me – perfect example.' Then Violet shuddered because her own old life was something that she didn't want her mind to wander to.

'It was a shock, that's all. Seeing her after all this time.'

'It was definitely her?'

Eve nodded. She couldn't mistake that face. Even when Marie smiled, her nose wrinkled slightly, giving it a lick of a scowl. She'd plumped out and her hair had grown, but it was unmistakably her.

Eve lifted the cup of coffee to her lips and the smell brought a shock wave of nausea that she only just managed to battle back, a nausea that felt different to any nausea she'd had before. *Tired, tearful, food aversions, heightened sense of smell . . . sick.* It was like the final piece of a jigsaw settling into its space, the one holding the key to the whole picture. *Oh my flipping heck.* Could she be pregnant after all? The realisation hit her like a brick.

Eve managed to sneak off in Boots and buy a pregnancy testing kit whilst Violet was caught up with choosing a nail varnish. She stuck on a smile and tried to be jolly and not spoil the day, but she wanted to be at home as soon as she could to do that test and was relieved when Violet had said she'd had enough by three o'clock.

Jacques was out when Violet dropped her off, which she was glad about. He'd left a note saying he'd be home about five. She had half an hour to do the test. She pulled one of the wands out of the packet and scanned the instructions, which were straightforward enough.

The test was positive without any doubt. She sat stunned, looking at the two strong lines that couldn't have been clearer. International shocker day. She didn't know whether to laugh or cry.

Jacques would go absolutely bonkers. He'd be an amazing father. But what sort of mother would she be? Her own had been useless; a fey, selfish individual more suited to satisfying her own needs before anyone else's. What if Eve had the same lack of maternal feelings towards the baby? Her mother's mother – Granny Ferrell – was an Olympic gold medallist at being a crap parent. How on earth her elder daughter Susan – Violet's mum – had grown up to be such a loving individual after the upbringing she'd had was anyone's guess.

Brain overload. Too much to think about. Today felt too big for Eve's head.

Then she heard Jacques' car pull up and quickly stuffed the pregnancy test into her handbag.

'Hello, *ma cherie*,' he greeted her, and opened his giant arms wide for her to walk into. 'Good day?'

'Lovely,' replied Eve, trying to hold on to her plastic smile because she could feel yet another headache start to pulse in her temple.

'I'm glad someone has,' Jacques said and slumped onto a chair at the table. The chair she'd vacated seconds ago after watching her pregnancy test result develop. 'You name it and it's gone wrong.' He looked beat and he never moaned, so that indicated to Eve how bad things might have been.

When prompted, he reeled off a long list of the day's disasters: orders that should have arrived being missing in transit, a bad leak in one of the holiday cabins, an owl with an eye problem . . . it went on and on and Eve knew that now would not be a good time to break her news to him. He'd need headspace for it. She needed headspace for it.

The grand reopening of the park was Jacques' baby for now and she wanted him to have his moment of glory without anything else getting in the way of it. Three and a half more weeks and then she'd tell him. Wrong or right – it was how she felt, so she went with it.

Chapter 23

Palma had really tried hard not to feel a thrill when Tommy texted whilst he was away at camp. His spelling and his grammar left a bit to be desired, but what did that matter. He was a rough lad and what you saw was what you got and she liked what she saw very much. Every thought of him that visited her brain brought a sweet warmth with it, and there were a lot of them which was dangerous because she hadn't told him the truth about herself and it would be a game-changer. From the tone of his messages, she could tell that he was feeling the same and it wasn't fair to lead him on. She promised herself that the next time she saw him face to face, she'd have to let him know about her pregnancy. She had no idea what words she would use but they'd be the last she'd say to him, that much was definite. He'd said he didn't want any complications in his life at the moment and she was just one big walking complication – well, two. She couldn't be more of an antithesis of what he wanted – *needed* – in his life at the moment.

It wasn't the baby's fault. None of this was *her* fault,

because Palma felt it was a girl. It was Palma who had made the bed and now had to lie in it. The baby was innocent of all charges of denying her the chance of having something special with the first decent man who'd made a play for her. None of it could be laid at the foot of the child growing inside her, of that she had no doubt.

She'd had an interview for an office job in a unit on an out-of-town trading estate that morning. It wasn't exciting or well-paid but beggars couldn't be choosers. The office was freezing and the body odour of the man who interviewed her was making her feel even more nauseous than the bus journey there had done. When she checked her face in her handbag mirror before she announced her presence, she saw that she looked rough, pale and puffy-eyed as if she were hungover. The first thing he'd said to her when they sat down at either side of his desk was, 'I'm not allowed to ask this legally but I'm going to anyway: are you planning to go off and have kids because we're only a small company and so I'm not training someone up only for them to bugger off and bleed me for maternity payments.' She'd lied and said no, but ten minutes after the interview was over, before she'd even reached the bus stop, she had an email from him thanking her for her interest but her application had been unsuccessful. She couldn't really blame him.

On the bus Palma rested her hand on her stomach.

'I think you saved me there. I'm not sure he would have been very nice to work for,' she 'thought' to the baby. She couldn't remember when she first started doing it but she often sent silent messages or questions such as, 'What shall we have for tea tonight, baby? Do we fancy a baked potato?' They'd connected. Palma cared for her. She wanted to give her the very best of what she had to offer and that included good food and some lovely music to listen to, a soothing, calm voice, warm baths. It didn't cost money to give the baby a peaceful place to grow in but, still, she needed to get some. It would have been nice for the little girl to be told one day that 'the lady who gave birth to you worked in a bakery,' or in an office, a shop, anything but 'she lived off benefits.'

As she was waiting in the station for the Dodley bus, a text from Tommy came through.

Ar you at home. Can I call up to see you. Missed you x

Something heavy landed with a thud in the pit of her stomach.

Out. Will be in three quarts x

Palma knew that sometime in the next hour, Tommy would be out of her life. She wasn't easily moved to tears but she felt a pain behind her eyes where they were gathering now. Even though it was all ending before it had barely begun.

He was there forty-five minutes later. His knock was a jolly *der-dum-der*, a non-threatening postman sort of knock. She opened the door and found him standing there smiling, wearing a look on his face that spoke volumes about how pleased he was to see her.

'Come in.' She stepped back, killing the moment when he might have hugged her. She lowered her eyes to his hands and saw he was carrying a long box of chocolates.

'Bought you a pressie,' he said. 'Didn't want to turn up empty-handed so ... here you go.' He put the chocolates down on her coffee table. 'Did you say you were putting the kettle on? Tea, plenty of milk but no sugar please.' Then he sat down squarely on her sofa.

'Thank you for the chocolates,' she said, though the thought of them wasn't doing much for her. Another strange symptom of pregnancy, going off certain foodstuffs like chocolate; tea tasted strange and the idea of pastry was enough to make her gag. 'Had a nice time?'

'Oh absolutely brilliant. I love working wiv 'em. How've you been? Anything exciting happening?' he called to her as she brewed the tea. It was a good job he couldn't see her face because he would have read a lot into her expression.

'Want a biscuit?' asked Palma, avoiding the question. For now at least, although it was stupid prolonging the illusion that all was as it appeared on the surface. And unfair on him.

'No. I'm counting the calories. I'm determined to hang onto that title. What are you drinking?' he asked, pointing at her cup as she set it down on the coffee table with his.

'Hot water. I've gone off tea and coffee.'

'Not pregnant, are you?' Tommy laughed.

'What makes you say that?' Her answer was too quick, too snappy.

'Because ... that's ... what happens ... ' His smile was waning before her eyes. 'Sorry, it was a joke.'

But the cat was out of the bag and had grown instantly to a size which would not permit it to go back in again. So what was the point in even trying?

'Yes, I am pregnant.' said Palma, sitting down firmly in her armchair.

'Right,' said Tommy. Just a word, just a sound – anything to puncture the air, also pregnant, but with shock. Palma thought she saw him swallow. He picked up the cup, took a sip from it, as if he needed to momentarily switch his focus to something simpler.

'I didn't know how to tell you. It's not mine,' she added hurriedly. 'I mean, I was acting as a surrogate.'

'Right.' He wasn't looking at her, but intently down into his cup. Then he blew out his cheeks and gave another small laugh that had no amusement in it at all. 'I wasn't expecting that.'

'It's for a couple who couldn't ...' *shouldn't* '... who couldn't have kids ...'

'They paying you?'

'Well ... expenses.' Another lie because she couldn't tell him that she'd blackmailed the father out of five thousand pounds so she could start a decent life – the irony of that wasn't lost on her.

'And how many months are you gone?' His voice was breathy and his smile had been wiped off.

'Two.'

'Two months.' He made an audible outward breath again, as if he'd been winded.

She didn't know whether to go on, tell him that it had all fallen through and now she was giving the baby up for adoption. It sounded worse in words than the mess it was. He saved her the trouble by standing up abruptly, an action that said he was going, that he didn't want to hear any more.

'Thanks for the tea. I better leave you in peace.'

He hadn't drunk above a mouthful of it.

'Oh, right. Well, just leave it on the table, I'll . . .'

But Tommy was already walking into her kitchen. Palma heard the tap as he swilled the cup out, the noise of him putting it down on the metal draining board.

'Look after yourself, Palma. I wish you a lot of luck, I really do,' Tommy said, warmth in his voice and something else she couldn't quite fathom. Whatever it was, it made her feel like shit.

'Thanks, Tommy. I hope you get on all right in your boxing.'

By the time she had stood he had opened the door. He turned there, gave her a flash of a smile and then shut the door behind him. It was a goodbye smile if ever there was one.

THE SECOND
TRIMESTER

The *Daily Trumpet* would like to point out an error in the article headed 'Local Doctor's Daughter's Wedding' in last Friday's issue. Dr and Mrs Biden's present to the couple was a holiday to the Maldives and a silver cafetière, not a silver catheter as stated. Deepest apologies to Dr and Mrs Bidet.

Chapter 24

Eve felt incredibly guilty being at the doctor's. The first person she told about the pregnancy should have been Jacques, not Dr Chan. Twice she had come close to telling her husband the news since she had done the test the previous week and twice she had chickened out. Fourteen more days and then the pressure would stop weighing down on his shoulders and interrupting his sleep and she would break the news and it wouldn't have to contend with caterers and security arrangements and press and everything else that went with lake-centred projects that featured A-list Hollywood stars.

'And what wonderful timing, because Dr Gilhooley has a new incentive for ladies like you,' said Dr Chan when he had finished taking some details from Eve. 'It's called the Christmas Pudding Club.'

'The what?' Though it sounded vaguely familiar.

Dr Chan laughed. He was a merry person, a smile always dancing on his lips.

'It's a club for pregnant women. The first one is tomorrow,

six for six-thirty in the evening. They're every three weeks at
the start, then every fortnight as you get nearer to the birth.
It's to give new mums a little bit more support and time with
other women in the same position. Are you interested? You
don't have to book, just turn up and it doesn't cost anything.'

Eve thought; Jacques and Davy would be at a charity
football match tomorrow evening. It would be easy for her
to slip out without any questions being asked.

'That would be lovely,' she replied, as Dr Chan handed her
over a pack of information with the leaflet about the club on
top. 'Yes, I'll be there.'

*

Gill was very much present in The Crackers Yard via
FaceTime on Iris's iPad. And delighting in telling them how
fantastic the weather was in Spain at the moment whilst it
was raining cats and dogs in Yorkshire.

'It's so difficult watching you all working so hard,' she
said, sitting at the table on her new patio and sipping from a
glass of something which had a small harvest festival resting
on the rim.

'You're looking sunburnt on your shoulders, Gill. You
watch to want yourself,' said Iris.

'Jealousy will get you nowhere, Iris Caswell,' chuckled Gill.

'Excuse me,' said Annie, walking quickly away towards
the loo.

'There she goes again,' said Gill. 'What is she now –
twelve, thirteen weeks? She should be stopping all that sicky
rubbish soon.'

'I hope so,' said Joe, opening up a box of newly arrived novelties. 'I hate to see her like this.'

'It's the best bit, the second trimester,' said Gill. 'She'll feel smashing, with any luck, and her hair will be all glossy and if she's anything like I was, you won't be safe in the bedroom, Joe.' She gave him her best wink.

'Really?' said Joe with a pair of raised, interested eyebrows.

'Yes, Joseph. I felt very sexy when I was pregnant. Both times. I'm surprised my girls weren't born with their eyes poked out.'

Joe chuckled softly and Iris feigned disgust. She was a lot more prudish when the smut wasn't coming from her own lips.

'I'll be switching you off in a minute, Gill Johnson,' she said.

'I'll have to go in a minute anyway. We're going to a barbecue down the road with Barbara and Alan. They're very posh.' Gill leaned forward as if to speak into Iris's ear in confidence. 'She has her bras made by Penn and Teller.'

'Ooh,' said Iris, impressed.

Joe hooted with a loud burst of laughter.

'What's up with him?' asked Gill, screwing up her face.

'Too much coffee. It's addled his brain,' said Iris. 'The queen goes to Penn and Teller.'

'I know,' replied Gill. 'Well, that's not strictly true because they go to the queen, Iris. Give Annie my love. Ted's waving at me, I'd better get off.'

As her face disappeared from the screen, Annie came from the bathroom looking as if she hadn't had any sleep for a fortnight and no blood was allowed upwards past her neck.

She really should be at home resting, thought Joe. And Iris, though she never complained, shouldn't be doing five full days a week at her age. He had no idea what they were going to do to survive. In this age when people were supposedly crying out for jobs, why couldn't he get anyone to work for them? With the best will in the world and with all of them working 24/7, all the orders on their books were not going to get made. He smiled at Annie as she retook her seat but inside he was on the verge of despair.

Chapter 25

The first Christmas Pudding Club meeting was held the following day at St Gerard's church hall next to the Royal pub in Dartley. The leaflet said that it was 'an opportunity for mums-to-be to mix and partners would be invited along in later sessions'. Palma thought she might miss those sessions. There was no way she was turning up as Billy-no-mates.

She'd hoped Tommy might have texted to say hello, but he didn't. She wasn't the type to dissolve into self-pity so she took a deep breath and blocked his number, then she deleted it. That way, she would kill off the stubborn part of her that held out some hope he'd want to talk it through with her, see if there was any chance there was a path through the mess she was in, because there wasn't. He had his career to think about and he couldn't afford to let anything get in the way of it, she understood that. She knew how passionate he was about his boxing and she would never have forgiven herself for diverting his focus anyway, so it was a no-brainer. For the next seven months, the baby would be her priority and she'd have to muddle through any which way she could.

Palma would make sure that she did her duty by her and delivered her to two pairs of loving hands that could give her the best of everything. Maybe even a private school and then university; a car, a big house with one of those Arctic cabins in the garden, a kitten and a puppy, a playroom full of toys, holidays in the sun, a pile of presents under the Christmas tree and lots of love.

She wasn't sure she would make the first session because she had spent hours that day, or so it felt, heaving into the toilet bowl. 'Come on, baby, enough now. Make it stop. I know you can hear me so play fair, no need for this,' she'd said. She'd almost worn out the flushing handle. Her jeans were hanging looser on her than they were this time last week. She thought pregnant women put on loads of weight, not lost it. Luckily she felt better in the late afternoon, and on the bus to the class, she had a brainwave: to look up jobs suitable for pregnant women. Someone somewhere was bound to have written an article about it on the net.

In the church hall, there was a table set out with cups and saucers and thermal jugs labelled 'tea' and 'coffee' and plates of biscuits. There were also jugs of juice: orange and lemon and blackcurrant and bottles of water. A woman with gorgeous dark curly hair was studying them to choose which one she wanted, and apologised for being in Palma's way.

'I'd have dived straight into the coffee a couple of months ago but I think I'll be hitting the juice,' said Palma, in an effort to break the ice.

'I've lost my taste for it too,' smiled the woman. 'This is

my second baby so I knew I'd feel like that and it does come back, but I can't even say that word' – she pointed to the tea flask – 'without gagging. I'm Raychel, by the way.'

'Palma.' She smiled and wished she could have wild gypsy hair like that.

'Oh, that's a pretty name. I might add that to my list of possibles, if it's a girl.' Raychel touched her stomach lovingly. 'I don't want to find out what sex the baby is until I give birth, though. I like the element of surprise.'

'Hello,' said another woman who joined them. 'I'm Annie. Bit nervous.'

'I'm Raychel and I'm a bit nervous too.'

'I'm Palma, and so am I.'

'Want one of these whilst I'm pouring?' asked Raychel, tipping the blackcurrant juice into a plastic cup.

'Thanks, but I'll have the lemon. Not those.' She pointed to the flasks, her finger fixing on the one that held the tea. 'I can't even say that word without gagging.'

Raychel and Palma both chuckled.

'Just said exactly the same,' Raychel explained. 'That's why we're laughing.'

'Awful, isn't it. I used to love a cup of tea so I hope I get the taste back.'

'You will. I know because this is my second baby. But I've forgotten so much so I thought I'd come to these classes when they were suggested.'

'I thought everyone here would be your age,' said Annie to Palma. 'I love your pink hair, by the way.'

Palma would rather have had Annie's colouring any day:

olive skin, black hair, pretty brown eyes. She'd dyed her hair black once and it made her look dead.

'Thanks. You look as if you should have an Italian accent,' said Palma.

'I'm a fake Italian,' said Annie. 'I look more Italian than my Italian husband. No idea why.'

A few more women had walked in now and were milling around the table.

'Help yourself to tea, coffee and juice, ladies,' said a small, rotund midwife in a blue nurse's top and navy trousers, 'and then we'll begin.' She was standing with the midwife Annie had seen at the surgery – Chloe.

Palma, Raychel and Annie took their places in the circle of chairs. Far more had been set out than there were people and so the two midwives started removing some and closing the gaps. Palma noticed that only one woman was holding a cup and saucer, all the others had glasses of juice.

'Do take your seats please, girls,' said Chloe, thinner and much taller than the other midwife and wearing thick-rimmed glasses. Together they looked like the medical version of Morecambe and Wise.

'Hello, ladies,' said Morecambe. 'My name's Chloe and this is Sharon and we are your Christmas Pudding Club mid-wives.' Sharon gave them a wave and a smile. 'Dr Gilhooley's idea – the younger, that is – I presume most of you are his patients?' Her tone somehow intimated that they register an affirmation with a raised hand. 'By the way, if you've brought your notes with you, you don't need them here.'

'I take them everywhere,' said a long-faced woman whose

ginger hair was scraped back into a tight ponytail. 'They're always in my bag.'

'Well, better that than forgetting them, but you don't need them here for future reference. So ... anyway ... it's a new one for us too, so you are the real suck-it-and-see ladies,' said Sharon, which caused a snort from the ginger woman, 'but it does seem a really great idea to us to have a longer time of interaction between you new mums-to-be, because you are very likely to build up your closest friendships through your children. In fact Chloe and I had our children at the same time, didn't we, Chloe?' Sharon turned to the other midwife, who answered, 'We did indeed, Sharon.'

'Twenty-six years ago,' said Sharon. 'And I'm still trying to get my baby weight off.'

A ripple of laughter ensued.

'So we thought we'd start by breaking the ice and you tell us your name and a little bit about yourself. Nothing too scary, just something so we can begin a conversation. Shall we start here?' She pointed to Palma, who gulped.

'Come on, first one gets it out of the way fastest,' Chloe encouraged her.

Palma cleared her throat.

'Hello, I'm Palma Collins. I'm twenty-two and this is my first baby. I'm single and I was recently made redundant.' She wasn't quite sure how much she should say but everyone was staring at her expecting more. 'I've been looking for a job but all I seem to be doing at the moment is being sick so I hope that goes away quick.' She dried up and her mouth opened and closed without anything more coming out.

'What would you like from these meetings, Palma?' asked Chloe, smiling at her.

'Er ... a bit of support. Some information. A job,' she chuckled but no one else did and then she felt stupid. 'I don't really know what to expect because I don't know anyone who's had a baby and I'm not really in touch with friends I used to have so ... I suppose ... not being alone through it all would be ... would be good.'

'How many weeks are you, Palma?' asked Sharon.

'Nine tomorrow.'

'Well in a couple of weeks, you should be through that sicky period with any luck and you'll feel much better. Thank you, Palma. Now you, love.' Sharon moved her eyes to the next woman on.

'Hi, I'm Raychel. I'm married to Ben, a builder, and we have a son but I've forgotten quite a lot about being pregnant so I thought it would be good to come. I really enjoyed my parentcraft classes the last time but my little boy was born early so I only got the chance to go to two. I thought this was a great idea having meetings much earlier on in the pregnancy.'

There was a chorus of nodding and a stray beat of a clap. Chloe nodded at Annie for her to begin.

'Hi, everyone.' There was a tremor in her voice. 'I'm Annie. Married to Joe and we have a cracker factory, the ones you pull, not the ones you eat. And I'm forty-eight. And I thought I was either going through the menopause or poorly. We've been trying for years to have a baby and it didn't happen. IVF failed – a few times – and we'd resigned ourselves to never being parents. And . . .' She beamed. 'Here I am. Better late than never. And . . .' She froze then. 'I can't think of anything else to say, except that it's nice to meet you all. And I look forward to sharing your journey.'

The next woman said that she'd been trying for a baby with her first partner but they'd split up before they'd actually gone down the IVF route. Now she was married to a policeman and she'd fallen pregnant straightaway. Her name was Cheryl. She said she was part-owner of Lady Muck, the cleaning firm.

Then there was Colleen who admitted that the baby had come as a real blow to her and her husband as both of them were totally focused on their careers and she felt shell-shocked and disorientated. She looked shell-shocked too. And trapped. She had great big brown eyes like a frightened fawn and dark circles around them as if she hadn't been sleeping properly. There was Di, the tall woman with the ginger hair and wide shoulders, who said that she'd split up with the father of her baby after she found him in bed with her mother (gasps ensued), and she was quite happy raising the baby by herself because she didn't need a man around – they were all useless tossers. And finally Eve, who told them that she was having her first baby with her husband and they ran the theme park Winterworld. She said that she had only felt sick once so far so considered herself one of the lucky ones, but she'd been having bad headaches and was so, so tired all the time.

'What a lovely bunch you all are,' said Chloe with a wide smile. 'We thought that for the first session we'd talk to you about eating and drinking. What's safe, what you should avoid. There are a lot of old wives' tales circulating, as you'll have heard. Sharon, have we got those handouts?'

The hour flew. Palma wished it could have gone on for longer because she'd learned lots and had a laugh. She didn't feel so alone in her predicament now and it was so much better being told things first-hand like what foods were okay to eat, without wading through lots of conflicting information on the internet.

'Some silly cow told me I couldn't eat any cheese,' said Di. 'And I bloody love cheese. I'm going to go home now to make myself a big plateful of cheddar toasties.'

'Oh, can I come?' said Cheryl.

'You'll have to bring your own cheese,' laughed Di. 'I'm not sharing my Cathedral City with anyone.'

'See you all next time,' smiled Eve. It was a bummer to learn that she should stay away from pâté because she and Jacques often had warm crusty bread and pâté for supper. She'd crave it now she wasn't allowed it. The law according to Sod.

Palma was about to walk out when a hand on her arm arrested her. It was the 'fake Italian' Annie.

'I hope you don't mind me asking, love, but were you serious about wanting a job?' she said.

'Yes, I was,' replied Palma.

'We're desperate for a cracker-stuffer in our company,' said Annie. 'It's not hard and you sit down so it would be ideal for you being pregnant. We've got a lovely working environment and though it's minimum wage, there will be overtime, cash in hand. We're on the industrial estate between Maltstone and Higher Hopp—'

'I'll take it,' said Palma. She knew where it was and that road was on a bus route. She could pick it up on Dodley High Street and be there in ten minutes. 'Do you need any references or anything? I've got one from my last employer. It's only a takeaway food place but I work hard . . .' She was gabbling, she knew it, but couldn't stop.

'Okay, if you have a reference, that would be good.' Annie felt as if she'd met a match on a dating site. 'When can you start? The sooner the better for us. Monday?'

'Tomorrow? If you don't mind me throwing up occasionally.'

Annie laughed. 'We might have to fight for the loo. We've only got the one.'

Palma's smile was radiant. 'What time?'

'We start at nine. Finish at five. We break for lunch, there's a lovely sandwich shop on the same estate. And there's as much tea and coffee – or juice – as you can drink during the day.'

It sounded perfect. Palma couldn't believe her luck. 'I'll be there,' she said.

And Annie knew she would be.

Chapter 26

As Joe and Annie's car pulled into the trading estate the next morning, there was the welcome sight of someone standing outside the factory door.

'Is that her, with the pink hair?'

'Yes, Iris, that's her.'

'Let's see how long she lasts,' said Iris with a sniff. 'What was her name again?'

'Palma,' said Joe.

'Palma? Well, at least she's not named after a plank of wood.'

Annie didn't have Iris's doubts, for once. She climbed out of the car quickly and greeted Palma with a smile. The girl's thin coat was wet through with rain.

'Come on, let's get you inside, Palma,' she said, pulling the keys from her handbag. 'You should have brought your umbrella today. Have you been standing here long?'

'Not really. I can either get a bus that gets me here at twenty to, or one at ten past and I didn't want to be late.'

'Oh, music to my ears,' said Joe, grabbing her hand and

shaking it vigorously. 'Welcome to The Crackers Yard, Palma. I am Joe, Annie's slave.'

Annie opened the door and disabled the alarm. 'Get that wet coat off and let me hang it up for you so it'll dry.' Palma gave it to her. She had a smart summer dress on, as opposed to Annie in her jeans.

'I didn't know what to wear,' she explained.

'Wear what you like,' said Joe, coming in. 'As long as you do the work, you can come dressed as Pinocchio. Can I introduce you to Iris, our next-door neighbour and star cracker-stuffer.'

'Hello,' said Iris, giving Palma the once-over. 'Going to stick around, I hope. These good folk are fed up of setting people on and them disappearing into a black hole.'

It appeared as if all the sins of the last would-be employees had been fashioned into a chain for Palma to wear around her neck.

'I'll not be going anywhere,' she replied.

Iris's head gave a little jerk, a gesture that said, 'we'll see.'

Joe rubbed his hands together. 'We always start off with a nice warm drink, Palma. What can I get you? We have some nice fruity teas now – or a hot chocolate maybe?'

'Just a glass of hot water please,' said Palma.

'Best way to start a morning,' said Iris, with a nod of agreement. 'Plus a squirt of lemon juice. Gets your kidneys stimulated. I'll have an undecaffeinated coffee please, Joseph.'

'So, you mean an ordinary one,' tutted Joe.

'Well, yes, but I'm making the point that I don't want one of those coffees from the jar with the green stripe on it.'

'And this is what I have to work with,' said Joe, with a flat palm extended in Iris's direction. 'No wonder no one stays around.' He walked off to make the beverages, still chuntering to himself.

'Palerma, come and sit next to me and I'll show you what to do,' said Iris.

'It's Palma,' shouted Joe from the kitchen, then he bobbed his head around the door. 'She called me Joe Pancetta for three whole years before she finally got it right.'

'For large orders we use those machines, Palma,' began Iris, 'but they can only glue in the snap and then roll, they can't stuff. It's the hand-rolling no one likes. Watch me. Sellotape the snap in first. Then I'm folding the flaps outside in. Make a nice round tube as you start closing the cracker. Then I push all three flaps into the corresponding slits over the top, middle one first to hold it, then give it a little roll to shape. Now I tie one end with ribbon, can you see? Then in goes my hat, my joke and my novelty. Then we close it by tying the other end with ribbon. And snip off the excess.'

'Looks straightforward enough,' said Palma.

'Make sure your bow is to the front. It's more of a craft than you might give it credit for. We do them properly in The Crackers Yard.'

Annie gave her new worker a wink. Iris was in her comfort zone being, well ... Iris.

Before half an hour had passed, Palma was stuffing crackers at the rate of knots and Annie felt a large chunk of weight shift from her shoulders. Palma was going to fit in perfectly with them, she could tell.

*

Effin was going out of his nut, he was sure. He and Thomas the train driver, Huw the engineer and Dylan were standing at the side of the Nutcracker Express train – which was a piece of engineering with a mind of its own – having the sort of conversation which should have been a *Monty Python* sketch.

'*Pam ddiawl bo'r cyfarwyddiade ma – sy, gyda llaw, yn y Gymraeg i chi bois o Gymru –yn cael eu anwybyddu? Ydw i 'di cal smac yn y chops? Ydw i di mynd yn hollol mental? Ydw i'n jabran yn Japanîs?*' He was gabbling so fast that not even his countrymen could understand him and looked blank. 'Oh for . . .' He bit off the expletive and began to talk slowly – in English, so that young Dylan could also enjoy his rhetoric. 'Why the hell are these instructions – which, by the way, are in Welsh for you Welsh lads – being ignored? Have I had a smack in the chops? Have I gone totally mental? Am I jabbering away in Japanese?'

Huw and Thomas exchanged baffled glances. Effin decided that he might have had more success if he *had* been jabbering away in Japanese.

'I told you to sort out the brakes, Huw.' Effin rustled a wad of paper in his face. 'I gave you a copy of these plans that should solve every problem this bastard train has.'

'When?' asked Huw.

'Monday. We was standing 'ere and we had a whole conversation about it,' said Effin, keeping a lid on his temper which was threatening to boil over. Huw, top-class worker as he was, had a brain the size of a wasabi pea. Ordinarily Effin would have had no doubt in his head that the discussion had taken place, but not at the moment. Not with all the lapses of memory he'd been having lately.

'Did we?' asked Huw, chewing on his finger as if that would help with his recall. 'Where did I put them then?'

'How should I know? And yes, we did. You were telling me you'd won twenty-five quid on the lottery,' said Effin.

'I did win it,' said Huw with a grin. 'But I can't remember telling you that.'

'How the bloody hell else would I know about it?' asked Effin. 'I don't have a crystal *bolycs* ball, do I?'

'My Auntie Rhonda had a crystal ball,' smiled Thomas, warmed by a sudden memory. 'She forecast the death of John Lennon in it. Only detail she got wrong was the place. She said one of the Beatles would get killed in York but—'

'Thomas, I couldn't give a flying fart about your Auntie Rhonda. Huw, I told you to mend the brakes, and because I suspected you were off in fairyland as usual,' he said as he turned towards Dylan, 'I asked young Dylan here yesterday to remind you.'

He didn't like the look that Dylan was giving him. Total confusion. 'What?' he barked at him. The first time he had ever raised his voice to the young man.

'I'm really sorry, Effin, but you didn't ask me to do that.'

Effin slapped his forehead. 'Not you as well.'

'We did talk, yes, but you never said anything about the train. If you had, I'd have told Huw straightaway because I was working with him.'

Effin felt the colour drain from his face as if someone had pulled a plug out from his neck.

'Are . . . are you sure?'

'I'm absolutely sure,' said Dylan, quietly, as if he didn't like the idea of contradicting his dad's friend.

'Are you all right, Effin?' asked Huw. 'You've gone very pale and—'

'*Ffycin 'el*, just mend the bloody train,' Effin yelled at top volume and stomped off quickly before anyone noticed that his lip had started to wobble.

*

Joe offered Palma a lift. It was no bother because they had to drive down Dodley High Street to get home. In fact, they could pick her up every day from the same spot and save her getting the bus, he said.

'If it's no trouble. I can give you some petrol money,' said Palma.

'Don't be silly,' said Annie. 'We aren't going to take petrol money from you when we're more or less passing your house.'

'That's really nice of you, thank you,' said Palma.

'Oh, you will be back tomorrow, will you?' said Iris, pursing her lips.

'Of course,' replied Palma with a broad smile. This job was perfect for her. At least for now. A boss who was also pregnant and so understanding and she'd save on bus fares, too. More than perfect.

'Then it's settled,' said Annie, locking the metal shutter over the entrance.

'If you could drop me at the Co-op that would be great. I'm out of a few things,' Palma asked, holding Iris's bag whilst she struggled into the back seat of the car.

'No worries,' said Annie with a smile of her own. All they needed now were a few more Palmas. She'd picked things up immediately and was quick and neat; she even passed the Iris test. As soon as they'd dropped her off in Dodley, Iris launched into talking about her.

'So, what do you reckon to her?'

'I think she will fit in perfectly,' said Joe. He gave Annie, in the passenger seat, a wink. 'What's your opinion, Iris. Do you give her your thumbs up?'

'I like her. I even got used to her hair by the close of day. She's got very deft fingers. And she listened to what I said. And she ties a good bow. Yes, she'll do.' She did one of her loud sniffs. 'Well, if she turns up tomorrow that is. I'll be disappointed if she doesn't.'

'I have a good feeling this time,' said Annie.

'I didn't see a wedding ring,' said Iris. 'Mind you, that's nowt fresh these days. They do it all in reverse order. They get pregnant, then they move in together, then they meet. Wonder what happened to the man who got her that way.'

'What?' said Joe with faux shock. 'Don't tell me you didn't get her whole life story out of her already.'

'There's tomorrow for that,' said Iris. And she sniffed again.

*

Palma didn't see Tommy until it was too late to avoid him. They were both in the tinned food aisle heading towards each other with full baskets. She thought he might ignore her but he didn't and she felt a mix of feelings that she couldn't quite untangle when he smiled and stopped to talk.

'How are you doing?' he asked.

'I'm good thanks, are you?'

'I'm always good. And I've just landed a sponsor.' He grinned.

'That's brilliant news. I'm so pleased for you.' And she was. He should be proud of himself for what he'd achieved.

'Carling Motors, have you heard of them?'

'That massive car place on Wakefield Road?'

'There's an even bigger Carling Motors in Leeds and in Harrogate and another in York. Owner is a proper boxing nut. It means I can give up labouring and concentrate on training full time.'

'You deserve it.'

'I do,' he said. 'What about you. How are you?'

'Busy, I've got a job at last, which makes me feel a lot better.' She was glad to get that in, in case he thought she was a lazy cow, although she didn't tell him that she'd only had it for a day.

'Oh, great stuff. What are you doing?'

'I'm at The Crackers Yard. They make crackers. The ones you pull, not the ones you stick cheese on.'

'Cheese,' he said, clicking his fingers. 'That's what I've forgotten. Thanks for reminding me.'

She'd given him his get-out word. As she thought, he started to wind up the conversation. 'Well, you take care of yourself, Palma.'

'You too,' she said.

He smiled again and she thought he was about to say something else, but he didn't. He walked off towards the cheese counter and she walked purposefully in the opposite direction towards the newspapers and magazines. She picked up a *Daily Trumpet* and put it in her basket as if it had been on her list of must-buys, then she went straight to the nearest till, packed her stuff quickly into her bags, paid and left without a backward glance.

She was glad to get home in a way that she never had been in Beckett Street. The little house almost felt glad to see her again, a fancy that she put down to pregnancy hormones making her hyper-sensitive.

'Tuna sandwich okay with you, miss?' Palma asked, placing her hand on her still flat stomach. She made it and sat at the table, spreading the newspaper open to read as she ate. She read every part of a newspaper, even the bits she wasn't particularly interested in. She always had, it was a thing she did. Same with books, too; she couldn't abandon one if she'd started it, she had to read it to the end. After the news, the lost and found columns, the 'would like to meet', articles for sale and coach trips, then there were the sports pages at the back and her heart kicked because there was a picture of Tommy 'Dynamite' Tanner – she tutted at the wrong name – holding up the Lonsdale belt in his right hand. *Sponsorship Deal for Tommy* was the header and underneath all the details and how proud Mr Carling was of the arrangement. The story continued overleaf so she turned to it and the words melted into an unreadable jumble because all she could focus on was the large colour photo of Tommy in a suit posing for the camera ... but this time his right hand was around the waist of a curvy, long-haired blonde in a skimpy black shimmery dress, showing off a cleavage that the Incredible Hulk could have drowned in. The caption underneath read: *Tommy with girlfriend Katie at the John Wade vs Lemit Kwapisz fight at Ponds Forge last weekend.*

Palma's skull exploded in prickles. Katie looked beautiful and perfect for the arm of someone who was up and coming in the boxing world. No wonder he couldn't get away fast enough from her in the supermarket.

THE TRUMPET TRIUMPHS

An unfortunate spelling mistake in last week's *Daily Trumpet* led to an unexpected success story when the Maltstone Over 60s club advertised their Tea, Cake and Mingle Afternoon in the weekend What's Happening feature. The article unfortunately appeared as 'Tea, Cake and Minge Afternoon'. Chairman Marjorie Thorpe-Horbury said, 'We were going to complain but so many people turned up that it was a ticket sell-out and £1752 was raised for the Sunshine House charity when we were only expecting £200 at most.'

Chapter 27

The next morning Annie and Joe sat in the hospital waiting room, him a lot more comfortable than her. Her bladder was about to burst from all the water she'd had to drink and Joe was doing his best to take her mind off the fact that fluid was about to come out of her ears. He pushed the *Women by Women* magazine into her line of vision. 'Look at this. Non-alcoholic tiramisu. What a joke.'

'Joe, I'm sorry, I can't concentrate on puddings. What time is it now?'

Joe didn't say that it was three minutes later than the last time she'd asked. And a full half an hour after the scheduled time of their appointment.

'I had a feeling they'd do this to me,' said Annie. 'I'm going to wee myself in a minute.'

Joe persisted with his dessert-disdain. 'Rum is what you should put in a tiramisu. That's what Italians do.'

Annie rocked back and forward. 'I'll have to ask how long they're going to be. If I start weeing I won't be able to stop.'

'I'll ask for you,' said Joe, putting the magazine down.

Just as he stood, the door in front of them opened and the sonographer called out Mrs Pandoro's name.

'Thank God,' said Annie through clenched teeth. She stood up carefully.

'Sorry about your wait,' said the sonographer with genuine apology. 'When someone is late, the system gets totally thrown.'

Joe knew that if Annie had got hold of the late one, she wouldn't have been responsible for her actions. She didn't get annoyed very often but Joe could recognise the signs that she was ready to blow like a geyser. But downwards.

The sonographer helped Annie up onto the couch. She was wearing a badge with her name on it: Vita Goodchild; a name not easily forgotten.

'If you could lift up your T-shirt for me,' said Vita. Annie did as she was told and shuffled into the position where she felt the least pressure on her bladder. Vita tucked some tissue over the top of her trousers and apologised in advance for the temperature of the gel.

'It can be a bit of a shock against the skin,' she said with a sympathetic smile.

'We don't want to know if it's a boy or a girl,' said Joe quickly. They'd decided they didn't want to be told in advance.

'Oh, it's too soon anyway,' said Vita. 'That info would come at your next scan. If everything is well and you don't need any interim checks, that'll be around twenty weeks.'

Annie felt stupidly nervous now and she reached for Joe's hand. She studied Vita's face as she moved the transducer through the gel on her stomach and looked at a screen above her head. Annie tried to read her expression to see if everything was all right, but it was as neutral as could be.

'I'm always thorough but even more so with an elderly primigravida, so no need to worry that I'll miss anything.'

'Elderly?' asked Joe and let out a laugh that made his lips judder.

'A very unflattering term for first-time mums over thirty-five,' said Vita. 'Sorry. Strangely enough, all I've had today are over thirty-five-year-old first-time mums. One was a year older than you. Would you like some photos of the baby?'

'Oh, yes please,' the Pandoros replied in unison.

After what seemed like an interminable silence, Vita smiled and said, 'We have two arms and two legs and a heartbeat and everything looks good so far. Would you like to see?'

Vita twisted the screen around and there – in beautiful black and white – was the unmistakable profile of a baby.

Joe made a sound halfway between a gasp and a gargle and when he spoke, his words were barely above a whisper.

'My God, look, Annie. Look at our baby. It's real.'

Annie understood what he meant. Until this moment she hadn't quite let herself believe it, but there was the indisputable proof that baby Pandoro was growing. She felt the tickle of a teardrop on her hand and wiped it away. It hadn't come from her eye but Joe's. He was laughing and crying at the same time, whilst she was calm and caught up quietly in the marvel of it all.

'And your dates are spot on. A nice Christmas present for you both.'

'The best,' said Joe. 'I can't believe it. Is that the heart?'

'Yes, there it is, beating away.' Vita handed over three freshly printed photographs. 'You pay for them at reception and they'll put them in a card frame for you. You'll be getting an appointment date for your twenty-week scan in the post. Any questions for me?'

Annie couldn't think straight. All she'd wanted to know was that the baby actually existed and was all right. And it did and it was.

Annie was all smiles when they got back to work and couldn't wait to show off her photographs to Iris and Palma, then they rang up Gill on FaceTime to show off to her. She was absolutely delighted and a little bit squiffy. They'd just come back from a boat trip with Mr and Mrs Penn and Teller and they'd been washing a swordfish lunch down with gin and tonics. It sounded wonderful but Joe and Annie didn't want to be anywhere else in the world at that moment than in their cracker factory holding the photographs of their baby. The next generation of Pandoros, which they'd thought they would never see.

Palma put the kettle on whilst they were conversing on FaceTime. It was only her second day at work but already she felt at home – the work equivalent of the little house on Rainbow Lane. Plus keeping busy helped drive that picture of Tommy and his blonde arm-decoration from her mind. He looked good in a suit. She'd have been proud to be on his arm too, and maybe she would have been had she not been up the duff with a stranger's kid. Why had she even trusted Clint in the first place? She knew he'd arranged the deal primarily for the money but she hadn't even questioned his 'pitch' to her, that the Stephensons were a couple with everything except the baby they so badly wanted. Once again she heard Christian's words echo loudly in her skull: *Desperate people do desperate things.* It was her only excuse.

That morning Palma had been working on a special luxury order for Rolls Royce where the crackers had to be hand rolled around a piece of pipe rather than the cheaper ones that were pre-cut and assembled in seconds. It was best done standing up at a table and Iris's back was playing up so she showed Palma how to do them. Iris had been impressed at how easily she'd mastered the technique and she was speedy too. Annie and Joe inspected Palma's production before they were packed into boxes.

'Palma, dear Palma, don't ever leave us,' said Annie. She couldn't believe how perfectly the crackers were constructed and how each hand-tied bow was exactly as it should be. 'I'm not sure even I could do as good a job in so short a time.'

'I got into the swing of them,' said Palma. She'd always given her best to whatever she was doing. *Except for your life,* said a nasty little voice inside her. *You're cocking that up left, right and centre, aren't you?*

'She even makes a nice coffee,' said Iris, slurping from behind them. 'Bit light on the biscuits though.' She winked at Palma who smiled and said, 'I'll take that on board for next time.'

'I'm craving something sweet; Jaffa Cakes, do we have any in the cupboard?' asked Annie.

'We did have ...' said Iris with eyes full of guilt.

'Oh my goodness,' said Joe, throwing up his hands. 'Tip number one, Palma, never leave the Jaffa Cakes in a cupboard when Iris is around.'

Annie laughed. She didn't care that her cupboard was empty of Jaffa Cakes because her soul was full of joy. Joy she didn't think for a minute would ever be hers. There was nothing that could be sweeter than that.

*

Palma was craving oranges ever since Annie had mentioned the Jaffa Cakes and asked Joe to drop her off at the mini supermarket at the other end of the High Street from the Co-op after work. It didn't have half the range of stuff and was expensive, but she didn't want to chance bumping into Tommy. Then again she did. Moth to the flame situation because it would hurt her to be near him, especially if he felt obliged to talk to her; if that happened she'd cut away as soon as was polite.

She'd see Joe and Annie tomorrow because they'd asked her if she would consider working a Saturday. They'd treat her to fish and chips for lunch, they said. She liked the Pandoros and thought the job suited her very well. Who would have known she'd have a flair for rolling crackers? She'd even volunteered to write some new jokes for them as the ones they were using were so crap they didn't even have a groan factor.

Minnie's Mart only had three aisles. She found some fresh clementines in the first and was heading down the second where the biscuits were when who should she see coming towards her but Tommy. She froze. *Shit. You couldn't make this up.* Her legs felt shaky and her jaw tightened with tension. She imagined how she'd look through his eyes: drab and flawed when compared to the dazzling Katie he had now in his life. She really wished he hadn't spotted her: she would have dumped her basket and walked out rather than have to pretend she was fine with being in a friend-zone, because she wasn't.

His twinkly eyes and customary grin had drifted into her mind more times than she would have liked. But that was an avenue which had closed and so the sooner she got her head around it, the better. *It couldn't have lasted anyway. Not when he can pull Katie-type girls*, said a voice inside her head that was attempting to comfort but evidently wasn't very good at it. She would rather not have met him at all than endure his forced politeness, his sympathy, his pity.

'You following me?' he asked, that smile making her legs feel incapable of holding her up.

'I . . . no . . .' she stammered. 'The Co-op didn't have any oranges.' The ridiculous lie was the first thing that came to her mouth. He must have known it wasn't true.

'I think we both must have magnetic bits inside us, Palma.'

She wanted to be first to break contact this time. To show him that she wasn't stalking him, because that would be beyond sad.

'Yeah, possibly . . .' a small burst of amused laughter. 'Anyway, hope you have a lovely weekend.'

'And you, Pa . . .' But she was walking away already, and

silently cursed herself for getting the timing so wrong. Now she just looked rude. She tried to compensate for that and called over her shoulder, 'See you, Tommy,' and she thought that she saw him wave from the corner of her eye.

She paid for the clementines and stuffed them into the carrier bag that she'd pulled out of her handbag. She always had one with her. She knew her desire to be organised and prepared came from the years when she lived in chaos with a mother who had no order or boundaries. Neither did the men that Emma brought home. Her mother had laughed it off when one of them lost his bearings and ended up in Palma's bedroom. She'd never quite rid herself of the memory of his hands pawing her young body and it was then she discovered – by accident – that a well-placed knee made the best escape route. Since that night, Palma never went anywhere without something she could use as a weapon, if it was called for.

As she walked home she wondered if Tommy had gone to that supermarket to avoid her too.

Chapter 28

Just when Eve thought that the day of the Half Christmas celebrations would never come, it did – and it was a total triumph – and then it ended and with it all the pressure that had threatened to blow everyone's head off for months.

'What a day,' she said, spearing a chip and delivering it to her mouth.

'The best day I have ever had in my life,' answered Jacques, as soon as he had cleared his mouth. 'A baby. A little tiny baby. Our baby.'

The amazing success of the opening had faded into obscurity when placed next to his wife's joyous revelation. Eve could feel the heat of his grin from across their dining table; it was so fierce, she could have barbecued a chicken on it.

Her original plan was to make them a lovely meal that evening and tell him about the baby over dessert, but best-made plans never ran smoothly. Eve had felt inexplicably sad when the crowds began to disperse, an inevitable comedown after months of living off adrenaline: the euphoria that the day's success had brought had dissipated and pregnancy hormones had flooded in, setting her brain into a spin. She'd taken herself off to the quiet of the animal quarter, where Jacques had found her. One kind word and a cuddle from him and the news came tumbling out in one big wordy rush instead of over a romantic candlelit supper.

She'd thought he would have raced around the park like a madman with his hands up in the air, but he didn't. He held her at arm's length and looked into her face to check she wasn't joking, then he had burst into tears. Man tears. A quick burst, as if they were a massive overspill of emotion, then he had hugged her tightly then swept her up and declared that they were going home immediately and would leave Myfanwy in charge of organising the lock-up. They called in at Sedgewicks for fish and chips to take home and celebrate.

Even going into Sedgewicks added to the weirdness of the day because the staff in the restaurant were full of the news that none other than Franco Mezzaluna had been there for his lunch. Eve doubted it, but today had been anything but sane, so maybe it was true. The waitresses certainly believed it anyway.

Home for Mr and Mrs Glace was an old farmhouse overlooking Half Moon Hill. It had been a wreck when they bought it. The man who sold it had been born in it eighty-eight years before and was selling up so he could spend his last years in Portugal with his expat family. The décor was two hundred and eighty-eight years old but both Eve and Jacques could see the building's potential. It had the most fantastic views and a huge fireplace that took up nearly the whole of one wall of the sitting room. Effin's men had had their work cut out turning it from a wreck into something cosy and structurally safe for them, but if Effin couldn't do it, no one could. As soon as the kitchen, bathroom and central heating had been installed, they'd moved in but there was still quite a bit of decorating to do and only two of the five bedrooms had been finished. Now they needed to get a move on and transform a third into a nursery.

'I want a proper wedding,' Eve announced as she tipped the teapot over Jacques' enormous Bagpuss mug.

His fork stopped on its journey up to his mouth.

'But we are married, Eve,' he said. 'Don't you remember? I wore a suit and you wore a red dress. Is this the onset of baby brain?'

'Of course I remember, you twerp,' she replied, 'but it was in the town hall and just the two of us.'

'As you wanted it,' said Jacques.

Eve gave a small grunt. Another of her stupid decisions. She'd said she didn't want a fuss. But, if she was really honest with herself, she had never felt properly married. A traditional ceremony would have made all the difference. They had a lovely wedding chapel on site in Winterworld and she knew that Jacques would have relished the idea of a big splashy celebration, but he'd not fought her decision to keep it low key.

'Well, I've changed my mind,' said Eve.

'Shall we get divorced first?' Jacques asked, eyebrows raised quizzically.

'Too expensive,' said Eve. 'What about a renewal of our vows in our chapel? And a massive party for our friends afterwards.'

Jacques studied her to see if she was serious. She answered his look.

'Yes, I do mean it.' She sighed long and hard. 'Look, Jacques, I know you wanted a full bells and whistles wedding and I know that I . . . that I . . .'

Felt guilty. Jacques didn't say it but in his mind he filled in the missing words for her. The short and easy answer was that a little part of Eve felt uncomfortable at the idea of having the sort of wedding she had been planning to have with Jonathan. It hadn't sat right with her then, but he also knew that it had nothing to do with her feelings for him. Eve loved him with her whole heart, of that he had no doubt.

'It's fine. It doesn't matter. We did the vows thing, we got married. That's all that was important.' He waved her words away with a slice of buttered bread.

'No, I was wrong,' said Eve. 'My Auntie Susan didn't get the chance to buy a new hat and I am absolutely in Phoebe's bad books for denying her the chance to be a bridesmaid.'

Jacques grinned. Eve's goddaughter Phoebe May Tinker didn't take any prisoners. 'So I've decided that I want a big Christmas wedding,' said Eve.

'But you can have a winter wedding any time. We have wall to wall wint—'

'No, Christmas. *At* Christmas,' said Eve, much to his surprise because when he'd first met her she was more anti-Christmas than a shed-full of Grinches. 'I want wall to wall

Christmas. Including Christmas itself. I want to be married properly, in our chapel, on Christmas Eve. No, make it the day before Christmas Eve, so that our guests aren't too inconvenienced. That's close enough to the big day.'

'Eve, the baby's due at Christmas. You'll be the size of a whale, darling,' said Jacques, with a cheeky wink.

'Then I'll go to a wedding-dress shop for whales. I want the big frock, the big cake, the big party and the big bouquet.' She didn't just want it, she *needed* it because she felt finally free of the past. She would never forget it because it was part of her journey to happiness, but she had let it go.

'Eve, you can't plan a wedding two days before your due date. That is absolutely *stupide,*' exclaimed Jacques, dipping into French, as he did sometimes when his emotions ran high.

'I can and I'll tell you why,' said Eve. 'Because I can guarantee the baby will be late. I was a fortnight late. So was my mother and my Auntie Susan and Violet. And my Granny Ferrell.' Her shoulders rippled with a small shudder at the name of her grandma who was the Devil Incarnate's much more horrible sister. The jackal carrying her was forced to have a caesarean because she had refused to budge from the womb.

'Are you inviting your granny?' asked Jacques, making his fingers into the sign of a cross.

'With any luck she'll be on a cruise,' said Eve. 'If it's a choice between a trip to the Bahamas and a visit to a chapel, I have a pretty good idea at what would win. Anyway, the sight of a crucifix would have her turning into flames.'

Jacques tried not to smile. 'Okay, if that's what you want, Eve.'

'It is. And as you are the Christmas expert, how do you feel about being the wedding planner as well?'

She saw his beloved mouth curve into a smile. She'd probably be given away by a snowman and have elves for bridesmaids, but what the hell – why not? He'd love this duty because he'd wanted a Christmas party wedding from the off, and he had bent so much to her will over the years they'd been together that now it was time to give a little back.

There was excitement at local theme park Winterland yesterday as Hollywood A-lister star Frank Mezzaluna opened the new lagoon named St Evelyn's Lake and then later was seen around the Penistone area with a mystery woman. Franco, who had been in the country to promote his new film which has the same title as the park, *Winterworld*, took off to see the local sights. Diners at Sedgewick's Fish and Chip restaurant on Half Moon Hill did not realise the star was in their midst eating from the 'ten per cent off Tuesday' menu. Waitress Sue Brown said, 'He said his name was Michael Bublé and he came from Ireland but I didn't believe him because he looked nowt like. I thought he was off *EastEnders*.'

The *Daily Trumpet* did hear that the mystery black-haired beauty was Chariot Walliams, a distant relative of TV star David Walliams.

Chapter 29

'Today I'm finally going to see what you look like,' said Palma inwardly to her baby as they sat on the bus. She was more excited than she thought she would be, but apprehensive too. She needed to know that the baby was healthy because she was slightly worried by the fact that she didn't seem to be putting on any weight. Considering she was at the end of her first trimester, so the baby book called it, she was as reed-slim as she always had been. She checked in her handbag to make sure she'd got the piece of paper with all the relevant bus times, but she was Palma Collins and so of course she had. As organised as she was, though, nothing could have prepared Palma for what would happen to her in the scanning room.

*

'You okay?' asked Jacques as Eve was walking at half her usual pace from the car to the hospital. It had been two days since she told him she was pregnant and he hadn't stopped grinning since. Eve had woken up to go to the loo last night and found him even grinning in his sleep.

She grimaced. 'No, I'm not okay. I feel like a balloon about to burst.'

'Uncomfortable?'

'That's not even close.' She felt like cancelling the scan and going to the toilet instead, but she'd already put one appointment off until she'd told Jacques she was pregnant, and by her reckoning she was fourteen weeks pregnant now, so she couldn't do it again.

As they turned the first corner past reception, in front of them was a slender woman with short, spiky pink hair.

'I think that might be Palma,' said Eve. 'She was at the Christmas Pudding Club.' She'd fessed up that she'd been there. She didn't want to conceal a single thing from him anymore.

They caught up with her at the reception desk. It was her. Palma recognised Eve immediately. Her husband looked nice, she thought. Very tall with one of those faces whose default setting was a smile. Like Tommy's.

Introductions followed. Palma noticed that Eve had put on some weight since she'd seen her last and mentioned it and they'd both laughed about how weird it was that they'd be happy to be getting fatter. But Eve couldn't say the same because Palma's stomach was washboard flat. But then Palma was much younger, with stronger stomach muscles; that had to have something to do with it.

'You look surprisingly comfortable,' said Eve, wriggling on the seat to find a position that relieved the pressure inside her.

'Bladder like an elephant, me,' came the reply. 'Good job because my appointment isn't for another half an hour.'

'Lucky you,' said Eve with a chuckle. 'You came early,

then? We left it until the last possible minute, didn't we?' She turned to Jacques but his attention was claimed by something he'd found in a magazine.

'I'm reliant on buses,' replied Palma. 'My life will be a lot simpler when I can afford to run a car.'

Eve nodded in agreement. She was lucky. She'd always had good jobs that enabled her to buy a decent car and run it.

'Any luck with a job yet?'

'Oh yes,' replied Palma. 'Do you remember Annie at the club? The one with the cracker firm, well she offered me a job. I've been there for two weeks now.'

'Non-alcoholic tiramisu. The world is truly coming to an end. An end, I say,' said Jacques aloud.

Eve rolled her eyes at him before continuing to talk with Palma.

'Is it a local firm?'

'Really local. Just outside Maltstone.'

Eve thought for a moment and then said, 'Will Annie be going to the Christmas Pudding Club next week?'

'I'm sure she will.'

'I'll have a word with her there. We should buy some crackers with our logo on them to sell. I can't believe we didn't know they were in the area.'

'Oh yes, of course, you own the big Christmas theme park, don't you?' said Palma, remembering their introductory speeches. 'If anyone should have crackers for sale, you should. Prices to suit all pockets, they do loads of really high-quality commercial stuff as well as the cheaper crackers. I'm working on some for Rolls-Royce.'

'That's a definite then. I'll talk to Annie and we'll fix up a meeting.' Eve committed that note to memory, or as much as her cabbage-brain hormones would allow her to. What a total find if they were so close. She did like to employ local firms wherever possible.

'What next? A banana split with no banana? A Pavlova with no meringue? *C'est nul!'*

A door to their left opened. 'Eve Glace,' called a woman.

'Thank goodness,' said Eve. 'Jacques?'

Jacques was still lost in the magazine. 'Surely it would taste as if something was missing?'

'Oh, will you stop talking about puddings and let's go and see our baby.'

Jacques sprang to his feet, wearing the expression of a small child who had just been promised the world's biggest ice-cream.

'Hope everything is all right,' said Palma.

'Thank you. Same to you too.'

*

Eve lay back on the bed with tissue tucked around her and gel on her stomach, which was showing a roundness she was sure hadn't been there a week ago.

'Would you like any scan photographs?'

'Oh, yes please,' said Eve and Jacques in unison.

'Right, let's have a look at your baby, Mrs Glace,' said Vita Goodchild, pushing the transducer around Eve's skin. Jacques was holding her hand.

'Everything okay?' he asked.

'Give her a chance to look, Jacques.'

'Sorry.'

'Let me check everything and then I can tell you,' said Vita, her eyes not leaving the screen. She was smiling, Eve noticed, and she felt comforted by that.

Eventually Vita said, 'Here you go. Here's your baby.' She turned the screen around and Jacques and Eve saw their child. It never failed to amuse Vita how that first sight affected people. For instance, the big guy in front of her staring open-mouthed at the black and white profile – she would have put money on it that he was the type to start blubbing or even running around the room shouting *yippee*, but instead he blanched. He gaped at the screen without moving as if he thought the image might vanish if he blinked. As for the dark-haired woman with the lovely green eyes – Vita thought she'd process the sight quietly, without much out-ward emotion but it was she who burst into tears and couldn't stop them falling. Vita handed her a box of tissues.

'We go through a lot of these in this department,' she said with a smile.

'Wow,' said Jacques, unable to think of anything that fitted the moment better. So much so that he repeated it twice more.

'Now you keep feeding yourself well and resting and growing that baby,' said Vita, picking up the three photos from her printer and asking the couple to pay at reception. She noticed the big man's hands were shaking as he took them from her.

*

Palma lay back on the bed and wondered what had been going through her mother's mind when she had her scan. Did she eat her five a day and give up the fags and booze and illegal substances? Obviously not, considering what a state she was in when she'd been born. They'd given her mother assistance so that she could keep her baby. They were idiots, they should have taken Palma from her on day one and given her to a family that would have cared for her properly. Blood wasn't thicker than water. It just made more mess.

The sonographer's name was Vita, Palma noticed. She knew that it meant life. It was a lovely name. Someone had chosen it with care for her. She'd never liked her own name. Her mother didn't even know Palma was Spanish; she'd thought it was a place in France.

Vita was concentrating hard as she moved the transducer through the gel on Palma's stomach.

'Would you like some photos of your baby?' she asked.

'Yes, please.' It would be nice for the baby to have them one day, and her new parents.

'They're three for five pounds. You pay on reception.'

'Thank you.'

'You're looking at a mid-January baby if you go to term. That's a wonderful new year present for you,' said Vita with a smile.

She carried on doing her checks and then she turned the screen around and when Palma saw the baby for the first time, she had no idea what emotion engulfed her, only that it seemed to start from her toes and wash upwards until it drowned her brain. She began to feel trembly and light-headed enough to faint. She heard Vita's voice as if it was in the far distance, 'Are you all right?' She felt Vita holding her hand, instructing her to breathe deeply, slowly. Vita asked again if she was all right and she answered with a silent nod that she was.

'Sit there for a few moments until you feel okay to get up,' said Vita.

'I'll be fine.'

'For a minute or so,' Vita insisted. 'I'll get you a glass of water, if you can fit it in.'

Palma sipped on the drink until she felt able to stand.

'There's a loo a few doors down,' said Vita when Palma handed her the glass back. 'I expect you'll be ready to use it now. Let me help you. Are you sure you're all right?'

'I am, thank you,' said Palma. But she wasn't all right. Not all right at all.

Palma sat in the hospital café, her hands drawing warmth from a cup of hot chocolate. She couldn't go back to The Crackers Yard without a sit-down and a think first. She opened one of the cards that the receptionist had slotted the scan photo into. She'd seen the picture of Annie's scan so it came as no surprise to her now that the baby was so 'baby-shaped' but it was an altogether different matter seeing *her* baby on the screen, moving around inside her. Christian didn't even enter her mind. He'd played such a small part in it all – she'd been more intimate with a piece of plastic than with him, anyway. He'd been written out of her personal history, the baby was all hers, created from her egg, growing in her womb. And seeing it inside her had knocked her for six. She felt tears well up in her eyes, and she didn't do crying, because she'd done enough of it for a lifetime in her earlier years and it'd got her nowhere. She fished a tissue out of her coat pocket and blew her nose, forced those tears back down.

All her cards had been flung in the air now. There was no way on this planet that she could even think about handing the baby over to someone else. This baby that she talked to in the bath and in bed and in the kitchen was her child and she was its *mother*. There, she'd dared to use the word. She tried it on like a coat and found it fitted her. They'd manage somehow. Other people did. Even Emma Collins had managed to raise her to adulthood and that was with bugger all care. Palma's child would be loved and looked after in a way she herself never had been. She couldn't let it go to someone else, it was her baby. Hers. Not even if they owned a yacht and a mansion and had the world's biggest Arctic cabin in their twenty-four-acre garden.

On the bus back to work, she wondered if she would have felt the same had she still been Tabitha's surrogate. Would she have been able to remain detached, seeing a baby on the screen that she had promised to someone else? *Sold* to someone else? A shudder rippled across her shoulders when she thought how stupid and naïve she'd been to think her emotions wouldn't have come into play. For someone as organised and base-covering as Palma had always prided herself on being, that had been a major oversight. One of many recently. Thank the Lord that Christian Stephenson had been a feckless, faithless arsehole.

Chapter 30

Jacques and Eve called in at a country pub for brunch before going back to Winterworld after the scan. Eve had ordered a breakfast from the waitress but couldn't for the life of her think of what hash browns were called.

'Those triangular fried thingies,' she said. 'What's the name of them?'

'Hash browns?' tried the waitress.

'That's it. Can I have a side order of those please?' As the waitress walked into the kitchen to give the chef the order, Eve shook her head at herself. 'How can you forget what a hash brown is called?'

'Baby brain?' Jacques suggested.

'How do you know about baby brain?'

'I've read about it in your Miriam Stoppard book,' said Jacques, who had ordered an Olympic-size breakfast because elation had given him a monster appetite.

'I think Effin has baby brain,' Eve replied. 'I'm worried about him.'

Jacques' eyebrows dipped in a gesture of concern and

he made a deep 'hmm' noise. Effin was in denial about his memory loss which was making him prone to even more mistakes. Jacques had warned Davy MacDuff against winding him up. He didn't want any more of those Santapark letters falling off and smashing someone's skull in.

'Do you think I should have a quiet word with Cariad?' asked Eve, after a few moments of contemplation. 'He might get himself checked out by a doctor if she persuaded him to. He'd listen to her.'

'I'm not sure,' said Jacques. 'Should we really put pressure on her to do that when Effin already knows he has a problem?'

Eve nodded. 'Maybe you're right. I hope it isn't the onset of Alzheimer's or anything like that. That would be so cruel.'

'It would,' Jacques agreed. That had crossed his mind also and it must have crossed Effin's.

Then the waitress arrived with their all-day breakfasts and snapped off that line of conversation.

'Ah, your thingies have arrived,' said Jacques, handing Eve the bowl of hash browns.

'Funny.'

'I know, I'm such a hoot.' He did an excited little dance in his chair. 'I can't believe I've seen our baby today.'

Eve shuddered with delight. 'What do you think it is, a boy or a girl?'

'I don't know and I don't care. Preferably one or the other. Have you thought of any names?'

'I've ordered a baby names book on the net. But I don't think you can really name them until you see them.'

'Okay, boss,' said Jacques, stealing a hash brown. 'I'll be guided by you. Six months to go. I can't wait.'

They both grinned at each other. They had grinned at each other more in the past two days than they had in all the rest of their relationship, and that was saying something.

*

'Yes, I like her a lot,' said Iris, constructing some cheap pre-cut crackers quickly and deftly. 'And her funny hair.' They were talking about Palma, who was due back from the hospital any time soon after having her scan.

'I think it suits her,' said Joe from the rolling table, where he and Annie were finishing off the crackers for Rolls Royce.

'She dyes it herself,' said Annie. 'She was telling me. Her hair is naturally very blonde so it absorbs the colour easily. She used to have it blue.'

'Blue hair? Mind you, Doreen Turbot's recently had a purple rinse and it looks nice. I never did understand why people want to spend so much at the hairdressers. When our Linda goes, it's over sixty pounds for a cut and blow.' She shook her head in disapproval.

'I bet blue hair suited Palma,' said Joe, stretching some stiffness out of his back. 'It would match her eyes.'

'What are you doing looking at other women's eyes, Joe Pandoro?' asked Iris with a stern expression.

'Oh come on, Iris, even I've been looking at her eyes,' said Annie. 'She's such a bonny girl.'

'I think she must have had it hard in her life,' decided Iris. 'And if I'm right, well, that's a proper shame. I sometimes get a waft of sadness coming from her, if that makes any sense.'

Annie understood what she meant. She'd felt it too but blamed pregnancy hormones for making her maudlin. 'It's her birthday next Friday. What do you think about getting her a pamper treatment for Glam Beauty Salon in Dodley? I don't suppose she has a lot of luxuries. And they're very good.'

'That's a lovely idea,' said Iris, reaching for her purse. 'You can put me down for twenty pounds. Here, Joe. Take it off me before you put the kettle on.'

Joe half-sighed, half-chuckled. 'I'm just a slave in this company,' he said, taking it from her and putting it in his pocket, just as Palma walked in through the door, huge smile on her face.

'Come on, let's have a look at the scan photo,' said Annie, thinking there seemed to be something different about Palma today. Something softer and brighter, as if a light inside her had been switched on. Or maybe that was her baby brain imagining the ridiculous.

The *Daily Trumpet* would like to apologise to the family of Peter Winstanley-Hughes for the unfortunate error which appeared in his obituary printed last Friday. Mr Winstanley-Hughes was a renowned drag racer appearing all over Europe and not a drag queen as stated. The *Daily Trumpet* has made a donation to the Winstanley-Hughes Young People's Foundation charity by way of recompense.

Chapter 31

Palma didn't find it half as scary going in to the second Christmas Pudding Club meeting and seeing everyone again. Especially as Annie had gone out of her way to give her a lift. Palma liked Annie enormously. She reminded her of her foster mother Grace in a way that she couldn't really explain because they looked nothing like each other, but kindness danced around them both like a perfumed aura.

They were amongst the last to arrive; everyone else was sorted with tea, coffee but mainly juice and water. They were down one member. Colleen, the one who hadn't wanted a child, wasn't there. The loud one, Di, had Raychel pinned in the corner. It was less conversation and more monologue delivered at high volume so that everyone heard.

'... *Come back?* I said. *Are you joking?* Why would I want to stay with a man who's slept with my own mother? MOTHER. I won't talk to her again either. My father's forgiven her. Then again, he couldn't wipe his own arse if he lived by himself ...'

'Hello again,' said Cheryl, the woman who part-owned the cleaning company. 'You both okay?'

'Yep,' Palma and Annie answered together.

'Had my scan this week. Amazing, isn't it?' said Di, joining them. 'I'm having bloody twins.' She tutted but she looked thrilled at the same time.

'I shouldn't tell you this but John fainted in the scan room,' said Cheryl. 'I was a bit scared before I went in and he was, "You've nothing to be scared of, Cheryl. I'm here." Then he goes and passes out. And he's supposed to have tackled Charles Bronson to the floor in prison once, he reckons he's *that* hard.'

They were chuckling over that when Eve rushed in. 'Hello everyone, I got stuck in traffic, thank goodness you haven't started.' Palma poured Eve a glass of juice because she looked flustered and warm.

'Oh, thanks, Palma,' Eve said, thinking that was kind of her and what a lovely young woman she was. Some people you really took to on sight, and Palma was one of those.

'Ladies, can we take our seats please?' said Chloe, clapping her hands to alert their attention. They all drifted to the chairs, arranged in a small circle now, as a new lady arrived and Sharon welcomed her. She was tall and black with the cheekbones of a model and a figure to kill for.

'It appears we have lost a sheep and found one,' said Sharon, then asked the new member of the group if she'd like to introduce herself. She did so very confidently.

'Hello everyone, I'm Ophilia – Fil for short. This is my first baby and probably my last, as I'm forty.' She was older than Di but looked half her age, thought Annie. 'My husband and I come from Nigeria and we've lived in England for four years now. He's a maths professor at the University of Huddersfield and I am a translator. I speak five languages but I can't get my head around Yorkshire. I'm nineteen weeks pregnant and I don't know how much detail you need ...' She looked at the midwives for advice.

'That'll do nicely, thank you,' said Sharon, thinking as they all did that she looked far too glamorous to be called Fil. She briefly filled in Fil on the session she'd missed. 'Last time we were talking about diet during pregnancy. I'll make sure to give you a handout. It's got all the information you'll need on it.'

'This week we are talking about things to buy during your maternity period, because no doubt you're itching to go shopping. And top of the list for you all will be clothes because I bet a few of you are busting out of yours already. How many of you sleep with a bra on?' said Chloe.

That prompted a few of the ladies to start patting their breasts as if it was a natural response to her words.

Sharon stood to attach a flipchart to an easel. She turned to the first page which featured a woman wearing a very comfy-looking brassiere and an old-fashioned nightcap.

'I've never heard of sleep bras,' Annie whispered to Palma.

'I've never heard of a belly band,' Palma whispered back when they got to page two.

Di, at the other side of her, shuffled in her seat quite a bit during the talk, obviously not that interested in this week's topic, but Palma was. It would be good to look stylish during pregnancy. She didn't want to slouch around in leggings and stained baggy jumpers like a lot of the pregnant women did in Ketherwood. Or pyjamas. She could never understand how anyone could venture out to the shops in a fleecy onesie and stupid bunny slippers, but she used to see it all the time there. There were at least two dressing-gowned customers a shift when she worked in Ketherwood Fried Chicken. She liked the idea of the empire line dresses or the pinafores with the large pockets. And the trousers with the expandable sides that she'd probably need by the fifth month. And she was sure she could put together a nice layered look to go to the local Co-op with, because it was hardly likely she'd have a fabulous social life over the next few months; but she didn't want to hide her bump away, she wanted to decorate it.

Chloe and Sharon had really done their homework and found some great pregnancy clothes sites, some with introductory money-off codes. Sadly Palma knew she probably wouldn't be buying anything from the store that sold floor-length gowns in velvet and shimmery materials, but it would be nice to browse through and fantasise that one day she'd be at a dinner where the men all wore suits and the ladies dazzled. The poshest event she'd ever been to in her life was the wedding of the daughter of the woman who owned the sandwich shop where she used to work. They'd hired Higher Hoppleton Hall and had a roast-beef reception for a hundred people and it was all very swanky. Then the groom was found in the toilets with one of the bridesmaids and the bride was arrested for trying to thump

the living daylights out of her – so not very classy by international standards.

Chloe said that their feet might grow half a size and water
retention would make them puff up, so investing in a decent
pair of slip-on shoes that supported their arches would be a
good idea. 'Like Fil's,' she suggested, noticing what Fil was
wearing. Beautiful flip-flops encrusted with sparkling crys-
tals. Her toenails were painted silver to match. Even her feet
looked model material.

'Fit-flops,' said Fil. 'I live in them.'

'Don't forget it's going to be hard to bend over so if you
have fiddly shoe straps that need tying and threading into
buckles, you'd better have someone willing to do it for you,'
said Sharon. 'Best to keep low and safe as far as heels go,
ladies. And that concludes our session for today, unless you
have any questions?'

No one did so the midwives wished everyone a good three
weeks until the next session, when they would be talking
about safe exercise.

Eve was talking to Annie when Palma returned from
a quick visit to the loo. Annie beckoned her into the
conversation.

'This is my star worker,' she told Eve, then turned quickly
to Palma, 'For goodness sake don't tell Iris I said that.'

'Please come and see us in Winterworld next week if
you're free, Annie.' Eve reached into her handbag for a business card. 'Ring me tomorrow and let's fix up a meeting. I'm
definitely free Monday, if you are.'

'I'd be delighted,' said Annie, with breathy delight.

'See you next time, Palma,' said Eve.

'Yeah, see you, Eve. Take care.'

When Eve moved off, Annie gave Palma a very large smile. 'I have you to thank for this, dear girl.' She fluttered the business card. 'You put in a good word with Eve in the scan department, apparently.'

'Well, I only mentioned where I worked.' Palma shrugged her shoulders modestly. 'But I did give your crackers a good shout out.'

Which was a great cue for her to go on and say what was on her mind, except that she wasn't quite brave enough. Then, as they were buckling up in the car, Palma gulped, took a deep breath and charged in.

'Annie, do you mind if I tell you something? You might hate me for it, but I really should say it.'

Annie's hand stilled on the ignition key. 'What?' Her face registered alarm.

'Your website's crap,' said Palma.

Annie burst into laughter. 'Oh, thank goodness. I thought you were going to tell me you were thinking of leaving us.' She twisted the key and started the engine.

'God no, not that,' said Palma. 'I've been wanting to say it since I saw it. It's all over the place. It's not easy to use and some of the links don't even work.'

'Joe hates updating it and I'll be honest, I'm not the best on computers,' Annie said. 'It's been on my list of to-look-ats for ages but I've been putting it off, if I'm honest. Don't mind if I take a detour into town to visit the cashpoint, do you?'

'No, not at all. And you have no presence on social media.

No Instagram pics, no Facebook account or Twitter,' Palma went on, emboldened by Annie's receptiveness.

'I have no idea about social media,' Annie confessed. 'I can't get my head around it. Do we need it?'

'I'd say so. Eve didn't even know you existed, which is tragic considering what she does and what you do all in the same area. You could have had a contract there from them opening.'

'We couldn't take the work on then, though. I'm not even sure we can now. Getting hold of staff is unbelievably difficult. I don't know why it's so hard, do you?'

'I have no idea.' Palma answered her honestly. 'But I think maybe that agency isn't doing you any favours.'

Annie had to stop sharply outside the town hall at the lights. They'd turned green and some idiot stepped out in front of her, eyes down on his phone. She couldn't believe it. *Him again.* Clint O'Gowan. That was twice now he'd stepped out in front of her car and twice now she'd regretted not ploughing into him. Maybe it was fate's way of trying to deliver him to her.

As Annie indicated to pull into a space, Palma turned to look through the back window. Clint was heading down the hill towards them, not looking at his phone anymore now. 'Please don't stop here, Annie,' she said, urgency in her voice. 'There's someone I don't want to see.'

It could only be him, there was no one else around.

'Clint O'Gowan? How do you know him?' Annie asked incredulously, driving on as Palma asked.

'I grew up with him,' Palma answered.

'Oh, did you.' Annie's tone had hardened. Tightened.

'How do you know him?' asked Palma, wondering how Annie's path could possibly have crossed with Clint's.

'He's the reason why Joe and I couldn't adopt, that's how I know him,' said Annie, her jaw clenched, her mouth a grim line. Then she swung the car around the corner too fast as if she hoped that Clint O'Gowan would be there and the chance to brake in time wouldn't be an option.

*

Cariad didn't recognise the mobile number but she answered it anyway. She had lovely manners; even when market research people rang her at unsociable hours, she always declined their services politely. She always thought that it must be a miserable job cold-calling and people wouldn't take it unless they needed money very much, so she didn't want to add to their misery.

'All right, Cariad?' It was Dylan. She wondered how he'd got her number, but she didn't ask because she presumed her flipping uncle had given it to him.

'Hello, Dylan, how are you?'

'I'm good, I'm good. I thought you might like to go to the pictures on Friday night. There's loads of new films out.'

Cariad winced silently. She wasn't convinced anymore that she and Dylan would be able to go out as friends. He was always staring and smiling at her and, as nice a boy as he was, she didn't fancy him at all. Plus she'd heard on the grapevine from Myfanwy that it was common knowledge that he'd taken a shine to her.

'Ah, the thing is, I'm flat-hunting this weekend ...'
she began.

'Oh go on, Cariad. Just as friends. Get your Uncle Effin
off my back, will you?'

Uncle Effin. He was a nightmare. She was busy at the
moment trying to find somewhere to move to. Her Uncle
Effin had said she could stay at the cottage for as long as she
wanted until she found a place but she'd declined his offer.
She had the feeling she might strangle him if she had to stay
in the same house with him banging on about how she and
Dylan would make a good pairing.

'I don't think so, Dylan. I'm a bit busy.' She felt rude turning him down but she didn't want to go.

'It's only a film, Cariad. I'll pick you up and take you back
home safe.' The pleading in his voice was making it even
more difficult. She felt guilty now as well as rude.

'I don't ...'

'You can pick the film and I'll pay. I'll even buy you popcorn. Oh, go on, Cariaaaad. Then I'll be able to tell your
uncle that we aren't suited to each other after all. He won't
take no for an answer.'

That sounded like her uncle all over. The emotional blackmail worked. Against her own wishes, Cariad found herself
saying. 'Okay, I'll go, Dylan. Thank you for asking me.'

*

In the time it took for Annie to pull some money out of the
cashpoint, she'd calmed down considerably. *That man*. He'd
even managed to taint Palma through association, and that

was unfair. She knew that Palma came from the rough end of the town but she hated him so much that she did not want to have any connection with him whatsoever, not even through a third party. She got back into the car, shutting the door harder than she meant to, as if she was venting her spleen at her young passenger and felt immediately bad for that.

'I'm sorry, I didn't mean to snap at you, Palma. I had no right.'

'It's okay,' said Palma with a tentative smile. 'Clint has that effect on people.'

'A friend of yours, is he?' Annie put the key in the ignition but she needed a couple more minutes before she had cooled down enough to drive.

'God, no. He's one of the reasons I couldn't wait to leave Ketherwood.' She didn't tell Annie the lengths she'd gone to in order to be able to do it though.

'What do you mean?'

'He's rotten,' said Palma. 'He's a user. In all senses of the word. I would be quite happy if I never saw him ever again. What did you mean about adopting?'

Annie let out a long, tired sigh. 'Six years ago, we had passed through all stages of the adoption process. We were in line for taking in two beautiful little girls, aged one and two. We had the room for them decorated and the week before they were coming to us, we went out for a meal. There were no spaces near the restaurant so Joe dropped me at the door because I had high heels on, and he parked a few streets away. When we came out, he went to get the car and I waited for him on the pavement and . . .' Annie's eyes narrowed as if she could see Clint in front of her '. . . that *thing* came from nowhere and ripped my handbag from my shoulder. And I didn't let it go, like I should have, let him have it. Instead I tried to hang on to it and Joe arrived and jumped out of the car. O'Gowan ran off and Joe ran after him; he used to box so he knows how to land a punch. O'Gowan would have got clean away if he hadn't tripped.' Annie sighed heavily once more. 'Joe tore into him and suddenly people came running out of the restaurant trying to drag Joe away. O'Gowan was covered in blood, insisting on an ambulance, the police. Joe was arrested. There was CCTV footage but only from outside the restaurant and all that showed was O'Gowan running with Joe in pursuit, falling and then Joe full-on battering him. Joe ended up in court. O'Gowan said that he'd only bumped into me and because I was drunk, I'd thought he was trying to steal my bag and that Joe was a maniac and he was terrified. I wasn't drunk, I'd had half a bottle of wine and I was merry and happy, but I wasn't drunk, Palma. Joe got a suspended sentence for assault. My Joe, my lovely gentle Joe. And the adoption was stopped.'

Annie's face dropped into her hands. Even now, after all these years it still hurt. The sunny back bedroom in their house had been redecorated and was now an office, but Annie could still see the seaside wallpaper with the mermaids and the crabs and fish and the sand-coloured curtains covered with brightly coloured starfish in her mind.

Palma had been sixteen then. She remembered hearing about Clint being put in hospital by some bloke. He'd knocked out one of his own teeth in the toilet there, apparently, to make himself look worse. He'd had his tooth fixed and it had been knocked out again a few months later by someone else.

Annie felt the warmth of Palma's hand on her shoulder.

'It was my idea to go out that night,' said Annie, wiping away a couple of stray tears with the heel of her hand. 'Joe wanted to stay in and cook for us but I insisted. I thought it would be a nice treat for us both. If only I'd listened to him.'

'How could you have forecast that?' asked Palma.

'It almost split us up,' said Annie. 'It didn't, but it nearly did. I've asked myself over and over so many times why didn't I let my handbag go? There was nothing in it but make-up and my purse. I could have stopped my bank cards easily . . .'

'It's in the past,' said Palma, searching in her handbag for a tissue for her. 'You can't change it and now you're having your own baby. Let it go, Annie. Don't let him spoil things for you again. He's a vile human being and he will get his come-uppance one day.'

Annie took the tissue and blew her nose, then started up the car.

'I used to be a believer in karma, love, but I'm not anymore. Not since that happened to us.' She slipped into first gear and they were away.

Chapter 32

Palma walked into work and straightaway saw the potted pink miniature rose plant on the table in front of her seat. She'd taken the bus in today because she had a dentist's appointment first thing. She told Annie she'd make up the time in her lunch hour and Annie told her not to be so daft. She knew that Palma was doing all sorts of things for them at home such as updating the website and setting up social media accounts.

'Happy Birthday, Palma,' called Annie and Iris in unison and then Joe emerged from the kitchen with a glass of Ribena with a lit sparkler in it. Palma hooted with laughter before gulping back a ball of emotion that rose to her throat.

'Blow it out and make a wish,' ordered Joe. Palma did as he asked and silently, as a chorus of 'Happy Birthday to you' erupted from her workmates, she wished the first thing that came into her head: that Annie and Joe's baby would be born fine and healthy without any troubles. She didn't save the wish for herself.

When she pulled out her chair from under the table, she

found the three envelopes sitting on it and smiled. She hadn't expected anything today from anyone. The sort of people she'd cut loose from weren't the birthday-card-sending type unless there was an ulterior motive to it. Nicole had brought her a card last year as a pretext for hitting her for a loan she had no intention of paying back. But somehow, she didn't think that these cards would have that purpose.

'Hurry up and open them,' said Iris with impatience.

'Give me a minute to get my jacket off, Iris,' Palma tutted, good-humouredly.

The first card was from her. A square arty one of a little blonde girl with a black cat on her knee.

'I thought she looked like you might have when you were a kiddy, before the pink hair,' said Iris.

'She does,' said Palma, 'thank you, Iris.'

Palma had never had a pet, apart from a goldfish that she'd won at a fair once. By the time she'd found something to keep it in, her mother had flushed it down the toilet, telling her it had died. It had stuck in her mind as the first time she felt a deep, resentful wave of hatred for her mother which scared and upset her for both its disloyalty and ferocity. One day she'd have a cat; a black one would have been her first choice too. The old lady next door to them in Hanson Street had one that used to sleep contentedly in her front window and Palma used to think that it had a more comfortable life than she did. The second card was from Annie and Joe and featured a woman in a deckchair, hat over her face as she relaxed in the sunshine.

'That's lovely, thank you,' said Palma. She'd found an old

stripy deckchair in the small shed in her back garden. If the sun carried on shining, she would get it out this weekend and emulate that picture, minus the hat. She opened up the third envelope, wondering who this one was from, and her eyes lit up when she pulled out the card inside.

'A pamper voucher? Wow.'

'From us all. There's a list of all the treatments. They do a lovely Indian head massage there. And you can have a hairdo and a manicure. Or something else if you prefer,' said Annie.

'Hot stones,' said Iris. 'That's my favourite. Doreen Turbot got me into those. They dip stones into warm oil and run them over your body. It's better than sex with Sasha Distel.'

'I'm speechless,' said Palma, grinning, though she had no clue who Sasha Distel was. 'This is lovely. Really, thank you so much.' She wasn't sure that she'd have a massage. She wasn't sure about having a stranger's hands on her, but she'd think about it.

'Right, now get to work,' said Joe, cracking a pretend whip.

'How were your teeth?' asked Iris.

'Fine, I only need a scale and polish,' said Palma, getting straight into making up the flat pile of waiting crackers.

'Typical,' huffed Iris. 'Just when you're entitled to get it free, you don't need anything doing.'

'You've got lovely teeth, Palma,' said Annie.

'Thanks,' said Palma. She'd always looked after them. She wasn't sure she could ever go out with anyone with horrible teeth. Tommy had nice ones. *Tommy Tommy Tommy*. Why was her brain insistent on trying to bring his name up all the time.

'Some of them people on *Jeremy Kyle*,' said Iris with a shudder. 'They wouldn't know one end of a toothbrush from the other.'

And they stuffed crackers and talked about *Jeremy Kyle* contestants until they broke for lunch: sandwiches from Bren's Butties and a chocolate birthday cake from the kitchen of Joe and Annie Pandoro.

*

Effin was grinning like a village idiot as he walked into the ice-cream shop and Cariad didn't need to ask why. Dylan must have told him that they were going to the cinema together that night.

The park was quiet and there were no customers so Cariad was cleaning the insides of the windows. She didn't like to stand idle.

'Fancy serving your old uncle some of his favourite, then and telling him all about what's happening?' He squished himself up into an excited little ball, making Cariad want to throw the bottle of Windolene at him. Instead, she washed her hands and picked up her scoop and plunged it into the chocolate and cherry without saying a word.

'What's up with you, Cariad? You've a face on you like thunder. I told your Auntie Angharad and she said—'

'She said, keep your nose out of it, Effin Williams. That's what my auntie would have said,' cut in Cariad. The look on Effin's face said that she'd hit the nail on the head and the lie he'd been going to tell died on his lips.

'I said I'd go out with Dylan once, to see a film. Don't start buying a suit for the wedding, Uncle Effin, because it's not going to happen.' She slammed the glass sundae dish down in front of him and he jumped a little in his seat.

'Dylan's dad Brynn was my best friend for years, did I ever tell you?' said Effin, loading ice-cream onto his spoon.

Cariad sighed. 'Only a few million times.'

'Oh, I had a lovely childhood.' His eyes took on a dreamy cast as his imagination whisked him back to the day when his one true love – Angharad Hughes – had reached for his hand at St Clydwyn's Sunday School during an Easter Lord's Prayer.

Cariad rinsed the scoop and picked up her cloth again. Her uncle was clearly deep in the warm pool of his idyllic past. She might as well not have been there.

'My mam and dad always felt a bit sorry for Brynn. His mam had buggered off and his dad was a *coc* and my mam bought more clothes for him than his own family did. He never seemed to have a lot of luck and then he met Dylan's mam Lin and it was like all his Christmases come together at once. Oh, she was a beauty was Lin. Tall and dark, just like Dylan.' Then his smile faded and he said, without meaning to, 'Poor Brynn.'

Cariad knew, because Uncle Effin had told her quite a few times, that Lin had run off with someone else and left Brynn to bring up Dylan. But he must have done a pretty good job of it because everyone liked Dylan. And Cariad couldn't understand why he was single because he was a hell of a looker. She could appreciate that, even if he didn't float her own particular love boat. She almost wished she did fancy him, but she didn't and you couldn't force affections to go where they didn't want to.

Then Davy MacDuff opened the door and barged into both the café and Effin's reverie. His voice carried urgency.

'Effin, can you come quick, there's a problem with the train. Thomas has been ringing and ringing you.'

'You watch your tone with me, boy,' said Effin, patting around himself for his phone. 'Where've I put my bloody mobile?' His frustration told in his grumbling tone. It wasn't like him to have mislaid it and Cariad knew that.

'Sorry to interrupt you, Cariad,' said Davy, sweetening his tone, which infuriated Effin even more than he was already, being shown up as off the ball by the haggis.

'That f . . . bloody train. It'll be the death of me,' said Effin, giving Davy a murderous look as he swept out of the door past him.

'Have a good time tonight, Cariad,' said Davy to her and it was her turn to look murderous then. Was there anyone who didn't know she was going out with Dylan Evans that evening?

Chapter 33

Palma treated herself to a Chinese takeaway that night. There was a lovely one around the corner – The Great Wall of China – where they served up your food in cartons, like in American TV shows; and somehow it tasted extra delicious that way, especially if you ate it with chopsticks. She devoured the lot and realised that was the first time in ages she'd finished a full meal. She was twelve weeks pregnant now and had enjoyed two full days without any queasiness. Her orange chicken and egg fried rice had pressed all the buttons, and for dessert she'd had half a Terry's Chocolate Orange. She couldn't remember the last time she'd had anything orange-flavoured before she was pregnant as it wasn't high up on her favourite tastes list, but pregnancy had sent her daft for it.

She was giving the cardboard cartons a swill with water before putting them in her recycling bag when there was a knock at the door. A knock she thought she recognised. A jaunty postman's knock: *der-dum-der. It couldn't be.* She went cold and hot at the same time. She wished she had the advantage of her bedsit window where she could spy on, unseen, whoever was standing on her doorstep.

She slid the chain on before opening the door a sliver, just in case it wasn't who she thought it was. She saw the flowers first: pink and yellow wrapped up in yellow tissue. Then her eyes flicked upwards and met with Tommy Tanner's.

*

Dylan picked up Cariad at six. He looked smart in a half-zipped black top and jeans and handsome with his soulful brown eyes and his thick dark hair which was the sort that women might want to rake their hands through. Other women – not Cariad. He opened the door for her like a gentleman both when she got in the car and when she got out at the other end. There was a bar in the cinema and Dylan bought them both a drink and two tubs of caramel popcorn. Cariad picked a Tom Cruise film because she didn't think it was fair to make Dylan sit through the musical she really fancied watching. He insisted on paying for the tickets and Cariad had to concede, though she didn't like it, because it made it feel as if she was on a date rather than a mates' outing where they'd have gone Dutch. Halfway through the film he reached for her hand and captured it and held it and she wanted to pull it away but felt mean. Her mind fell away from the film, she just wanted to go home. She felt annoyed with him that he'd persuaded her to come out under false pretences, but she was more annoyed with herself that she hadn't stood firm and said she didn't want to go to the flipping cinema, because she'd suspected all along that this was what would happen.

*

'Come in,' said Palma, after Tommy had pushed the flowers into her hand without saying anything more than, 'These are for you.'

'Thank you.' Had he remembered her birthday? How could he have known? The answer to that came after he walked in and saw the two cards on the mantelpiece, either side of the pink rose plant.

'Is it your birthday?'

'Yes. Today.' He hadn't known. So what were the flowers for? 'Would you like a cup of coffee or something?'

'Tea, please. And Happy Birthday.'

'Thanks.'

Tommy sat down on her sofa and his hands reached for each other as if he were nervous about something.

'I'll go and get you one.' She remembered how he took it. Whilst the kettle was boiling she put the flowers in the vase he'd brought full of freesias the last time he was here. She'd arrange them properly later and snip off the bottoms, but they'd do for now. She set them down in the middle of her small dining table then went back into the kitchen to brew the tea, all the time wondering why he'd come because he was sitting in silence and she wasn't going to prompt him.

'Thank you, they're lovely,' she said, delivering a mug to his waiting hands, hoping he wouldn't notice how shaky her own hands were. Then she sat on the other side of the sofa, with a good space between them, and waited for him to explain what he was doing here because he seemed to be in no hurry to. He took a sip before putting his drink down on a coaster on the coffee table slowly, as if stalling for time. Or building up courage.

'How's things with you?' she asked eventually before the tumbleweed starting blowing across the room.

'Palma, I'm really sorry,' Tommy said, looking down rather than at her. 'I haven't really known what to say to you.'

'About what?' she asked.

'You, your ... situation ...'

'It's okay,' she replied, impressed at her own coolness. 'It must have come as a bit of a shock. I didn't know how to tell you.'

'I've been thinking about it a lot. I shouldn't have walked out on you like that.'

'Really, I understand.'

'You helping someone out like that. It's massive.'

Ah. She gave it thirty seconds before he walked out again.

'My situation, as you put it, has changed,' she said.

Tommy's head snapped up. 'You haven't ... you know, got rid of it, have you?'

'No,' said Palma quickly. 'I mean, it all fell through. The couple split up. They don't want the baby anymore. So I'm keeping it.'

'What? Really?' He seemed shocked.

'Yes, Tommy, I am.' She felt slightly annoyed by his tone. What business of his was it anyway? He'd made his feelings clear the last time he was here, so what did he want? Why the flowers? Why the questions? She could start asking him a few of her own. Did 'Katie' with the knocker-showing dress know he was here, for a start?

'That's a shame,' he said, reaching for the mug, lifting it to his lips again, putting it back down. 'For the baby I mean. Not being wanted.'

'The baby is wanted,' said Palma, her jaw tightening. 'I want her. She's mine. She doesn't need a feckless knobhead of a father who only agreed to it all for a quiet life. And no, I didn't know that before I entered into the arrangement, before you ask. I thought I was giving a childless couple something they were desperate for and couldn't have themselves, not saving a woman's bloody figure and—'

'Whoa ... whoa.' Tommy held his hands up to stem the flow of her ever-increasing agitation. 'You don't need to defend yourself to me.'

'Why are you here, Tommy?' Palma demanded.

'Because I haven't been able to get you out of my head, Palma, that's why.'

Well that shut her up.

'Since that night in the park, you remember?'

'Of course I remember. I've got the scars to prove it.'

She saw a smile quirk his lips and it spread to her own, annoyingly, even though she fought it.

'I even switched supermarkets so I wouldn't bump into you and I still did and I knew you'd switched supermarkets so you wouldn't bump into me.'

'I didn't,' said Palma. 'I told you, I needed oranges.'

He wiggled his finger at her. 'You big liar.' His smile closed down. 'I hurt you, I must have done and I'm really sorry.'

'Don't flatter yourself,' she said. But he knew by the defensive snap in her voice that he'd called it right.

'You and me, Palma, we're from the same garden,' Tommy said. His hand twitched as if it wanted to reach for hers but wasn't quite brave enough. 'Shit soil, rocks, no water, no sunshine, but somehow we managed to grow into strong plants. I'm doing okay, but I've had help, breaks. You haven't, have you?'

'I have recently,' she said. 'I've got a great job, lovely people around me, I'm doing all right actually. And I love this little house, so don't you feel sorry for me, Tommy Tanner.'

Now his hand did reach for hers and take it and hold it between both of his.

'I don't feel sorry for you, you daft bint, I like you. I really like you. I couldn't believe that I'd bumped into you again, you know. I've never forgotten about you from school and then that night in the park it was like ... like fate. The best kind.'

'But that was before you knew I was having a baby. A baby that I'm now keeping,' she said quietly, expecting him to pull away from her, but he didn't, his hold tightened.

'Don't you think I've thought about it all, Palma?'

'You don't want complication in your life, Tommy. You made it clear and of course I respect you. I didn't blame you at—'

'Shut up, Palma and let me speak. I don't want complication,' he said. 'But I want you, and if you come with complication then I'll take it. I weighed everything up after I left here last time: what I'd feel like if I was with you and you had to give the baby up to those people, or you deciding you didn't want to hand it over and keeping it, or them running out on you. I went through every possible scenario, and I kept coming to the same conclusion . . . that it didn't matter, because if you and me were together we could sort it. Somehow. I want you, I really do. Give me a chance, Palma.'

He was caressing her fingers. She couldn't remember anyone ever touching her so tenderly before. It flooded her brain with such an alien sensation, she couldn't work out if it was pleasurable or painful. What was he asking? Give him a chance to what?

'What do you mean?' she asked.

'Give me a chance to be with you,' he said. 'Just, see what happens, see where it goes. Honest, Palma, you're stuck in my brain. I nearly dropped my shopping basket when I saw you in the Co-op. I didn't want cheese. I wanted to get away from you.'

'Charming,' said Palma, deadpan.

'I wanted to get away from you because I wanted to be with you. I've never felt anything as strong. It was like being in the ring, a massive wave of emotion. I was standing there looking at cheese and shaking.'

Palma half-wanted to laugh but he was deadly serious, his eyes were glassy as if he were on the verge of tears.

'You and me, Palms, we don't get things the easy way, not like other people. And that little baby, I thought, it's going to be hard for Palma giving it up. I wanted to be there for you. But now . . .'

'Yeah, now, it's—'

'Palma, will you let me finish. Now, more than ever that little baby deserves to have someone who loves him from the off and is on his side.'

'The baby has – me,' said Palma.

'He can have me as well. I'll take him on. I'll be there for him an' all.'

His words weakened her and so her defences came up. She pulled her hand away from his.

'I saw you in the paper with a woman. Your girl-friend, it said.'

Tommy tutted and then gave an impatient huff. 'She's one of the ring girls. She asked me to pose for a photo with her, that was all, I didn't even know her name. She must have spoken to the press, because I certainly didn't. Ask my bruvver when you see him, I went with him and Jackie to the fight. She's not my type for a start. More plastic than Barbie. I like my women more natural. But with pink hair.'

He was smiling now. She stole a look at his face and saw the splash of freckles over his nose, his warm grey eyes taking her in.

'So, do you fancy being my girl, Palma Collins? We'll work everything out that needs to be worked out as we go along.'

'I don't want to get in the way of anything for you,' said Palma. 'I'd never forgive myself. It wouldn't be right.'

'You didn't answer the question: will you be my girl, Palma Collins?'

His arm reached around her shoulder, he shuffled towards her on the sofa. She felt him turn into her and the press of his chest against her own and she didn't resist and that seemed to answer his question for both of them without the need for spoken words.

*

When they got into the car, Dylan had suggested they go on for a drink after the film.

'I'm a bit tired, thanks, and I've got an early start in the morning,' Cariad replied. It was a lie but delivered convincingly, she thought.

'Just one,' said Dylan. 'I know a lovely place.' And he had swung out of the car park and driven them off to a pub in the middle of nowhere, despite what she'd said. 'We should come here for something to eat sometime,' he said as he opened the door for her and offered his arm because the ground was full of potholes.

He'd bought a glass of wine for her – large, even though she'd asked for a small one – and a pint of cola for himself. 'I don't drink and drive, you'll be safe with me,' he said, sitting down opposite her and reaching for her hand across the table. It wasn't the drinking and the driving that she was worrying about.

Cariad was withering inside herself. Dylan was looking at her like a love-sick pup, asking her what she liked to do on her days off and she was politely fobbing him off at every pass – too politely because he wasn't taking the hint. And he was taking one sip of his pint every five minutes.

In the loo, Cariad gave herself a talking to in the mirror above the sink. She had to stop trying not to hurt his feelings because she'd hurt them a lot more by making him believe this was the first of many dates. If she had to knock the point home with a sledgehammer, well then she'd just have to. When she came out again, it was to find that he was buying another round in, even though he hadn't even shifted a quarter of his drink. It was then that Cariad grew really cross because this was definite manipulation. It galvanised her into saying what she really felt.

'Don't get me another drink, Dylan. I haven't finished the last one and I want to be at home by . . .' she swept her eyes down to her watch and did a quick calculation '. . . ten thirty at the latest. As I told you, I've got an early start.'

'Oh one more won't kill—'

'I said no, Dylan. No.' Cariad cut him off with a tone in her voice that brooked no misinterpretation and the smile dropped from his face. 'I've had enough, thank you. So when you're ready, we'll go. I've had a lovely evening but I'm tired now.'

She sat down at the table to give him a chance to finish his drink but she didn't want any more of hers. He followed her over, his movements slow. If it was an attempt to infuriate her, it was working.

Dylan lifted the glass to his lips and took the tiniest sip before replacing it on the coaster. 'You might have to wait for me, Cariad, if you want a lift,' he said, sounding like a very different Dylan to the one she'd been sitting with before she went to the ladies.

Cariad sat stiffly in her chair holding her handbag in her lap, her body language making it plainer than plain that, as far as she was concerned, the evening was at an end. She looked anywhere and everywhere but at Dylan, making her displeasure blatant. He didn't speak either and at the periphery of her eye corner she occasionally saw him lift his glass, take a sip, set it down again.

At ten to eleven, Cariad took her phone out of her bag. 'I'm going to ring for a taxi, Dylan, so you can stay here as long as you want,' she said.

Dylan stood, scraping his chair back on the rustic floor. 'All right, I'll take you home now. I thought we'd have had a nice drink and a talk but obviously it wasn't to be.'

She didn't like his tone or the way he marched towards the door, leaving her in his wake. *If he lets it swing back in my face, I'm ringing that taxi*, she said to herself, but he didn't. He held it open for her, but he didn't open the car door for her as he had done before.

She thought he'd set off like a maniac, but he didn't do that either, although he was driving at speed on those winding country roads and she tried not to react because she thought that might further fuel his annoyance with her. The silence that filled the car had a thick, heavy, unpleasant weight and Cariad turned her head so she was looking out of the window the whole time. That she couldn't wait to get home to a house she shared with the biggest pair of bitches on the planet said it all. The relief that she felt when they reached it was ridiculously intense.

'Thank you for seeing me home, Dylan,' Cariad said, her tone polite but tight. She pulled the handle to open the door, but it was firmly locked. She snapped her head around to Dylan, totally out of patience now.

'Can you open it, please?'

Dylan didn't move for a long few seconds and then he said in a measured, even voice, 'You know what the trouble with girls like you is, Cariad? You don't give anyone the chance.'

'What do you mean, *the trouble . . .* ?'

'I haven't finished. You women all want a gentleman and then when you get one, you turn all feminist, moving goal-posts, leading them on . . .'

Cariad opened her mouth to protest but thought better of it.

'You want the bits of rough, the ones that don't respect you, then you get them and start bleating when they hurt you. You want to turn them into the nice guys, which is ironic because there are nice guys out there already but you lot don't want them ready-made.'

Cariad remained silent. It sounded as if he was mixing her up with someone else.

'Maybe it's catching because your uncle is out of his head too.' Dylan tapped his temple slowly.

Now Cariad did react.

'What do you mean?'

'He's losing it. Everyone's talking about it.'

Cariad felt pressure hot and fierce building quickly inside her. She needed to get away from him before she cried or screamed or flew at him because she had no idea which would happen if she blew.

Then Dylan suddenly reached forward and pressed a button releasing the lock on the door and Cariad snatched the handle and threw herself out of the car. She heard the word at the moment that she slammed the door shut: *hwren*. He spat it out, then crunched into first gear and took off down the road as if he were in the Batmobile chasing the Joker.

Hwren. He'd just called her a whore.

Apologies for the article that appeared in last week's *Daily Trumpet* Arts supplement. The exhibition at the Town Hall features a painting by Dick Van Dyke, not David Icke as reported.

Chapter 34

'You okay, *ma cherie*?' asked Jacques, heavy on the French accent as Eve stretched out to ease the ache in her back. She was standing in the corner of the office leaning on Gabriel the elk, who seemed happy enough to be of assistance.

'I'm starting to feel some extra weight dragging me forwards now,' Eve explained.

'I'll give you a nice massage later tonight,' Jacques offered.

'Don't expect me to lie flat on my front though,' said Eve. 'Look at me.' She framed the mound of her stomach with her hands. 'I think I'm putting on half a stone per day.'

'You sit down and I'll put the coffee through,' said Jacques. Their machine was ancient and spat aggressively through the filtering process as if it resented its purpose but it delivered a superb offering. When he had poured the jug of water into the machine he crossed to the window, hearing the chug of the Nutcracker Express behaving itself for once. It was rolling down the track as obediently as if it were on a choke chain. He could see Thomas smiling as he drove it and behind him, Joe and Annie looking from one side to the other, taking in as much of Winterworld as they could during the journey from the front gate to the office. They'd been scheduled in for a meeting at eleven that morning.

Then Jacques looked beyond the train because something had caught his eye: the unmistakable figure of big Davy MacDuff with his arms around someone. A female with long black hair. And there was only one uniformed female with long black hair on the payroll – Cariad Williams. He hoped that Effin wasn't in the vicinity because he didn't even like Davy breathing the same air as his niece. Davy was a good bloke but he didn't always think as logically in the civilian world as he had in the military one. He was much more suited to the latter and it had taken him a long time to adjust back into the former. He was an attractive man, Cariad was a pretty woman and he had no right to tell either of them how to conduct their business but he was very fond of Cariad and he didn't want to see her consumed alive. She was certainly flavour of the month, what with Franco Mezzaluna's pupils the size of black holes in space when he'd seen her, young Dylan Evans throwing his cap at her and now Davy MacDuff getting physically close. The charm of Cariad was that she thought of herself as a Ford Fiesta whereas men thought of her as a Ferrari Fiorano.

He snapped off his thoughts about them to answer the door and invite Annie and Joe into the cabin. Eve bounced over, shook Joe's hand and gave Annie a hug, trading info on how the other was.

'Come and sit down,' said Jacques, taking another crafty peek through the window to find Davy slowly walking off with Cariad, his arm hanging loosely around her shoulder in a friendly rather than an intimate fashion, not that Effin would see it like that if he spotted them. He turned his attention back to the room and offered everyone a drink. Then, after some general chit-chat, Joe opened the sample case he had brought with him which was full of different crackers from the large luxury ones to the cheapest. He handed over a catalogue of their goods and a price list, which he explained gave a ballpark figure but no order was standard. He worked best when people gave him their budget, he said, and he'd tell them what he could give them for that. A technique that had always served him reliably. Eve picked up the sheet of numbers, Jacques picked up one of the crackers and asked if he could test it. Joe offered to take the other side and they pulled, resulting in a beautifully crisp bang. Jacques won the main body of the cracker and poked inside with his finger, pulling out a black and silver folded crown, a small round tin of moustache wax and a joke that made Jacques snort with laughter.

'That seems to have gone down well,' said Eve with amusement.

'Brilliant,' said Jacques. 'I love it. Look, Eve.' He passed the joke to his wife who smiled when she got to the punchline. The joke was right on his level.

What do you call a hen staring at a lettuce?
Chicken Caesar salad.

'Palma wrote that,' said Annie. 'She decided our jokes needed updating.'

'Palma?' asked Jacques. 'The girl we met at the scan? With the pink hair.'

'Yep, that's her,' said Eve. 'Our Christmas Pudding Club buddy.'

'It's like two worlds colliding,' said Jacques, clapping his hands together. 'Crackers and Christmas puddings. I love it. We should all be married to each other.'

'We think we could have a cracker shop in the park, don't we, Jacques?' said Eve, bringing him back to earth. 'You can brand them with our Winterworld logo, can't you?'

'Of course,' said Joe. 'Anything you like.'

'Maybe two qualities for two pockets,' decided Eve. 'Fun ones and luxury ones.'

'We also have these for special occasions,' said Annie, putting a sparkly box on the table housing two much larger crackers. 'These are his and hers crackers or his and his or hers and hers or undecided and undecided. And we also have individually boxed ones for super-special occasions. I can't tell you how many engagement rings we've packed into them.'

'I wish I'd thought of that,' said Jacques, slapping his forehead with his hand. 'Imagine the surprise.'

'There was no surprise. You told me you were going to marry me the first time we met,' Eve reminded him.

'And I was right, wasn't I?' he dabbed the top of her nose affectionately. 'Just as I'm going to tell you that your next wedding is one you'll never forget as long as you live.'

'We are renewing our vows,' Eve explained. 'I like these a lot.' She picked up a square-sided cracker.

'They sit very good in the box,' said Joe.

'Yes, these for the more expensive ones and these' – she picked up a round one – 'for the cheaper lot.'

'Both the same quality of snap though,' said Joe. 'It's all about the snap.'

'No, the toys,' argued Jacques. 'And the jokes. Chicken Caesar salad . . .' and he let loose a fresh burst of laughter.

'It's everything,' said Annie. 'You don't want to be let down on any of the components.'

'Hand-rolled or not?' Eve turned to Jacques.

'If I might advise you on that,' put in Annie. 'The hand-rolled are a lot more labour intensive and that pushes up the price. These days the pre-cut cracker templates are very good and we can do you a much better deal on them.' *Plus we don't have the workforce to do the hand-rolled at the moment,* Annie didn't say. 'I mocked up some white ones for you.' She pulled a glossy white cracker out of her bag with holographic snowflakes printed onto the card. The ends were tied with glittery white ribbon, 'Winterworld' had been written on it with a silver pen, and there was a 3D sticker of a snowman stuck on the front.

'It's a rough prototype, but you get the idea. You can have Winterworld printed on the ribbon or we can have it printed on the card. It can be obvious or subtle so it shows up only when the light catches it.'

'I like the ribbon idea,' said Jacques. 'Glittery crackers though.' *Subtle* was a swear word to Jacques.

'We can do that of course,' said Joe, flapping his hand as if to imply he could do glittery crackers in his sleep.

'I agree,' said Eve. She looked at the novelty samples which were so much better than the usual tiny plastic combs and rubbish spinners. Not to mention the sexual–expertise–predicting red cellophane fish. The tiny books and miniatures were fabulous.

'Let's start with a small initial order,' she said. 'Ten thousand for December, staggered delivery from October, is that okay?'

Annie and Joe did a synchronised gulp. 'Of which sort?' Joe asked.

'Both. Ten thousand of each. To begin with. Is that okay?'

'Can we do it?' asked Joe after the train had deposited them at the front gates.

'Of course we can. At a push. We couldn't turn the business down,' said Annie. 'The machines can handle the rolling, it's the stuffing and the tying that is going to be the main problem – as always. I'd better get cracking on a design straightaway.'

Joe muttered something worried and Italian.

'We *will* have to find some outworkers,' said Annie. 'Either that or put some speed in Iris's hot chocolate.'

Joe shook his head. 'I can't believe we've said we can do this.' He dropped his car keys, his hands didn't feel capable of gripping anything. 'We're struggling as it is with the orders we need to finish already, and we have a workforce of one Italian slave, two pregnant women and a pensioner.'

'We will do it, Joe,' said Annie. 'If this year has taught us anything it's that the impossible is doable.' She reached up and placed her hand on his dear cheek. 'We are going to expand and grow along with my waistline, Joe Pandoro. There are other Palmas out there and we will find them.

And what's more, I think that Miss Palma Collins is our lucky charm. She'll help us to get what we need, I'm sure of it.'

'We can but ask her to try,' said Joe, opening the car door for his wife and their heir incumbent.

Chapter 35

'What are you grinning about?' asked Iris, as she studied Palma from across the table.

'I'm just happy,' came the reply.

'Sex,' Iris exclaimed, as if she was suffering from a rogue spasm of Tourette's. 'That's what it'll be. Who with, that's what I want to know?'

Palma laughed. 'No, it's not sex.' She screwed the top off her bottle of pink lemonade and took a long sip, knowing that Iris was desperate to find out what it was then, if not sex.

'Come on, spill the beans,' said Iris impatiently. 'I might not be here much longer and I don't want to die not knowing.'

'Okay,' said Palma, standing to reach a reel of ribbon from one of the shelves behind her. 'I have got a fella.'

Now it was Iris's turn to grin. 'Aw, what nice news. Not one of those internet men though? Sally Birtwistle at Golden Surfers got herself involved with one of those. Turned out to be a conman. Stole all her mother's jewellery when she had him up to the house for a roast.'

'He's an old school friend. I ran into him recently.'

This was the most Palma had talked about her personal life and Iris was going to take full advantage of the flow.

'Come on, you'll have to tell me a bit more: name, what's he do for a living and does he know you're up the spout?'

'He's called Tommy Tanner and he's a boxer. He's the British welterweight champion and lives at the top of Dodley. You might have seen him in the papers. And yes, he does know I'm having a baby.'

Iris lifted up her glasses and studied Palma's midriff. 'You'd have had to tell him though because you aren't showing yet, are you? I bet you're one of those who doesn't. Our Linda didn't show much. I think it was because what she lost in fat she gained in baby. She's always been a big unit, has our Linda.'

Palma laughed again. She'd had a smile on her face since Tommy had turned up on Friday. He hadn't stayed for long after he'd asked her permission to call them a couple, because he had a big training session the next morning and then a night out with his sponsor. But he was free on Sunday, he said. Could he take her for lunch? Then he'd kissed her, a short, sweet kiss on the lips and left her grinning, much as she was doing now.

'He took me out for lunch yesterday,' said Palma. 'I can't believe I didn't put on a stone with what we ate. Well me, anyway.'

'Anywhere nice? We sometimes have a carvery. My little great grandson Freddie loves them. He has a plate a grown man couldn't shift and straight after goes bouncing in the play area. How he doesn't throw up in the ball pool, I have no idea. Anyway, less about us and more about you – where did he take you?'

'The Little Cygnet, do you know it? On the road to Wakefield.'

'Not come across it,' said Iris after a quick hunt through her mind. 'Was it one of those posh places where they stick a piece of lettuce on your plate, call it summat fancy then charge you a tenner for it?'

'Quite the opposite, Iris. It was a lovely country pub with everything home-made. I had a mushroom stroganoff with wild rice. And onion. Then I had a piece of cheesecake that was more slab than slice and I wolfed the lot. Tommy said that if he'd known I could eat so much, he probably wouldn't have asked me.' She sighed a Disney princess sigh and Iris was glad to see her looking so cheerful. There was no sad aura hanging about her today.

'I'm glad for you, love. And enjoy it whilst you can because once you get to thirty, you only have to look at a cheese and onion crisp and your hips will start swelling.'

They heard a car draw up outside.

'Boss is back, best look busy,' said Iris with a chuckle.

Annie walked in, Joe lingered behind, talking on his phone.

'Yes, Jacques, we can do wedding crackers. How many you want? . . . Yes, we can do those for you . . . Okay, I meet with you in secret . . . I'll tell her not to say anything . . . Goodbye.'

'How did you get on?' called Iris.

'Very well,' said Annie with a doleful tone that didn't match her words. 'Too well in fact. A starter order of twenty thousand by Christmas.'

Iris's busy hands stilled. 'How the heck are you going to do those?'

'We're going to have to get more staff. Palma, can you help us? Where do we go? I'm not asking the agency again.'

'Let's advertise via the website' said Palma. 'I'll update it to invite people to apply and then spread it on social media.' She thought of how hard it had been for herself to get a job, especially when she had first found out she was pregnant. Maybe there were a whole lot of people out there who couldn't get a job because they were housebound – or even pregnant – despairing that they were on the scrapheap when in fact their services were very much in need. 'If you'll let me have fifteen minutes to do it, I can set the ball rolling now.'

'Go right ahead,' said Joe. 'Use my office.'

'Palma, we bought you a sandwich, do you want it now?' asked Annie.

'No, I'll have a break when I've finished,' said Palma, disappearing. 'Okay to shut the door so I can concentrate?'

'Of course, love,' said Annie, before turning to Iris and Joe. 'She's a wonder, isn't she?'

'Aye, she's a good lass,' said Iris, leaning forward to impart a confidentiality. 'She's got herself a fella. A boxer. Someone she's known from school. He's a British champion, she says. Tommy somebody or other.'

'Not Tommy Tanner?' asked Joe, who was a boxing afi-cionado. 'He's the British welterweight champion. She'll be able to get tickets for the ringside. We have to stay on the good side of Palma now.'

'And he knows she's up the spout,' Iris went on. 'I think I

like him already. I hope he doesn't bugger her about. He'll have me to deal with if he does.'

'What were you saying on the phone to Jacques, Joe?' asked Annie.

'He wants us to make some wedding crackers because he and his wife are getting married.'

'Eh?' said Iris.

'They're renewing their vows, but he doesn't want Eve to know what he's planning, so I'm going to meet with him in secret to discuss a design. I'll go and put the kettle on.'

'You renewed yours, didn't you?' said Iris.

'We did, in Jamaica,' said Annie.

'Why though?' asked Iris. 'I'm just curious. Our Linda's friend Gaynor says couples only do it when one of them has done the dirty. That model . . . the one with the big boobs . . . she's renewed them every time her and her husband have got back together. They must have clocked up fifteen ceremonies because he can't keep it in his trousers. I bet she's bloody sick of the sight of wedding cake by now. I'd have booted him out because you can't patch up a marriage with royal icing and marzip—' Iris's hand flew up to her mouth. 'I'm not saying you two are like them. I only wondered what other reasons people had to go and do it.'

Iris and Gill had both started working there five years ago, after all the trouble. They'd never known what the Pandoros had been through.

'We had a rough patch, Iris, and we wanted to start again on a new footing. No one else involved, just life and pressure and all that disappointment that we couldn't have a baby.'

'And look at you now, eh?' beamed Iris. 'You're not half starting to show. You'll be feeling it soon. Nineteen weeks I was when I felt this little thing shift in my stomach. Scared me to sodding death.'

Annie knew she was starting to show now. The skirt she had on was one she'd kept – for whatever reason – from when she was at her fattest and it was snug. She'd ordered some clothes from a pregnancy store on the internet and they were due to arrive that week. Some nice empire-style dresses, expanding trousers and loose-fitting tops. This old skirt was going straight in the bin when she got home. She pulled out the order book and slotted the Winterworld crackers into the schedule. Now all they needed was the manpower.

Palma emerged from the office. 'Okay, I've put an advert on the website and I've tweeted it and spread it on Facebook. Maybe you could get in touch with the *Chronicle* and the *Sheffield Telegraph* and the *Trumpet* because it would make a great story.'

'The *Trumpet*?' exclaimed Iris. 'The only thing they get right is their name and I've seen a couple of times when they haven't even done that.'

'Anything is worth a shot,' said Annie. 'I'm on it.'

'The numbers and the email addresses of the features editors are in the back of the telephone book on the desk,' said Palma. 'I thought it might be good to have them to hand so I wrote them in.'

Annie gave her head a small shake. 'I absolutely do not know how we managed before you came along,' she said.

'She's not that great at sticking a kettle on though,' Iris's voice rang from behind. Hint taken, thought Palma.

The Knackers Yard, the cracker-making firm on the Maltstone Business Estate are looking for home-workers to assemble and stuff crackers from the comfort of their armchairs.

Joint managing director Jose Pandoro said that he was hoping that people would apply who might be finding difficulty in getting work because they were housebound or pregnant when finding employment might be difficult.

Jose Pandoro told the *Daily Trumpet* he is looking for workers from homes with no smoke or pets. 'Cracker erections and stuffing might sound simple but they have to be right,' he said. 'We pride ourselves on the quality of our products.'

In the first instance please phone or email. Details in our Weekly Directory page on page 4.

Chapter 36

Whilst Eve was at her antenatal appointment, Jacques was busy planning the wedding with the help of Myfanwy. He had discussed the crackers with Joe Pandoro, he had the cake arranged already; Eve's cousin Violet and her mum, Auntie Susan, were sorting out the dresses. He had flowers ordered, the reception menu chosen and the weather booked. Of course there would be snow because the snow machines would take care of that. He still had plenty of time to do other mad things and Jacques being Jacques would take full advantage of any Christmassy element he could stuff into the proceedings. That included getting Stephen, one of the rescued snowy owls, to fly to the front of the chapel with an eternity ring when he'd chosen it. He thought he had a handle on what Eve might like: something classy and beautiful, like her, with emeralds as green as her eyes. He was clicking through some pages on his iMac when the door opened and in she walked so he flicked over to the Sky news page.

'Hiya, darling, how did it go?'

Eve was grinning from ear to ear. Her face was getting chubbier, though he didn't mention that in case she thumped him.

'All good,' she said. 'And I heard the baby's heartbeat. It was going ten to the dozen but apparently that's quite normal. It was so strong, I wish you could have heard it too.'

'I'll hear it soon enough,' said Jacques. 'I can't wait.'

Eve looked tired today. She'd not slept well. She was having dreams about the baby being born with two heads, or no head. Then a few nights ago, she dreamt she had given birth to an enormous slug. Watching *The Fly* hadn't helped.

'Is there anything going on with Davy and Cariad?' asked Eve, as she hung her jacket up on the coat stand. 'I've just seen them both outside the ice-cream parlour. Davy was pacing up and down and he seemed very agitated and Cariad looked as if she was trying to calm him down. What do you think all that is about?'

'I have no idea,' said Jacques, thinking back to the beginning of the week when he'd seen them together in a close embrace. He wondered if he should try and find out, though.

*

Following the advert in the *Daily Trumpet* – which might have got some of the details wrong, but thankfully neither the email address nor the telephone number for applications – there were quite a few enquiries about the position of 'cracker erector'. Iris had also had the foresight to ring Hilda, who cleaned her daughter's house once a week, to ask if any of the girls who worked for Lady Muck might fancy a spot of outwork which they could do at a time to suit. Hilda said she'd ask around. Within the half hour someone introducing herself as Astrid had phoned Joe asking if she could apply. At first he thought it was a joke phone call because Astrid had the strangest accent he'd ever heard in his life – a cross between broad Yorkshire and deepest Black Forest German.

'Oh, that'll be Astrid,' said Iris, when Joe came out to report the conversation to them: *'Iz ziz Mr Pandoro.'* 'Yes?' *'Eyup, have you any of ze jobs left stuffing crrrackers.'* 'She works with my cleaner Hilda. She's had . . .' she left a dramatic pause and whispered the tail end of the sentence as if she was scared of being overheard '. . . the op.' She made a snipping scissor gesture with two fingers, blades pointed downwards to the groin area.

'What op?' asked Joe. 'Honestly. Everyone thinks Italians are a little crazy . . .' he rotated his hand at the side of his head '. . . but people from Yorkshire are totally *pazzo*.'

'Her bits have changed sex. But . . . oh, she's lovely. Very tall, very amazonian. You'd never tell she used to play rugby for Frankfurt. She's getting married to an antiques dealer called Cutthroat Kevin. He's an expert in old barber's shop memorabilia. I bet she'll want some extra work for money to put towards her wedding.'

Joe's jaw dropped. '*Pazzo*' he said again.

'Don't employ anyone called Clamp,' said Palma. 'Especially Alaska and Nepal.'

'Oh yes, we know that,' said Iris, pushing up her bosom.

'Nepal Clamp,' repeated Joe, shaking his head. He still hadn't got his head around that one. '*Pazzo*, absolutely *pazzo*.'

The phone started ringing and Palma picked it up and began speaking into the receiver. 'Yes, that's right, we are looking for outworkers ... can I take your name, please?'

The exhibition currently at the Town Hall does not feature a painting by Dick Van Dyke as reported in the recent *Daily Trumpte* Arts supplement but a painting by Jan Van Eyck. We offer apologies for the misleading information.

Chapter 37

By the third meeting of the Christmas Pudding Club, Annie and Joe had set on four outworkers but it still wasn't enough. Annie picked up Palma early so she could have a conversation with the midwives Chloe and Sharon to ask if they knew of any pregnant ladies who might want to do some cracker stuffing in between bouts of morning sickness. They said they'd ask around but two names instantly came to mind, because the two women in question had recently asked the midwives if they knew of anyone who employed home-workers. Annie was now nineteen weeks pregnant. Her baby was the size of a mango, so the internet told her. She hadn't experienced any of the leg cramps or abdominal pains that her book said she might at this stage, but her bladder had shrunk to the size of an ant's head and she wished she had a fiver for every time she needed the loo during the day and annoyingly, through the night.

She knew it would pass but she'd been feeling ultra sensitive and moved easily to tears. She'd dreamt about her mum sitting on her bed, holding a tiny baby and saying that she didn't ever think she'd see this day and was so glad she had. It had felt so real and Annie woke up disorientated, sure that her mum had followed her out of the dream and would be there, even for a second, an imprint in the dark, a faint echo of her voice, the briefest trace of her Blue Grass perfume . . . but nothing. She broke down in tears and hadn't wanted Joe to know she was so upset so she sneaked off into the bathroom and sat on the toilet seat where she sobbed freely. Annie had never known her dad but her mum was parent enough. They'd been friends as well as mother and daughter and Joe had adored her too. She'd died suddenly not long after their last round of IVF had failed and Annie missed her so much. She would have made the best grandparent.

Annie knew what Iris meant when she said that the feeling of a baby moving around within her had scared her to death because the first time it happened, last week, it had felt like insect wings vibrating softly inside her, or − less romantically − trapped wind. But she had known immediately what it was and she'd shrieked with delight. Joe had leapt from his chair and put his hand on her stomach, but the fluttering was too gentle for him to experience from the outside. He'd feel it soon, he said. He could wait.

Palma was fifteen weeks pregnant. Her baby was the size of an apple and she was still able to wear the same clothes that hung in her wardrobe but she wished she couldn't. She wanted to be like everyone else in the group who were proudly showing off their baby mounds; gobby Di was swelling up like an inflatable dinghy. She looked cheerful, partly because she'd found herself a man. Not just any man but her 'lying, cheating bastard of a husband's half-brother who'd always fancied her', she said.

'Talk about keeping it in the family,' said Eve under her breath to Palma and Annie and they'd had to fight to keep the giggles in.

'Arseface was livid when he found out,' Di was broadcasting to everyone. 'It's caused a right old falling out. I'm not talking to my family and now he's not talking to his. But Daniel and I are happy as pigs in shite.'

'And long may it last,' said Annie to her new friends. 'Why shouldn't she have a bit of happiness?'

'I'm lucky,' said Eve, peeling back the top from a packet of Polos and handing them around. 'Once upon a time I didn't think I'd find anyone to love.'

'I've been with Joe since I was twenty,' said Annie. 'We saw each other across a crowded Valentine's night disco floor. Whitesnake was playing "Is This Love" and it was, from that first moment.'

*Aww*s ensued. 'And our Palma is courting now, aren't you?' Annie went on.

'I am,' Palma said proudly with a smile the size of a giant croissant. 'Three weeks on Friday.'

'It's obviously going great guns, judging by that sparkle in your eyes,' said Eve and gave her an affectionate nudge.

'Ladies, can you bring your drinks and biscuits over and we'll get started,' said Sharon, clapping her hands. 'We're going to talk about exercise today because it's important that you do some. It'll help combat stress and any backaches and tiredness and build your stamina for the big day. Obviously we aren't talking abseiling or water skiing. We've got a film to show you and then we thought we'd do a practical session of yoga on the mats. Okay?'

Palma liked the look of the aqua-natal classes that were held at a private pool on the outskirts of Higher Hoppleton. She'd always liked to swim. She and her school friends used to go often, although Nicole soon lost interest because she preferred to stay dry and hang around with older lads. She'd lost touch with her swimming buddies since they'd left the gutter of Ketherwood: Libby had gone travelling after college and settled in New Zealand and Sam had gone down to study in a London uni and never came back. They'd emailed and texted for a while but it had lessened off until it stopped completely. Sam and Libby didn't even keep in contact with each other. It was a friendship which had served them well through school but was never meant to stretch further than that.

They practised some yoga stretches on the mats although they had trouble keeping the giggles in after Di dropped a very loud fart.

'I shouldn't have had that cauliflower for me tea,' Di said, dispersing the air around her with windmill-like arms. Raychel was laughing so hard she ended up trumping too.

'I go to Pilates regularly and a lot of wind-breaking goes on there,' said Fil. 'It's almost compulsory to fart.'

It came as no surprise to anyone that the gorgeous Fil exercised. Annie wished she'd taken it up years ago if it would have made her look like Fil.

Chloe distributed some leaflets. 'There are some links

to YouTube sites on here as well as a recap of all the stuff we have done– or at least tried to cover in between all the laughing – today. *Preggers Yoga* is my particular favourite because the woman on the videos does exercises suitable for every stage of pregnancy in fifteen-minute bites. And if anyone wants to book one of the private Aqua Mama classes, then the telephone and email contacts are on there. Don't forget the next Pudding Club meeting will be a fortnight today, not three weeks. Has anyone got any questions before we finish?'

'I have,' said Di, sticking her hand straight up like a keen kid in a classroom. 'Can we have sex?'

'I'm very flattered, Di, but I have a husband,' said Chloe, much to everyone's amusement.

'I mean can I personally?' Di went on, when the laughter had died down. 'You know, whilst I'm pregnant, only me and Daniel are gagging for it and I thought I'd check.'

'Yes, you can have sex, Di. The gentleman's . . . er, penis, doesn't go beyond the vagina so it won't touch the baby.'

'You haven't seen him,' said Di with a smirk. 'He could brush my teeth from the inside up.'

'Lucky you,' chuckled Fil.

'I'd advise not swinging from the chandeliers though,' put in Sharon. 'But yes, sex is fine. Not *Red Room of Pain* stuff though.'

'Smashing,' said Di, marching to the exit as if she were on a mission.

'Do you fancy going to those aqua classes in the private pool?' Eve asked Palma and Annie as they were walking out with the info sheets. 'I want to but I don't fancy going on my own.'

'I'd love to,' said Annie. 'I can give you a lift, Palma.'

'Then count me in,' said Palma.

*

Tommy was waiting for Palma when she got back from the club. He was leaning on his car, wearing a T-shirt that showed the profile of his toned body underneath. Something fizzed inside her with happiness at the sight of him, as if someone had poured a glass of champagne into her heart.

'Where've you been?' he said, tapping at his watch. 'Thought you'd have come back by now.'

'We went on a detour to find out where a swimming pool was,' said Palma. 'I didn't know you'd be over tonight.' She took her key out of her handbag to unlock the door.

'Before you go in, I want you to come with me,' said Tommy. 'Hurry up, get in the car. That's a good girl.' He took her arm and guided her gently to the passenger door.

'Where am I going?'

'Hungry?' he asked, not directly answering the question.

'I'm starving.'

He let out a sigh of relief. 'Good, get in.'

Palma did as he asked.

'I've cooked you a meal, I hope it's not flipping burnt,' said Tommy, sliding the gearstick into first.

'You should have rung me, then.'

'It was supposed to be a surpriiiise,' he chuckled.

'What if I hadn't been hungry?'

'You're always bloody hungry. Fasten your seat belt.'

She hadn't visited his house yet. They'd been taking it slowly. He hadn't even touched her below the neck and that suited her fine. She didn't take it as a sign that he didn't fancy her because she knew he did. Their first proper kiss had happened exactly a week to the day after her birthday. It had been tentative and gentle and so very, very sweet.

Tommy's house was situated at the top of Dodley in a select new estate: 'The Bluebells'.

'Bit girly,' scoffed Palma.

'Shut up, you,' Tommy threw back.

He pulled up the drive of a small, neat detached house and parked in front of a garage door. The front lawn had been freshly mowed and there were flowering plants in the borders.

'Who does your garden?' she asked.

'Me. Why?'

'I just wondered. I didn't think you'd be the gardening type.'

'I like it to look nice,' he said. 'What did you expect – a Ketherwood rockery?'

He meant one with a sofa, broken TVs and old bikes in it.

'Looks lovely,' she said.

'I know. Come on in,' he said and she thought he looked slightly nervous as he got out of the car, as if he might be worried what she'd think about his home.

Palma walked into his hallway and detected the smell of polish in the air and she tried not to let him see her smile. He'd obviously been giving it a clean and a dust before inviting her up. She felt touched by that. She kicked off her shoes and left them by the door.

'You don't have to do that,' he said.

'Yes I do,' she returned. The carpet was bouncy-new and pale mouse-brown. It felt luxurious underneath her bare feet.

'There's a downstairs loo there if you need it,' he said, pointing at a door to his left before opening the other one straight ahead. A lovely rich casserole smell greeted her as she walked into his light and surprisingly spacious kitchen. There was a dining area to the right and a glass table set for two there.

'It's fab, Tommy,' she said, doing a full circle. The kitchen units were top notch: glossy and ice-white.

'I've not got a bad eye for décor, have I?' he replied, the cockiness in his tone belied by a nervous scratch to the back of his head. He took a couple of long strides to the table and pulled out the chair from underneath it.

'Sit down and I'll dish up before it's cremated.'

'Can I help?'

'No, you're my guest.'

Palma sat down and he tucked her under the table and then started darting around almost manically as if he didn't know what to do first. As he opened the oven door, he made a noise of pain and started waving his hand around before running cold water on it.

'Burnt yourself?' asked Palma.

'I'll live,' came the reply.

She turned away from him, suspecting that her scrutiny

was making him jittery, and settled her attention on the room instead. The lounge led off from the dining room, the whole downstairs, apart from the hallway and stairs, was open plan. Large blue-grey tiles covered the floor and walls of the kitchen and dining area and this colour carried through to the walls of the lounge. Framed and mounted mono-chrome pictures of boxers hung everywhere – his heroes, she guessed – Muhammad Ali, Joe Frazier, George Foreman, Lennox Lewis and Tommy himself, the Lonsdale belt slung across his shoulder, hand held high in victory. A single shot that captured the uncontainable feeling in his heart.

Her attention snapped back to the immediate area when he put down a plate in front of her. Chicken and tiny mushrooms and onions in a reddish-brown thick sauce, mangetout, miniature whole carrots and an ice-cream scoop of mash with green bits in it.

'It's colcannon, before you say your mash is mouldy,' he said.

'I wouldn't have said anything of the sort,' Palma pro-tested. 'It looks delicious.' And it did.

'Can I get you a drink? I've got that pink lemonade that you like.'

'That'd be smashing, thank you.'

Tommy opened up a fridge, a huge American-style one. Palma had always wanted one of those. He poured the bottle into a tumbler for her and brought it to the table along with a glass of milk for himself.

'I like milk when I'm eating mash, is that daft?' he asked, sitting down opposite to her.

'No, why should it be? This is great, by the way.' No man

had ever cooked her a meal before, but she didn't say that because it might sound a bit pathetic. Apart from school dinners, she couldn't even remember having any 'proper food' when she lived at home; it all came out of a can, a packet or a Pot Noodle carton. Grace Beresford had been totally different, everything fresh: meat and fish from the market, lots of vegetables from her own garden or neighbours' allotments. She made her own custard and jam roly-polys from scratch, which warmed up the cold winter evenings, and lots of one-pot stews with rich, hearty sauces.

'Potatoes went a bit dry, so I added extra butter to soften them up,' said Tommy.

'It's perfect, will you stop worrying.'

He took a sip of milk, missed his mouth and it went all over the table. He jumped up to fetch some kitchen roll.

'Tommy, relax. It's only me, not Nigella Lawson,' Palma called to him.

'I'd be less nervous in front of her.'

'Yeah, 'course you would.'

'I don't fancy her.'

A warm feeling pinged inside Palma's breast. 'That's nice,' she said. 'I fancy you too.'

'Do you? Do you really, Palma?'

She pulled a face. 'Course I do, dummy. I wouldn't be here otherwise, eating your Coq au Vin.'

'Actually, Miss Know-it-all, it's Chicken Chasseur.'

'Who taught you to cook, then?' asked Palma.

'I learned most of it at Forestgate. Somebody who was there when he was a kid became a chef at the Ritz in London and he used to come back and run a course. I learned all sorts. I can make my own bread. I don't, but I could. I cheat, Jackie bought me a breadmaker a couple of Christmases ago.' He cut a piece of chicken and after he'd finished eating it said, 'I'd like you to meet Neil and Jax. I've told them all about you.'

Palma huffed. 'I bet they were thrilled. You copping off with a pregnant woman taking your focus away from your boxing.'

Tommy dived straight in to protest. 'You don't. In fact if anything it's given me more focus. Because I'm not only doing it for me, I'm doing it for you and the baby. I want you all to be proud of me.'

Palma felt a lump spring to her throat. She was gob-smacked that he felt so deeply and strongly. They were only at the beginning of their relationship, but they fitted together so well. She felt it too. But she also didn't want him to feel burdened, so she was giving him plenty of space to change his mind and get out. She was holding back from running down the relationship path at the speed her heart was urging her to, just in case he did.

'I am proud of you already, Tommy. You're the British welterweight champ, for God's sake. That's a massive achievement. And look at the lovely home you have and the car – at your age.'

Tommy grinned. 'Aw, shuttup and eat your tea,' he commanded.

*

Davy and Jacques were having a beer at the Crown, the nearest pub to Davy's lodgings. It was an 'old man's pub' but served a good pint and every day was pie day on the menu. It refused to kowtow to trendy cocktails and sizzling platters and did what it did best: provide a quiet, restful respite for workers after their day's toil without any of the fancy stuff.

With all the build-up to the launch of the Winterworld lagoon and then the news about the baby, Jacques hadn't had much opportunity to catch up with his old friend, properly, over a pie and a pint. He wanted to ask if he'd be set for acting as best man. He felt he'd cheated Davy out of the position when he and Eve got married in secret with only a couple of strangers as witnesses and so he had some making up to do. As did Eve. Denying her Auntie Susan the opportunity to buy a new hat was borderline unforgivable.

Davy, of course, agreed. He was looking forward to it. In his own words, he hadn't been in a good place when Jacques and Eve first tied the knot. It had taken Davy a lot longer to adjust to civilian life than it had Jacques; he hadn't left the army with a physical disability like his friend had done, but he'd had a mental one for a long while.

'I saw you and Cariad getting quite close recently,' Jacques could not resist saying.

'Don't be daft, she's half my age,' said Davy, lifting the beer to his lips.

'Quite a few of the girls have been swooning over you. Some of them even younger than Cariad,' replied Jacques.

Davy gave a lopsided grin. He was a good-looking man now he'd got himself sorted out. He'd looked like a skinny

Rasputin when Jacques had caught up with him last year. He'd let himself go, didn't know how to fit into the world anymore. Now he was groomed and toned and back in the driving seat of his life. 'Well, you've either got it or you haven't.'

'Seriously, come on. What's going on between you two?'

'Nothing,' said Davy. 'I swear to you. She needed a bit of experienced man advice.'

'She's got her Uncle Effin for that, though,' said Jacques.

'Effin isn't experienced, Jacques. He married his first love and has never had any complications, he hasn't been around the block at all. Plus he's an uncle, who ... maybe isn't the best person to talk to about some things,' Davy replied, putting his glass down on the table. 'It's between Cariad and me, Jacques. I'm not betraying any confidences. I like Cariad and yes, I'd be in there like Flynn if I thought I had a chance, but ... I think she's got her eye on a higher prize.'

'Dylan Evans. I see your point. Young, fit, handsome ...' Jacques chuckled.

'No, not that wee ...' He shook his head, bit off his words. 'I don't understand why Effin's got him on a pedestal. There's something about him.'

Davy did have a tendency to take against people for no explicable reason, Jacques remembered then. It had caused a couple of problems, as it would, when you were supposed to work together as a unit. He had always blamed it on his instincts being too strong. Their commanding officer at the time had told him to unwire those instincts and wire them back up properly or he would be out on his arse.

'He's Effin's one-time best friend's son, I do believe,' said Jacques.

'Another pint?' said Davy, draining his glass, pushing his chair back and standing.

'Don't mind if I do,' said Jacques. He could take a hint. The subject of 'the Welsh lot' as Davy called them collectively, was closed.

*

Dessert was a Pavlova. A bought nest but Tommy had whipped up the cream and loaded the fruit in it himself, he explained, as he put a dish down in front of Palma.

'Don't believe in small portions do you?' she said, puffing out her cheeks.

'You should have left some room. I didn't expect you'd stuff the whole of your main course down in one mouthful. You can shift your grub, can't you? I don't know where you put it.'

'It would have been rude to leave it,' Palma picked up her spoon.

'I've got cheese and biscuits to come after, so be warned.'

And he wasn't lying. He brought a cheese platter to the table after the pudding, complete with sticks of celery and grapes. It was like something out of an expensive restaurant, she thought.

'You're eating for two, aren't you?' Tommy chuckled, seeing her eyes widen in surprise.

'Two humans, not two blue whales.'

'I thought you'd be slapping weight on by now,' said Tommy. 'How many months have you got to go?'

'There's about forty-one weeks from start to finish and I'm fifteen tomorrow.'

'So twenty-six then, six months exactly.'

She raised her eyebrows, impressed at this speed of calculation. She seemed to remember him not being that bright at school. Mrs Digley, their maths teacher, made them sit in order of academic ability and Tommy was always in the last row. The old cow did wonders for kids' confidence.

As if he could see into her head he said, 'Do you remember that old cow who used to teach us maths? Mrs Digley?'

'Yes I do. Horrible old bat.'

'She sent me a letter to Forestgate. She said that she was most disappointed in me but always knew I'd end up somewhere like that. The phrase that really stung – and I remember it word for word – was "I pride myself on forecasting the fate of those whom I teach and I knew from the off you would never amount to much".'

Palma's hand froze on its way to pick up a stick of celery. 'She didn't?'

'It was the kick up the backside I needed. Forestgate was okay, bit too okay. It was better than home, but . . . but that letter made me cry. It changed me. I thought, fuck you, Mrs Digley, I'm going to show you what I'm capable of.'

He was angry and upset at the same time; there was a determined tightness to his jaw and a waver in his voice.

'And you did, Tommy. Look at you.'

'Yeah, between her pushing me down and our Neil pulling me up, I did it, didn't I? I should thank her really.'

'No you shouldn't. If you hadn't been so bloody-minded,

she could have had you slitting your wrists saying something like that, the old bitch.'

'Stay with me here tonight. We don't have to do anything, but just stay.' He reached for her hand across the table. Palma felt the warmth from it spread through her whole body. She nodded.

'I'll stay.'

Chapter 38

Annie, Eve and Palma arranged to go to 'Aqua Mama' the following week. In their maternity swimming costumes it was obvious that Annie and Eve were pregnant but Palma had the tiniest bump and was wearing an ordinary one that she'd bought from the supermarket. Cheryl, from the cleaning company, and Raychel with her wild dark curls were there too. Palma felt like a pretender at the side of all the round stomachs. She was definitely pregnant though; she had felt a very delicate fluttering inside her. Mind you, since she and Tommy had been an item, she'd had quite a few butterflies beating their wings against her stomach walls. She'd stayed at his house three times in the past week and they'd finally made love on the third occasion. He'd been gentle and reverent and loving and she hadn't wanted to leave his arms in the morning. She was falling for him and it was getting harder to hold a little of herself back in reserve. The part that she'd need to prop her up if it all went wrong.

The woman who ran the sessions was very jolly hockey-sticks. Her name was Shona and this was her own personal pool, built in the garden of her own personal very large house. She was slim and gorgeous with bright copper hair and the figure of an Olympic swimmer. Surprisingly, she had seven children, she told them, and no tummy tuck needed.

'She must have grown them in a jar,' said Eve for Palma's and Annie's ears only, which set them all off giggling like naughty kids.

The water in the pool was blissfully warm and the first exercise was a simple bobbing up and down, enjoying their weightlessness in the water. One woman at the front was very large and pregnant. Even her legs looked pregnant. Palma wondered if she would ever get that big. Her body would have to get a move on if she was. She felt slightly cheated that she was sixteen weeks pregnant already and hardly showing.

'Okay, I'm going to put on some music and I'd like you to run on the spot, kicking your legs behind you like this,' said Shona, from the poolside.

'Oh, I like this,' said Annie, getting right into the groove of KC and the Sunshine Band. 'I wonder if it would feel like this if you were exercising in outer space.'

'How are you getting on with your cracker stuffing, Annie?' asked Eve.

'Wonderful,' she replied. 'We have a full workforce hard at it now, including four pregnant ladies who were crying out for some work to do at home and four of Cheryl's cleaners who wanted some extra money.'

Palma had interviewed the women at the factory and the ones who sounded promising were given some crackers to roll. Three of the people who turned up hadn't been suitable: one couldn't even grasp the basics and another had been extremely hungover and slapdash. Palma thought she looked vaguely familiar but hadn't been able to place her and the third silly bint said that she was happy to do everything but touch ribbon because she had an aversion to tying knots. Two men were also working for them: a single dad who was struggling to find work that fitted around his kid and a lonely pensioner who wanted something to do. Astrid was their stand-out favourite – what a fabulous person she was. And so quick and precise, despite the size of her fingers. Annie had her hand-rolling some luxury crackers after only a few days and she'd been helping Palma do the white ones that Jacques had ordered for the renewal of his and Eve's vows.

'Twenty-week scan tomorrow,' said Annie, with an excited little hop.

'And now we are going to do some resistance work on our arms,' said Shona, demonstrating on dry land.

'I'm next Tuesday,' said Eve.

'I'm next month,' huffed Palma. 'I'll be glad when I start slapping some timber on. I want to wear big frocks like you two fatties.'

'Oy,' said Eve and Annie together.

'You'll be swelling soon enough,' said Cheryl at her side. 'Enjoy it whilst you can. My back is breaking from all this weight already. How the hell I'm going to last until November, I have no idea. You see that big woman at the front? She's not even eight months pregnant yet.'

'Bloody hell,' said Eve.

'Thank the lord we aren't elephants,' Raychel butted in. 'Twenty-two months, they're up the spout.'

'Think of twenty-two months' worth of free dental care though,' replied Cheryl, surprisingly puffed from what sounded such an easy exercise. 'I could have a full set of veneers done.'

'*And stop,*' said Shona from the front. 'It might not be so tiring for you if you did the exercising without gossiping, ladies.'

The naughty five firmly closed their mouths as Shona distributed some foam noodles and proceeded to show them some stretching exercises designed to tone up their 'down belows'.

*

Effin helped Cariad move into her new home in Little Kipping. 'The Old Vicarage' had been thoughtfully converted into four flats and Cariad's was at the back with a small private garden. Her uncle, always swift to dismiss shoddy workmanship, was very impressed with the standard although he was much happier when he spotted one of the kitchen cupboards was out of alignment with the next. His lads wouldn't have got away with that and his status as king of the refurbs was no longer threatened.

After all the boxes had been carried in, Cariad took the kettle out of one, filled it up and plugged it in so they could have a cup of tea together.

'You could have stayed at the cottage with me, you know,' Effin said. 'Saved yourself a few bob.'

'I know,' said Cariad. 'I didn't want to trouble you.' Which was partly true. More than not troubling him, she didn't want to be responsible for murdering him either. He might have thought he knew what was best for her, but he didn't always. Take Dylan Evans for instance.

'So, have you seen anything of Dylan then?' asked Effin, trying to sound casual.

'Nope,' replied Cariad flatly. 'Please, Uncle Effin, I don't want to talk about him.'

'Oh, okay,' said Effin. 'But—'

'But what I might want to talk about is your memory,' she said, not giving him an inch. 'I've been hearing all about you misplacing stuff and forgetting things.'

Effin pulled himself up to his full height of five foot four. 'What ... who the bloody hell has been saying stuff about me? Bastards.' He was incensed and when he was incensed his skin changed colour like a chameleon who had been shifted from a white blanket to a bright red one at speed.

'People told me because they thought you might listen if I said something to you,' said Cariad.

'Who told you? Was it the Poles or the bloody Welsh boys. Pricks, the lot of them.'

Effin started to pace up and down.

Cariad tried to shake the picture of Dylan tapping his temple out of her head, telling her that her Uncle Effin was losing it. After he'd told her that on their night out, she'd done some private investigating to see if he was telling the truth and she hadn't liked what she'd found out.

'I heard about the letter falling off the Santapark sign

from someone who cares about you a great deal,' said Cariad, gently.

'Dylan?'

'No,' screeched Cariad, 'not bloody Dylan. Why do all roads lead me to Dylan Evans with you? People are worried about you, Uncle Effin. I think you should tell Auntie Angharad. Go have a holiday and take some time off.'

He should go take some time off before he kills someone, were Thomas the Tank's exact words.

'There's nothing wrong with me,' said Effin, now leaving red and acquiring a bruised-purple tone to his face. 'And don't you dare tell your Auntie Angharad,' he snapped. He had never used that tone with her before, which spoke volumes.

'People are worried about you, they care. And despite the fact that you call them all a bunch of useless wankers—'

'Cariad! Your language,' gasped Effin.

'Oh, Uncle Effin, I'm not a child anymore. And I'm bilingual, in case you've forgotten. When you are standing there shouting "*Ffycin hel. Ffycin cocs y cwm. Chi 'di darllen y planie ben i waered! S'ech chi ddim yn cachu heb cyfarwyddiade!*" the Polish lads might not understand you, but I know you're shouting, "Fucking hell. Fucking valley cocks. You've read the plans upside down! You wouldn't shit without instructions", BECAUSE I'M WELSH MYSELF IN CASE YOU HADN'T NOTICED.'

Effin fell silent. An occurrence that happened only in the most extreme of circumstances.

'And every one … well, nearly every one of those *fucking valley cocks* knows that in that great big beating heart of yours, you love them, and they love you. And they care about you. And they want you to go and see a doctor.'

Cariad's words hung in the air long after she had finished saying them, like the tail of a bell peal. She stood in the thick hush, hating that she might have hurt him but also cognisant of the fact that it needed a mallet to knock the words into his head and she was probably the only one who could wield it at the moment.

Eventually he spoke. 'Right then. So ...' he coughed, sniffed, swallowed, '... now you're all moved in, I'll be off. I'll see you at work. I won't stay for a cuppa.'

'Oh, Uncle Effin ...'

'You ring me if you need anything, Cariad love.'

He turned from her and walked briskly to the door. Not even her mallet was big enough, it seemed.

Chapter 39

Annie lay on the couch and let the sonographer move the transducer around her stomach. It wasn't Vita this time, but someone older, less smiley, with deep marionette lines from mouth to chin, revealing that the natural set of her expression wasn't a very happy one. 'Lesley' wasn't as talkative either and Annie felt duty-bound to stay silent whilst she did what she had to.

'Is everything all right?' said Joe, feeling that the silence needed popping with a verbal pin.

'I'm looking now, Mr Pandoro,' said Lesley.

'You're very quiet.'

'Joe.' Annie grimaced at him.

'I'm quiet when I'm concentrating,' said Lesley. 'It's important I check everything and we can chat when I have finished.'

Joe pulled a 'Well, that's me told' face at his wife and Lesley carried on.

'I'm presuming you'd like some photos,' said Lesley eventually.

'Please,' said Joe and Annie together. Then Lesley twisted the screen around and they saw a very different baby to the one they'd seen before. There was so much more detail: a clear spine, little fingers, perfectly formed feet.

'There's a lot to check on the anomaly scan, you see,' said Lesley. 'I couldn't see what I needed to see at first but then he twizzled for me. I call them all "he" by the way. Saves all that *he* and *she* nonsense. Do you want to know the sex of your baby?'

'No,' said Annie, a split second before Joe.

'I didn't want to know either,' said Lesley and she smiled. Her face changed totally, softened, when she did so. 'I've got five, including a set of twins, all girls. Every pregnancy different. "You're having a boy this time," my mother said because my second pregnancy was so different to my first. I didn't. She had me lying on the floor dangling a needle over my stomach telling me the third was absolutely a boy and it wasn't. So don't you listen to all those old wives' tales.'

'Oh my, I can't believe how big he's grown. Or she, of course,' said Annie, taking the photos that Lesley handed over. Joe didn't say anything, but stared at the image on the screen, a look of wonderment on his face.

'Halfway now,' said Lesley, wiping the gel from Annie's stomach with a single accomplished sweep. 'Now the fun really begins.'

'What did she mean by "now the fun really begins"?' asked Joe as they made their way out of the hospital.

'I expect it's because we're on a countdown,' said Annie. 'I have to say, this past twenty weeks has flown by.'

'I feel so much more comfortable now that we have a reliable bank of staff for when you and Palma have to stop working,' said Joe. 'I think we should give her a raise. She works so hard. And she has done so much on the website and twittering or whatever they call it. We have over three thousand followers now.'

'Is that good?' asked Annie.

'It sounds good,' said Joe. 'Palma said that the *Daily Trumpet* and the *Chronicle* are both following us.'

Annie laughed. 'I suppose I ought to get au fait with all this stuff because our baby will be born into a technological age, won't he, or she. Iris is better at it than we are. Maybe we should join her Golden Surfers group.'

Joe turned and gathered her into his arms and his espresso eyes were full of love for her, she could see that. 'Oh, Mrs Pandoro, I feel like a young man every day when I am with you. My pension years are centuries away.' He kissed her and two teenagers walking past in their green school uniforms smirked at each other.

'Hey, I'm Italian,' Joe yelled after them, causing their grins to broaden further.

'Joe!' Annie admonished him. But only half-heartedly, because he wouldn't have been Joe Pandoro if he wasn't a little *pazzo*.

Chapter 40

Palma eventually gave in to pressure from Tommy to meet his brother and sister-in-law. They invited her for Sunday lunch, the day after she had booked in at Glam to spend the voucher that the 'cracker crew' had bought for her. She said she'd love to and her delighted acceptance disguised her fear. They were checking her out, she knew. The forthcoming fight was important. Sky were showing it as a pay-per-view so there was a lot of money involved as well as prestige. This was Tommy's first defence of his title and he wanted to prove to the world that he hadn't merely got lucky last time.

Palma had booked an Indian head massage and a hair colour at the salon. She could easily have laid flat on her small stomach for the hot stones massage that Iris recommended, but she didn't want to squash the baby. For the head massage, she sat on a chair with her shoulders naked, towel wrapped around her chest. She doubted she would be able to relax but she was wrong. She felt herself drifting off as 'Julie' smoothed all the knots out of her back with firm, experienced hands and made her head sing from the double onslaught of the beautiful fragrance released by the oils and the scalp massage.

Since she'd learned that she was going to be meeting Tommy's family, she'd changed her mind about having her hair re-pinked and had the colour stripped out and replaced with a more conventional silvery-ash shade. It was lovely when the stylist had finished; strange, because she'd had pink hair for years, but nice. It made her look more responsible, less frivolous and – she hoped – more acceptable.

Tommy didn't see her that night because he was attending a prize-giving for the boys and girls at the Personal Development Centre and was really excited about it. One of the kids had discovered a love of photography and been offered an apprenticeship working with one of the big shots in the photography world based in London.

Tommy said he couldn't wait until they went to some big swanky event together. He wanted to show her off, he said. And his baby. He always referred to the baby as *his*.

He picked her up at quarter to twelve on Sunday. She'd been awake since seven and couldn't count the times she'd slapped her hands away from her mouth to stop herself worrying her nails. She painted them lavender, the same shade as the Laura Ashley dress she'd chosen to wear. She'd found it on a seconds stall on the market a year ago; it had been dirt cheap because there was a tear under the arm and a discoloured collar where some clumsy customer trying it on had stained it with make-up. She'd managed to get it off with some Vanish and the seam had taken five minutes to stitch up. She loved the dress, it made her feel girly and delicate and as near to sophisticated as she was ever likely to get.

Shock registered on Tommy's face when she opened the door.

'Where's your hair gone?' he said, amending it immediately to, 'The pink, I mean. Don't get me wrong, you look lovely but so . . . different.'

'I thought I'd have a change,' said Palma, locking up.

'I like it,' said Tommy, viewing her from a choice of angles. 'But I liked the pink. It was you.'

'I thought I should be a bit more sensible now,' she said, getting in the car.

'I hope you aren't changing for me,' he said and trilled a line from the Billy Joel song 'Just the Way You Are'.

'Don't be daft.' Palma's mouth was watering with nerves. She wished that moment of Neil and Jackie seeing her for the first time was over and done with. Tommy commented on the lack of conversation as he was driving.

'I've never heard you as quiet,' he chuckled.

'I'm scared,' she answered.

'What of?'

'What they'll think of me.'

He turned to her. 'Seriously? They'll love you.'

'You never told me what they said when you dropped it on them that . . . that I'm pregnant with someone else's kid.'

There was a telling pause before Tommy spoke again. 'I'm not going to lie, Palma, they shot me a look, but Jackie was a teenage mum. She had a son when she met Neil. Both of them know that life doesn't always run on a smooth track. I don't need to remind you of our family history, do I?'

That made her feel better. At least it did until they pulled up outside Neil's house. It was a new build on a half-finished estate, double-fronted with a long front garden. On the drive was a tiny, shiny vintage sports car and a brand-new black Range Rover, judging by the number plate. Her legs felt wobbly as she got out of the car.

Tommy caught her hand. 'Come on, they're great, you'll be fine.'

She wanted to tell him to wait a minute, let her breathe but she knew she'd sound pathetic. She could feel her heart rapping inside her as he did his jaunty postman's knock on the door and walked straight in, shouting, *Hello, we're here.*

Jackie came down the hallway first. She was tall, straight-figured with wavy bottle-blonde hair cut off at her shoulders. She had a no-nonsense stride and hard features but her smile of welcome was warm and wide.

'Hello, Palma,' she said, and held out her hand. 'Nice to put a face to a name.'

'Smells good, Jax. You had outside caterers in?' said Tommy cheekily.

'I'll ignore that,' said Jackie. 'Take Palma into the conservatory, Tom, I'm just nipping to the loo.'

Tommy led Palma forwards into a large kitchen which opened out into a conservatory. There was a brocade-upholstered sofa and chairs there as well as a dining table. Tommy knocked on the window to alert the attention of a man standing in the middle of the back garden. He had a totally different build to Tommy: heavier set, thicker arms, shaved head, bull-like neck. He waved, then wandered up towards the house. He shook Palma's hand also. 'Nice to meet you at last, Palma,' he said with a small, but not unfriendly, smile. 'Nice to meet you too,' she replied.

'I've lost a pair of dumb-bells' said Neil to his brother. 'Have you got 'em, Tom?'

'I have. You bloody lent them to me,' said Tommy, turning to Palma and adding, 'He's getting old.'

'I've been searching for 'em all weekend,' said Neil.

'I told you he'd have them,' called Jackie from the hallway.

'Neil built a gym at the bottom of the garden,' explained Tommy.

'It's his man cave,' said Jackie, returning to them.

'Can I get you a drink?' asked Neil. 'Wine or . . . sorry . . . we have tea, coffee, water . . .'

'I've got some pink lemonade in,' Jackie took over. 'Tommy said you liked that so I bought some.'

'Oh, you didn't have to get it in specially,' said Palma. 'I'm fine with water or orange juice or . . .'

Tommy had opened the fridge. 'I'll choose for you or we'll be here all day,' he said, taking a bottle of pink lemonade out. 'Jax? Neil?'

'I remember when I was pregnant with our Jacob,' said Jackie. 'I couldn't even drink water. It made me gag. I craved grapefruit juice but the doctor told me off. Said it would rot my teeth and make my heartburn worse than it already was. As if it could be. You getting any heartburn yet, Palma?'

At last the elephant in the room had been acknowledged.

'Not yet,' she said.

'You're lucky. Very small, aren't you? You can't even tell.'

'Have a seat,' said Neil, as if this line of conversation was something he wanted to move away from.

'Enjoy being waited on,' said Jackie. 'Don't get used to it, you,' she directed at Tommy. 'It's a one-off.'

Palma and Tommy went to sit at the table.

'Lovely here, isn't it?' Tommy said. 'I'd like a house like this one day with a big garden and a conservatory.'

'Your house is perfect,' said Palma.

'Yeah for a couple, not a family. I've been thinking about having a conservatory though,' said Tommy. 'I can visualise it as a sort of playroom for the baby. It'll be lovely and sunny.'

She smiled but she worried that he had fallen too quickly and easily for her with plans for their future already forming. Nothing had ever gone smoothly for her and she didn't trust that it all seemed so rosy now. She would have liked nothing better than to wake up every morning in Tommy's warm, comfortable house with the bouncy carpets and huge picture windows, but she also wanted to take things slowly. Sure steps. Nothing rushed. She didn't want the rug pulled from under her feet again.

'Here we go, I've put everything on so what you don't want, leave,' said Jackie, putting down two huge plates in front of them. Roast lamb with carrots, green beans, puffy Yorkshire puddings, roast potatoes, nothing elaborate but plain home cooking. Neil followed behind with a gravy boat carried in both hands and Tommy laughed at him.

'You'd make a rubbish waitress,' he said.

'I don't want to spill it,' explained Neil. He wasn't smiling but there was a chuckle in his voice and Palma realised he was one of those people who had a drier sort of humour. She hadn't thought them much alike but, sitting across from Neil, she noticed that their eyes were the same, grey and large with thick dark lashes and they both had high cheekbones and a small gap between their two front teeth. Neil looked older than his years, though; he and Tommy could have been father and son, rather than brothers.

'And don't eat all yours,' said Neil to Tommy. 'She's put too much on your plate.'

'Give the lad a day off,' tutted Jackie.

'He can't have days off, he's a boxer. It's like saying have a day off life, Jax.'

'I'm having a day off, so get lost,' said Tommy, turning to Palma as he did so. 'Look how he nags me.'

'Good job I do though. You wouldn't have a title if I didn't. Or a career. You'd be working in a shop selling bloody fried chicken.'

Palma felt herself colouring. Did Neil know that's what she used to do and it was a dig at her, or was it an unlucky guess? She willed Tommy not to say *Palma used to sell fried chicken*. Thank goodness he didn't.

'I'm not a fancy cook,' Jackie explained to Palma. 'We don't usually have a roast on Sunday, not for the two of us. Only on special occasions.'

'Ooh, you are honoured,' said Tommy through a mouthful of Yorkshire pudding, causing the gravy to dribble down his chin.

'Scruff,' said Neil. 'I hope you eat better than that if you go out for romantic meals.'

'I'm a gent, me,' said Tommy.

'Aye, maybe too much of one,' said Neil. 'Can you pass me the salt please, Palma love.'

Palma knew he'd given a piece of himself away then and had hurriedly tried to cover it up with an endearment. No one else noticed it, but she did. *Too much of a gent.* Taking on another man's child, that's what he meant. Her guard cranked up. Despite the gracious invitation, despite the specially bought lemonade, despite the politeness there was an undercurrent of something spiky and protective of their own and it had just broken through the veneer of their hospitality.

Pudding was a home-made apple pie with shop-bought custard. Tommy teased Jackie about turning into Doris Day. Jackie brought Palma into the conversation a few times with questions: was she a baker? Did she watch boxing? Could she remember Tommy from school? But Palma couldn't relax. She was waiting for them to put their cards on the table and thought it might have happened when Tommy went to the toilet and left the three of them alone. It didn't. When he returned, Jackie began to clear up the plates and Palma rose to help her.

'No, you're a guest,' said Jackie. 'He can help me . . .' she stabbed a finger in Tommy's direction and then nodded at her husband. 'Neil, go and show your shed off to Palma. He's so proud of it he gives everyone a guided tour.'

'It's not a shed,' protested Neil.

And Palma knew that this had been arranged beforehand.

Take Palma down to the gym and give her the hard word. She played along, admiring the flowers in the borders en route, commenting how much bigger the gym looked close up. Neil opened the door and led her inside. One wall was completely mirrored. There were weights and equipment everywhere and a whiteboard, which had been scrawled on with red pen.

'Tell him I want my dumb-bells back,' said Neil. 'He'll conveniently forget.'

'I will,' she said, looking around and trying to dredge up something to say. 'Is it cold in here in winter?' *Pathetic*.

'It's got a heater.'

'Looks really good. Did you paint it inside?'

'Me and our Tom.'

Just say it, please, Palma begged inwardly. The walls were bulging with the pressure of the unsaid words.

Neil walked to the rack with the missing weights and started to straighten the others above the gap.

'He's done well, hasn't he? British champion,' he said and Palma knew this was the start of it.

'It's amazing. You must be very proud of him.'

'I am,' said Neil. 'He's worked hard to get where he is. Now he has to stay there.'

'I hope he does.'

'This next fight is the big one for him. Really big. He has to keep focused.' Neil turned to her then, sought eye contact. 'This is his chance to prove to everyone that last win wasn't a fluke. He can't afford to let anything get in the way of that, do you understand what I mean, Palma?' He didn't wait for her to answer before continuing. 'It's not my place to say this because he's a grown man but don't cock him about. We want him to be happy but . . .'

That 'but' hung in the air, full of threat and judgement.

'I wouldn't,' said Palma. 'I know how important it is.'

'Okay,' said Neil. 'It had to be said, I hope you understand.'

'I do,' said Palma.

'Our Tom feels things deeply and I know he's fallen hard for you. I'll not lie and tell you I'm thrilled about it. The timing's off and . . . you know . . .' His eyes made a dart to her stomach.

'I do know,' she said. 'I'll not get in the way.'

'Good. Because I'll do anything to protect our Tommy. Anything.'

That 'anything' was so much more than a word. It had an importance and a depth of meaning that was much greater than the sum of its letters. Palma felt a rush of anxiety course through her veins.

Then Neil smiled and clapped his hands together and the sound signified a full stop on the matter. 'Anyway . . . don't forget to remind him. My OCD kicks in if everything isn't in its place.'

That was clear, thought Palma as they wended their way back up to the house, talking about how the desire to have a nice garden lay dormant in the brain until someone hit their forties, when it leapt out like a surprise.

Palma thanked Jackie and Neil for the meal, which had been less of the consideration that Tommy had been led to believe and more about setting out the family stall, something he seemed blissfully unaware of. She feigned the beginnings of a headache on the way home, telling Tommy she'd rather go to hers than his and rest because she was tired and had eaten too much. He was disappointed but understood, he said. She knew if she'd asked him to stop off halfway home and move a mountain, he would have. She really really liked him so much, but the conversation with his brother troubled her. She'd been right to keep something in reserve; although it wasn't her cocking Tommy about that would be the problem, it was more that she wouldn't be enough for him. He was going places and she was standing still. He'd smash her heart into bits if he dumped her for a 'Katie'.

He opened the car door for her, helped her out, made sure she was in the house safely. He kissed her tenderly before saying goodbye as if she were something precious and she knew that she had nothing to worry about. But she was worried, all the same.

Chapter 41

It was Palma's antenatal appointment the following afternoon so she left work at two-thirty and, despite her protestations, Joe insisted on dropping her at the surgery. It was the least he could do, he said, for helping to ease their staffing problems. Iris had now gone back part-time and Astrid came in two afternoons per week. She was wonderful company and only too happy to share all the details of her journey from unhappy male rugby player to ecstatic gorgeous woman.

'*Einmal war sie eine hässliche unglückliche Raupe. Jetzt ist sie ein wunderschoener glücklicher Schmetterling,*' she said, then apologised for slipping into her native language as she sometimes did without thinking. 'Once I wor an ugly unhappy caterpillar. Now I am a beautiful happy butterfly,' she said in her funny half-and-half accent.

Astrid made them all laugh lots. Joe had been unsure of her at first but now Annie was (mock) afraid that they'd run off together.

The fake headache Palma had pretended she'd had the previous day had become a reality within a couple of hours and she'd gone to bed early crippled by it. She'd had horrible dreams about Tommy hating her and not believing that she really liked him, even though she was screaming it in his face. She'd woken up cold and shivering and been so physically sick, she'd almost had to ring Annie and ask for the day off. Luckily it had subsided after a warm shower and a couple of paracetamol and when Annie and Joe picked her up, they were none the wiser she'd been through the mill for the past twelve hours.

Palma handed over her phial of urine to the midwife who thanked her with a cheery, 'Ta love' and screwed off the top to test it. 'That's fine,' she said at the sink and returned bringing a fresh phial for Palma to use next time.

'So, how have you been?'

'Good,' nodded Palma. 'But I still don't seem to be growing. Everyone I meet is saying how small I am.'

'Some people don't show much all the way through, all women are different, but we'll have a proper look at you in a minute. Let's do your blood pressure first.'

That was fine too. The midwife told Palma to lie down on the bed in the corner and pull up her T-shirt. The midwife checked her notes. Then she took out her tape measure, wrote down her findings, felt Palma's stomach and asked if Palma had felt the baby moving yet.

'I think so. Just a little bit, at night when I'm quiet.'

'That's the way. Soon as you're ready for rest, they're ready for play. Get used to that,' said the midwife. 'Both when they're in and out of you.'

The baby was the size of an avocado now. She could close

her fist and suck her thumb and yawn, according to Palma's book, but she didn't look big enough to have anything even that size inside her.

The midwife pulled out a small machine from a drawer. 'Let me see if I can hear the baby's heartbeat,' she said. She moved the transducer around Palma's stomach and a racing thump filled the air.

'There we go,' said the midwife.

'Oh, thank God,' said Palma and laughed with relief.

'I think, to be on the safe side, we'll bring your next scan forwards so we can check everything's okay.'

'The last scan was fine though, wasn't it?' Palma asked.

'It was, but there's things on the twenty-week scan that wouldn't show up on the twelve-week one,' said the midwife. 'The anomaly scan picks up a lot more detail that can't be seen until the baby is at least eighteen weeks old.'

'Should I be concerned?' Palma asked.

'Never worry until you have to has always been my motto,' said the midwife.

Chapter 42

'Look at our baby,' yelled Jacques as Vita the sonographer twisted the screen around. 'I can't believe it. Look how he's grown.'

'Do we still want to know what sex it is?' Eve checked with him.

'Yes, let's ask, Eve. I want to know.'

'So do I.'

'Sure?' asked Vita, waiting for them to confirm. 'Okay . . . it's a boy.'

'A son.' The word felt beautiful and sweet in Eve's mouth. She didn't mind if it was a girl or a boy, but now she knew it was the latter, she was as delighted as if it had been her first choice. She had a vision of Jacques carrying him on his wide, high shoulders and travelling on the wayward Winterworld train, trying not to fall off. *A son.* Now she could buy blue things and decorate the nursery. Sod the PC brigade, it was going to be full of planes, trains and automobiles.

'Everything okay?' asked Eve.

'It all looks grand to me,' said Vita. 'I am very thorough.'

'Thank you,' said Jacques, grabbing Vita's hand and shaking it as if she had built the baby herself and was receiving a quality control award for it.

'My pleasure,' said Vita, chuckling. She handed Jacques the scan photographs and then swiped the gel from Eve's stomach.

Jacques waited outside the toilet, thankfully only a few strides from the sonographer's room.

'Nice wee?' he asked as his wife emerged.

'The best,' said Eve. 'I think if I ever feel depressed in future, I'm going to fill up my bladder until it nearly bursts and then enjoy the sensation of letting it go. It's euphoric.'

'I don't want to go straight back to work, let's go and have a nice coffee somewhere. And cake.' Jacques' face lit up with boyish glee at his own suggestion.

'I'm good with that,' said Eve. 'I might as well enjoy being fat.'

'We can talk about names now we know. What do you think about Jacques Junior?'

'Top of the list,' Eve nodded.

'Really? I thought you'd laugh me out of town.'

'I love the name Jacques,' said Eve. 'And if he turns out to be half the man his father is, I'll be happy with that.'

Jacques crooked his arm for her to take.

'A son,' he said. 'I can't wait to meet him.'

Neither can I, thought Eve. She couldn't get her head around the fact that she was carrying something that could hear her heart beat from the inside. It was both scary and wonderful. If they'd waited for the 'right time' they might never have found it. Thank goodness, it had found them instead.

*

Someone knocked on Palma's door that evening – a chirpy 'Tommy knock', even though he was training and she wasn't expecting him. He didn't come straight in as usual which made her wonder if he was carrying a big bunch of flowers and his hands were too full to open the door. He'd bought her a lot of flowers since they'd been a couple. She'd laughed once that her little house looked like the waiting room in the crematorium.

She pulled the door open and her glad expression dulled because it wasn't Tommy, it was Nicole standing there with her yellowing smile and long lank hair.

'Hello, pal,' she said. 'I hope you don't mind me calling in to see you.' She took a step forward but Palma didn't move aside to let her in, leading Nicole to shuffle awkwardly back again.

'I'm expecting someone, Nicole,' said Palma, overriding her naturally polite inclination to invite her in.

'I just thought I'd say hello. I caught the bus up. Bit chilly today, innit.'

It wasn't chilly. It was a lovely summer evening. The first day of August – Yorkshire Day – and the sun had shone on them all day. Cool to someone who had screwed up their system with drugs maybe.

'Nicole, I don't have any money to lend you,' said Palma. She was under no illusion why Nicole would have caught a bus up here. 'How did you know where I was?'

'Our Jaz came to the cracker place for a job. She recognised you. She didn't want to say who she was in case you felt obliged. She should have though, because she didn't get it.' She chuckled and Palma saw that she'd lost a tooth, second from the front. She'd have none left in five years. 'Mind you, she says she was nearly sick on all the crackers.'

The hungover girl. Palma had thought she recognised her. Nicole's younger half-sister.

'She goes out with a lad who lives round here. She's seen you in the Chinese around the corner.'

It was that easy to find someone with a morsel of fortunate timing, thought Palma. 'I don't want to trouble you,' said Nicole. 'I'm in a bit of shit, Palma.' And she wiped at her eyes which were spilling out real tears; but then again, knowing Nicole, she'd probably put an onion up her sleeve. Despite her strongest reservations and everything that looked out for Palma screaming at her, 'DO NOT LET HER OVER YOUR THRESHOLD', Palma moved aside and said, 'You'd better come in.'

'Ta.' Meekly, Nicole stepped inside the tiny lounge. She brightened immediately.

'Oh, this is nice. Much nicer than Beckett Street. How much do you pay for all this?'

She sat down on Palma's couch and gazed in wonder around her, much the same as Palma had gazed in wonder at Tommy's house when she'd first walked in there, except she hadn't been casing the joint for stuff to nick. 'Is this the same furniture you had before? It seems more comfortable in here. Is it expensive living here?' The same question, reworded.

'So what's up?' asked Palma, avoiding answering her.

'I'm pregnant,' said Nicole. She gave a watery smile. 'You don't need to ask whose it is.'

Palma closed her eyes and shook her head. Clint had at least six kids that she knew of and he took responsibility for none. Which was lucky for them really.

'I'm going to have it,' said Nicole. 'I might even get a house like this out of it.'

'Are you joking?' said Palma.

'Why? You've not done so bad,' returned Nicole.

Palma laughed; she couldn't help herself. 'I'm not having a baby to get benefits. I'm having a baby to love and bring up decent. I'm working to provide for us. I won't just sit on my arse and expect everyone to pay for it. It's not like having a pet, Nicole.' Was she really having to explain this to a woman who was twenty-three?

'But you didn't get pregnant to do all that. You got pregnant to sell it and get some money,' said Nicole, 'so don't give me that holier-than-thou shit.'

Palma opened up her mouth to counter that but it was the truth. Coming from Nicole's mouth, what she had done sounded awful, heartless. No soft flesh on those hard bones of words.

'I'll be doing my best by this baby, Nicole. It'll be hard work but I'm not going to be the same sort of mother that mine was. And what the hell are you doing sleeping with Clint O'Gowan?'

Nicole shrugged. 'Dunno really.'

'Are you using?'

Nicole shrugged again. 'You can't just stop like that.'

Palma almost fell down onto the armchair. 'You need some proper help, Nicole.'

'I know,' said Nicole, with a weary sigh. 'That's why I came here. I've been reading up on it. I need some vegetables and fruit but I'm skint.'

She needed to read up to find out she should be eating well during pregnancy? That poor, poor little baby. If there even was a baby. Nicole had a capricious relationship with the truth.

'Clint doesn't know where you are, but he's been asking around. Says he wants to talk to you sooner rather than later.'

Palma's skull prickled. 'What for?'

'Dunno. I doubt he'll come to Dodley though. He was a bit pissed off that he couldn't ring you. So was I if I'm honest.' She feigned hurt, but Palma wasn't taken in. Nicole wasn't that naïve that she didn't know their friendship was long gone. All that existed of it were a few tenuous threads of nostalgia that gave Nicole a way in when she wanted a favour.

'Why wouldn't he come to Dodley?' asked Palma.

'I shouldn't tell you this, Palma, but the Webbs are after him, so he said if I saw you to ask if you'll ring him.'

The Webbs were another of the 'families' in the area and they made the O'Gowans look like the Brady Bunch. There were a few notorious criminal clans in this part of Yorkshire: the Bellfields who were pretty low key these days, but in their heyday were brutal; the Clamps and the Crookes who were mainly rough and skanky rather than dangerous; the O'Gowans who laughably aspired to be the Webbs, but didn't have the brains to even spell their name – and then the Webbs themselves. They'd risen out of the gutter, loved tailor-made suits and glittery events where they could flash their cash. They had nice houses, classy cars and 'respectable' businesses around Maltstone and Higher Hoppleton. They kept their hands clean and paid heavy, nasty people good money to do their dirty work for them. Clint would have been an idiot to cross them, but then he *was* an idiot. Palma really didn't want to know the details, but she did take a gram of comfort knowing that Dodley was a no-go zone for him.

'You've changed your hair. Looks nice. Sophisticated,' Nicole went on. 'I won't tell him, if you help me. I need a hundred quid. To sort myself out,' she said.

'I haven't got a hundred quid, Nicole,' said Palma. 'I've got things to buy for my baby.'

'A hundred quid and I'll go,' said Nicole. 'I promise. You won't have to see me again. I don't think you want to, do you?' Her expression was set as she looked at her one-time best friend.

'We've chosen different paths, Nicole,' said Palma. 'I've left Ketherwood. I don't want it following me here. I don't even want to hear the name Clint O'Gowan again.'

Nicole sniffed. 'You always did think you were better than the rest of us.'

Palma wasn't having that. 'What, because I didn't do drugs? Because I didn't want to shoplift? Because I looked after my stuff? Because I wanted to work and better myself?'

'Some of us haven't got a choice,' spat Nicole.

'Of course you have,' countered Palma, with force. 'My home life was worse than yours. I didn't say to myself, "Well,

I was born in Ketherwood and so I have to live like the worst of them do for the rest of my life." I wanted more for myself than I had, not less, so yes, of course you've got a choice, every bit as much as me.'

'Nobody paid me to carry a kid for 'em though,' Nicole sniped.

'If I hadn't done it this way, I'd have done it another. It wasn't how I wanted it to happen, but yes – I took the short-cut whilst it was on offer.'

How had that beautiful girl turned into this, thought Palma. She'd been stunning and funny and clever once. There *must* be a vestige of the old her that still existed in that scruffy, venal shell and Palma appealed to it. 'Nicole, please tell me that you've got more ambition in you than just to be a single mum opening your legs every time Clint O'Gowan clicks his fingers. Can't you remember being at school and teachers telling you that you could really make something of yourself? Can't you remember wanting to open up your own beauty salon or be a WAG?' She'd been pretty enough to accomplish it too.

Nicole looked suitably sheepish for all of thirty seconds before she asked, 'So, are you going to let me have it? I need stuff. Vegetables and things. For the baby.'

She was trying to manipulate her, hoping to appeal to her as one caring mum-to-be to another. She probably wasn't pregnant at all and if she was, Palma didn't think the baby had much chance of surviving her selfishness. She couldn't get involved. She wouldn't be dragged back down the sink.

'Look, I'm not daft,' Nicole went on. 'You don't want

to see me again, I get that. When I walk out of the door, I won't come back here. I promise. And I won't tell Clint where you are.'

'And if I don't help, you will, is that what you're saying?'

Nicole's shoulders jerked. 'I need . . . things.'

'Wait there,' said Palma with a huff. She went into the kitchen and took a soup can out of the cupboard. She'd used the contents and washed it out and it had a hundred and twenty-four pounds in it for emergencies. This could be classed as such. She did it quickly, so that Nicole didn't have the chance to slip anything into her bag whilst her own back was turned because she couldn't help herself.

She held out five twenty-pound notes to Nicole.

Nicole's hand came out slowly, almost in wonder that she'd asked and it had been given.

'Thanks, Palma. I mean it. And I'm sorry. I feel ashamed.'

'I hope you do, Nicole. Because that shame might make you reach for better things. Please think about what I've said. Get some help.'

'Have you any change for the bus back? They won't take a twenty.'

It was laughable, but then again it wasn't. None of her words had hit home. Nicole lived in the here and now; the future extended only as far as her next fix. Palma went back into the kitchen and scooped all the change out of the coin part of her purse. 'That's all I've got,' she said.

'I hope it goes all right with you and your baby,' said Nicole at the door. 'I won't trouble you again.' She was gone within a minute of the coins touching her open hand.

Palma felt like crying. She'd been blackmailed, just as she had blackmailed Christian. Not for as much money but the resentment of being dangled on the end of someone else's string ran as deep. *As ye sow shall ye reap.* She couldn't argue with karma when she'd hoped and prayed it existed, even if she had fallen foul of it now.

On Monday, the *Daily Trumpet* unfortunately reported that Arthur Shafton, who died last month aged 97, was once a famous Sinitta tribute act on the variety club circuit. We would like to point out that Mr Shafton was in fact a Sinatra impersonator. We apologise unreservedly to the family for any distress caused and have made a contribution to a charity of their choosing.

Chapter 43

The next night, at the fourth Christmas Pudding Club meeting, they were discussing drugs – if that wasn't ironic, thought Palma.

There were a few more loose dresses around today because the ladies of the Christmas Pudding Club were a little more rotund than they were when they'd last met; with one exception. Palma was wearing one of the two pinafores she'd bought, even though it was very baggy, but she wanted to stop anyone marvelling at her flat stomach. She was starting to worry about it now and wished her scan date would hurry up and arrive in the post.

'You'll be starting to consider your birth plans very soon,' said Chloe. 'All I will say is to keep an open mind, because what you think you want might be something very different to what you will want on the day, when you're trying to squeeze out what feels like a Nissan Micra. Hands up anyone who doesn't want any pain relief at all.' No one did.

'Well, there's a first,' said Sharon, sharing Chloe's surprised laughter.

'I want all the drugs they can give me,' said Fil.

'And me,' said Di.

'I might have a water birth,' said Cheryl. 'Especially after we went to that aqua aerobics class last week. I thought it might be nice and relaxing.'

'I had a water birth,' said Sharon. 'And I would highly recommend it. We have two in the labour suite so it's first come, first served and I was lucky because it was free when I wanted it.'

'We've brought a film about some births to watch today,' said Chloe. 'And I've got a sample gas-and-air mouthpiece to try. We'll show you some puffing exercises, though we will do these again nearer the time. Won't hurt to do them twice.'

'I got all my breathing wrong last time,' said Raychel. 'I knew what I had to do but I forgot everything.'

'This is where a clued-up birth partner comes in handy,' said Sharon. 'Co-breathing with them.'

'I think my Daniel might be a good one to have by my side. I've got no complaints so far,' said Di.

Chloe dragged their attention back to the matter in hand or the session would have been hijacked by Di outlining her present situation, which everyone presumed was more than acceptable, judging by her smiley demeanour.

'As you'll see in the film, breathing can help a lot. When you're scared, your breath tends to be shallow and everything tenses, which leads to lack of oxygen and even more panic and it'll wear you out very quickly. Rhythmic breathing like this . . .' Sharon demonstrated '. . . is what you need to remember most of all. You're going to need a lot of energy and you don't want to waste any. Try and make sure your out-breath is longer than your in-breath. I've put lots of tips on the fact sheet this week for you. Anyway, let's watch.'

The films had come on a long way since the one that Annie was shown at school that scared her half to death. That film was French and everyone got a fit of the giggles because the woman poohed as the baby came out. The film had to be stopped before the end because Mick Eckersley and Peter McClaren started trading hard punches when Mick said that Peter's mother had thrown the baby away and raised the turd as her son because it was better looking. Annie had forgotten all about that until this moment. Funny what the brain stores away, she thought.

The epidural needle looked scary but Eve's cousin Violet had had that and said it was fantastic; totally took all the pain away. Still, she wished she hadn't seen the length of it. Sometimes too much information wasn't such a good thing.

Annie had hoped to survive the birth with gas and air, but after listening to Gill's and Iris's tales of childbirth, she'd made up her mind to go with the flow. Palma hadn't even let herself think about the birth stage yet; she'd start doing that when she knew everything was all right. She knew it would be, she was being silly worrying.

'A fortnight till our next meeting, ladies,' said Chloe at the end of the session.

'Anyone going to Aqua Mamas class tomorrow?' asked Cheryl. 'A few of us went last week and it was very good.'

'Not me,' said Di. 'I'm getting enough exercise at the

moment, if you know what I mean,' and she winked and gurned like Les Dawson.

'Oh, I'll come,' said Fil.

'It's a fiver and the pool's lovely,' Annie butted in. 'I'm ringing up to book in the morning if anyone else wants me to do it for them as well.'

That was six of them, then. All of them except Di. Dr Gilhooley's aim to help mothers-to-be claim support and friendship from each other was working a treat.

Chapter 44

Iris, who'd been off for a few days, hadn't seen Palma since she had her hair changed and she made a real song and dance about it when they met at work the next morning.

'My goodness, I didn't recognise you, Palma,' she said, arms akimbo. 'When I first met you I thought, *what bloody colour is her hair?*, but it's so you. I mean, that's a lovely colour you've got on, but that pink hair looked so much more natural.'

Annie hadn't said anything because she didn't want to upset Palma, but she'd thought the same. Palma and pink hair went together perfectly.

'I went for lunch with Tommy's family at the weekend and I didn't want them to judge me on my hair colour,' said Palma.

'Well, they aren't worth bothering with if they do that,' said Iris. 'Get that pink put back in and be Palma again. You look far too normal,' she went on. 'And you don't want that.'

The trouble was, Palma did. She wanted the 'normal' that Iris and Joe and Annie took for granted because they'd always had it: food in the cupboards, a little bit of money in her purse and that feeling of being accepted and loved. That stuff was boring to other people but for her it was something to aspire to. She wished she could have wiped out her past and started life again from the moment she moved into the house on Rainbow Lane. One thing was certain, her baby would never know what it was like to go to school in an unwashed uniform with a stomach grumbling from hunger. She'd come home to a cheerful house and a hot meal waiting for her and she'd have to eat up her vegetables. On winter nights, they'd have spaghetti Bolognese and home-baked jam roly-poly and custard made with eggs and double cream. She'd sleep soundly in clean sheets and never have to prop her chair against the door for fear of a stranger bumbling in. Her child would not have to turn a comatose mother over on the sofa so that if she vomited in her sleep, she wouldn't choke herself. Normal equated to wonderful in Palma's world.

She hadn't told Tommy what Neil had said to her in the gym at the bottom of his garden because she didn't want to stir up any trouble. She loved him, she wanted everything for him that he wanted for himself and more; and she wanted to prove to his family that she wasn't the sort of woman who would divert Tommy's focus, so any worries she had about her pregnancy, she kept to herself. He was going to take her out for a meal tomorrow, he said, and try and fatten her up a bit. She'd not meant to, but she'd snapped at him for bringing it up again that she wasn't putting on weight and he'd been mortified that he'd upset her. And then she'd been mortified that she'd upset him and apologised, saying it was her pregnancy hormones at play and to ignore her and that she'd love to go out for a meal with him.

At least in the Aqua Mama class she could forget all about the Neil lecture and have a laugh. Fil was last into the water and strolled out from the changing room in a golden bikini, looking like a Bond girl. Everyone's jaw hit the bottom of the pool. She even made Shona look like a munter by comparison.

'You have no idea how beautiful you are, have you?' said Annie after the session and Fil had thrown her head back and let loose a laugh that wouldn't have sounded out of place in a *Carry On* film.

'Same time next week, ladies?' asked Cheryl. 'Fil, try to look a bit ugly, you're showing us all up.'

'Natural beauty is a curse,' said Fil, and gave her a cheeky wink. 'I suffer every day.'

Palma thought she was falling in love with these women, as surely as she had fallen in love with Tommy.

When Tommy arrived to pick her up the next night, he brought with him an enormous yellow teddy bear.

'I couldn't resist it,' he said. 'We should start buying things for the baby, shouldn't we?'

'Let me get the next scan out of the way first and make sure everything is all right,' she'd answered. He couldn't wait to come with her but she hadn't told him the date had been brought forward.

Over their main course Tommy asked her if she'd like to move in with him.

'I know it's early days, but you and me, we're meant to be, aren't we? I can feel it, can you?'

Palma did feel it. She loved being with him, loved the feeling of anticipation when he texted her and said he was on his way over. But Neil's words had made her extra wary and she wanted to be sure – for both of them – that every step forwards they made was a solid one. She knew he craved the family thing: the wife, the kids. And she knew that was because he wanted to be the dad he wished his own had been, as if that put the past right for him. But she had to make sure he wanted these things with her and not just anyone. In short, she couldn't really believe her luck.

'I love you, Palma. You're all I could want,' he said, trying to lighten up the weight of his words by buttering some bread at the same time as he said them. 'You've only got one bedroom. I've got three. The middle one would make a perfect nursery. For now, anyway, because I want to move to somewhere with a massive garden so we can have that Arctic cabin you want.'

She laughed, 'Oh, now you're bringing out the big guns.'

'Oh come on, Palma. What's the point in hanging about when we both know I'm right?'

Because Neil's words were perched on her shoulder like a raven, that's why.

'Tommy, hold your horses. We've got plenty of time before we need extra space so there's no rush. You've got to keep your head on your fight, not on redecorating, and I've got to keep mine on having this baby. Don't run at this, Tommy. We've got all the time in the world, so let's get it right.'

Tommy took her hand and held it between his. 'I know, I'm sorry. I just can't believe my luck.'

Palma couldn't help the laugh that escaped her. She had more right to think that than he did. 'Are you joking? I could understand you saying that if I looked like that ring girl and I was driving an Audi R8; but I've got nothing, Tommy. I stuff crackers for a living and let's not even mention—'

Tommy thumped his chest, where he imagined his heart lay. 'I wish you could feel what I do in here,' he said. 'I've never been so sure of anything in my life. Actually, scrap that, I have. When I knew I was going to win the title. I walked into that ring and there was no doubt in my head at all.'

'Eat your steak and shut up,' said Palma.

A couple passed by their table. She: slim, plastic boobs and hair extensions and half the age of her companion, who had a sharp suit on and was tall, powerfully built and lantern-jawed.

'All reight, Tom,' he said, his voice rough, deep, his accent as broad as his white-toothed smile. 'How's tha gooin'?' He shook hands with Tommy as if he was absolutely delighted to see him.

'Good, mate, good. Are you?'

'Nivver better. I'm coming down and see thy Neil. Tell him to watch art for me.' He pretended to box with Tommy who reciprocated with the same moves and said: 'Dream on if tha' trying to tek me title off me.'

'I want some tickets for t'feight. Ringside. Save me six. Naw, eight. Full job. Dinner and drinks. I mearn it,' said the suit.

'I will. I'll be in touch when I gerram.'

The suit turned to Palma. 'Sorry, sweetheart. I'm disturbing your meal. I'll leave you alone. See thi', Tom. See you, love. Look after him.'

'See thi', Dion,' said Tommy. 'Have a nice evening,' he said to the woman, who was really a girl with shovelfuls of make-up on.

'Awreight,' she answered through blown-up lips. It was evident that theirs wasn't a relationship built on sparkling conversation.

'Dion Webb,' explained Tommy, when they'd moved on to their table.

Palma hadn't heard the surname in years and now she'd heard it twice in three days.

'He looks hard,' said Palma.

'He is. I wouldn't like to be on the wrong side of him and his lot but he loves our Neil and he's boxing mad. And he loves me, of course. But then again, how could you not?' He grinned a Tommy grin and Palma had to agree with him. It would be very hard not to love Tommy Tanner.

'He takes a lot of 'roids,' Tommy went on, smile closing. 'He's doubled in size since last time I saw him and it weren't that long ago.' He shook his head. 'Fool's game.'

Palma reached for a piece of bread. Her appetite had just switched up a notch having seen Dion Webb. She could understand why Clint wasn't likely to come sniffing around trying to find her with him in the area.

Tommy liked to talk in bed. He liked to lie on his back with his arm around Palma and converse in the dark. Palma savoured the feel of him holding her; she loved the smell of him and the smoothness of his skin taut over his muscles. But that night he fell to sleep more or less as soon as his head touched the pillow. Palma lay still, listening to his breathing, her own in tune with it. The baby had brought them together, in a mad way. She might never have bumped into him again had she not been cutting through the park that night after being at the Stephenson's house. Christian and Tabitha and that episode of her life felt like a million light years away.

The baby twitched inside her, making her presence known and Palma pressed her hand against her stomach. She was there and alive, warm and safe and her little heart was beating. Everything would be all right, she told herself. She knew it would. She was worrying over nothing.

Chapter 45

Palma had a letter to say that she had to attend the hospital on Tuesday, 15 August at 2.30 p.m., the day before the fifth Christmas Pudding Club meeting. She was less concerned than she had been, though. She'd noticed as she lay in the bath that her stomach was definitely standing a little more proud. The baby liked to move around when Palma's body was submerged in the water. Palma had a vision in her head of her baby, like a tiny mermaid, swirling and twirling inside her.

The Aqua Mama classes were now a weekly event. They did try and take it seriously but their 'naughty corner' of the pool contained too many gigglers. Fil was the worst of them all. She had nearly drowned during the 'frog legs' stretches. On land, she was elegance personified, gliding from the changing rooms to the poolside in a variety of fabulous swimming costumes, but in water, she was like a submarine with holes in it.

Life was better than Palma could ever have expected it to be. She had broken her rule about shopping for some baby clothes because there was a sale on in Baby Palace in town. It sold seconds from chain stores like Marks and Spencer and Gap, though it might only be a thread that needed cutting off or a mark that could be dabbed away. She bought some white babygros and socks and cute white satin shoes and a yellow cardigan with duck-shaped buttons. She cleared her bedside cabinet to store the baby things and sat the big yellow teddy that Tommy had bought on top as if he were guarding them.

The day of the scan eventually arrived. She had only told Joe and Annie that she was having blood tests up the hospital as the midwife thought she might be anaemic. She hadn't told Tommy anything because he would have insisted on coming with her, making sure she was okay. He certainly wouldn't have allowed her to go on the bus to the hospital with a bladder full of water.

Palma lay on the couch, her stomach covered in gel, ready to see her baby again.

'So you're nineteen weeks,' said the sonographer. Not the same as the last one. This one was called Lesley and gave off a cooler vibe. 'Now, relax.'

Palma tried to do as she said and stared up at the ceiling, keeping her eyes away from Lesley in case she saw something in her expression that disturbed her. The room was full of silence and anticipation broken only by finger-taps and clicks on the keyboard below the screen. Eventually Lesley spoke.

'I'm afraid I'll have to ask you to drink some more water and take a little walk,' she said, giving Palma's stomach a deft wipe with a sheet of tissue from a roll. 'I can't see the baby properly and hopefully it'll move position if you do that. Okay? I'll see the next mum and then we'll have another go. There's a water machine outside to the right. Take two cups and then walk up and down the corridor for me.'

'Is that normal?' asked Palma.

'It usually does the trick, yes,' answered Lesley.

Palma felt fit to burst when she was called in again. She passed the couple who had just exited the room holding their scan pictures. The woman was half-laughing, half-crying and the man had his arm around her shoulder.

'Come in, love,' said Lesley to her and smiled and Palma tried not to think that Lesley didn't look like the sort of person who would call someone 'love' and so if she did, there would have to be a reason for it.

Once again she lay back on the couch with her trousers pulled down below her small fundus, her T-shirt pulled up and her anxiety levels in orbit.

Lesley moved the transducer through the gel. 'That's better. That's much better.'

'Can you see if it's a boy or a girl?' asked Palma. 'I'd like to know.'

Lesley was concentrating. Palma wasn't sure if she'd heard her then Lesley said, 'It's a girl.'

She'd known it. Her little mermaid swimming around inside her. Her little girl, her daughter who was going to wear the white babygros and the cutesy shoes and be photographed with the giant yellow teddy.

'Is she all right?'

Again that silence punctuated with the odd click, click, click. *Please tell me everything is all right.*

'I'm ... making sure,' said Lesley, her eyes not leaving the screen. Until they did and she smiled and Palma burst into tears.

Chapter 46

The fifth Christmas Pudding Club was taken up with the subject of equipment.

'Walk into Baby World or Mothercare or anywhere like that and you will be absolutely overawed with everything, so we thought what might make a good session would be to discuss stuff that you might find really useful and worth the outlay and things that are non-essential luxuries,' said Chloe.

Sharon was trying to open some windows. There were so many of them, all south-facing, that the room was like a greenhouse from the mid-August sun. Everyone, without exception, was fanning themselves with the help sheets that Chloe had given out earlier. Di was the size of a house and sweat was running down her face. Even her breasts seemed to be leaking because there were two large circles on her light grey dress. She'd made a joke about it when she'd first walked in. That and the fact that she couldn't lean over and shave her legs anymore and that Daniel had two choices: shave them for her or share a bed with a mountain gorilla.

'A lot of equipment you can buy second hand as well,' said

Sharon, giving up the ghost on the window-opening front and closing the curtains instead.

'I wish I'd have kept hold of all my stuff,' said Raychel. 'We were only going to have one child and then . . . da dah!'

'Dr Gilhooley is trying to set up a shop to buy and sell good quality baby things,' said Chloe.

'Dr Gilhooley is chasing a sainthood,' laughed Fil.

'I'd give him one,' said Di, snorting with laughter when she realised her words had a double meaning.

Annie stole a look across at Palma and saw that she was chuckling too. She was very pale and though Annie hadn't made mention of it, her young friend didn't seem to be blooming like the rest of them who were plumping and glowing. She knew that Palma had been to the hospital the previous day and they'd found out that she was anaemic, which explained her pallor. Annie hoped the iron tablets they'd prescribed would sort her out. Her hair colour didn't help – she suited the pink so much more and it made her look fresher, whereas those shades of ash bleached her. They'd given her a scan whilst she was there, Palma had said, and she'd found out she was having a girl. Annie had a mental picture of Palma's daughter being born with pink hair.

The midwives' handout included a list of all the important basics. Baby clothes with poppers at the crotch that a lot of cheap versions didn't feature; a changing station (*you could live without it, but it'll save your back*, said Chloe and so she considered it an essential). Nipple shields were cheap but vital because breastfeeding could be painful at the beginning, said Sharon – they were covering feeding in the next session.

Di had found out the previous week that she was having two boys, so her shopping list would be slightly longer but at least not doubled, according to Chloe.

'I can't wait. I'm going to raise them so they aren't twats to women,' she said to Raychel beside her, but everyone could hear anyway. 'And they don't shag their in-laws.'

'I would consider a feeding bra an essential,' Chloe went on and produced one from a box at her side where she had a host of gadgets and other aids to show them. 'Have you all applied for the freebies that came in your pack from the doctor? If not, you should. And there's a list of other things you can get for free from the internet on those sheets you're all presently fanning yourselves with, so please read them.'

'I love a freebie,' said Cheryl to Annie. Even though she had plenty of money these days, in her mind she was still a woman who had never had much and so she didn't squander any on daft things she didn't need. She was carrying a girl and she and John had decided to call the baby Edith after the dear lady who had changed her life. If it hadn't been for Edith, she would never have had 'the year of the sunflower' as she liked to call it. More had happened to her that year than all of her others put together. Losing a love, losing a friend, being stolen from, being cheated, having her heart broken, fighting with Edith's dickhead nephew, nearly being arrested by a policeman called John Oakwell who made her cry in a supermarket. It had been a busy one, to say the least. The worst and the best year of her life and because of it she was the most contented woman on the planet, married to a man who thought the world of her. Whoever said that life was a rich tapestry had hit the nail right on the head. Her tapestry just happened to be full of policemen, paintings, Cillit Bang . . . and sunflowers.

'Good to have a bag packed ready for the hospital nearer the date,' said Sharon. 'There's a list of what it should contain on your sheet as well. Lists, lists, ladies, because *get organised* is our motto. It must contain the three "bigs": big baggy T-shirt nightdresses, big knickers and a big bar of fruit and nut.'

Raychel nodded. Her Aunt Elizabeth had slipped a huge bar of fruit and nut chocolate into her bag when she had her first baby. 'Trust me,' she'd said. 'You'll thank me for it.' And she had. Her aunt had been pregnant at the same time as her two best friends from school and the three of them had been at her first birth because her husband Ben was stuck in the snow in the Midlands. This time, he'd promised to take only local jobs from late October onwards. Her aunt was more like a big sister to her, even though she hadn't known her until a few years ago. She thought more of her Aunt Elizabeth, and her two adopted aunts – Helen and Janey – than she did her own mother whom she hadn't seen for years and never wanted to see ever again. She'd told her the sort of lies that would have denied her the joy of motherhood had they not been uncovered. Raychel had loved being pregnant but if it hadn't been for Elizabeth, she would never have felt a child grow inside her. Although now she was riddled with heartburn and had a pea-sized bladder, insomnia and backache, she wondered how she'd conveniently forgotten the downside of her first pregnancy.

The session ended in good time before everyone wilted. Fil reckoned they had all lost a pound in sweat each, Di probably two. It had been so hot she had barely spoken. That hot.

'There's no Aqua Mama tomorrow,' said Cheryl, when they were outside. 'It was on the website. She's had to have the pool drained for some reason.'

'Oh, that's a shame,' said Eve. 'I was looking forward to seeing what colour swimsuit Fil was going to wear.'

'It would have been tangerine,' Fil chuckled. 'I look so hot in orange.'

'You'd look hot in a black bin bag, sweetheart,' said Annie. 'You're like the Girl from Ipanema.' She was showing her age now because no one knew what the heck she was on about.

Fil's husband was waiting for her outside, leaning casually against a beautiful silver Mercedes sports car. He had on a snow-white shirt and aviator shades, and the group of ladies sighed collectively at him because he looked like Idris Elba's taller, more handsome older brother.

'If my maths teacher had looked like him, I'd have had a string of A-stars in trigonometry,' said Cheryl.

'I wouldn't,' said Di. 'I'd have been so naughty he'd have had to keep me back every night for detention. Or spanking.'

'He snores badly,' said Fil.

'I'd have quickly learned to live with it,' said Di.

He smiled over at them and waved.

'He doesn't know this yet but he's going to have to trade that car in for a baby-friendly vehicle very soon,' whispered Fil. 'I'll let him have another couple of weeks of fun then I'll hit him with the news.'

'Wear your tangerine swimsuit when you tell him, it might soften the blow,' Eve advised and Fil walked towards him, mile-wide smile sitting on her lips.

'You're quiet,' said Annie in the car. They'd almost reached Palma's front door and she'd hardly spoken a word.

'It's the heat,' said Palma. 'I might not be as big as you lot but I'm feeling it.'

Annie nodded. 'It's like having a central heating radiator inside you, isn't it?'

'Yep.'

'Are you seeing Tommy tonight?'

'Not tonight. I want an early one.'

As Annie pulled up into Rainbow Lane they both spotted the bucket on the doorstep.

'What the hell ...' said Palma, getting out of the car to investigate. She found it was full of ice and placed in the centre of it was a bottle of the elderflower pressé that Palma had taken a liking to. Tommy had left it for her to come home to.

'And it's not a bad bucket either,' said Annie with a smile. That was the sort of thing Joe would do. You couldn't teach that level of consideration, it came right from the heart. If Tommy was even a fraction of the man that Joe Pandoro was, Palma should cling onto him for all he was worth.

Palma waved Annie off, went into the house and locked the door. She lifted the bottle out of the ice and poured herself a glass and felt it course all the way down her dry throat. *Tommy, Tommy, Tommy.* The house was full of signs that he loved her: the furry throw he'd bought for her in case she had a nap on the sofa and wanted to cover herself, the flowers in the vase, the chocolates on the coffee table, the card on the mantelpiece with a house in rainbow colours on the outside and on the inside the message: 'To my favourite girls, from your favourite boxer.'

She had more love in her life now that she'd had in the all the preceding years put together and it was starting to panic her. She couldn't give like he could; she couldn't trust anything to work out. She expected the ground to fall away for every forward footstep she took because so far, that's all it had done. His glass was always half full; hers wasn't only half empty but likely to be smashed by someone she hadn't seen coming at her from behind. She'd hold him back, just like Neil had thought she might and she wouldn't do that to him. If she couldn't keep to his pace, it was better that she let him go now.

Chapter 47

Eve was now twenty-three and a half weeks pregnant and the more unsavoury aspects of pregnancy were starting to encroach on her enjoyment of the experience. The heartburn was terrible and she was swigging Gaviscon from the bottle. She was sick of having to go to the loo every five minutes and wished she could poo as easily as she could pee. Constipation, bad dreams, sleep problems, leg cramps, fat ankles that she had to elevate as much as possible and thank goodness it was hot weather because there was no way she could bend over to get a pair of tights on. And the sheer act of breathing was starting to make her breathless. Jacques was a darling and gave her nice leg massages and didn't want her going into the spare room in the middle of the night even though she knew she was disturbing his sleep with her tossing and turning.

'Struggling, darling?' he asked her, peering over the top of his iMac in their shared office at her strained expression and back-stretching.

'What have you done to me, Jacques Glace?' she replied with a mock homicidal expression.

'From what I remember you rather enjoyed me putting that baby in there,' he winked at her and she let rip with a peal of laughter. 'Can I get you a coffee or a juice or anything?'

Eve used to love coffee from their temperamental old machine and she had a sudden liking for one.

'Do you know what, I think I will have a coffee, please.'

'Coming right up.' He put a fresh coffee through and Eve sniffed the air, in the manner of a bloodhound picking up a track. Her sense of smell had become ridiculously sensitive since she had fallen pregnant.

'Are you using a different brand?'

'No, why?'

'It doesn't smell the same as it usually does.'

'Your nasal receptors are off target. You can experience a lot of miswires where smell and taste are concerned; I've been reading about it,' said Jacques. 'And your baby brain will be terrible at the moment. And you're especially prone to infections too.'

'Thank you, Doctor Glace,' said Eve, sniffing the air again. That coffee didn't smell right, and she wasn't imagining it. There was an acrid, unpleasant note to its aroma.

'Baby's the size of a cantaloupe in case you're wondering. Another week and a half and he'll be a cauliflower. And what is slightly worrying is that in three and a half weeks he'll be the size of a cucumber,' Jacques went on, pointing to the 'fruit and veg chart' he'd run off from the internet and stuck on the wall. Eve felt much heavier than if she had a cantaloupe inside her. If the baby took after his father, he'd be more the size of a Chernobyl watermelon by now.

The coffee machine began to deliver its brew to the waiting jug with spluttering objection. 'Finally. A watched pot . . .' said Jacques with a smile.

'You'd have got it sooner if you'd flown to Brazil,' said Eve.

'Look, I have it here,' said Jacques, reverentially carrying a mug over to her and setting it down on the coaster he'd recently bought for her, printed with the photo of their baby at his twenty-week scan. Eve didn't like using it; she said she felt as if she was burning him. She lifted the mug to her lips and drank – then made a face.

'You'll get your love of coffee back, don't you worry,' he said. 'I've been reading about it.'

The smell wasn't coming from the coffee though.

'Is something burning?' asked Eve. The odour seemed to be growing stronger by the second. She got up and started sniffing again and her nose led her to the outside door, much to Jacques' amusement. She opened it and turned right.

'It's coming from Effin's office, Jacques.'

Jacques could smell it now and he could see smoke through Effin's window. He yelled at his wife to stay back as he opened the door. A patch of Effin's carpet at the front of his desk was ablaze. Jacques picked up the metal waste paper bin, tipped the contents out, filled it up from the sink in the corner and poured it over the small fire. Smoke started to plume and Jacques stamped the life out of it, then he reached down and pincered up the end of a now very soggy cigarette and put it in the ashtray on Effin's desk.

'What's going . . .' said Eve, but Jacques wasn't in the mood for explaining, instead he marched past her, his expression furious.

Jacques caught up with Effin by the train where he and Huw and Thomas were having yet another conversation about how it was running.

'Effin, can I have a word,' said Jacques and Effin knew by the way that he said it that the word wasn't going to be a very friendly one. Thomas and Huw took their cue and melted away.

'What's up, Captain?' said Effin.

'You've nearly burned your office down, that's what,' said Jacques, doing his best to rein in his temper. 'Your cigarette rolled off onto the carpet.'

'Cigarette, what cigarette?' said Effin.

Jacques' patience with Eve's baby brain did not extend as far as his site manager's negligence. 'The cigarette you obviously lit and left to burn.'

'Hang on, I never smoke inside,' said Effin. 'In fact, I haven't had a cigarette in months. I've given up. Angharad says—'

Jacques cut him off.

'Effin, if I hadn't been married to a woman who seems to have developed superwoman abilities during pregnancy, I have no idea what the extent of the damage might have been.'

Effin was shaking his head.

'Jacques, I have not even bought a packet of fags for . . . as long as I can remember. I need to see this.'

'Yes, let's see it,' said Jacques tightly. 'I'll show you, shall I?'

Effin set off walking briskly towards his office, Jacques at his side, neither of them saying a word. Inside, Jacques pointed to the cigarette.

'There it is. I put it in your ashtray. Why would you even
need an ashtray if you don't smoke inside?'

'I use it for paperclips,' said Effin, scratching his head in
confusion. 'This can't be. I haven't smoked in ...' He tried
to think back. 'Well, I had one last week, I caved in ...'
which didn't help his argument. He pulled open his drawer
where he used to keep his smoking paraphernalia, hoping to
prove that the space was now full of pens and Post-it notes
and other office detritus, but there sat a box of matches and
a packet of twenty Benson and Hedges minus one.

'I ... but I ...' Effin started spluttering like Jacques'
coffee machine.

'Look, Effin, I have no idea what is going on but you need
to stop pussyfooting around the fact that something is wrong.
You're the talk of the park. I wasn't even going to mention
the sign falling but coupled with this, you're a danger and I
can't have that.'

Eve, hovering around the door, had never seen her usually calm Jacques so furious. And she had never seen Effin
so cowed, either.

'I'm so sorry. I don't know ... what's up ...'

'Take the rest of the day off, Effin. Go home, get some
sleep, make a doctor's appointment. This' – Jacques picked up
what was left of the cigarette – 'is the second strike against
you and I won't have a third, do you hear me?'

Eve had to turn away. She knew Jacques was right but
she couldn't stand to see Effin so reduced. She went back
into the office, sat at her desk and tried to remember what
she was doing before she'd started smelling the smoke. Baby

brain was one thing but Effin didn't have that, which meant it could be something far more serious and that would break all of their hearts.

*

That night Palma put on her pyjamas instead of the lovely dress she'd bought for the night out that she and Tommy should have been going on. A big flashy event in Sheffield hosted by Tommy's sponsor. She was letting him down, she knew she was. Deliberately.

The taxi drew up outside and she felt sick at what she was about to do. He walked in wearing a gorgeous blue suit, white shirt and tie and the aftershave that made her senses sing. His smile shrivelled when he saw her.

'What's up, Palma? Aren't you going?'

'I'm sorry, Tommy. I just don't feel like it.'

'Aren't you well, sweetheart? Look, sod the evening, I'll stay with you . . .'

He would say that. He'd throw what was important away for her because she and the baby were his priority, he'd told her she was, and she couldn't have that.

'No, you won't,' she said firmly. 'I'm not having that on my conscience. You go and enjoy yourself. I'm tired and I'm not up to a late night and I'm not hungry. Really. It's important. People will want to see you, not me. It doesn't matter if I go or not.'

'I'm not that bothered about it though,' he said. 'I was mainly looking forward to it because we were going together.'

Their first big outing. The event where she would be introduced to his sponsor and everyone else who was important to Tommy in the boxing world. *This is my girlfriend and our baby.* And he was lying for her benefit, because he had really been looking forward to this evening. The speaker was Mikey Hyde, a boxer he'd looked up to and was desperate to meet and have the obligatory boxing photo taken of the two of them: smiling with their fists butted together. Neil and Jackie would be there too. Neil and Jackie who knew that *his* baby was someone else's.

'Go on,' she said. 'I'll be okay. You have a great night. I'm going straight to bed.'

He didn't want to leave her but he didn't want to let people down either. He enfolded her in a tender hug, planted a long kiss on her cheek because she'd turned her head from him. Then he left and she felt shit, but the truth was that she'd realised recently how deeply Neil felt when he'd said *I'll do anything to protect our Tommy. Anything.* Because you did what had to be done when you cared about someone that much.

*

It wasn't dark until ten thirty that night. Palma wasn't tired and had spent the evening listening to music through her headphones. She felt the tunes soak inside her that way and was sure the baby responded to them too, settled, drifted off to sleep to the songs that made her mother the happiest – music from shows: *Joseph, Sunset Boulevard, Evita.* Not *Blood Brothers* tonight. 'Tell Me It's Not True' – she couldn't listen to that one. She was about to turn in for bed when there was a quiet knock on her door, so quiet that she thought she'd imagined it until it happened again. She remembered to slip the chain on too late and tried to shut the door again and do it, but it was pushed forwards at speed from the other side and she was thrown back.

'Let me in quick for fuck's sake.'

Clint O'Gowan was closing her door from the inside.

'What the . . . ?'

'Well I can't fucking ring you, can I, because your old number's dead.'

Her heart was beating fast. She crossed her hands in front of her pyjama top, held it closed at the neck, aware that she had nothing on underneath it.

'Why would you need to get in touch? We've no connection anymore.'

'But we do, don't we?' he said, flicking a finger out towards her stomach. 'I thought you were getting rid.'

It wasn't hard to guess how he knew she was still pregnant, or where she lived. As if she could have trusted Nicole. She'd wasted her money there.

'You can hardly tell,' he added, studying her form.

'What do you want, Clint?'

'Don't use that fucking tone of voice with me,' he said, taking a step forwards; she took one back. She dropped her eye contact, didn't challenge him.

'I've found a buyer for you,' he said, jiggling on the spot in that irritating way he had.

She had no idea at all what he meant. 'A buyer for what?'

'I know a couple who can't have kids.'

That's what he'd said last time, when she should have recognised that nice couples didn't use people like Clint O'Gowan to help them.

His words tried to sink in but couldn't. He had to be joking, even though Clint didn't joke. He didn't do small talk. He traded and he cheated and he took from people.

She couldn't help the laugh that escaped her. It had nothing to do with humour and everything to do with incredulity. 'Are you serious?'

'There's three grand in it for you,' he said.

Of course he was serious and she didn't want to know any more. She wouldn't even let her brain entertain a single detail.

'No, Clint. No.'

'I hear you're seeing Tommy Tanner. Is that right? Is that why you're suddenly playing happy families?'

She didn't say anything, she let her silence answer for her.

'Think about it, Palma. Three grand and that's not counting everything you'd save over the years. No point in getting all above yourself now. You were quite happy to sell it to Christian bastard Stephenson.'

Now she did answer; it spiralled out of her like a fired bullet and she couldn't have stopped its passage if she'd tried. 'Fuck off, Clint.'

Clint moved towards her so fast he was a blur: he pressed his face up to hers, his hand, a bony clamp, on her throat. She could smell his foul breath, feel his spittle land in her eye as he spoke.

'Who the fuck are you talking to? I don't care what state you're in, I'll kick your fucking twat in.'

'I'm sorry, I'm sorry,' said Palma, pins and needles prick-ling her hands, her arms, her scalp.

Then the front door opened again and in walked Tommy and Clint sprung away from Palma. His nerves were already on edge from the crap in his system before you could even throw in his being in the Webb stronghold of Dodley.

'What's going on?' Tommy said, his neck blotching before her eyes. Palma knew how it must have appeared to him.

Clint made for the door, Tommy caught his arm, Clint shrugged him off. 'You're a fucking mug,' he said to him and attempted to leave but Tommy grabbed him again and pulled back his fist. Palma screamed and threw herself in between them.

'Don't hit him, Tom.' Her body was protecting Clint only because Joe Pandoro's fists had made contact and look what had happened to him. Tommy Tanner would be even richer pickings.

Clint took advantage of the moment to slip outside like the greased rat he was. Tommy followed but Palma clamped her hands onto his arm to anchor him and even in his enraged state, he was aware enough of her not to push her off.

'Come around here again and I'll kill you, you piece of shit,' Tommy shouted down the road, but Clint had disap-peared into the shadows.

'He's not worth it, Tommy,' Palma said, releasing her hold.

Tommy rounded on her then, hurt, confused. 'What was *he* doing here, Palma?'

'Nothing, Tommy. Less than nothing.'

How could she tell him? Tommy would kill him and she couldn't think of a lie that would appease him. Her heart was beating like a bass drum, her whole body shaking with adrenaline. Tommy's mood was reflected in the way he barged back into the house and she followed, not knowing how to mend this.

'I thought you were going to bed?'

'I was, I was. But I stayed up listening to some music.'

'I was going to post this through the door for you and saw the light on.' From his jacket pocket he pulled a photo of himself and the boxer Mikey Hyde. *Big love to Palma and baby – Mikey x* had been scrawled on it in black Sharpie. Palma opened her mouth and nothing came out. His thoughtfulness never failed to stagger her, humble her. He would have been so excited, imagining her finding it on her doormat in the morning, she knew that, because she knew him. He deserved so much better than what little she had to give him in return.

'What did he want? What did he mean by "I'm a mug"?' Tommy was agitated, upset.

'I don't know what he meant,' Palma yelled back. 'He was just spitting words.'

Tommy's head was spinning. He was pacing up and down her small room like Clint would, but it was pain powering his steps, not drugs.

'He meant that I was a mug for taking you on, didn't he? Why would he think that?'

'Because I'm nothing, Tommy,' she shouted back at him. 'You're going places and I'm just me and he thinks I'm still one of his ... someone who ...'

'What're you saying? "He thinks I'm still one of his"? One

of his what?' The whites of Tommy's eyes were standing out against the red of his face.

'He brokered the surrogacy deal,' said Palma, crying now. 'That's all the connection I have with him. Had.'

'He did? Clint O'Gowan? Palma, what the hell were you thinking?'

'Because that's how desperate I was,' she yelled back at him.

'Why was he here tonight? It must have been something important for him to come all this way. Is that why you didn't want to go out?'

'I didn't know he was coming. Honest, Tom.'

'What did he want, Palma?'

'Don't ask, Tom. Please. Let it go. I haven't seen him since I left Beckett Street.'

'And I just happened to turn up on the one night he's here?'

'Yes. Yes yes yes,' said Palma.

Tommy fell into the armchair. He nipped the top of his nose as if he were trying to numb his tear ducts.

He wanted to believe her and he didn't and she couldn't blame him because it didn't sound like the truth. Sometimes lies were swallowed whole and sometimes the truth was too convenient to be believed.

'You've been funny with me recently. Distant,' he said, the fire leaving his voice, anger giving way to reason. 'You haven't wanted to see me, I can tell. Holding me off.'

It was true. She bent her head and didn't even try to deny it.

'There was nothing up with you tonight, was there? You just didn't want to go, did you?'

She hadn't wanted it to happen like this. She shook her head, small movements but enough for there to be no doubt.

Tommy sniffed. 'Why, though? What have I done?' His bewilderment was palpable; it was agony for her to witness.

'Nothing, you haven't done anything,' said Palma. 'Timing, I think.'

'Timing? What does that mean?' he yelled, getting up. She couldn't look at him, she couldn't bear that tremor in his voice. As he rose, she sank onto the sofa as if they were at either end of a see-saw.

'Tommy ... I just ... I just don't feel that it's right, that *we* are right.' *Now, do it now,* said a voice inside. 'I think we should ... I think we want different things.'

'Like what?' There was pleading in his voice, in the way he stood, in his grey eyes that weren't sparkling with amusement now but with tears.

'I don't know what I want. I don't ...'

He broke in again. 'Am I moving too fast, Palma? I'll back off ...'

'*Break* off, Tommy, not *back* off. It's too much. You've found where you need to be, I haven't. I feel caught up in something that isn't what I want.'

Silence followed her words. It felt louder than the words she'd thrown at him.

'Break up. Is that what you want, Palma?' Tommy said eventually, breathlessly, as if he'd been physically winded.

Palma sighed. 'I'm sorry. It's for the best, trust me.'

Tommy walked to her door. Palma waited for it to open but he simply stood there.

'I can be a bit full-on, I know. I'm sorry.'

Palma didn't look up. She didn't want to see his face. She kept her head bowed and felt her tears sliding down her cheeks, watching them as they landed on her pyjamas.

'I wish I hadn't come round to drop this off. I wish I hadn't seen him leaving. We wouldn't be here if I'd gone straight home instead, would we?'

'Yes we would, Tom,' she replied quietly. 'It just brought it all to a head.' She heard a small noise come from him, a small sad noise of pain in his throat as if it was echoing the sound of his heart cracking. She lifted her head, opened her mouth to say his name, but the door was closing behind him. He was gone.

THE THIRD
TRIMESTER

The *Daily Trumpet* would like to offer its most sincerest apologies to Beautician Sarah Mills of Glam beauty salon in Dodley for an unfortunate mistake in last week's Saturday review of 'We Recommend'. The wording should have read that Sarah attributes her complexion to using *Oil of Olay* for over thirty years and not Oil of Ugly. Ms Mills would like to remind customers that this weekend all products in her salon are 2 for the price of 3.

Chapter 48

Annie was early when she called for Palma to take her to their tenth Christmas Pudding Club meeting. She knocked, but there was no response. She tried the door and it opened as far as the chain would allow it to.

'Palma? It's Annie.'

'Coming. Hang on. Not quite ready.'

Annie waited, expecting Palma to let her in but she didn't. A couple of minutes later she appeared with her bag, only opening the door wide enough to let her exit.

'Got a man in there?' Annie chuckled.

'It's a mess,' replied Palma, locking up.

Annie doubted that. Or at least she would have done once, but since she and Tommy had split up a couple of months ago, Palma wasn't the same girl. Though she smiled as usual on the outside, Annie knew she wasn't smiling on the inside. Little tell-tale signs gave the game away: she'd stopped going to the Aqua Mama classes, saying she didn't really like them; and her hair, that was always so perfectly ruffled, looked unbothered with. She walked, talked and acted like herself, but she wasn't herself. Almost as if a pod had grown in her bedroom and taken her over, as happened in *The Invasion of the Body Snatchers*.

Palma hadn't given them any more detail than she and Tommy had decided to call it a day and that was that. Annie had hoped that Palma might have confided in her but she hadn't. Even Iris had been upset for her.

'It can't be because it's someone else's baby, can it, because he was all right with that,' she'd asked Annie, when Palma was out of the way at her last ante-natal. 'Do you think it finally dawned on him that he couldn't handle it?'

Possibly, but Annie knew there had to be more to it. A man who went to the trouble of putting an iced bucket of pressé on Palma's doorstep wasn't someone who was flippant with his emotions, she was sure of it.

'That's a nice dress,' said Annie as Palma got into the car. It was a grey pinafore, fully let out at the sides, although it was very loose and her belly wasn't pushing at the material the way her own dresses had started to.

Annie was thirty-three weeks pregnant now and glad that the summer had segued into a much cooler autumn. Baby Pandoro was punching and kicking her from the inside so much that Joe had made a joke one day that she must be carrying a boxer inside her, then winced and wished he could have recalled his words back into his mouth. Palma hadn't reacted, but carried on hand-rolling the last of the special Christmas crackers order for a hotel in Sheffield. Annie hadn't told her that they would grace the dining tables of those who had purchased the VIP package for the fight card on which Tommy Tanner was the main event.

Di was gargantuan now. She had stretchmarks on her stretchmarks and they could all see them as she had switched from big dresses to crop tops and leggings. She'd also been to a professional photographer to have the 'Demi Moore' naked pregnancy shot done and she pulled out her phone to show them the four-foot-square canvas of it gracing her living room wall. The first ten minutes of their meetings had officially become *The Diane Ogden Love-Life Show*, in which she regaled them with the latest news. This week it was a shocker.

'I'm back with Lee, my husband,' she said, to a sea of open mouths. 'It's better for the kids. I've patched it up with my mum. She swears blind that they only did heavy petting and not shagging.'

'What about Daniel?' asked Cheryl with a touch of disappointment, equally felt by the others. They'd all liked the sound of him.

'He served his purpose,' sighed Di, inspecting her nails. 'It was nice whilst it lasted but I didn't really want the lads being brought up asking why their uncle was sharing Mummy's bed, or why their grandad was constantly trying to duff up their father, so we agreed to start again on a new footing. Blood is thicker than sperm, as they say.'

No one corrected her.

'I'm so glad that it worked out for you,' said Fil, which summed up the feelings of them all. From dreading Di trapping them in a corner to deliver her woes at first, they had started trapping her in corners to force her to spill the beans.

'Aye. Lee's got a smaller willy but he can keep it up for longer than Dan.'

No one could say that she spared them the detail.

'Looking swell, ladies,' said Chloe.

'Feeling fucked,' said Di.

'Well, that's how you all got here,' Sharon winked and made a clicky sound. 'As some of you might give birth early, we thought we'd have a general chat this week, talk through anything that's been bothering you. I know we said we would revisit that old chestnut, pain relief. Have any of you changed your minds over what you originally said you'd have?'

'I'm not having a water birth,' said Cheryl.

'And I now would like one,' said Fil.

'Are you sure, Fil?' Raychel turned fully to her. 'You aren't good in water. You're like a mermaid would be on land.'

'Water is definitely not your medium, Fil,' Cheryl agreed. 'Please rethink.'

'I'll settle for a tin opener,' said Di. 'Has anyone ever burst open because their skin's split? That's what I feel like is going to happen to me.'

'When you think you can't stretch anymore, trust me, you will,' said Sharon. 'The human body is an amazing thing.'

'What's going to happen to all the excess skin, is what I want to know,' said Di, rolling up her sleeves as if she were complaining at a customer service desk and holding Sharon directly responsible for the problem.

'All mine shrunk back the first time,' said Raychel, 'though I'm not sure the same thing is going to happen again.

That's the worst thing I found: the day after you give birth, your stomach is like a massive collapsed balloon. And you feel cold, as if you were carrying a radiator around with you and it's been whisked away.'

'I wish I'd stayed in my lesbian phase,' tutted Di. 'I could have been settled now with a pretty woman and a chocolate Labrador.'

Just when you thought there was nothing more to learn about Di, she came up trumps with yet another revelation.

'I'm worried about dying in childbirth,' said Cheryl. 'I have terrible dreams about it.'

'You'll be in the best possible hands,' said Sharon. 'All those hormones racing around your body make you anxious, so try and offset that with the breathing exercises we practised a few sessions ago. The calmer you are, the more you'll enjoy the birth experience. It's natural to be scared when you don't feel in control.'

Raychel didn't want to frighten the others by questioning that word 'enjoy'. But she'd enjoyed looking back on the memories of it, more than she had 'enjoyed' going through it at the time.

It was a good session, full of warm camaraderie, laughs and more of Di's disclosures. She'd had a threesome with two rugby players once, she told them and highly recommended it. Cheryl said she should write a book and Di had replied that she wouldn't want her sons knowing about all her exploits. She'd got all her wild ways out of her system and simply wanted to be a normal boring mam now.

'We thought next session might be a good time to bring your

other halves or your birthing partner,' said Chloe as the meeting came to a close. 'We will go over the breathing and teach them how to help you,' added Sharon. Eve wasn't alone in thinking that she could have sat there talking with the group for another half hour at least. She took a lot from the club, friendship and support and comfort. Dr Gilhooley had proved he was every bit as wise and intuitive as his father by setting it up.

'Have you thought about who you'll have as a birthing partner?' said Annie to Palma in the car.

'I'm going to ask Iris if she's free,' replied Palma.

She sounded so serious that Annie had to say, 'Really?'

Palma smiled. 'I don't need anyone, only the doctors and nurses,' she said. She wasn't being stoic, she really didn't want anyone but professionals to be there. Professionals who knew what they were doing.

Palma had a hot chocolate, watched half an hour of TV and then went to bed. She curled up into a ball and felt her baby moving around inside her. She'd decided to call her Gracie, after the most wonderful, loving woman she'd ever known. If there was a heaven, she would be looking down on her now and saying to her in a kind, but concerned voice, *'Oh, Palma Collins, what have I told you about letting people into your heart? Open the doors, love. Don't keep the sunshine outside.'* But she'd let Grace Beresford into her heart and she'd left her and it had broken her. *In the end, the only person you can really rely on is yourself,* so someone wise once said. Palma's comfort zone had room for just one person in it. That way she didn't get let down, but her baby would always be able to rely on her. She smoothed her hand over the compact

mound of her stomach. She spoke to Gracie all the time. She lay
in the dark and told her how much she loved her and would do
anything for her. What she couldn't imagine was Gracie being
born, leaving her ultimate protection, when she wouldn't be
able to keep her safe anymore.

She was in a deep sleep by ten and so she didn't hear the
quiet first knock on her door, or the insistent second one or
the steps walking away when it seemed as though there was
no one at home.

*

After the club meeting, Annie and Joe watched some TV
and halfway through a repeat of *Cracker*, she found herself
thinking about prawn crackers which revved up a compul-
sive craving for a Chinese meal. And when Annie craved
something at the moment, she *craved* it. Her cravings were
legendary and something they'd still laugh about in years
to come: toasted currant teacakes slathered in Nutella and
slices of banana, hard-boiled eggs dipped in Marmite, crispy
lettuce leaves soaked in vinegar – which did nothing for
her heartburn but she didn't care – and cauliflower mashed
up with double cream, Laughing Cow cheese triangles and
tuna. Up until her pregnancy, Annie had hated cauliflower.
It was on her list of 'vegetables to be outlawed', but for some
reason, she was eating her way through the cauliflowers of
the UK single-handed. Tonight her passion was for sweet and
sour pork balls with noodles and a side order of crispy won
tons. Her mouth was slavering at the prospect of her teeth
crunching into the fried pastry.

The best takeaway around by far was the Great Wall of China on the High Street in Dodley but they didn't deliver.

'Oh Joe, it doesn't matter,' said Annie, watching him slip off his dressing gown and put on his trousers.

'Of course it matters,' he said, pulling his black jumper on. 'My God, look at me. I am like a burglar. All I need is a baka ... balal ...'

'Balaclava,' laughed Annie. He never could say the word. That and 'certificate'.

'I'll be back in about half an hour,' he said, threading his feet into his trainers – also black.

*

Clint O'Gowan was full of cocaine and walking brazenly up Dodley High Street towards his car. *Fuck the Webbs*, he thought. They'd gone soft anyway. Fat from all their fancy meals. Who the fuck did they think they all were, telling him to stay away from Dodley *or else*. If they'd really meant business, they'd have come after him but they hadn't. Spineless bastards.

Palma was obviously at the boxer's house which was a nuisance. If she hadn't changed her phone number he wouldn't have had to come.

The High Street was empty apart from a man across the street getting into a black Audi. Nice. Dressed head to foot like a fucking ninja, a thought that made him snigger to himself. Out of the far corner of his eye, he saw the man cross the road to his side. Then he felt a hand on his shoulder, swinging him round.

'Oy. What the . . .'

He looked into ninja man's face and it took a long second for his brain to travel from faint to full recollection. His smile spread to its widest potential.

'Well well well. We meet again, Mr Pandoro.'

*

Joe returned over an hour after setting off. Annie had rung him once but he hadn't picked up.

'They'd given me the wrong order and I had to wait until they made the right one,' he explained.

'What have you done to your hand?' asked Annie. His knuckles were bleeding.

'I fell over the pavement,' he said. 'I hurt my knee as well.'

Annie laughed. 'I bet you were glad you volunteered to go and get me a Chinese.'

Surprisingly the contents of the containers needed heating up in the microwave. She didn't think anything more about it. Not until she heard the news about Clint O'Gowan.

Chapter 49

Gill popped up on FaceTime to see how everyone was doing. She couldn't believe how big Annie's bump had grown.

'Right little fatty now, aren't you?' she chuckled. 'How's your weather?'

'We're having a bit of a cold snap,' returned Iris.

'So are we,' said Gill. 'I've had to put a thin cardi on today. There was an actual cloud in the sky this morning. I'd forgotten what they looked like.'

'Really,' said Iris, trying not to sound too jealous. 'How's Penn and Teller?'

'Oh, we don't bother with them anymore. All they did was brag. Handmade bras and handmade shoes and Jag this, Porsche that.' She leaned in close so her face filled the screen and whispered, 'That sort are only bothered about being the top dogs. We've hooked up with the people across the complex – Dougie and Maureen – who are exactly like us except they're from Birmingham. They don't look down on you for owning a set of pans from Argos.'

Annie smiled. 'They sound more like your sort of people.'

'Oh, they are, Annie. And they've got a lovely pool. If the weather picks up, we might have a swim there later after our lunch but it's dropped to twenty-two degrees.' And she shuddered.

'I'm surprised it's not snowing, aren't you, Joe?' Iris turned to Joe who had deposited a coffee in front of her.

'What?'

'I'm saying . . . oh, it doesn't matter.'

'Where are you going for lunch then? McDonald's?' snipped Iris, turning back to the iPad screen.

As Iris and Gill continued to gossip, Annie quietly observed her husband. There was something troubling him and there had been for a few days now. She'd asked him and he'd replied that she was imagining things, but she wasn't. Him and Palma both. They smiled, they talked, they were sociable but occasionally the façade slipped and she could see the hint of something dark underneath that was eating at them.

*

That evening, Palma had just sat down to her tea when there was a timid knock at the door and her heart did not know whether to rise or sink. She looked through the window and the disappointment felt like a rock in her stomach. Nicole. She'd have to be hard now, no more pay-offs. No more Mr Nice Guy.

She threw open the door and Nicole lifted up her hands as if to ward off the unfriendly words she knew were about to come her way.

'I'm not here for any money, before you say. I thought you might want to know about Clint,' she said.

'Nicole, I really don't want to know anything—'

'He's dead, Palma.'

'What?'

'Can I come in?'

It was dark and raining and bitter. With an outward breath of annoyance, Palma moved aside. As Nicole stepped past her, Palma could smell her pronounced odour – fishy and sweaty as if she hadn't washed for a long time. She had a sudden flashback: she and Nicole shopping in Boots on a Saturday afternoon, testing out all the perfumes. Nicole always had some Impulse in her bag which she would spray into the air and then step into. She took pride in herself back then.

'You didn't know?' asked Nicole, sitting straight down on the sofa, after moving a carrier bag full of baby clothes onto the carpet. 'Nice and warm in here.' She was shivering. She had lost weight since Palma had last seen her, her legs were like sticks in her jeans.

'Can I get you a coffee or a cup of tea?' Palma asked, immediately cross with herself for being so damned polite.

'A tea would be good,' said Nicole. 'Four sugars and plenty of milk.'

The kettle had not long been boiled. She put a teabag in a cup whilst trying to keep a discreet eye on Nicole and her light fingers, but Nicole remained on the sofa with her hands pressed between her knees. When Palma delivered the mug to her hands she noticed how bitten down her nails were. Another memory: being in Nicole's bedroom with a big box of nail varnishes, nicked from various chemists and the market. Palma hadn't understood the exhilaration that Nicole found in shoplifting. She didn't want to be around her when she did stupid things like that. Those stolen nail varnishes had hammered the first nail into the coffin of their friendship.

'Been shopping?' said Nicole, looking around the room.

'Yeah,' but Palma wasn't interested in talking about that.

'Your dinner'll get cold,' said Nicole, nodding to the table.

'I'm not that hungry anyway. What happened?'

'They found his body in a wheelie bin up by the railway track. Awful, innit.'

An undignified end to suit his undignified life. She was more shocked than she thought she might have been. 'Where?'

'Here. Dodley. They found him last Thursday morning. Police had had a tip-off, apparently.'

'What was he doing over here? I thought he had to stay away from the Webbs?'

'That's Clint for you, in't it? Once he gets some snow inside him, he thinks he's fucking Iron Man.' Nicole slurped on her tea. 'Nice this, thanks.'

'You told him where I lived, didn't you? After swearing you wouldn't.'

Nicole shrugged. 'I didn't set out to but he found out I'd been here and . . . you know what he's like. Was like.'

She was lying and Palma had lost all patience with her.

'You talk a load of crap, Nicole. Is this another of your stories? Is he really dead?'

'He was over here to see you. He had someone who

wanted to ... do a sort of deal. I did tell him you wouldn't be interested,' Nicole added hurriedly.

'He'd already been round to say that,' said Palma. The night that Tommy had come round and found Clint in her house. *Come around here again and I'll kill you,* Tommy had said. Palma felt something dark and chilly pass like a cloud over her heart.

'He doesn't take no for an answer easily though.'

'He didn't come here again.'

'Well that's why he was in Dodley. I'm glad you said no. I heard what they wanted to buy it for.'

Her words conjured up something horrible in Palma's head and she tried to expel it before the picture took root. An impatient car horn bipped outside.

'I got a lift,' said Nicole. She stood up, opened the door, called outside to someone, 'Gimme five minutes.' Then she came back inside and said, 'Sorry, patience isn't his virtue.'

'Who did it, do they know?' asked Palma.

Nicole shrugged her shoulders but she was looking at Palma with non-blinking eyes.

'You don't think it was me?' Palma laughed, a dry humourless sound. 'What planet are you on?'

'I never said that. It was a single blow to the head, I heard.' She didn't miss a beat before adding. 'You still seeing that boxer?'

Palma swallowed, tried not to show that Tommy's possible involvement had even crossed her mind. 'You think that Tommy Tanner would risk everything he's worked towards for that piece of—'

Again Nicole started waving madly. 'I didn't mean him, but he's friendly with the Webbs, isn't he? I told Clint not to come here but he thought he was Teflon. "Fuck the Webbs," he said. I thought you might have heard something.' She tilted her head, looking at Palma as if she expected her to give something away in her expression, but there was nothing to give away.

'I'm not going out with him anymore. I haven't been for a couple of months.'

'Oh. I'm sorry to hear that.'

Again the car horn sounded.

'I better go before he wakes up all the neighbours,' said Nicole. 'I had to find out if you knew about Clint.'

'Are you still having his baby?'

Nicole's eyebrows gave the slightest quizzical dip before she answered. 'Oh, I lost it.' And Palma knew then that she had never been pregnant at all.

Nicole's eyes travelled over Palma's shopping-cluttered lounge. 'I hope everything goes all right with you and your baby,' she said. 'It'll not want for anything will it?' A small smile. Just a hint of the girl she'd been showing in the curve of her once-beautiful lips.

Palma stood there long after she had heard the exchange of voices outside, long after she heard the impatient wheels spin off, looking at the room through Nicole's eyes: the bags of clothes, the baby bath, the bouncy chair, the toys and books made out of material, the car seat. She didn't even have a car and she'd bought a car seat. Every single item bought with more love than money and with more hope than both of those put together.

Chapter 50

Relations had been strained between Cariad and Effin for a while but after the fire in the office, Effin took a long hard look at himself and didn't like what he found. He didn't want to worry his wife about his memory loss but he also realised that keeping it all in wasn't doing him any good either. Then he'd mended the snow machine and tested it and it was working fine, but the day after it wasn't again. The screw that he'd replaced was missing and it seemed to be indicative of a screw missing in himself too. That had finally pushed him to visit the doctor, expecting to be given some pills and sent on his way; which is what had happened the last time he'd seen the doctor about anything, too many years ago to count. But Effin was sent for a dementia test, which he passed with flying colours. And surprisingly his blood pressure was rock solid too. The doctor recommended he speak to a therapist – maybe there was an underlying reason why he felt he was – to quote himself – 'losing it'?

Speaking to a total stranger was something Effin would never have considered in a million years, but he needed to function competently, and something was obviously standing in the way of that. He had become a danger to other people and himself and so it was definitely time to drop the macho act and meet with someone, though he'd keep it under wraps and not tell anyone. So he'd booked a session with Dr Alex Cousins, a stress counsellor. He'd found his name on the internet when he typed in 'recommended therapists for memory loss near Penistone' in the search bar. He had his first session tomorrow and he was terrified at what they might uncover. Or not, because if there was no underlying psychological reason then it *had* to be a medical one.

Effin waited until the ice-cream parlour was empty of customers before going in with a box of chocolates.

'*Helo, Cariad, cariad. Shwd wyt ti?*' 'Hello, Cariad, love. How are you,' he asked, meekly, worried that she would tell him that she wasn't speaking to him. What business had he to try and run her life for her when he couldn't even run his own properly? But she didn't, because she was Cariad and she loved her uncle. Interfering old sod that he was, she knew that he only had her best interests at heart.

'Hello, Uncle Effin. Haven't seen you for a while.'

'No.' Never before had he been tongue-tied in front of family. He really wasn't himself. 'Er . . . how's the new flat?'

'It's lovely,' she said. 'Next time Auntie Angharad is up, you should bring her round. I'll make us tea.'

She waited for him to suggest inviting Dylan Evans as well, but he didn't. All he said was, 'Great.' Then, as if a hand from behind had pushed him forwards, he took a step towards her and held his hand out. 'I brought you some chocolates. Truffles from the place in Penistone that makes their own. I know you like them. Just a little box because I know they're fattening.' Adding quickly: 'Not that you're fat or I'm tight, mind.'

'Oh, that's very nice of you. Do you want to take a seat and have some ice-cream?'

'No, I can't. I'm going over to look at the grotto. There's been a leak and it's saturated all the wooden floorboards and made a big hole.'

'Oh, okay.'

'Can't have Santa falling down it and breaking his neck, can we?' He smiled, hesitantly for him.

'No, we can't.' Cariad smiled back at him.

'Anyway, nice to see you.' He turned to the door.

'Uncle Effin.' Cariad ran over to him, put her arms around his bulldog-like neck and planted a large kiss on his cheek. 'You can always count on me if there's anything on your mind, you know.'

'Nothing on my mind, love,' he said and exited the ice-cream parlour, thinking that these therapy sessions were going to be hell when he couldn't even open up a chink to his nearest and dearest.

Chapter 51

Palma had been in two minds whether to tell Annie and Joe about Clint. She didn't want to dredge up anything unpleasant for them, especially now they were going to have the child they thought they'd never have and life was good; but at the same time maybe it would be cathartic and they'd feel that the universe had punished him when they couldn't. Before she had worked out what to do for the best, fate delivered. The front page of Friday's *Chronicle* carried the story and the headline was suitably ignominious.

LOCAL MAN FOUND DEAD IN BIN

Palma always bought the *Chronicle* from the Co-op on Friday mornings before Joe and Annie picked her up. She didn't say anything until they had reached The Crackers Yard because she didn't want Joe to crash the car with shock. She pretended it was the first she had heard of it when she unfolded the paper whilst Joe was making the drinks.

'Clint O'Gowan's dead,' she said. 'It's the lead story.' She handed it over and Annie took it from her slowly, disbelief registering on her features. Annie read silently but her mouth moved over the words.

'He died in Dodley?' she asked, shifting her gaze to Palma and there was a question in her eyes.

'It's nothing to do with me, in case you're wondering,' replied Palma quietly. Annie had told her to keep it between themselves that she had a past association with Clint. Joe carried a raw spot for him that would never heal.

'Palma, I didn't mean that,' Annie hastily assured her.

'I'm just saying it though.'

Annie carried on reading.

'Convicted drug dealer Clint O'Gowan, of White Street, Ketherwood was found ... cause of death was a blow to the head ... bundled into a wheelie bin ... dumped in a field at the side of the railway line ... missing since the previous night ... People appealing for witnesses ...' She took the newspaper through into the kitchen and passed it to her husband.

'Joe, look. He's dead. Clint O'Gowan.'

Annie noticed how hard he gripped the newspaper to read it, then she took in the dark scabbing on his right hand which suddenly acquired a terrible relevance. Her brain started spinning. Had O'Gowan died the same night that Joe was in Dodley picking up her takeaway? The night he took over an hour to come back. The night he'd returned with a lukewarm meal and bleeding knuckles.

'Good,' said Joe, tossing the paper on the work surface. 'I'm glad he's dead,' and he returned his attention to the kettle.

*

Palma had a hospital appointment that afternoon to check on her anaemia, and Annie was glad she was out of the way because she needed to talk to Joe in private. She knew that whatever was troubling him was big and sensed he was trying to protect her in some way, and it frightened her why that might be. As soon as Palma had left, she walked into the office and found Joe sitting with his head in his hands.

'Joe, what's wrong? It's something to do with Clint O'Gowan, isn't it?' she said. 'I knew it as soon as I saw your face when you read the paper.' She reached for his arm and he moved it away before her hand made contact. 'You have to tell me, love.' Urgency in her voice now; she felt a shudder of pain through her soul.

He lifted his head and she saw the despair etched on his face, 'I as good as killed him, Annie,' he said.

*

Effin was having his first therapy session with Alex Cousins, who he presumed would be a man but she wasn't. She was a very nice woman, it had to be said, with a welcoming smile and a beautiful calming voice, but he'd have felt more comfortable talking man to man.

When they were halfway through their session, Alex thought a change of position might help, because Effin had erected more barriers than there were on the Thames. Effin needed to relax before he could let her into his head and, she suggested, the best way to do that might be for him to lie on her very comfortable couch whilst she conversed with him from outside his line of sight. With his eyes closed, and her soothing tones now coming from somewhere behind him, Effin immediately felt as if his shredded nerves had climbed down off a ledge and could take a break.

Effin didn't realise he had given away as much as he had, chatting with Alex Cousins, but after only the first session she had it figured out that whatever was happening in his present life had deep roots in his past. She didn't enlighten him on this for now but made notes that for the next session, they needed to go back in time, maybe to things he didn't know he was carrying as baggage. Because somewhere in the junk file of his head lay the answer to why Effin's mental state was in such turmoil.

*

Annie had never seen Joe look so crushed before. Not even when he stood shamed in court, not even when Annie was inconsolable after the adoption process was terminated with such sudden ferocity. But here he was sitting at a desk littered with cheerful novelties and he was sobbing.

'What did you do, Joe? Did you ... was it you ...?' She couldn't get the words out. *Joe, her Joe?* It wasn't real. Clint O'Gowan was dead and still he was casting his stinking shadow over their lives.

'That night when I went for the Chinese. I had just come out with the order and I saw him, across the road at the side of the pub there, walking up the High Street. I knew it was him straightaway because he has been in my head for years, but he didn't see me until I was at his side. And then he turned to me and he recognised me and he smiled and he said, "We meet again, Mr Pandoro".'

Annie couldn't feel a beat in her heart.

'Did you hit him, Joe? I understand why, if you did.'

'I wanted to . . . but . . . no, I didn't,' said Joe and Annie's heart kicked hard, as if his denial had restarted it. But now she was confused.

'It happened so quickly . . . I saw his face change. He was looking over my shoulder and then he started running and I was knocked off my feet . . . two men came from nowhere, out of the pub, I think, shouting at him . . . shouting his name. They disappeared up an alley that goes to a field and I . . . I . . . I don't know what made me do it, Annie, but I followed them. I saw one of the men shaking his hand as if he had just hit something and he was laughing and he said to the other, "Well that was easy." That's when I noticed *him* lying on the grass, face down and I knew . . .' Joe took a deep breath '. . . I knew he was very hurt. And I was glad. And I went back to the car and I started to drive home but . . .' Joe sighed, buried his head in his hands again, jabbered a mouthful of heartfelt Italian. '. . . I had to ring someone, I couldn't . . . not do it. I took out my mobile but . . . God forgive me, I was afraid I'd be traced. They'd find out our history, we'd be dragged into it all again. So I drove to the call box in Hodroyd. I rang the police and an ambulance from there and then I hit a wall with my fist because I felt ashamed that I might have had a part in something that I had imagined so many times in my head. I shouldn't have driven off, I should have rung straightaway. Because I didn't, they couldn't find him. Because of me, these men had the chance to hide him . . . move him like rubbish into a bin ... a bin! Oh God. I might have saved his life had I ... had I not ...'

'Oh, Joe,' Annie threw her arms around him. He was shivering, her dear kind Joe. 'This wasn't your fault. You should have told me all this when it happened.'

Joe was distraught, inconsolable. For years Clint O'Gowan had been dangling on the edge of Annie's consciousness: turning up in the newspaper with a mention, bringing him back to the forefront of her mind when he'd sunk to the back; through his association with Palma, or a chance sighting and now this. She wasn't going to let him ruin another moment of their lives. She wasn't going to let him bind his rancid self to her husband through guilt.

'Joe Pandoro, Clint O'Gowan is dead and it was nothing to do with you. Let him go, love. In nine weeks max we will have our baby, he didn't stop us having one. He was a hurdle in our lives and we cleared him. Because of you, *you*' – she forced him to look at her – 'his family will at least be able to bury him. Think of that. You did more for him than he deserved. Your conscience is clear. You're a good man, Joe.'

'I was going to hit him. I don't know what I would have done if I hadn't been pushed out of the way.'

'Yes you do, because you could have punched him, but you didn't, you held back. *What ifs* can drive you mad, Joe. What *did* happen is that someone else killed him, not you. Don't let him spoil anything for us anymore. He is gone and we are here. Think of us and the future, not him and the past.' She lifted his hand and placed it on her stomach and said again, with gentle firmness. 'Let him go, Joe. Let him go.'

Chapter 52

Palma was thirty weeks pregnant now. She had her bag packed at the side of the door in case the baby came early: big T-shirt nighties, big pants, big bar of fruit and nut, nursing bra, nappies, cotton wool balls and nappy bags, a magazine to read. She had everything she and her baby could possibly need in the house, not only for those early days, but beyond. She had built up the cot and fastened the mobile of pastel-coloured farm animals above it. Sometimes she wound it up and let the tinkly lullaby play and she imagined her tiny daughter smelling of Johnson's baby powder snuggled up in her pink 'Gracie' blanket closing her eyes and falling to sleep.

She could hold everything together away from the hospital, keep all her worries and fears packed away in the maternity bag in her head. All her life she'd been able to put on a front, pretend that her life wasn't crumbling behind a brave façade. She'd gone to school like normal kids, doing her adding and subtracting and no one ever knew that every day, she was terrified she'd arrive home and find her mother with her head smashed against the stone hearth or in a crumpled heap at the

bottom of the stairs. She'd washed and ironed her school uniform, pretended to herself that her mother had waved her off
looking pristine, when in reality she hadn't seen her for days.
She'd pretended to everyone that being in care was no big deal,
when she was dying inside with shame. Then Grace Beresford
had come along. She'd never had to pretend anything with her.
But Grace was gone and she was on her own again, pretending
that everything was fine in Palma's world.

She finished reading the *Chronicle* on the bus home from
the hospital. On the back page there was a full report on
Tommy Tanner and how his training regime had cranked
up considerably now there were only seven weeks until the
defence of his title: hard runs every day – sometimes three
miles, sometimes ten – eight to ten rounds of sparring every
night with tough southpaws to prep him for fighting with
Frank Harsh, the contender for his title. And then ... words
that were magical to her: *On Monday, Tommy returned from a
week-long intensive training camp in Poland.* He hadn't been in
the country when Clint had met his end. She felt a bomb of
relief detonate inside her, but it was too dark a place there
for its flash to last long and it was snuffed out two lines down
by a quote from Tommy: 'I have nothing in my mind but
what is happening on 23 December. The only face I have in
my head is Frank Harsh's. There is no room for anything or
anyone else.' He had said the words to the newspaper but she
knew they had been meant for her.

The *Daily Trumpet* would like to apologise to Mr Gilbert Philips for an article that appeared in the Gardening Special supplement last weekend for unfortunate wording under the photograph where he was won best in show for his giant peonies. He did not win best in show for his giant penis as the article stated. We apologise for any embarrassment sustained by Mr Gilbert.

Chapter 53

Effin worked late on the Sunday, mending the hole in the grotto floor, though he had absolutely no idea how a trickle of water could have rotted the wood as badly as it had. Come next weekend, Winterworld would be open seven days a week in the run-up to Christmas. They were already in the first week of November and he had no idea where the year had gone to, but he wished it would hurry up and bugger off because it had been awful. Next year would be better. Angharad had persuaded him to take a cruise – three whole weeks. Seven nights sailing across the Atlantic where he would be forced to rest, seven nights sunning himself in the Bahamas and then seven nights home again. He didn't know how to relax without doing anything; but he'd have to learn. His elder son was getting married and Angharad was on a diet so she could compete in the fashion stakes with the mother of the bride. She'd lost four stone so far and was looking less like a middle-aged woman – whom it had to be said he loved dearly – and more like the foxy young thing he had married. But whatever was wrong with his mind had spread to other regions and his trouser soldier wouldn't stand up on duty. He was far too young for that to happen and he knew that Angharad, who had always been so wonderfully demanding where sex was concerned, was looking forward to making that cruise ship rock.

He'd checked the wages seven times now to make sure they were right and not cocked up like they were again last week. He couldn't understand how he could have got it so wrong: Thomas, who'd only worked one day had walked away with more than Arfon and Mik combined, who had worked their bollocks off. This time, he'd taken no chances and saved the calculations to a memory stick, after being shown how to do it by the Missus, and mailed them to himself as a backup. But it was all so time-consuming and brain-knackering.

After he had finished for the evening, he locked up the office, pulled his car keys out of his pocket and set off walking out of the side gates when he heard a noise to his left. Just a small one but he'd always had the ears of a bat. It was a noise with an echo attached, as if it had been made in a cave and so there was only one place around here that it could have come from. He turned towards the source of it, Santa's Grotto, where he had spent more time than he'd wanted to today, repairing the dratted hole that had so mysteriously appeared. He'd mended it, checked it was mended and then mended it a bit more, to be absolutely sure. A herd of morbidly obese elephants could tap dance on it now.

'Hello,' he called. He was answered only by silence.

'That you, MacDuff? I'm watching you watching me, you bloody haggis, just so that you know.'

Still nothing.

A nice cup of tea, a pasty and beans then a bubble bath and a chat with Angharad before bedtime would sort him out, he decided. His bloody brain was playing tricks with him. Now he had thwarted his forgetfulness with OCD checking, it was trying to introduce ghosts and ghoulies into the equation. Well, he wasn't going to let it. Besides, ghosts couldn't undo holes, so he was safe to go home and forget about things. So he reckoned.

Chapter 54

It felt like a new week in every sense of the word to Annie. She had a lightness in her that hadn't been there for a long time, years maybe. As if a splinter, which had wormed its way under her skin and defied reaching, had unexpectedly drifted into a position where she could pull it out. It could have been hormones of course, the same ones which had given her the energy to clean the house from top to bottom at the weekend, including changing all the curtains. Joe would have been furious if he'd seen her, but he'd gone off to do the big shop. Annie felt invincible, euphoric. She'd read about the nesting phase in her Miriam Stoppard book but she hadn't expected it to grip her with such fervour. She wished she could bottle it and sell it.

Joe was still wracked with guilt; he had considered driving to the police station to tell them what he knew.

'Which is what exactly?' asked Annie. 'You saw two men who you can't describe chase O'Gowan up to a field. If the police had any CCTV footage they'd have checked it and know that already. You owed him nothing and still you gave him more than I would have done. There's no debt to pay, Joe.'

He was a good, decent man who knew right from wrong and they'd bring their child up to know it too. They could guide and teach and give him or her the smoothest runway possible and hope that when they lifted their wings, they would follow the best flightpath and head for the sun. She was more than ready for motherhood to properly begin. She felt like Boudicca as she squeezed herself into the car to drive to work.

*

Palma took a deep breath and rang Annie's mobile. She didn't need to fake an 'ill voice' because she genuinely had one. Her throat was hoarse from throwing up, her eyes raw from crying.

'Get back to bed,' Annie had told her. 'We're ahead of schedule, plus Iris and Astrid are both here so now they can spread themselves out at the table if you're not coming in.'

Palma knew she was trying to make her feel better and she was grateful for her consideration, but it would take more than that to lift her. She couldn't sleep for her dread of the day when she would have to give birth; she was terrified of it. And it was getting harder and harder to hide the fear.

*

Effin was handing out the work sheets for that morning. For Arfon and Mik and their crew it was checking all the electrics. For Ifor and Stanislaw and their crew, carrying on with the snagging list; Barry and Karol, the security cameras needed looking at because they weren't working – and for MacDuff and young Dylan, a spot of pointing. He knew that young Dylan was as happy with that job as MacDuff hated it. Effin's morning started off well, seeing Davy MacDuff's disgruntled expression.

Effin found the Missus and Santa talking outside the offices. Eve was looking beautiful, Effin thought, with her stomach protruding. She reminded him of how Angharad had been at the last stage of both of her pregnancies: dark hair glossy, skin dewy and stomach the size of a beach ball.

'Morning, Effin,' she called.

'Morning, Missus. How are you? You're looking fabulous.'

'I'm heavy, that's what I am,' chuckled Eve. 'I'm not sure I can get any bigger.'

'My Angharad said that. I thought at one point she was going to pop like a spot, but she kept on growing.' He didn't add that she had kept on growing after she'd given birth, too. She'd only recently started to lose her baby weight and their youngest was twenty-five.

'We're heading over to the grotto,' Eve said. 'The hole's fixed, isn't it?'

'All good and mended.'

'I had an idea what we can use that space at the side of Santa's throne for. And, whilst you're here, where do you think would be a good place for us to put a crèche in the park?'

Being pregnant had opened up whole creative portals in her head. Her body might be tired but her head was buzzing.

'A crèche? For babies?' asked Effin.

'Er ... yes,' replied Eve, wondering what else they could put in a crèche.

'My Angharad says there should be a crèche for husbands in supermarkets.'

'And she's right. You lot get in the way.'

'Until you want something reached from the top shelf,' Effin threw back.

'Ha, you'd be no good, would you? Some of my elves are taller than you, Effin.' Nick laughed, a proper deep Santa guffaw and Effin's laughter joined it. He felt good today, in control.

'Behind the grotto would be ideal. We'd need to clear some trees for it.'

'Next phase, next year,' said Eve. 'No rush. Come on then, Nick. Let's see if my toy machine idea is feasible.'

Effin went into his office and put on the kettle and whilst it was boiling he checked in his top drawer to make sure that he hadn't bought himself any more cigarettes and matches that he couldn't remember. Thankfully only paperclips, rubbers and other stationery items were present.

'Your Aunt Evelyn would have loved all this,' said Nick. 'She handed the reins over to the right people. And I'm so proud that I'll be conducting—' He slapped his hand over his mouth. 'Whoops.'

Eve grinned. She knew that there was a wonderful conspiracy of silence going on behind the scenes about the wedding. She didn't feel guilty about leaving it all to Jacques because whatever he would arrange would be wonderfully mad and if she interfered, she might bring some sanity to the proceedings and she didn't want sanity this time around. She didn't want sensible, she wanted full-on bonkers. And there was no man who could do bonkers better than her husband.

'It's okay, Nick. I kind of figured you'd be officiating anyway. In full-on Santa gear, I do hope,' Eve said, lifting crossed fingers so he could see them.

'I couldn't possibly say,' said Nick with an involuntary wink that gave the game away.

They entered the grotto and switched on the light but it wasn't working.

'Better tell Effin to add that to the snagging list,' said Nick.

'What a nuisance.' Eve pulled her phone out of her pocket and switched on the torch, shining it in front of her as they walked. 'Anyway, we're here now so I might as well show you what I mean. Look . . .' But she didn't finish her sentence because she fell, a second before Nick did, through the patched-up hole in the floor that Effin had mended only the previous day.

Chapter 55

Jacques sat beside Eve's hospital bed, holding her hand. He had so many emotions blasting through his brain he didn't know where to start untangling them. Concern being the dominant one, closely followed by anger. Eve hadn't broken her leg, but she'd sprained her ankle and ripped a massive gash in her thigh. She'd also hurt her arm, breaking the fall of poor Nick, whose full weight had crashed down on Eve. He'd been shaken badly and was beside himself with guilt that he had let Eve lead the way with her torch when sense should have told him to insist they wait until after the lights had been looked at.

'I'm going to have to tell Effin to leave,' said Jacques.

'You can't do that to him.'

'For his own safety,' said Jacques, with a growl in his voice, 'because if I see him again soon, I'm likely to throttle him. He told you that the floor had been mended, didn't he? And he told me too. In fact, he stood in my office this morning and was rabbiting on about tap-dancing elephants being able to stand on it safely.' He slapped his forehead. 'I'm as much to blame. I should have checked it. Why didn't I? After all that's happened?'

Eve didn't know what to think, except that as much sympathy as she had for Effin, this was the third serious mistake and it couldn't be ignored. She hadn't even told Jacques about him losing all the wages on his computer twice now, and how she'd had to ask Arfon to sort out the snow machine that Effin was supposed to have fixed.

Jacques was angry enough at the moment to tell anyone who had any connection with Effin to get out of his sight. She knew he would calm down but he was right, they'd have to insist that Effin took sick leave and found out what was wrong with him.

Luckily for Effin's neck the baby was fine. All the monitors connected to Eve were bleeping in the proper places, the Doppler machine reported that the baby's heart was pumping ten to the dozen and the consultant was happy to let her go home that afternoon with a bandaged foot encased in a very unglamorous giant sandal; but, he'd said, to be on the safe side, he wanted her to have an ultrasound.

A porter wheeled her down to the department half an hour after she'd drunk two large glasses of water, Jacques at her side carrying the crutches that would be her friend for the following couple of weeks at least. Eve felt ridiculous and indulgent being transported in a chair. Bathtime was going to be fun, she thought.

Jacques picked up a magazine and offered it to Eve, but she refused it. She preferred to people-watch. A woman approached the reception desk asking, in a none too happy

tone, when her scan was going to happen because she was
bursting for the toilet and couldn't hold out much longer.
A doctor presumably, judging by the stethoscope around
her neck, walked briskly past talking medical lingo into a
mobile. An older woman was trying to control a toddler
bouncing around. 'Tierlon, come 'ere and behave.' *Where
the hell did that name come from?* mused Eve. She wondered
if he'd grow up to like his name or change it to something
ordinary like Duncan, as Zowie Bowie had done. Then the
door to one side of her opened and a male doctor came out
and behind him a young pregnant woman with ash-grey hair
and a complexion to match. It was Palma from the Christmas
Pudding Club. Eve opened her mouth to call, but something
stopped her. Palma's head was bent; the doctor had his hand
gently on her back and was speaking softly to her now,
whilst Palma was flicking tears from cheeks that looked red
and salt-burned. Then they turned down the corridor and
disappeared from sight.

Chapter 56

Jacques was ridiculously excited about going to his first Christmas Pudding Club meeting.

'I don't know what you expect to be there other than adults, yoga mats, tea and biscuits,' said Eve, reaching for her crutch.

'It makes the baby so real,' said Jacques, clapping his hands and jumping up and down.

'Isn't this real enough for you?' said Eve, pointing at her massive baby bump.

'I mean hearing how to prepare for the big day, knowing what to do to help you,' said Jacques, lifting up Eve's handbag.

Eve wondered if Palma would be there. She didn't have a partner so maybe not. If Annie and Joe were there though, she'd ask if everything was okay. It hadn't looked good news from what she'd witnessed.

They were the last to arrive. Palma wasn't there but all the others had their partners with them. Eve was surprised to see the love god that was Di's husband. She'd imagined someone in the mould of Ben Affleck, based on how Di had described him. She wished she had the same glasses that Di owned because all she could see was Stan Laurel's lankier brother. But they were holding hands as they sat in the circle and Di looked radiant and smiley, so did it really matter that her descriptive powers were slightly askew.

'Getting near now, ladies and gents,' said Sharon. 'Anyone getting tightenings around their fundus?'

Jacques stuck up his hand and everyone laughed.

'Braxton Hicks. Your stomach will feel rock hard but it's not uncomfortable, just odd. It's your body gearing up for the birth.'

'How will we know the difference between these Braxton Hicks and the real thing?' asked Cheryl.

'Trust me, you'll know,' said Raychel at her side.

'Your Braxton Hicks contractions may start to get stronger now and so it's a good time to practise your breathing. And I'm delighted you've all brought your partners along today. So can you move your chairs so you're all facing your loved one.'

'Or your husband,' said Di, then she nudged him and added, 'Only joking, darling.'

'I'll never remember all this,' said Joe.

'There's always a fact sheet,' said Annie.

'Breathe out and as you do so, imagine your breath as a thin thread leaving your mouth,' guided Sharon. 'Visualisation helps you to focus and move your mind away from the pain.'

'Did you do this last time?' Ben asked Raychel.

'No, I fast-tracked to Pethidine,' she replied.

'Now imagine a contraction coming, take a deep breath

to prepare yourself for it and then pretend you are trying to blow out your birthday candles on a cake,' said Sharon. 'Imagine every time a flame goes out, it takes your pain with it.'

'My pain will be nothing to the pain you'll be in if you get caught in another snowstorm,' Raychel warned her husband Ben, before taking in that deep breath.

'You're breathing in through your mouth and blowing out through your nose, Di,' said her husband Lee. 'You sound like a horse.'

Fil's husband Henry was taking it all so seriously it was giving her the giggles and she ended up doing more snorting than breathing.

'Let's try some panting,' said Chloe.

'I do a lot of panting,' said Di, with a cheeky grin. 'I should be good at this.'

At the end of the session, Di made an announcement. 'It's my thirty-fifth birthday on Saturday. Anyone fancy having an afternoon tea with me because I'm not sure that I'll be back here again. My belly button is sticking out. They think I might be a bit further on than they first thought. Four o'clock, Sunflower Café, Pogley Top. Don't bring a present, just bring yourselves.'

'That sounds nice,' said Eve. 'I'd like that.'

'That'll be lovely,' said Cheryl. 'I know it well.' Oh, she had some happy memories attached to that place.

'Right, see you all Sat'day then,' and off Di waddled towards her man.

'And what happened to you?' asked Annie, nodding towards Eve's bandaged foot.

'I fell down a hole in Santa's grotto on Monday,' she replied. 'And Santa fell on top of me.'

'Avoiding all the jokes I could make, I presume you're all right?'

'Sprained ankle, cut leg, bruised arm, that's all; Santa is totally okay but then he had a soft landing. I went to hospital straightaway obviously, but the baby's fine.' She paused, hoping she wasn't about to break any confidence. 'I had an ultrasound and I saw Palma there.'

'Really?' replied Annie. 'That's worrying. She's been off all week. She felt sick so I told her to rest up.'

'I didn't try and get her attention because she looked very upset.'

'I rang her yesterday to see how she was and she didn't mention anything. You're sure it was Palma?' Annie asked, but she knew that Eve wouldn't have mistaken her.

'It was definitely her, Annie, and I'm not just saying this, she was with a doctor and she was crying.'

Annie nodded. 'Thank you for telling me. I'll call round and see her on the way home.'

'For obvious reasons I won't be at Aqua Mama tomorrow,' Eve said with a smile. 'So see you on Saturday for afternoon tea?'

'See you then,' said Annie.

'Give my love to Palma. I hope she's okay. And if she isn't, let me know if I can do anything.'

*

Effin wasn't up for any visitors. Not even Cariad would
have got past his threshold at the moment. He had booked
a crisis appointment with Alex Cousins for first thing in the
morning and he just wanted to go to bed and kill time until
then, which really hit home as an indication of how low he
was. So when he heard the knock at the door, he wasn't in
the best of moods and went to tell whoever it was to bugger
off. Then he opened it and standing on his doorstep was
MacDuff, of all people. What did that stupid haggis want?
He asked him, in Welsh, forced out a smile, made it look as
if he was saying a polite hello.

'*Be ti ishe, yr hagis hurt?*'

Davy gave a small laugh, shook his head in a 'give me a
break' way and answered him. '*Daeth yr hagis hurt yma i dy
helpu di, ond gei di fynd i grafu nawr!*'

Effin looked suitably gobsmacked. Not only had MacDuff
understood him but had replied in fluent Welsh. He'd said
that 'the stupid haggis came here to help you, but you can
get stuffed now.'

'Eh?'

Davy answered his shocked expression.

'My mother and my granny, who lived with us, were
Welsh speakers. I was raised tri-lingual: Glaswegian, English
and Welsh – listed in order of importance.'

Effin tried not to wince. He couldn't count the number of
Welsh insults he'd flung at MacDuff in front of his face and
the haggis had understood every one. Duplicitous bastard.

'Come to gloat, have you?' said Effin, defensive walls up.

'Not at all, quite the opposite. I came to ask you a question.'

'No, you can't run my teams, is the answer,' said Effin, anticipating the only question he thought MacDuff might pose. 'There's loads of people I'd ask before you and that includes the fucking owls.'

Davy ignored the insult. 'My question is, do you have any enemies working at Winterworld?'

'What?'

With more patience than he felt, Davy repeated the question. 'Do you have any enemies working at Winterworld?'

'You're all my enemies,' snarled Effin. 'All of you wanting to take my money for doing bugger all work.'

'Drop the façade, Effin, for fuck's sake. I've been watching you.'

Effin smiled nastily, opened his mouth to spit some choice Welsh at him and then stopped himself because it would be no fun now, knowing that MacDuff was in on the game. Instead he delivered it in English. 'I knew it. I knew you'd been watching me. I could feel your beady haggis eyes on me.'

'And you should be glad I was, because I checked the snow machines after you'd mended them and they were working fine.'

Effin's hands came to his substantial waist. 'Oh you did, did you? How very thoughtful of you to check to make sure I'd done them corr—'

'Oh shut up, Effin and listen. I checked them straight after you did them,' said Davy again, 'but when Arfon tried them, they were strangely broken again. There seemed to be quite a few things you'd worked on that suddenly stopped functioning soon after. It flagged up to me, so I thought I'd ... trail you for a wee while.'

Effin's face was starting to glow. The cheek of the man. That he could … Then he realised what Davy was saying to him. As comprehension dawned, his mouth opened and closed wordlessly like a confused fish.

'If I'd known you were going to mend the grotto floor, I'd have checked that as well but I didn't know until it was too late.'

Effin remembered something then, and he looked accusingly at Davy.

'Was it you up in Winterworld, loitering about when I left on Sunday night?'

'Nope. I was tucked up in bed with a wee lassie,' and he winked.

'Cariad?' Effin's eyes widened so much they almost popped out of his head.

Davy gave him a mischievous lop-sided grin. 'I wish. My landlady's white cat. I'm in charge whilst she's sunning herself in Lanzarote, so you can hold your fire. I, like you, only have Cariad's best interests at heart. It's quite possible for a man and a woman to be friends, Effin. But you need to take a look at *your* friends, pal, because one of them has it in for you. And it's not me. So I'll park that with you and be on my way.'

And with that, Davy turned from him and walked to his car, leaving Effin dazed by his benevolence. Or was it merely a ruse by the haggis to screw with him? He didn't know – his brain was fried.

*

After the Pudding Club meeting, Annie dropped Joe off at home before going over to Dodley Bottom by herself. She knocked on Palma's door, prepared a smile in readiness. Palma opened it a slit, half the length of the chain, and said a cheery, 'Hello, Annie.'

'I brought you a fact sheet,' Annie said, holding it aloft. 'You missed a very funny session and probably Di's last appearance there. She's invited us all for afternoon tea for her birthday on Saturday.'

'Thanks.' Palma's hand came out through the gap to take the sheet. Annie wanted that door open so she kept it out of her reach.

'Aren't you going to let me in?' she asked.

'The house is a bit of a mess, Annie.'

'Let me in, Palma,' Annie said, gently but firmly.

Palma slid the chain across and opened the door fully. She looked terrible. Pale and poorly and her eyes were puffy and sad.

'Sorry, I haven't tidied up,' she said, apologising, moving bags off the sofa to allow Annie to sit down.

Annie couldn't believe what she was seeing. Baby things were everywhere; on the dining table, under the dining table, against the sofa, piled up in the corner. A toddler buggy, a beautiful pink Moses basket and a Tell-the-Time child's clock in a box. She noticed the baby jigsaw and the plush octopus with every foot a different colour and texture.

'Can I get you a drink of something?' Palma asked as Annie sat down in the armchair.

'A glass of juice, anything you have.' Palma went into the

kitchen and Annie looked around. Something was not right here at all. The lounge was chaos, the room equivalent of Dorian Gray's portrait, offsetting something, but she didn't know what.

'I never had the chance to ask you about Joe and what he said about Clint O'Gowan,' said Palma, as she poured out a glass of orange squash. Her voice had a forced normality.

'He said it made him feel guilty for wanting him gone,' said Annie, but her mind was on her immediate surroundings and not on O'Gowan. There was nothing normal about this situation. There were bags of baby clothes at her feet, all with the labels still attached.

'I heard ... heard that he'd got on the wrong side of a family who live in Maltstone. Real hard-nuts. He handed himself to them on a plate, coming to this end of town.'

'Where did you hear that?' asked Annie, wanting to believe it was true.

'Someone who'd know told me. Someone from Ketherwood that I ... I bumped into. Sorry, I haven't been shopping, I've only got orange.'

'Thank you,' said Annie, taking the glass from her, noticing her bitten nails. She must be feeling so very alone now that they were so near to their birth dates, Annie thought. Maybe all this stuff was nest-building, a protective wall around her and her baby, over-compensating for not being able to supply the baby with a second parent.

'Do you want to tell me about Tommy, Palma?' Annie asked softly, seeing how her hands formed a nervous knot as she sat down on the sofa.

'There's nothing to tell, Annie,' said Palma.

'I think there is, Palma. Why did you really split up?'

'He needs to concentrate on his boxing,' said Palma, her voice level as if delivering a rehearsed answer. 'I didn't want to get in the way. It wouldn't have been right. I've got nothing to offer him.'

'You had yourself, Palma, and the baby. That's what he wanted.'

Palma's face creased. Whatever scaffolding was propping up her composure was failing under the strain.

'I can't give him the baby that's inside me, Annie. I can't keep her.'

Annie moved across to the sofa to be next to Palma.

'Oh love, you can, Palma. Joe and I will see to it that you get as much help as you need. You'll make a great mum, don't doubt yourself . . .'

'I don't mean that, Annie. I have to let her go, I have no choice.'

Chapter 57

Palma had known from the moment that Lesley the sonographer smiled at her that something was wrong because it was a smile that was frayed at the edges and there had been no eye contact.

'I need you to stay put for a couple of minutes so I can check on something,' she'd said. Palma had lain on the couch, a heartbeat pounding in her brain. 'Please God, make everything be all right,' she had chanted like a mantra, over and over until Lesley came back with a man, shirt sleeves rolled up, Asian, black hair shot through with white at the front like a Mallen streak. He exuded experience and the pair of them talked quietly whilst looking at the screen, the words a blur apart from the odd one that stood out from the others. Hard medical words. Bilateral. Renal. Agenesis.

The Asian doctor had a soft voice; he'd introduced himself as Dr Jindal. He turned the screen, explained what was there. No amniotic fluid around the baby. Absence of kidneys, no bladder. He wanted Palma to see this for herself first. Then he asked her to follow him out of the scan room. She passed a woman waiting to go in and see her own baby on the screen, cushioned in fluid, floating around in it and protected by it. A cushion her baby didn't have.

It was rare, Dr Jindal said, once they were in his consulting room. It was nothing she had done, it happened sometimes. It couldn't be picked up in the first scan.

Her body was the only thing keeping the baby alive; once she was born, she would die. Palma had two major options: to abort or to carry on with the pregnancy and give birth. There was a sensitive third option: if the baby was born at 5lb 5oz, Palma could consider donating her tissue, heart valves, pancreas. It was something to think about, Dr Jindal said. It wasn't an easy decision but it might help her to think that her daughter could help other babies to live.

'I don't want other babies to use my baby,' she'd screamed at him, tears rolling down her face and Dr Jindal hadn't shouted back at her. He'd handed her a tissue and said he understood, but to take time to think all the same.

He wanted her to come back tomorrow and discuss the options, have another scan. Did she have someone she could bring with her? She'd said no, she was alone.

She'd tried to look the condition up on the internet but she couldn't stand to see the images and the words gave her no hope . . . She didn't sleep. She tried to hold it together as she walked into the hospital the next day, sat in a sea of heavily pregnant women in the waiting room like a damaged boat about to sink.

An MRI scan had only confirmed that the baby could not survive outside the womb.

There was no question of aborting the baby, she said. She could feel Gracie moving inside her, snuggling to get comfortable underneath her skin. She watched her stomach change shape when she lay in the bath. Babies responded to light, her book said, and when she shone the torch of her phone down onto her, it was as if Gracie turned to face it. She told Dr Jindal that she would have the baby. There was always the chance that they'd made a mistake, wasn't there? That when she was born, they could check properly? Dr Jindal had told her that, unfortunately, there was no mistake.

Chapter 58

'I finally accepted it this week, Annie, after my last scan. There is no hope. Gracie will be born in six weeks, that's all the time I have left with her.' She cast her eyes over all the boxes and bags in the room. 'She won't ever use the bath, I won't be teaching her how to tell the time on the clock. I don't know what I was doing. Hope can be very cruel. Is there anything here you can use?'

'My darling Palma,' Annie put her arms around her young friend. 'Let me help you deal with this. You can't do it on your own.' She made Palma's shoulder damp from her own teardrops and pulled away and apologised.

'Daft as it sounds, once it had finally sunk in, once I knew for sure . . . I could make plans. I was born needing medical help, Annie. If someone hadn't donated blood, I wouldn't be here today. I have to pay that forward, it's the right thing to do. I'm going to write some letters for the children who will benefit from what she leaves them. I have a recording of her heartbeat and I'll put it in a teddy bear.' The big yellow teddy that Tommy had bought, the first thing her baby 'owned'.

'I'm eating all I can, Annie, because I want to make sure she makes the weight. I don't want all this to be for nothing.'

Annie snapped a tissue out of a box on Palma's coffee table. 'What about counselling? Have you been to see anyone?'

'It's hard,' said Palma. 'There's counselling for bereavement, there's not much to help you prepare for the loss of a baby that's presently living inside you. All the midwives and the doctors have been so kind, though. Dr Jindal has given me his mobile number. I can ring him any time.'

'Does Tommy know all this?' asked Annie.

'God, no. I couldn't drop this on him. This would have broken us up anyway, all that pressure. He'd have resented me in the end, so what would have been the point?'

'You should have told him, Palma, given him the choice.'

'It's complicated. He—' She broke off abruptly. She couldn't tell Annie that Clint had called over that night and how his presence had added to the mess. 'It's for the best.'

'Pack a bag, you're coming home with me,' said Annie. 'You're not staying here by yourself.'

Palma smiled. 'I'm fine, honestly. I'll be in work tomorrow. I need to keep busy during the day.'

'But what about the nights, when you're alone? Please, Palma.'

'That's our time together,' said Palma, hand on her stomach. 'I tell her things, you know, about me, to take with her when she goes. Do you believe in heaven, Annie? I don't know if I do anymore. But just in case, I talk to her, read her stories. I tell her what her life would have been like and all the things we'd have done together.' *We would have bought wellingtons and splashed in mud, picked bluebells, grown tomatoes. We'd have had a cat called Cinders, a black one. I'd have brushed your hair until it shone. We'd have read books about folks in Faraway Trees and chocolate factories. I'd have taught you how to make the best spaghetti Bolognese in the world.*

'I can't leave you,' said Annie, unable to wipe the tears as fast as they were flowing. 'Please stay with us for a night at least.'

'Go home to Joe and I'll see you in the morning.' Palma smiled, gave Annie a gentle kiss on her cheek. 'Thank you for being my friend,' she said. 'I may need you in a few weeks. But for now, I'm okay.'

'I – we – will be there for you, Palma.'

She had to stop off twice on the way home because she couldn't drive for the tears clouding her eyes.

Chapter 59

When Annie had returned from seeing Palma, Joe had wept too. He couldn't imagine anything so cruel. He had thought not being able to have a child the biggest slap nature could administer, but to conceive and then to discover that by giving birth you consigned your baby to die was worse. Annie had said they should tell Tommy. Joe had advised her to think about that. They couldn't put themselves in Palma's shoes, he said. They shouldn't be the ones to over-rule her decision to not burden him with this. Sleep on it, he'd said and though Annie had slept on it, she was still of the same mind.

They'd told Iris when she got into the car the next morn-ing. For all her age, Iris was a woman with a great heart and she was a loving mother who'd had a miscarriage at seven months sixty years ago.

'Poor lass,' she'd said and foraged in her bag for a tissue.

Palma was waiting for them in her usual spot.

'You okay, love?' asked Annie, then cursed herself for the most inane question in the universe. People said it to her

when her mum had died because they didn't know what
words to use. Tragedy robbed everyone of the ability to say
the right thing, even the most eloquent. Shakespeare himself
would have come out with, 'You all right?'

Joe didn't know what to say either. He couldn't do his
usual jokey '*Buon giorno*, isn't it a beautiful day today, Palma,'
whether it was thunderstorms or sunshine.

Iris, despite the size of her mouth, could be surprisingly
sensitive. She put her hand on Palma's, gave it a squeeze, and
said, 'You'll be all right love. In time.'

*

Effin lay back on Alex's couch and closed his eyes. Davy's
words had been circling in his head all night, like a flock of
confused crows. He didn't have any real enemies that he knew
of. The only person he didn't get on with – and he could see
the irony in it – was MacDuff himself, who'd warned him
that he'd got an enemy. He knew the Welsh and the Poles
both took in good humour what he said to them. He had
about as much chance of putting the fear of God into any
of them as he did getting an Olympic gold medal for pole-
vaulting. He paid them more than fair money – no funny
business or fuss; if they needed any time off for the dentist or
family business, it was theirs. He felt he was a good boss. And
a good husband, a good father, good uncle and a good friend.

'So, Effin,' began Alex in her rich, pleasant voice, like his
favourite honeyed lamb made audible, 'you felt as if you were
in crisis? Can we start from there?'

'I've been booted off my job until I get sorted out.' The

words stung the inside of his mouth as he said them and he had to clear his throat before continuing. 'My boss's heavily pregnant wife fell down a hole that I'd mended and I *had* mended it. I tested it out, a herd of pregnant elephants with wild rhinos on their backs could have danced on that after a full meal and it would have held. But the next day, it was as if I'd never touched it. I don't think I'm losing my memory, I think I'm going mad, except—' He stopped and squeezed the bridge of his nose with his finger and thumb.

'Except . . . ?' coaxed Alex.

'I had a visitor. A hagg— . . . a bloke I can't stand who works for me. He said that he'd checked one of the jobs I done and it was right, I had done it. He thinks someone broke it again to make me look bad. He thinks I have an . . . *enemy.* ' He weighted the word with dry amusement.

'It sounds as if you don't like this man.'

'I don't. He's a tw— . . . a . . . I don't know what he is, but I don't like him.'

'Describe him.'

'He's tall, younger than me, beard, a Scot. Military.' He wrinkled up his nose on the last word.

'Military?' Alex questioned, picking up on the distaste.

'Ex-military, actually.'

'Decorated?'

'He's got a swanky medal, so I believe.'

Effin heard Alex's pen move on paper. He could imagine what she was writing: that he was jealous. Of a haggis.

'Is it the Scot part or the military connection that bothers you most?'

Effin quickly protested. 'Neither, I'm not racist or . . . or jobist. It's just him. His personality. He thinks everyone likes him.'

'And do they?'

'Well . . . probably.'

Scribble, scribble, scribble.

'Does he remind you of anyone?'

There was a definite pause before Effin answered, 'Yes.'

'Someone from your past.'

'Yes.'

'Who is it?'

'Stu Stirling.' The name came out in a hiss.

'A soldier?'

'He became a pilot. With medals,' said Effin through gritted teeth.

'And how did you and Stu know each other?'

'We all went to school together. Carmarthen Boys Primary and Senior.'

'A close friend?' asked Alex.

'Yes. There were three of us. Tight. Me and Stu and Brynn Evans.'

'Tell me about the friendship.'

'We were like brothers. We did everything together; walk to school, go to chapel, play out. Until . . . until I starting spending some time with a girl I'd known for a lot of years. Angharad. Beautiful girl. I liked her from the off, but she was a bit younger than me. It was just kids' stuff, but when we got older . . . I knew she was for me.'

He suspected that Alex had noted how his features had softened.

'And how did your friends take that?'

'They weren't happy. But I enjoyed being with her. Always at me they were. "Come out with us, Effin. Plenty of time for girls later. Break it off."'

'And did you?'

Effin bowed his head. 'I was stupid. I was nearly twenty but stupid. And I broke it off with Angharad and she was heartbroken. And guess what, bloody Stu Stirling asked her out. And she accepted. She told me later that she'd done it to teach me a lesson, but I didn't know that at the time.'

'You must have felt very betrayed.'

'I was fuc— ... furious. Then she broke it off with him and he ran off to the forces. Sent me a letter saying he was ashamed and that's why he'd left. Hoped I could forgive him in time.'

'Did you ever meet him again?'

'No I bloody didn't. After what he did to my An— ... what he did to me.'

'You were going to say, "After what he did to my Angharad." What did he do to her?'

'I don't know. She wouldn't talk about it. To this day. She left home and went to work in Llanelli and a few months later, I got a job working there for a builder and our paths crossed again and they never uncrossed.'

'Tell me about your parents.'

'Oh, they were lovely people. Really kind. My dad could be a bit strict but he loved us. Used to take me and my brother fishing early on Sunday mornings. Then Mam would cook what we'd caught for tea and we'd have it with fresh bread she'd make every weekend. My four grandparents lived either side of us. Really happy childhood I had. They had us late, me and my brother. All of them gone now, except me.' There was a tremor in his voice that Alex picked up on.

'All?'

'All of them. My younger brother died in a car crash. Left a lovely wife and a beautiful daughter. She's like our own. She works up at Winterworld with me. I keep an eye on her.'

'You're protective over the women in your life?'

'I am. After Stu attacked my Angharad – at least, that's what I think happened. He was someone I trusted. Someone I'd known all my life. And because she refuses to talk about any of it, my brain thinks it must have been the worst thing I can think of that he did to her.'

'What about Brynn? Do you keep in touch?'

'When I moved away, we didn't see each other much again. He lived on a farm and when his dad died, it was up to him to take it over. There was always that pressure on him, you know. He never enjoyed farming, he was so clever with his hands. My dad taught him loads of things but he was a natural at constructing and he could teach my dad a thing or two in the end. The pair of us could have built a house from the foundations up at fifteen. I thought he'd sell up but he resigned himself to his fate. He really wanted to be a pilot, in fact it was him talking about it that made Stu want to do it, but Brynn had a funny eye. His dad hit him, dislodged something inside. Horrible man he was. Brynn spent more time at our house than he did his.'

'Now, our session is coming to a close today, Effin,' said Alex gently.

'*Duw,* that's gone fast.'

'Well, as I explained on the phone I had to squeeze you in between appointments this morning so it was a shorter than usual meeting, but I think we're making great progress.'

'Are we?'

'Yes, we are. It might help if you revisit those early days in your head. Try and remember anything you'd put away, locked away because you didn't want to face it.'

'There's nothing,' Effin answered immediately.

'Think of your mind as a loft,' said Alex. 'You've switched on the light and seen a lot of familiar things of not much interest. But then you go in closer. Open boxes, move objects and there are things underneath and inside that you'd forgotten about, each one with a host of memories attached.'

'Loft, eh?' said Effin, pulling himself to his feet. He felt lighter than when he came in. Talking did help. The doctor was right. He might not be so quick to scoff again about psycho bollocks.

'Book in with the receptionist, Effin. I think another session soon would be best,' said Alex, her pen going ten to the dozen in her notepad, and Effin would have loved to have been a fly sitting on her shoulder and seen what it was she was writing.

Chapter 60

The Sunflower Café wasn't much to look at on the outside but push open the door and you could immediately feel the cheery welcome the place afforded. Bright yellow walls and blue curtains patterned with sunflowers, the interior really took a theme and ran with it.

Annie was the last to arrive at Di's birthday do on the Saturday afternoon. 'Sorry, couldn't find a parking space,' she said to the others, already seated at a long rectangular table and drinking tea.

'Park your bum,' shouted Di. 'We were only killing time until you arrived. Lee's paid for this so you won't need to get your purse out. No Palma?'

'No, she couldn't make it,' said Annie. Palma had said to tell them why she wasn't there and why she wouldn't be going to another Christmas Pudding Club. Whilst she had still had hope dancing in her heart, she had felt part of them, carried along with them as they journeyed together towards motherhood; but now, she felt cut adrift, she'd be a spectre at their feast and she didn't want to dampen their joy. Annie had cried for her every one of the three days since Palma had told her. Not in front of her, but thinking about her at night, talking to the baby that was living inside her, reading to her, bathing with her . . . Annie's heart broke for her.

'We've ordered the full shebang,' said Cheryl, budging up so Annie could sit down on the bench.

'I have never had a cream tea before,' said Fil. 'Am I in for a nice experience?'

'Bloody marvellous,' said Di. 'And this place does the best. Pass that teapot down to Annie, Cheryl.'

'I haven't had a pot of tea in ages,' said Annie.

'It's magic, I tell you. I totally lost the taste for it, but I'm really enjoying this today,' said Eve.

'How's the leg?' asked Annie.

'Bit sore, but I'll live. I'm more upset about my dress. Whopping great unmendable rip in it, and it was my favourite.'

The waitress came over with two stands full of sand-wiches, cakes and scones and then returned a minute later with two more, then jam and deep bowls of clotted cream.

'Oh, my.' Fil's huge eyes opened wide as dinner plates. 'This is a banquet.'

'Don't you have these in Nigeria?' asked Cheryl.

'I think some of the big hotels in Lagos have started to put them on the menu but I haven't been. I have had an African afternoon tea in London, though.' She reached over for an egg mayo finger and the ecstasy showed on her face when she bit down. 'It wasn't like this.'

'She makes these scones with clotted cream, does Patricia

the owner,' said Di, nodding at a woman behind the counter. 'And she gives you butter. I can't stand an afternoon tea where they don't give you butter for your scones.'

'Greedy bugger,' snorted Raychel.

'Which do you put on first, cream or jam?' asked Fil.

'Depends on the weather,' replied Di.

'The weather?' asked Fil.

'Aye, whether the cream's nearest to my hand or the jam.'

Fil threw back her head and laughed. The joke wasn't that funny, but the atmosphere was sunny and warm and hitting her jolly spot.

'I'm so glad I met you all,' said Di. 'It's been a roller-coaster this nine months but I wouldn't have missed it for the world.'

'You and your husband seemed loved up on Wednesday,' said Eve.

'Aye, it's better than ever now. We're all friends again. We're having Daniel as one of the godparents. He's going out with my sister now and she's one of the godmothers, so it seemed right. Mend bridges and all that. Pretend it never happened. Sweep it right under the carpet.' She sighed then and smiled. 'But I've got some cracking memories of a night in with a bottle of olive oil and a can of squirty cream.'

Eve and Annie exchanged telling glances and then quickly broke eye contact before they started giggling.

Annie joined in the banter but half her mind was on Palma. She should be here with them, talking about epidurals and Di's love life and laughing until it hurt about breathing techniques and worrying about poohing when pushing whilst the tea flowed and the scones were buttered. She left it to chance whether or not she should say something – if she was meant to, the opportunity would present itself, she thought. If not, she was meant to stay quiet.

When the third refill of tea arrived, Di said, 'If we wrap up some of these scones, Annie, can you take them to Palma? Might make her slap on a bit of weight and look as fat as the rest of us.'

Annie took a deep strengthening breath. Chance had turned up and given her the opening. 'There's something wrong with Palma's baby. That's why she's stopped coming to the meetings.' She had their full attention.

'What's up,' said Raychel. 'Not serious, is it?'

So Annie told them.

*

Effin's mind had spent a lot of time in the past since the meeting with his counsellor. He'd only admitted to one person how much Stu's treachery had hurt him. As much as he had loved his little brother, Stu had been as close as his twin. When Stu and Angharad had their brief interlude, Effin had got really drunk one night on his dad's home-made cider and ending up kissing Mai Jones whom Brynn was sweet on. Brynn thought it was hilarious. He said Effin had saved her from him because she was obviously a whore, which he thought was a bit harsh. He'd felt so guilty that he'd broken down and cried on Brynn's shoulder, said it was no excuse for what he did with Mai but he was missing Stu and Angharad terribly. Brynn had said that he was best rid of both of them.

The therapist had made Effin realise that he was – and he

hardly dared admit this even to himself, because it shamed him – jealous of Davy MacDuff, who reminded him of Stu Stirling with his cocky confidence and likeability. That's why he didn't want to take to MacDuff and he certainly didn't believe he had his back. It was easier to suppose that MacDuff was double-bluffing him, making him think he was on his side when really it was him sabotaging his life. He couldn't trust him because it would be like trusting Stu all over again.

But still, it set him off wondering again what had really happened between Stu and Angharad to make him join the forces and her to run off to Llanelli.

*

There wasn't a dry eye around the table when Annie had finished telling them about Palma, about her houseful of toys and baby clothes, about the letters she was going to write to children who would have a life because her daughter had lost hers. Because she was going through it all alone.

'And that's why she broke up with the boxer? Because she didn't want to burden him with it all?' asked Eve.

'That's why.'

'And he doesn't know any of this?' asked Cheryl, black rivers of mascara running down her face.

'He doesn't. I wanted to tell him but Joe said I shouldn't interfere,' said Annie.

'Fuck that for a lark. He needs to be told,' said Di, her neck jutting in and out with indignation like an angry emu.

'I'm torn, Di. It's Palma's secret to tell, not anyone else's, that's what my brain is saying to me, anyway. But my heart . . .' She didn't need to finish off the sentence for it to be clear which of those two organs had the louder voice.

Di had no inner contradictions. 'If he had accepted this baby as his own, then surely he should have the right to know?'

'I agree with Di,' said Fil. 'Palma has the whole facts, Tommy doesn't have any. He should be given the information – the truth.'

'I have to agree too,' said Eve, putting her hand on her very pronounced mound of stomach. 'Just imagine if Tommy is giving her space until the baby's born and then hoping they'll get back together and be a family. Palma hasn't given him the option to prepare for losing the baby.'

'Don't shoot me, but I'm throwing this in the mix,' said Raychel. 'What if Tommy finds out and it doesn't bother him and he thinks that he's had a lucky break?'

'Then at least he's made a decision based on all the facts,' said Fil.

'And she's well rid because he's a bleeding twat,' added Di.

'I don't think he is a twat though,' said Annie. 'I think he adored her.'

'Someone has to tell him,' said Di. 'And I know who.'

The others waited for her to enlighten them.

'Us,' said Di.

There was a bomb of silence dropped in their midst and then Annie spoke.

'You're absolutely right, Di. I felt it from the off.'

'Mother's intuition,' said Di. 'I bet he'll be at the gym now,' she went on, taking her phone out of her bag. 'He's bound to be. He's got a big fight coming up so he'll be training every day, twice a day.'

'How come you're so clued up?' asked Eve, forcing a fork down her tight bandage to scratch an itch on her leg.

'My dad was a boxer. His nose went from one side of his face to the other but he loved it. He was never quite good enough to win the belts so he became a professional heavyweight sparring partner. He worked with some of the greats: Joe Bugner, Henry Cooper, Marvin Hagler. There's not much you can tell me about the boxing world that I don't already know.'

She keyed in a number on her phone and lifted it to her ear. 'Lee, what's the name of the gym where Tommy Tanner trains? Get the number for me and ring me back.'

'Are we really doing this now?' said Fil, grinning wildly with excitement.

'Why not? It'll be open, so if he isn't there, we'll go back tomorrow when he will be. And we'll keep going back until we get hold of him.'

Di's phone rang and she answered it whilst scrabbling in her bag for a pen and pulling a napkin towards her. 'Got it. Ta love,' she said. 'Come on, girls. We've got some fate to interfere with.'

Chapter 61

Di pushed open the front doors of Tanners Boxing Gym and the other five heavily pregnant women followed, waddling like ducks behind the big momma. The gym was a massive space and well stocked with equipment. One man was skipping, two were punching bags, one sitting down lacing up a red boot. There were two elevated boxing rings, one empty, the other with two men sparring and two more at one corner watching, guiding.

'Excuse me,' shouted Di and all activity stopped. 'Can you tell me where we can find Tommy Tanner?'

'Wahayyy,' red boot guy cried. The men outside the ring shared a joke the women couldn't hear and the two boxers inside it chuckled. The heavier-set of the corner men walked over. 'Can I help you, ladies?' He had his arms wide as if preparing to shepherd them out.

'He thinks we're fans,' said Raychel. 'He's going to fob us off with a signed photo.'

'We want a word with Tommy Tanner, please,' said Di.

'He's a bit busy, I'm afraid. Can't be interrupted. Can I help?'

'No,' said Annie, jumping in and not leaving it all to Di. 'Only Tommy can.'

'Sorry, ladies,' said the man, smile slipping a little now.

'That's him, isn't it?' said Di, pointing at one of the boxers in the ring. 'I recognise his legs.'

'You're fans, I presume?' said shepherd-arms.

'I went to his last fight when he battered the shit out of Brendan Barlow in the eighth round. I know this one coming up against Frank Harsh is even more important because it's all right winning a title but it's defending it successfully that will mark him as a champion. Harsh's got a long reach so you'll be using sparring partners with the same. Harsh is also better at distance so Tommy will have to get into his personal space and hit him close up, won't he?' Di gave him a triumphant smile that said *so don't class me as a pregnant bimbo.*

'You know your stuff,' said shepherd-arms, blowing the air out of an impressed pair of cheeks.

'We're not here for a pair of autographed shorts for a raffle prize is my point,' Di went on.

'We *need* to speak to Tommy,' said Cheryl, stepping forward.

'Unless you tell me what it's about—'

'It's Tommy's business only. Private,' said Annie, cutting him off.

The man scratched his nose, appealed to Di. 'Look, you've just said how important—'

'What is it?' shouted Tommy, who had stopped his sparring.

'Nothing,' said shepherd-arms.

'Tommy Tanner, come 'ere,' Di yelled and her voice carried right to the back of the gym. 'It's you we want. You'll thank us.'

Tommy shrugged at his partner in the ring, climbed out of it and came towards them. He was grinning, clearly amused.

'A private word with you, if you don't mind, Tommy,' said Di, giving shepherd-arms a losing-patience look of her own.

'G'is a minute, Neil,' said Tommy. Shepherd-arms, or Neil as he was now, melted away from the group and went back to the ring, shaking his head. 'What's up, girls?' He was expecting a request to sign a photo for a dad's birthday or a charity request for a couple of tickets, but not what came next.

'We're friends of Palma's,' said Annie.

Tommy's smile slid from his face. 'Is she all right?'

'I'm afraid she isn't, lad. Not at all,' said Di.

*

Tommy didn't even knock. He walked straight into Palma's house and stood on the doormat taking the whole room in: the stacks of boxes, the bags taking up every inch of space. And Palma, sitting at the table, trying to marry receipts to goods. Her eyes registered him but the information was on a delay to her brain because it was seconds before she said his name. And the same amount of time lapsed for him before he said hers.

He was still in his shorts and boxing boots. He'd grabbed his half-zip from the locker along with his car keys and driven here on automatic pilot. He hadn't known what to expect when he walked in, he wasn't even sure he had understood properly what the six pregnant women were telling him. All he knew for certain was that he had to get over to her, without thought getting in the way.

He didn't know what to say to her. It had been two months since he'd seen her and in that time he'd tried to convince himself that he didn't care but his eyes swallowed her up and relayed the sight of her down to his heart which wanted to leap out of his chest to her.

'Is it true? About the baby?' he said, his voice robbed of strength.

'Who told you?' she said, her own voice barely above the volume of her breath.

'Your mates came to the gym. I've just left them there. They're all pregnant.'

Palma's head turned towards the receipt in her hand. Boots. Three packets of Pampers for newborns and some baby lotion. She couldn't get a refund on the lotion because she'd spread it on her hands, closed her eyes and sniffed and imagined she was holding a baby with the same gentle perfume.

'I don't know what they told you.'

'That she can't ... that once you ... once you give birth ...' He gulped. It felt as if his throat had swelled up.

Palma bit her lip. 'Yes, it's true. There's no hope. I thought there might have been, which is why ...' Her eyes swept across all the baby items. 'I went a bit loopy for a while, Tom.'

He took a step towards her. 'I'm not surprised.'

She turned her head away from him, tried to wipe her eyes without him seeing her but his were locked on her.

'Your friends said you didn't want me to know.'

'I didn't,' she replied. She couldn't look at him. Someone else she couldn't have, like a cruel illusion.

'Why, though? I don't get it.' Her friends had told him why, but he didn't buy it. There had to be more to it than that because it was plain stupid.

'I didn't want you bogged down with all this. A baby that wasn't yours and then . . .'

'You know I bonded with her as well. I wanted to see her when she came out. I'd have still looked after her . . . and you. Will she be born . . . al . . . alive?'

'I'm going into hospital when I'm thirty-eight weeks for a caesarean. If I go to term she might not be. I can hold her till she goes,' said Palma, tears sliding down her face. 'She won't be in any pain. Then they'll take her and . . . they can use some of her to help other babies so they don't die.'

'Why can't another baby help ours,' said Tommy, his face creased up now. If he'd been in the gym, he'd have hit something hard.

'Because she's been unlucky. There's nothing more to it than that. It's nothing I've done, nothing I haven't done. She's just not destined for this world.'

Slowly, Tommy cleared the space remaining between them.

'Let me be part of the life she will have, however short it is,' he said. 'Let me be part of yours. I've been so fucking miserable, Palms.'

His arms opened and closed around her and Palma's heart both rejoiced and broke a little more at the same time.

Chapter 62

Davy, Jacques and Eve were all having Sunday lunch together at the old farmhouse, Jacques was cooking. Eve was tired now and Jacques thought she should stay at home and rest from now on but she'd protested. At least she had until that morning. Now she wasn't sure she had more than another week left in her to work in an office. What she really wanted to do was scrub things: cupboards, skirting boards, wash bedding, generally *fettle* and she thought that this coming week might be her last at Winterworld for a while.

Arfon had taken over the running of things from Effin. Jacques hadn't been as forgiving of Effin as Eve had and he was glad the man was out of his sight. If only he'd taken time off after the cigarette incident his wife wouldn't be hobbling around on crutches, and he didn't even want to let his mind dwell on how much worse it could have been.

'How's the new boss?' Eve asked Davy, passing him what was left in the bowl of roast potatoes. She couldn't get enough of them at the moment. She had started to wonder if it was possible to overdose on them. She was eating for twelve, never mind two.

'Well, I don't get as many dirty looks or haggis comments now,' Davy grinned.

'Oh yes, he used to call you a haggis, didn't he?' Eve laughed and then reined it in when Jacques shot her a look. Nothing to do with Effin tickled any part of his funny bone presently.

Davy waved the haggis comment away with a flap of his hand, 'It's the way he is. No one takes offence. Although, I must admit, he has a strange charm he doesn't even know he possesses, which is why he gets away with so much. I've punched men for far less.'

'I like Effin and I am worried about him,' said Eve. Jacques humphed.

'I went to see him last Wednesday,' said Davy, spearing a floret of broccoli.

'Whatever for?' asked Jacques. 'I would have thought you'd be the last person he wanted turning up on his doorstep.'

'Obviously I am, but I've been doing some investigative work on his behalf.'

'Investigative work?' questioned Jacques.

'I don't think Effin's losing his memory or his mind. I think someone is trying to discredit him.'

'You've been watching too many conspiracy films,' said Jacques, reaching for the apple sauce.

'I'll tell you why I think that, shall I?' said Davy. 'I watch people. And what I see of Effin is someone really conscientious and bloody good at what he does, and then suddenly he's making mistakes all over the shop. Big ones. Dangerous ones. But something didn't quite ring right about the whole thing so, when I got the chance to do it without being seen, I checked on a job he'd finished – the snow machines, as it happened. He made a big show of insisting he did them because, he said, everyone else was useless. So, in other words, everybody knew that he'd mended them by himself. I stayed behind that same night and I tested those machines and they were working fine. But in the morning, they weren't again. They were tampered with, I'm sure of it. The security cameras are always going down and I will bet you anything the ones at fault are coincidentally in areas where Effin was working.'

Jacques listened to what he had to say, out of respect, but what Davy was implying was ridiculous.

'Why would anyone do that? And, of course, who?'

'I don't know. But they got what they wanted, Effin trashed and out of the way. I presume he was the target because, as far as I know, no one else has been going around complaining that the work they've done has suddenly become undone. Effin said that when he was going home after mending the hole in the grotto floor, he thought he heard someone moving about.'

'Well, he would, wouldn't—' Jacques bit off what he'd been going to say, because this was Davy he was talking to and Davy did not make wild assumptions.

'Given a wee bit more time, I could have got to the bottom of it, but there won't be any more incidents, I reckon,' Davy went on. 'Someone very clever and very quick is behind this.'

'And sly, if it's true,' added Eve. She didn't want to think anyone could be so hateful. Then again, she didn't want to believe that Effin was losing it. She knew he would be out of his head with worry about what had happened to her in the grotto.

'Stanislaw used to work in the circus, didn't he?' mused Jacques. 'On the trapeze. Then again, Arfon's got the top job now. And he's like a spider monkey on roofs. Mik and Effin had that massive disagreement at the beginning of the year. Or what about—'

'Oh stop, Jacques,' said Eve. 'These people have worked with Effin for a long time. If you start to look at who has had an argument with Effin, everyone has; but they're like his family.'

'And your Granny Ferrell is your family,' Jacques threw back at her. 'Talk about the enemy within.'

It was a bullseye point. Eve's Granny Ferrell was the most wicked old bag on the planet. She made the Antichrist look like Anne of Green Gables.

Davy cut into his giant Yorkshire pudding.

'I'll keep my eyes and ears open because I want to solve this. Arfon knows what he's doing but he isn't half as much fun to work for.'

'If anyone else but you had come up with this theory, Davy, I'd have laughed it out of town,' said Jacques. But they hadn't – Davy MacDuff had.

Chapter 63

Joe had been furious at what Annie and the Christmas Pudding Club women had done on Saturday, turning up en masse at Tommy's gym.

'We made a unanimous decision to interfere,' returned Annie. 'And it must have worked because he ran straight out.'

'How do you know he went to see Palma?' Joe said, throwing his hands up in an expansive Italian gesture. 'He might have gone to throw himself off a cliff.'

'Oh Joe, it was obvious,' said Annie.

'How do you know you haven't done more harm than good? *Per amor del cielo,* Annie, how do you know they are together now?'

Annie didn't, not for sure, but she had a feeling that they were.

Then, Joe's opinion made her start to doubt herself and she had a terrible night's sleep. She rang Palma's mobile on Sunday mid-morning to check on her.

'I'm fine, Annie.' She was quiet but there was a lift in her voice. 'Thank you for what you and the girls did yesterday. It was kind of you all.'

'Did . . . did you see Tommy?' She hardly dared ask.

'Yes, he came to see me. And we talked. A lot.'

Annie held her breath.

'I should have told him. I shouldn't have cut him out of what was happening. I know that now. He was lovely to me,' Palma went on.

'Is he there with you?' Annie unconsciously crossed her fingers.

'No, sadly not.'

Annie's heart fell two feet. 'I'm so sorry, love.'

'Not at the moment, I mean. He's training. We have to work out how to combine what is happening for us both, but somehow we'll manage it.'

Annie hiccupped and a pocket of tears tumbled out.

'I've been so worried about you,' she said.

Joe was gesticulating madly behind her.

'Joe's asking if you'd like to come up and have Sunday lunch with us,' Annie said.

'Tell him thank you, and I'll see him tomorrow at work, but I'm packing up the stuff I bought. Most of it is returnable.'

'Can I come and help you?'

'I'm on the last leg. Tommy's taking the parcels to the post office tomorrow. The things I can't send back I'll donate to the hospital. Their gym supports the premature baby unit up there.'

The sooner all that stuff was out of the way the better, thought Annie. What a terrible situation, to be surrounded by items bought for a baby that could never use them.

'Annie, thank you for caring,' said Palma. 'Thank you for the job, the support, the coffee, the laughs – everything. I'm not sure where I would have been if it hadn't been for your kindness.'

Annie started to well up again. 'You know where we are if you need us,' she said.

'If you can pick me up as usual tomorrow that would be grand,' said Palma. 'I think it might be my last week, Annie. I need to . . . get ready.'

'Of course, sweetheart. Whatever you want. You decide. I'll see you tomorrow. If you change your mind, it's fine.'

'Annie,' Palma said again, as Annie was about to end the call.

'Yes, love?'

'I heard that it was definitely the people I told you about who caught up with Clint O'Gowan. They would have done it sooner rather than later, they wouldn't have let it go.' It was common knowledge in Dodley what had happened, although no one would be so foolish as to grass on the Webbs. Tommy had told her in confidence what he'd heard from reliable sources, but it wouldn't have been right to keep it from Annie. 'He made it too easy for them, turning up on their patch. It was never going to end up any other way for him. One single punch and he was gone, Annie. I thought you might want to know that.'

Annie did. She would tell Joe and it would be the last time Clint O'Gowan's name would ever be mentioned in their lives. His memory would be as dead as the rest of him.

The *Daily Trumpet* would like to take this opportunity to point out that the notice last week in 'Lost and Found' should not have read that 'Mrs Burton had not seen her Siamese twins for three days, last sighted on Dodley Road', but her Siamese cat. Fu Manchu has since returned after being found in the neighbour's garage.

Chapter 64

'I just need you to tell me what is going on in my head,' said Effin as he reclined on Alex Cousins's sofa first thing that Monday morning. 'I need an end to all this.'

'Did you try visualising the loft?' she asked.

'Yes, I did. I peeled back covers and tried to open boxes and all of them were bloody locked,' sighed Effin.

'The key is somewhere in that loft, Effin. You will find it.'

Effin doubted her. All that airy-fairy nonsense wasn't him at all, but he'd been desperate enough to give it a go. It had worked to a certain extent because he had seen himself climbing into a loft that looked suspiciously like the one that stood over the row of the three cottages where his parents and grandparents lived in in Carmarthen. He'd pulled the dusty covers back from objects in the corners and seen plenty of memories that he'd forgotten were there: the best man at his wedding, Will Davies, spilling red wine all over Angharad's mother's pale cream outfit; his dog Hywel dying; Angharad screaming at him when their first-born was crowning. She made that girl on *The Exorcist* look like Shirley Temple. And lots of other inconsequential rubbish that made him wonder why his brain had hung on to it. The significant stuff was all in the big black sealed trunk standing cocky and proud in the middle of the floor space and no amount of bashing it with his dad's old sledgehammer – also in the loft – would release the catch and give him access to its contents.

'Tell me about the most traumatic experiences of your early life,' began Alex. 'Up to the age of twenty-five.'

'My Grandad Williams dying,' said Effin. 'I felt a weight of guilt because I'd always preferred my Grandad Jones and I thought that, now he's passed, he'd know that and it'd hurt him. I don't think he was aware of it when he was alive because I made up the difference with pretence, if you like.'

'Interesting,' said Alex, though Effin didn't know what she meant by that. 'Go on.'

'Hywel, my dog dying, I wept buckets. Stu and Angharad going off together. And . . . *Oh, God.*' He thrust his head into his hands. Alex had to push him to reveal what had triggered his exclamation. 'It was all my fault that Brynn's dad hit him that time and damaged his eye. He'd been told he couldn't go to the visiting fair in case his dad needed him to help with the lambing and I persuaded him to sneak out and his dad lost a sheep and her twin lambs because he wasn't there to help.'

'It wasn't your fault that he did that, Effin.'

'His dad said it was.' Effin wiped his face, hoping Alex wouldn't see the emotional leakage.

'Tell me about some of the happier times that stick in your mind from that period.'

Effin cheered instantly. 'The fishing and bird watching

with my dad, my mother's baking, Angharad and I getting back together again after that ... that Stu incident. We were married the year after. She had a beautiful white dress on and the bridesmaids were all in pink and I had a pink tie on and so did my best man Will, but my dad wasn't going to wear pink for anyone.' He chuckled.

'Your best man Will?' questioned Alex. 'Not Brynn?'

'No,' said Effin. 'We'd started to drift proper apart by then. I did ask him but he wouldn't.' He paused, searching his memory. 'It was lambing season and his dad put his foot down. So I asked Will Davies ...' A picture wandered into his mind of he and Angharad planning the wedding. Will had been her suggestion.

'Tell me a little more about Brynn,' asked Alex. 'When was the last time you saw him?'

'Oh *gad imi weld* ... sorry, let me see, I mean ... must be seven years ago now. I went to his uncle's funeral. Lovely man he was.'

'And before that?'

Effin couldn't recall. Years before was the nearest he could get to it. 'The last time I saw him for a proper chat was just after his wife left him. My, she was beautiful. But then, Brynn could be a charmer. He got this one up the aisle and pregnant before she could find out ...' He stalled and again Alex prompted him, picking up on his reluctance to be disloyal.

'Brynn could be strange with girls,' said Effin. 'His mam had left him and his dad was a control freak. He was desperate for a good woman but his skills weren't very refined so he put on a front, a veneer, if you like. He was very handsome, strong, but girls didn't seem to like him and off they all went after only a short time of knowing him. He should have left his dad and come with me to work away but his dad said if he did that, he'd cut him off without a penny. Anyway, Brynn charmed Lin and they had a son but . . . he didn't treat her with a lot of respect, is what I heard, and so she went off with another fella. Didn't even try and take the baby with her, so Brynn said, which clearly demonstrated what sort of whore she was.' *Hwren*. Brynn had used the word a lot. Every girl that ever rejected him was a whore. It was one of the few words he used in Welsh because he'd taken to speaking English more. He wouldn't speak Welsh at his uncle's funeral. He said . . . something about everyone who spoke Welsh being a . . . well, a word beginning with c that not even Effin used.

Hwren.

He hadn't thought much of it at the time. He put it down to sour grapes and saving face, but Brynn got nastier about each girl the more he was dumped.

Alex's voice pulled his thoughts back. 'Did you ever see Brynn's boy?'

Effin's face brightened. 'I did and I do. I sent him presents every birthday and every Christmas. He's working with me at the moment. I had hoped that he and my niece would get together.'

'Why's that?'

Guilt. The word slammed into him from left field and stung him with its harsh impact.

'Because he's a good boy. Very good worker.' Something

was jumping up and down at the side of his head now, waving madly at him to notice it but it was just out of sight. Something about that word *hwren*. Something about a dog. Something horrible.

Alex brought Effin back to his wedding for the rest of the session but there was nothing of significance there. It didn't matter though, because Effin had felt the lock give on that big black box of secrets. He needed a couple more people to help him heave the lid and then, he knew, it would be opened; but he wasn't sure if he could bear to see what was inside it.

Chapter 65

There wasn't even time for a mid-morning coffee break at The Cracker's Yard. Annie and Joe were filling boxes, Palma was on ribbon-tying, Astrid was hand-rolling and Iris was on sticker duty. The Leeds Gentlemen's Club needed an emergency order of five hundred gold crackers with black and gold hats, male-suitable gifts, dirty jokes and the company sticker on the front. International Crackers had let them down at the eleventh hour and they needed – with a capital N – these for their AGM. Name your price, they'd told Joe on the phone. So Joe did, hoping to put them off because they were working to capacity as it was – and they snapped his hand off. And that was why sweat was pouring off every brow that morning.

Annie, despite her bulk now, had buckets of energy so she was savouring it whilst it lasted because she knew it wouldn't go on forever. Securing the Gentlemen's Club's order was a big one for them because it was a countrywide concern with money to burn.

Palma's fingers were flying. If someone didn't know what was going on in the background of her life, they would have seen only a pretty young woman concentrating on the job in hand. Secret concerned glances zipped to her often from her fellow workmates but she seemed okay – at least on the surface. She needed to prepare. None of them could help her do that. How could any of them know what it was like to be her and have to go through what she would have to? Not even Iris pretended she could.

*

As soon as Effin got into his car, he rang Angharad. Coincidentally she had just come down from the loft with the big box of Christmas decorations.

'What the bloody hell are you doing up there? I'll be home soon and I'll get them. You'll break your neck.'

'Effin Williams. I've been getting the decorations in and out of this loft since before I can remember so don't you go all macho on me all of a sudden,' she snapped, then added proudly. 'I was up on the roof shifting the satellite dish last week.'

'Pfft, what the . . . ffffbloodpffft . . . ?' Effin couldn't get his words out. 'That's it. We are moving to a bungalow.'

'I want to move up there to be with you,' said Angharad. 'There's nothing much for me here anymore. The lads have moved away, my family have all passed and I want to see more of you. I love the countryside there. I love it when we go for walks.'

'Really?' He was surprised by that.

'Yes really. We'll talk about it at Christmas, eh?'

How could he tell her that he'd have to leave here? And in disgrace.

'No more climbing.' He had a vision of her falling through the loft hole and had a momentary flash of how mad the Captain must have gone when the Missus had her accident. The one everyone thought he'd caused. He wanted to be at home with Angharad now but if he turned up, she'd know something was wrong and he couldn't tell her what had been happening. He felt ashamed.

'Angharad. I have something to ask you and I want you to tell me honestly.'

'Go on,' she said, warily.

'Why did you and Stu split up?'

'Oh, not this,' said Angharad with a loaded sigh. 'I don't want to—'

'It's important, really important. I can't tell you why but trust me.'

There was a plea in his voice that troubled her so she didn't cut him off, as she had before.

'He felt guilty. He said that as much as he'd fancied me, he'd crossed a line in friendship that shouldn't be crossed and he had to get away.'

'But why did you go to Llanelli? You didn't have to if he'd gone.'

'Because I did, Effin. And that's all I'm saying.'

'Please. What did Stu do to you? Why did you break it off with him?'

'He didn't do anything,' replied Angharad without even having to think about it. 'What do you mean? He broke off with me. I'd have married him.'

'What?' Effin's heart rate went through the roof.

'I'm joking. He was lovely but he wasn't you and that's why we would have split up eventually anyway, but it was him that broke it off, not me. And for the reasons I've just said.'

Effin's blood pressure nudged back down again. 'Didn't you once start to tell me that he'd been a bit rough with you?'

Angharad took a breath. 'Effin . . . I never said that was Stu.'

*

It was Davy MacDuff's turn to find a surprise visitor on his doorstep that evening.

'Well, well, well. To what do I owe this pleasure, Mr Williams,' he said. 'Would you like to come inside? There's no one else in so we can have exclusive use of the lounge.'

Effin, all too aware that his hospitality was more than he offered Davy, walked meekly past him inside with a thank you.

'Coffee, tea, biscuits?' asked Davy.

'No thank you. I won't be staying. But . . .' he took a deep, fortifying breath, 'I need a favour. A big one. Please.'

'A big yin?' smirked Davy. Quite a turn-up for the books, this contrite, polite Effin. Then he realised that he shouldn't have fun at the man's expense because he must be in a bad way to ask for his assistance. 'Please, take a seat.'

As soon as Davy sat down, his landlady's white cat jumped on his knee and he was infused with a Blofeld-type power rush.

'It's about Cariad,' said Effin.

'You want to be best man at our wedding?' asked Davy. 'Sorry, sorry, couldn't resist.'

Effin started to insult him in Welsh then remembered that Davy knew all the words for 'smug bastard haggis'.

'I'm asking you to betray a confidence,' he said.

He had Davy's interest now. 'Oh?'

'I wouldn't ask if it weren't important. I know Cariad thinks of you as a friend. And she'd tell you things that she wouldn't tell me.' He paused to see Davy's reaction but he remained neutral.

'Go on.'

'Did she say anything about the date she'd had with Dylan to you?'

'No,' said Davy, but his answer was too quick to be believed. 'But if she had, if she wanted *you* to know, she would have told you.'

'I know,' said Effin. 'It would take me an hour to tell you the background and why I'm asking, but it really does matter.'

Davy studied Effin, saw the worry in his eyes, the way he was swallowing nervously.

'Okay, she didn't tell me everything, but enough. Seems your super Dylan couldn't quite believe his charms fell on stony ground. Insisted on paying for everything as if that gave him a right to control how her feelings went. Cariad agreed to go to the cinema on a friends-only basis but Dylan wanted more than to be friends. He thought a wee box of popcorn and a ticket to see a film gave him access all areas and when it didn't, he got a little bit . . . annoyed.'

Effin's spine straightened. 'How annoyed?'

'Oh, nothing physical. I would have jumped in myself if there had been. Just verbal. But names can really wound, can't they, Effin?' He looked at Effin pointedly. 'Cariad made me promise I'd not make it my business and I stood by that, but I warned her that the gloves would be coming off if it happened again. Even if it was only words.'

'What sort of names?' said Effin, trying to will his face not to colour.

'She was a little sketchy on the detail but she did mention one – ironically a name reserved for a woman who gives it away rather than one who isn't prepared to.'

Hwren.

The big black box in his head suddenly sprung open as if the hinges had been greased with melted butter.

Chapter 66

The Christmas Pudding Club was two members down that week. Chloe, on her phone, had a video message from Di. She was in hospital looking knackered and joyful with a baby in the crook of each arm.

'Hello, you fat cows,' it began. 'Meet Jacob and Jesse. Born naturally, with a bit of gas and air and some panting because my fanny more or less spat them out. Three quarters of an hour from start to finish. Do not forget those nipple shield things because my tits are in bits. Breastfeeding might be natural but it chuffing hurts. Hope to see you at the Summer Pudding Club because there's only five weeks and two days before me and Lee can start having sex again. Good luck girls,' and then she blew a kiss.

'I saw her yesterday,' said Chloe. 'She gets this week's prize for most profanities in one minute. She had a surprisingly easy time of it, I have to say.'

'And Fil had a little girl this morning,' said Sharon. 'Ayo. Absolutely beautiful.'

'Like her parents, then,' said Raychel.

'You know about Palma, presumably?' Cheryl asked the midwives. They nodded with sad smiles.

'I think she's incredibly brave,' said Raychel. 'We don't know how lucky we are, do we?'

Annie had tried to put herself in Palma's shoes a few times, questioning what she would have done had she had the same devastating news. Probably the same, she concluded, but what a dark place to be.

'She and Tommy are back together at least,' Annie told them.

'Oh, thank goodness,' said Cheryl. 'I was afraid to ask. John said we were mad to do what we did.'

'Ben said much the same,' said Raychel.

'I won't even begin to tell you the torrent of Italian that I got from Joe,' said Annie, 'but then they didn't have our pregnancy sensitivities. I swear they make us borderline psychic.'

'We did good,' said Cheryl.

'Yep,' replied Annie, 'we certainly did.'

There was no special topic of discussion that session, just a general chit-chat over drinks and cake, because Cheryl had been baking. Her nesting had mainly taken the form of cooking and she'd made lots of meals and frozen them for the next weeks.

'I feel quite sad that one by one we will be dropping off. Like that book by Agatha Christie,' said Raychel with a smiling sigh.

'Except we won't be murdered,' chuckled Eve. 'I'm getting married on the twenty-third in the chapel in Winterworld. You're welcome to come, but I understand if you are otherwise engaged.'

'My, that's cutting it fine,' said Chloe.

'All the babies in my family have been at least ten days late,' replied Eve.

'Babies do not stick to patterns, Eve.' Chloe wagged her finger.

'My intuition is telling me that I'll be okay, though, so I'm going with that.' Her intuition was also telling her that the wedding was going to be loop the flipping loop. She had a vision of herself drifting down the aisle in a dress not dissimilar to Alice's in *The Vicar of Dibley*. But then again, she had left it up to Jacques, and so she couldn't complain if that's what happened.

As they walked out to their cars, the four remaining Christmas Pudding Club women hugged each other, in case they weren't at the next meeting. None of them were going to the Aqua Mama classes now that their little group had broken up; it wasn't the same. Plus the ordeal of getting dressed afterwards was now too much. There were *Good luck*s all round. Cheryl's due date was coming up next and she was ready for it, she said. She was sick of the heartburn and of trying to roll herself out of bed in the middle of the night to go to the toilet. She was sick of having to use ten pillows in strategic places to be comfortable at night and sick of not being able to put her own socks on.

'John says the first thing that comes out of my mouth when the baby is born should be its name,' she laughed.

'I look forward to being at Bloody-Hell-That-Hurt's christening, then,' said Annie. She felt ridiculously tearful as she zapped open the car to drive home.

Chapter 67

'*Shwmai, Dylan bach*? Sorry, we'll speak English, I know you prefer it. How are you? Come in, come in,' said Effin, herding Dylan into his cottage.

'I'm good, Effin, how are you?' said Dylan. He handed over a four-pack of beer.

'Very kind of you, boy. Sit down. We might as well have one of these now. I made a stew for tea. Not as good as Angharad's but not bad. Less honey, more cider in my sauce.'

Dylan sat at the table and opened two of the cans. He really was a good-looking boy, thought Effin. Dark, thick hair like his dad but tall and fine-featured like his mam. He hoped he wasn't too late.

'How've you been then?' asked Dylan as Effin got the plates out of the oven using a big glove.

'Very down, as you can imagine. Very down,' said Effin. 'I think I'm going to leave here because I've probably lost the contract at Winterworld so my business will inevitably fold. I don't know what I'm going to do. I can't carry on working because I can't be trusted. That's what everyone thinks.'

He noted how Dylan shifted awkwardly in his seat.

'I'll have to sell my house. I'll buy a much smaller one and take early retirement. I was going to settle up here with Angharad. We sit on the terrace at night and watch the birds hovering over the fields. Buzzards, sparrowhawks, barn owls . . . and the kestrels. They're my favourite. Remind me of my childhood. My dad took all us boys on my birthday to see *Kes* at the pictures, including your dad. I cried my bloody eyes out. You ever seen it?'

'We read the book at school.'

'He came from round here, Barry Hines, the man who wrote the story. The place didn't look much on the film, so never thought I'd fall in love with Yorkshire when I came here. Never thought I'd make it my home, but I have. I've read the book too, many times. *A Kestrel for a Knave*. I still get upset at the ending: all that hope and potential in one boy completely destroyed by a total and utter twat. A family member too. You'd think he'd have his back, wouldn't you? His fate could have been so different.

'"See that boy Billy Casper, he had a passion," my dad told me. "He found something that made his heart want to beat. We all need a passion in life."' Effin laughed. 'I don't know if he was trying to make me feel better but he told me he knew what happened to Billy Casper after the film had ended. That his passion never left him and he grew up and escaped from his past and ran a sanctuary for injured birds and was happy. "Never let your past dictate your future," he'd say.' Effin gave a long, sad outward breath. 'I don't know what my future will be now. Go back to Wales. Might buy myself a dog.'

Dylan ran the edge of a finger across the bottom of his nose. 'That's not good,' he said and bowed his head.

'Your dad got a dog these days, Dylan?'

'A couple of sheepdogs.'

Effin started to ladle stew onto the plates. 'I remember a dog his dad – your grandad – had. A female sheepdog. He called it *Hwren*. Horrible name. Do you know what *Hwren* means in English?'

'Er, no,' said Dylan. His neck was blotchy-red, Effin noticed.

'It means whore. He used to kick it. I once told him to stop and he slapped me. And my dad went round to the farm and he had your grandad up against the wall. Told him if he ever touched me or that dog again, he'd find himself drowned in his own sheep dip. Very handy with his fists, your grandad. Although, funnily enough, he only ever used them on those much weaker than himself. That's how your dad ended up nearly blind in one eye, did you know that?' He put a plate down in front of Dylan and smiled. 'Help yourself to bread. It's from the bakery just down the road from here.'

'It's . . . it's nice bread.' Dylan was uncomfortable and Effin was glad. He wasn't uncomfortable enough yet, though. Not by half.

'Miserable old fucker, your grandad,' Effin went on, noting that Dylan hadn't answered him. 'Bitter man and a proper control freak. Eat up, boy.'

Dylan took a piece of bread and dipped it into the gravy with the reticence of one who suspected it might be poisoned.

'Your dad wanted to be an aircraft pilot, did you know?'

'Dad?' echoed Dylan, with the tone of one who didn't.

'Our friend Stu became one, but because of your dad's eye, he couldn't. What he could do was things with his hands! He was so clever, could turn them to anything. You've got his gift, I see that, you can do it all, can't you – electrics, brickwork, joinery and you love it, don't you, Dylan?'

'Yes. Yes, I do.'

'Brynn did too. Got so much enjoyment out of making things. He should have been my partner in the building trade. I did ask him, but he stayed on the farm and he had to hear about Stu being a hero in the air and see me making a success of myself, all because your grandad said he'd cut him off without a penny if he didn't. It would have done your dad good to get away without a penny because he'd have made his money with his talent. But instead he stayed and your grandad filled him up with his bitterness. Taught him wrong. Taught him that women were nasty things not to be trusted or respected. Every one of them a *hwren* – a whore.'

Dylan's eyes were fully down on the stew and the redness had crept up to his cheeks now.

Effin took a spoonful of the stew, ate it, drank some beer.

'Stu the pilot used to go out with my Angharad before he suddenly went off to join the forces. I always thought he'd run off in shame because he'd done something nasty to her. In fact, as I started to remember, it was your dad that told me.' That recollection had been in the big black box. He'd been too quick to believe what Brynn had told him and pin it on Stu because he was still smarting from him and Angharad getting together. He'd have forgiven Stu in time because they were only young, silly boys – and he loved him. But he would never forgive him for hurting Angharad, and Brynn knew that. So Brynn had seen to it that the door on their friendship was not only closed, but bolted and then cemented over. It had been Brynn, though, who'd come on roughly to Angharad and then begged her not to say anything. It was a one-off, he'd said to her. He wasn't like that. And because Angharad felt guilty about the part she'd played in splitting up the friendship between Stu and Effin, she didn't want to play a part again in splitting up Effin and Brynn; so she'd kept quiet but the sight of Brynn made her feel sick and she'd moved away.

'No, Dad never told me anything about anyone called Stu,' said Dylan.

'Your mam was a lovely woman,' said Effin, taking some bread.

'Dad said she was a . . .' Dylan started quickly then shut up.

'I bet he did. Well let me tell you, Lin was a beautiful girl. One day you should find out her side of the story because there will be one and it'll be very different to the one Brynn told you. I used to love your dad but he changed into someone I don't know and it took me a long time to realise that. He'd have been a different man had he told his father to go fuck himself. Life would have straightened him out, but instead he stayed on the farm doing a job he loathed and got all twisted up.'

Dylan stood up, scraping the chair across the floor as he did so. 'I think I'd better go, Effin.'

'You sit down and you eat and you listen,' snarled Effin,

wearing an expression that no one had ever dared to defy. Dylan sat, picked up his spoon again.

'Every woman was a whore to your grandad and that's how it became with your father. He despised himself for staying on that farm but the brain is wonderful at self-preservation. Your dad needed to hate something else instead of himself to survive the hell he was in. So he hated Stu for following his dreams and he hated me for following mine and being happy and finding a nice woman, one that moved away because she couldn't stand the mere sight of him. He hated your mother for rejecting him. It was always someone else's fault, never his, that's how he excused himself for all the mistakes he made, never taking any of the respon-sibility himself. I bet he did tell you about his eye, Dylan. And . . . and I bet he blamed me, before the man who made his skull shake with the blow he delivered, didn't he?' Dylan was unmistakably suffering from subtext overload and the redness had reached his scalp by now, but Effin wasn't letting up. 'His dad might have had him trapped for the first half of his life but he trapped himself for the second. You're a clever boy, Dylan. Whose idea was it to ask if you could work with me, eh? And why – so you could level the playing field for your dad? Pay me back for having the gall to be content and successful? Make me look like an incompetent idiot so I'd end up as miserable as him?'

Effin noticed a splash in Dylan's stew.

'You going back to the farm to live? Same bitter, lonely life as your grandad and your dad? Seeing all your friends go off into the world and meet girls but you'll stay and get older and more unfulfilled and angrier at life and label every woman a whore before she's even looked at you?'

Another splash. Dylan swiping at his cheek.

'That where your passion lies, Dylan? Sheep farming?'

A silent slow shake of the head. *No.*

'The world is your oyster, Dylan *bach*. My late brother had a saying: *Don't look down at a little moon in a muddy puddle, when you can look up and see it hanging there bright and huge in the sky.* I love my kids, Dylan. And I know your dad loves you, but when you raise a child, there comes a time when you have to let them fly off. It's wrong to load their wings with your own baggage so they're forced to stay in the coop.'

Effin raised his eyebrows at himself in surprise. He had no idea where that had come from. Another open box in the loft, no doubt.

Dylan's spoon fell from his grip and clattered into his dish and his head fell into his hands.

'I don't know how to put it right,' he said. 'I'm so sorry, Effin.'

A tidal wave of relief washed over Effin. He hadn't been going loco, he'd got the nail bang on the head. Sherlock Holmes, fucking move over. He had the urge to do his first ever fist pump.

'Write a letter to the Captain. I'll smooth it over somehow if you tell him the park sign was your fault and the hole, because I'm not losing my reputation for anything or anyone . . .'

'I never thought it would cause anyone to get hurt,' said Dylan, openly sobbing now.

'Dylan, boy, the park sign falling off could have killed someone and you could have made the Missus lose her baby.

You ought to thank your lucky stars that didn't happen. And I'll have that set of keys you've got. Borrow mine and have a set cut did you?'

Dylan blew out a long breath. He didn't have to confirm it.

'You could use your skills for good not bad, boy.'

'I'll have to leave, won't I?'

'You will. But I have another unit in France doing up a manor house. Why don't you take up my offer of a job there. There will be more. In fact I don't know what I'm doing in this fucking freezing hole full of grown men walking around dressed as elves and snowmen when I could be there myself.'

'I don't deserve that,' said Dylan. 'I don't know myself anymore.'

'Time to be another self then,' said Effin. 'Time to be the self you should be and not the one anyone else wants you to be.'

Effin caught sight of himself in the long mirror by the door as he saw Dylan out and for a split second he looked just like his dad, which made the corners of his mouth twitch into a smile. He wouldn't go far wrong if he was channelling Goronwy Williams. His hero.

'Effin Williams,' he said to his reflection in the mirror. 'Private detective, philosopher, businessman and, above all, sane and well: I salute you.'

His dad had always said you should be able to look at yourself in a mirror and see a person you were proud of; and if you didn't, change until you could. Goronwy Williams had loaded his son's wings with nothing with flight dust and Effin hoped he'd done the same for his own boys.

Chapter 68

Raychel was out Christmas shopping in Meadowhall with her real aunt and her two adopted ones. Saturdays there were mad enough as it was, and Saturdays near Christmas were manic, but it was the only day on which they were all free.

'This was a bloody stupid idea,' said Janey as they stood in the queue in Debenhams. 'I don't even know why I'm here. I've done all my Christmas shopping online.'

'You're here for our scintillating company,' said Helen. 'And a slap-up lunch.'

'Everywhere will be packed,' grumbled Janey. 'We won't find a table.'

'We will,' said Elizabeth. 'And if we don't we'll drive off to a nice country pub. You okay, love?' She turned to her niece who was stretching whilst holding her back. Raychel was very large now. She looked as if she had nicked half the stock from Debenhams and was hiding it under her dress.

'I'm ready for a sit-down,' she answered.

'Look, we're parked just outside here. It's madness to walk to the other end to the food court. Let's do the country pub option,' suggested Helen.

'I'm good with that,' said Raychel. 'This is the last thing I have to buy.' She held up the burgundy dressing gown and stroked it. 'Ben will look like Noel Coward in this.'

'We'll get him the matching pipe and slippers,' smiled Elizabeth. 'What the hell . . .'

She moved backwards, feeling the splash on her legs.

'Oh, shit.' Raychel stood stock-still, not knowing what to do. Water was pooling around her feet.

'Your waters have broken,' said Helen.

'I am going to die with embarrassment,' said Raychel.

People in the queue had moved back so Raychel was totally exposed to what felt like a hundred pair of eyes. 'I can't move,' she said.

'No need to gawp, love,' said Janey, to the woman with the gob-dropped-open stare. 'She's pregnant and her waters have broken. It's all perfectly natural. Nothing to see here.'

'I've been standing in this queue for ten minutes, I'm not leaving until I've bought this dressing gown,' said Raychel stubbornly.

Elizabeth grabbed it from her hands and pushed in front of a man heading for the end till.

'Sorry, emergency. Could you ring this through so my niece can go and give birth, please?'

'Nothing like getting your priorities right,' said Helen, linking Raychel's arm and leading her off out of the store, her shoes squelching horribly with every step.

'A mop might be an idea,' Elizabeth said to the till assistant, scooping up the dressing gown and then moaning Janey-style at no one in particular, 'Once upon a time you used to get your shopping free if your waters broke. Now they don't even give you a carrier bag.'

They shoehorned Raychel into the back of Janey's SUV.

'I'm going to wet your seat,' she hollered.

'Sod the seat. Let's just get you to hospital.'

'I'll ring Ben,' said Raychel, but she dropped her bag on the floor of the car and let loose a few choice expletives.

'What's this pillock doing?' barked Janey, as the Mercedes in front decided to block her exit. She couldn't reverse because she had a Renault up her backside.

'*I'll* ring Ben,' said Elizabeth. 'Where is he?'

'Working in Leeds,' said Raychel. Her stomach was rock hard with Braxton Hicks contractions except they'd never hurt before and now they were becoming uncomfortable.

Janey blasted her horn at the Mercedes, which had absolutely no effect.

'It's waiting for that parking space,' Elizabeth growled. 'They're like gold dust at this time of year so it's not going to budge until it's got it.'

'I think my contractions might have started,' said Raychel.

'Right,' said Janey, pulling on the handbrake, throwing off her seat belt, snatching something from the recess in the dash and opening the door. 'I'm going to shift this bell-end in front if I have to shove the car out of the way myself.' She marched – battle-ready – over to the driver's window of the Mercedes and rapped hard on the glass.

The middle-aged woman on the other side of it tried to ignore her.

'Police,' said Janey, flashing an open black wallet with a badge and ID. 'Move this car immediately. You're causing an obstruction and we have a medical emergency.'

The Mercedes immediately started edging forwards and Janey swaggered back to the car, grinning.

'What the hell did you say?' asked Helen.

'I held this up,' she passed the wallet to her. 'Our Robert's toy police warrant card.'

'Impersonating a police officer, Janey Hobson, you naughty girl.'

'Right, we're off. Finally.'

In the back Raychel laughed. 'These are definitely not Braxton Hicks. Ohhhhh my.'

'Remember your breathing,' said Elizabeth. 'In through your nose, out through your mouth. Make a sound, that helps.'

'Fuuuuuuuuuuuuuck. Yes, you're right, it does.'

'Christmas sodding traffic, spare me,' said Janey. 'Roads full of idiots. Why isn't he moving when the lights are at green?' Janey blasted her horn again, which had the desired effect.

Elizabeth started speaking into her mobile. 'Ben, it's Elizabeth. Raychel's in labour ... Just leaving Meadowhall, we're on our way to the hospital, so meet you there. I'll ring again when we land ... yes, I'll tell her.' She turned to Raychel. 'He says hang on until he arrives.'

'Shove a cork in it,' chortled Janey.

'Ooooooooooo,' said Raychel.

'Good girl. You're doing fine.'

'They're doable. I'm okay,' Raychel assured them.

They were on the motorway, at last. The other carriage-way was gridlocked but their side was fairly clear.

'Do you remember when we all turned up for your first, Hels,' said Elizabeth as she rubbed Raychel's back. 'You were pulling on the gas and air pipe and you'd thrown your TENS machine in the corner of the room.'

'I remember. It was totally useless,' said Helen, clicking her tongue.

'All I can say is that you must have liked gas and air, seeing as you went back three more times,' said Janey.

'Mother Nature makes you forget the bad bits, otherwise no one would ever have more than one,' replied Helen.

'It didn't make me forget, that's why I only had one,' said Janey, overtaking a Porsche. 'If I get a speeding ticket, I'm splitting it four ways.'

'I saw my dad that day,' said Helen. 'Clear as anything. Standing at the side of me telling me to push. You can tell me it was the pethidine but I know he was there.' She smiled.

'I'm seeing nothing but stars and floating things. I think my eyeballs have burst,' said Raychel. 'Here comes another one.' And she took in a very deep breath.

'I couldn't go back to being fertile,' said Janey with a sniff. 'Now passing junction thirty-six, one more to go. These days I spend all the money I don't need for tampons on gin.'

'Yeah, 'cos the menopause is really plain sailing,' tutted Helen.

'I never thought I'd be old enough to go through menopause,' said Janey. 'I thought it was something old women did.'

'It is,' Elizabeth threw back. 'We are ancient old bags.'

'I know one thing, I'm getting too old for these dramas,'
said Janey.

'Are we nearly there?' asked Raychel after a few minutes
trying to remember what sort of breathing she should be
doing. She kept confusing her birthday cake candles with
her thin threads.

'We are, love. I'm signalling to come off as we speak.'

Elizabeth's phone rang. 'Hello ... Ben ... just coming
off at thirty-seven, where are ... bloody hell, are you
in Concorde? ... Okay, love, see you in about quarter
of an hour.'

Soggy and in pain, Raychel went straight into the labour
suite and daughter Beth was born forty minutes after her
father arrived. He was not helpful during the breathing
exercises.

Raychel decided they needed to reassess their contracep-
tive choices from now on.

Chapter 69

Effin showed his visitor through to the back of his house and retook his seat on the patio at the side of a blazing fire pit, huge pot of tea on the table in front of him, next to a pair of giant binoculars. He looked like a man at peace with himself. He looked like the Effin Williams Jacques knew.

'This is a hell of a view, Effin.'

'I like to sit here and gaze,' he said. 'And watch the birds of prey hunting for mice in the fields.' He nodded his head towards a kestrel fluttering in the air. 'Very underrated birds. But to watch them properly, you have to become part of the silence ... Cup of tea? Freshly brewed.'

'Thank you, yes, black, please,' said Jacques. He wouldn't have thought that Effin and silence went together, but in this tranquil spot – maybe, just maybe.

'Take a seat. I'll fetch you a mug.'

'I expect you can guess why I'm here,' said Jacques when Effin had returned from the kitchen.

'I can.'

'I . . . we . . . are dumbstruck. Effin, I should never have doubted you. I should have done more invest—'

'Shhh now,' Effin poured out a tea and set it on the table.

Jacques pulled a letter out of his pocket. 'I could take this to the police.'

'Can I see?'

Jacques handed it over. Dylan had admitted trying to trash Effin's reputation and given a profuse apology for what had happened with the grotto floor. The letter was very heartfelt and honest.

'What on earth was going on there?' asked Jacques.

'A lot of history, that's what. I'll tell you about it one day when you've got a spare year,' said Effin. He let out a long breath. 'Hardest work of your life, raising a child. You and the Missus will realise that when yours arrives. It's like owning a fresh piece of sculptor's clay and it can be made into something beautiful with time and care or it can be twisted into a mess. But if it's the wrong shape and you get to it before it's fired, it can be remodelled, put straight.' Effin smiled. 'Once that baby comes out you're bound to it all your life. You'll worry about it and want the best for it. It's the ultimate lesson in selflessness is parenthood, if you do it right – and mark my words, you'll get so much wrong. But you'll do a much better job of it if you put your child before yourself, because if you do it the other way round, it's not fair.'

'And did you untwist that piece of clay?' asked Jacques, taking a sip from the tea.

'I hope so,' said Effin, passing the letter back to Jacques, who put it on the fire and watched the flames eat the words.

Chapter 70

Hello Little One

    I'm the mum of a baby girl who sadly died just after she was born. She wasn't able to live herself because she was too poorly but she could help to make other children well. You are one of those very special children.

    It broke my heart to lose her but to know that my Gracie could be there for you mends it more than you could ever imagine. To me, it means that her time in this world, short as it was, was a truly wonderful gift.

    Life is precious and amazing - so be happy. Leap high, laugh lots, dance, sing loudly, kick footballs into goals, love - most of all enjoy.

    With my fondest and best wishes for a long and beautiful future.

    Gracie's mum.

It was hard writing letters to children Palma didn't know, children that might benefit from the death of her own baby. It was hard writing them when she could feel Gracie shifting – *living* – inside her.

As soon as Tommy had gone for his morning run, she had taken out her new writing pad and hand-written seven letters. It had to be done. She slid the folded sheets into their envelopes, sealed them and then she put them in her hospital bag which was waiting at the side of the door. She hadn't thought she had any tears left inside her until today, but she had. Oceans of them. All she could hope for was that Gracie was born at the weight the doctors needed so she could live through others who needed her. Palma could just about bear it if that happened.

Chapter 71

The last Christmas Pudding Club meeting consisted of the two midwives, Cheryl, Annie and Eve.

'Raychel had a little girl – Beth,' announced Cheryl, showing them the photographic proof on her phone. 'Seven pounds five ounces. I popped up to see her. Her waters broke in Debenhams apparently. She gushed over six pairs of Christmas shoppers' shoes.'

They all had a good laugh at that.

'I've had such a brilliant time at these meetings,' said Annie. 'Do thank Dr Gilhooley for his brainchild.'

'You'll meet up at clinics and mother-and-baby groups. Then there's Aqua Babies with Shona if you fancied it,' said Sharon. 'It's not goodbye, just *au revoir*.'

'Now that will be great fun if Fil goes,' said Annie.

'Have you all stopped working now?' asked Chloe.

'I flipping have,' replied Cheryl.

'Me too,' said Eve. 'I'm too tired and fat to even say the word *work*. I may possibly be too fat to walk down the aisle, and don't tell my husband this, but I think I've had better ideas than to renew my vows when I was nine months pregnant.'

'I'm still working,' said Annie. 'We have an intensive week of giving it all we have to finish off the rest of our orders then we are closing down until January.'

'How's Palma, Annie?' asked Eve.

'I'm seeing her on Saturday for coffee,' said Annie. 'She sounds okay on the phone but . . . you know.'

The nods of the others said that they did.

'We have these for you all,' said Sharon, reaching in her bag and bringing out a blue foolscap file. 'I was hoping to give them out to everyone on the last meeting, but I'll send them on to the others. Not sure what I should do about Palma's.'

She presented the three pregnant ladies with an A4 envelope each. Annie opened hers up and pulled out the piece of card inside.

This is to certify that Annie Pandoro was a member of the Christmas Pudding Club. Chloe, Sharon and Dr Gilhooley had signed it at the bottom next to a cartoon of a woman whose pregnant stomach was a Christmas pudding.

'It's a silly daft thing I know,' said Chloe and excused herself because she was filling up.

'I think it's lovely,' said Annie. 'Let me take Palma's and I'll see how the land lies when I'm with her.'

Her new-found mother's intuition would guide her to do the right thing, she was sure of it. It hadn't let her down so far.

*

On Saturday Joe picked Palma up from the house on Rainbow Lane because he wouldn't allow Annie to drive anymore.
Plus she couldn't fit comfortably behind the steering wheel.

Palma had a discernible bump now and her face had
plumped too but she was so very pale. Her usually bright blue
eyes were dull and though she smiled at them as she walked
out to the car, sadness seemed etched into her face.

'I hope I don't say the wrong thing,' said Annie.

'Just be yourself,' advised Joe. 'Be the Annie she knows.'

Palma opened the car door and clambered into the back.

'Hello love,' said Annie, cutting herself off before she said,
Are you all right?

'Hello, you two,' she replied.

'Is Tommy training?' asked Joe.

'Twice a day. Runs in the morning, spars at night.'

'I might have a few pounds on him to win,' said Joe, pulling out onto the High Street.

'You should, Joe. He's determined.'

Annie opened up her mouth to speak and then closed it
again. She'd been about to ask if she'd heard about Raychel.
Everything that was in her head was related to babies.

'How are the Christmas Pudding lot? Anyone had their
babies yet?' Palma asked eventually, before the silence
choked them all.

'Erm . . . well . . . everyone now but me and Cheryl and Eve.'

'What did they have?'

'Di had twin boys, Fil had a girl and Raychel had a girl.'
She didn't go into the detail she would have had it been Eve
in the car.

'Oh, that's lovely.'

'Here we are, ladies. I'll pick you up in an hour and a half, okay?' said Joe, drawing up in front of the Sunflower Café.

'Bloody hell, Annie, you're massive,' laughed Palma when they got out. She put her hand on Annie's stomach; the baby kicked, as if affronted. Annie reciprocated without thinking, placed her hand on top of Palma's mound, felt the baby stir.

'Into the café,' ordered Palma, seeing Annie's composure start to crumble. 'Come on.'

They picked a seat in the corner by the window and ordered afternoon tea for two. Annie wasn't even hungry now. It seemed so incongruous having scones and pretending everything was fine whilst underneath the surface was a chaotic torrent of despair.

'I apologise in advance,' said Annie. 'I'm going to say the wrong thing, I know I am.'

'No one knows what to say, Annie. Not even Tommy. So just take off the filter and talk to me normally because normal is what I could really do with at the moment.'

'How are you doing?'

'I'm numb, Annie. And I'm in limbo. I've written some letters to children who might benefit from what Gracie can give them. It was hard but I felt a . . . little bit of light turn on inside me, if that makes any sense. It gave me something to focus on, because I know what it's like to be scared that you'll lose your baby and I know how grateful I'd be if there was something, or someone, that could give her a chance to live.'

'Here you are, ladies. Enjoy. Cream tea for four,' said the waitress, putting down the frame with three tiers of plates.

'I'm trying to eat for four by myself at the moment, even though I don't really have an appetite,' said Palma. 'Gracie has to make the weight.'

'If she doesn't, you must not think you could have done anything different, Palma,' said Annie. She was worried that Palma would be inconsolable if what she had hoped for didn't happen.

'I know, but I'm doing my best. I'm not sure it makes any difference stuffing myself, but anything's worth a try. This looks lovely,' said Palma. 'Tommy's on a very strict diet. A regime. It's a way of life for him: diet, hard training. I think Neil and Jackie worried that I wouldn't be able to tolerate it but I'm happy to stand with him, be his support, be in his corner, as they'd say.' She reached for both a cucumber finger sandwich and a cheese and pickle.

'Have they been all right with you?'

'Yes, very kind. I haven't seen too much of them because I don't want to put them in a situation where they feel awkward. They have no idea what to say to me either so they send me things – a cake, a scarf, books, magazines. It's very touching. I know they care.'

'You're so incredibly brave,' said Annie, coughing away the swell of emotion that was lodged in her throat.

'Trust me, I'm not, Annie. If I couldn't feel her living inside me I'm not sure I wouldn't throw myself off the nearest bridge. You can't wait to meet your baby, I'm trying to delay meeting mine for as long as I can. Every day I have with her is precious. I have to do all the things before she's born that I wish I could do afterwards with her: walk in the park, storytime, singing nursery rhymes. I'm not strong, I'm not brave, I'm just making the best of what time I have. I don't want to cry because she'll feel it and wonder why I'm doing it.'

Annie pushed down the tears prickling the backs of her eyes, annoyed at herself. She was here to be a comfort for Palma, not a blubbering wreck. She pulled the envelope out of her bag.

'We didn't know if you'd want this or not. It's a certificate to say that you were in the Christmas Pudding Club.' She handed it over tentatively. Palma took it out and smiled.

'Yes, I was part of it all. And it's where you and I met so I would like it, thank you. Now, tell me about the world of crackers,' said Palma, reaching across and giving her 'fake Italian' friend's hand a squeeze. 'Tell me about Astrid and Iris and all the daft things that have happened since I went on my leave. And can I come back when . . . well, you know . . .'

'We will welcome you with open arms,' said Annie.

Chapter 72

'Five ... four ... three ...two ... one. And that's the last.' Everyone applauded as Joe put the last cracker in the box and then placed the lid on it.

Every order complete and this last one would be picked up by the courier first thing in the morning, one day ahead of schedule.

Astrid reached for a mince pie. She, along with all the others, was wearing a festive crown.

'Who wrote t'jokes for the Gentlemen's Club crackers?' she asked. 'Zey were disgusting.'

'Palma,' said Joe.

'Oh, bless,' said Astrid. 'Funny, but disgusting. Zey will love 'em.'

'How is she doing?' asked Gill from out of the iPad. 'I can't imagine what she must be feeling.'

'She's got a good man beside her and us as friends and she'll get through it,' said Iris. 'How's your weather?'

'Chilly and wet,' said Gill. 'My girls are coming out at the weekend. I've told them not to bother bringing their bikinis.'

'We've got brilliant sunshine today.' Iris grinned smugly. 'It's like spring, give or take the brass bands everywhere you look. You can't go into any shop without someone singing "Silent Night" at top volume and rattling a tin in yer face.'

'You all right, Annie love?' said Gill, peering into the iPad for a closer look at her old boss.

'Yup. I'm having those Braxton Hicks contractions. My stomach's as tight as a drum top.'

'You look in pain,' said Gill.

'Not pain exactly but I feel like I've got really bad trapped wind. I'm trying not to embarrass myself.'

'Oh, just do a big fart,' said Astrid. 'We promise to excuse you.'

'Not a chance. I don't even fart in front of Joe, never mind the internet.'

'I fart anywhere I feel like it nowadays,' chuckled Iris. 'They expect you to do it at my age. I once cleared a whole aisleful of shoppers in Morrisons with a silent but deadly.'

Annie doubled over. That Braxton Hicks contraction took her breath away. 'Flipping heck,' she cried.

'Annie, Braxton Hicks contractions don't cause that face,' said Gill, watching her via the wonders of FaceTime. 'Are you sure it's not a proper contraction?'

'I don't know,' Annie answered her. 'But if the baby is even thinking about coming today and not letting me have a week off at least, we shall have words.'

Sitting around a table eating mince pies and talking about old ladies farting in supermarkets was not how Annie had imagined her first stage of labour. Gill had told her not to bother going to the hospital yet, but to stay there, talk, do some breathing until the contractions were nearer together. Astrid and Joe busied themselves by shrink-wrapping the final order onto pallets in readiness for the following morning's collection, although Astrid had done most of the work because Joe was starting to flap. She sent him off to make tea; he made four lots. By then, Annie's contractions were fifteen minutes apart.

'It's so exciting,' said Astrid, clapping her hands and reaching for another mince pie.

'I'm having another one, Gill,' groaned Annie. 'Dear God, that hurt.' She took in a long breath, pretended there was a cake in front of her and began to blow out all the candles one by one.

In Spain, Gill checked her watch. 'That's twelve minutes since your last one. Joe, I'd get the car out, lad. Have you got your hospital bag?'

'It's in the boot,' said Annie, blowing out more imaginary candles.

'Okay, okay,' Joe was flustered, looking for something though he couldn't remember what.

'Joe, give me ze unit keys. I vill lock up. What time are ze couriers coming in t'morning?'

'Between eight and nine, Astrid. I don't know where my keys are.'

'They're in your hand, Joe. I can see them from Fuengirola,' said Gill, pointing at them from the screen.

'Joe, go. I vill take Iris home and I vill be here in ze morning.'

Gill blew a kiss. 'Let me know what flavour you have. Good luck, Annie love. I'll leave you all to it.'

'Wages, Joe. Presents for Astrid and Iris. They're in the office,' puffed Annie.

'Everysing can vait,' said Astrid, crooking her arm for Annie to hold onto. 'Everysing but ze babby.'

*

Massimo Vitale Pandoro was born at seven o'clock that evening. He was seven pounds and twelve ounces and had a full head of thick, dark Italian hair. He was the best Christmas present his mother and father could have ever wished for and as big a miracle to them as the birth of the baby Jesus. Probably more so because Mary was years younger and hadn't been through what they had to get a son.

Chapter 73

Three days before Tommy's fight, it was time for Palma to go into hospital. Time for her to say hello and goodbye to her child. Tommy was by her side, gowned, scrubbed up, holding her hand when the doctors performed the caesarean. Palma heard her daughter's cry as she left the sanctuary of her body.

'She's cute as a button,' said a midwife who lifted her straightaway onto the scales, cleaned her up quickly.

'We're filming this for you,' said another.

'And we have a baby girl at five pounds seven ounces,' came a call and it was then that Palma cried. Burst into tears that had no place in any single emotion: happiness, sadness, relief, despair.

'Here's your little Gracie.' Palma felt the beautiful weight of her baby on her chest. She had soft white hair and butter-soft skin. She felt Tommy collapse into himself as he held on to her arm.

The doctors had warned them Gracie might not breathe well as her lungs were underdeveloped, but she did. Taking in the scent of her mother the baby settled, gripped her daddy's finger with her tiny perfect hand.

Tommy took photos on his phone, his hand trembling. He held her and breathed her in and she couldn't have been any more his than she was at that moment. A nurse snipped a lock of Gracie's hair, took a video of them all together, of the baby reaching out, touching her mother's lips.

Gracie drifted away forty minutes later, fell gently into a sleep that she would never wake up from, her last breath against her mother's full, warm breast and a nurse with tears streaming down her face lifted her away after her parents had said their final goodbyes and told her they loved her and would never, ever forget her because she would always be their first-born, their little girl, their Gracie.

Palma heard someone in the room cry, a howl, a keen, an animal sound of pain. She hadn't realised it came from her until she felt the raw ache in her throat.

Chapter 74

The immediate lead-up to her wedding day was bittersweet for Eve because Annie rang to tell her about Palma. Tommy had called round to the house, Palma had asked him to. She wanted Annie to know that Gracie had made the weight and that would help her to cope.

'I'm glad you told me, Annie,' said Eve. 'I've been thinking about her.'

'Life is to be treasured,' said Annie. 'Grab it and run with it and have a lovely wedding day. I'm sorry I can't be with you but I'm sure you understand. I've got my hands full.'

'Totally and utterly,' smiled Eve.

She wasn't convinced she'd sleep the night before the big day. She'd long since given up on having a night where she didn't have to roll out of bed three times at least, but throw in wedding nerves too and she had no chance. But sleep she did and woke up to the sound of Jacques in the shower. He was singing 'Going to the chapel' at full volume. Michael Ball certainly had nothing to worry about.

They'd agreed that they wouldn't do the traditional 'night

before the wedding apart' thing because Jacques wanted to be there with her just in case she went into labour, even though she continued to insist that the baby would be late in arriving.

Eve was off crutches now and only had a small hobble to show for her injury. She hoped that her wedding outfit didn't include skyscraper stilettos. Then again, Auntie Susan was designated dresser and she did favour a sensible heel.

'I'm going to make you a full English breakfast,' said Jacques, slipping on his enormous white dressing gown that made him look like a polar bear.

'I'm too nervous to eat,' said Eve.

'So am I,' said Jacques.

Eve pulled a face. 'You are never too nervous to eat.'

'I know, I lied. I'll see you downstairs in ten minutes.'

She came down to a feast. The table was groaning from the weight of food. Eve surprised herself by making quite an impact on it.

'I am presuming my Auntie Susan hasn't got a tight-fitting dress so I might as well enjoy it whilst I can,' she said, putting away her second bacon buttie.

'I'm looking forward to the wedding night,' said Jacques with a saucy wink.

'Jacques, if your sexual organs come anywhere near mine for the next year, I will cut them off.'

At lunchtime, when her Auntie Susan and Violet arrived, Jacques kissed her and left to go to Effin's cottage – the designated male headquarters. Her Auntie Susan was carrying a hat box bigger than Eve's lounge. The bridal and bridesmaids'

gowns had all been stowed in one of the new nursery ward-
robes without Eve's prior knowledge.

'I hope you like your dress,' said Susan.

'Bit late if she doesn't,' said Eve's cousin Violet. 'Stop worrying, Mum. Start flapping about the flowers. Weren't they
supposed to be here by now?'

'Oh my GOD, where are they?' shrieked Susan, searching
wildly in her handbag for her phone.

'Looking swell, cuz,' said Violet with a grin. 'Bet you
haven't heard that one before.'

'I can't remember you being this "swell" when you
were pregnant,' Eve returned, running her hands over her
baby mound.

'I wasn't. Not even half. I'm not sure the chapel aisle is
going to be wide enough for you.'

'Bloody cheek.'

'Flowers are here, flowers are here,' Auntie Susan zoomed
past them en route to the door.

'Oh, and the make-up and hair woman will be here in
ten minutes, apparently. It's snowing at the other side of
Penistone. White Christmas, here we come.'

'I hope it's not too bad. Effin has to drive some of the
lads to Wales after the wedding. If they don't get home for
Christmas, their wives will kill them – and us.'

'Sprinkle tonight, worse tomorrow,' said Auntie Susan.
'Have you any gin? For my nerves.'

Two hours later, Eve slipped on the gorgeous white velvet
gown that her aunt had designed for her. It had an impressive

train, scalloped neckline and the bell sleeves and white cape were both edged in soft faux-fur. The shoes were low-heeled boots with buttons up the side. There was a bit of a struggle to insert her still slightly swollen damaged foot; Prince Charming wouldn't have accepted it as a perfect fit, but eventually – success. The make-up woman went for subtle on the eyes, with holly-berry red lipstick. She swept up Eve's hair at the sides, securing it with pins with snowflakes on them, then fitted the plain white veil which was edged in the same fur. Violet and Phoebe May Tinker, her very excited goddaughter, were in red ballerina-length dresses with dark green beribboned ballet pumps. They carried posies of red roses and holly and Eve's bouquet was a huge teardrop of white roses and mistletoe.

'So far, so good,' said Eve as she posed for photographs. It was all beautifully tasteful.

Outside, stray snowflakes were bumping into the windows, heralding more to come from the thick blanket of low cloud in the sky.

'Here's the car,' chirruped Auntie Susan.

'Auntie Eve. Uncle Jacques said that he was riding into the chapel on a giant penguin, is he telling the truth?' asked Phoebe. She was ten, and mentally so was Jacques.

'I really wouldn't put it past him, darling,' replied Eve, picking up her dolly bag.

The Silver Ghost Rolls-Royce deposited them at the gates of Winterworld and a uniformed Thomas was waiting for them there at the side of the Nutcracker Express train, which had been decorated with balls of holly and laurel leaves. He saluted with a grin and such gusto he nearly knocked his hat off.

'Welcome aboard, everyone,' he said, looking up at the snow falling in soft large flakes.

'Oh, Auntie Eve, the train is too slow,' grumbled Phoebe. 'I like it best when it goes mad.'

'Trouble is, Phoebe, this train should have six speeds but it only likes two – this one and the one we don't talk about,' said Thomas. 'I'm not sure your Auntie Eve would appreciate it if I hit the accelerator.'

Slowly but surely the train chuffed to the side of the chapel. The snow machines had been working at full throttle for an hour, puffing flakes into the air which danced with those falling from the sky. There was a red carpet leading from the drop-off point to the chapel and six snowmen at either side of it.

'This is where it starts to get like a bad drug trip,' whispered Violet.

'Auntie Eve, what sort of drug trip?' asked Phoebe.

'LSD,' Eve answered her.

'Are they the mind-altering ones?'

'Eve, she's too young to know about stuff like that,' tutted Auntie Susan.

As they walked along the carpet the snowmen raised their umbrellas to form a ceremonial archway. An elf appeared to sprinkle white rose petals where they were to step.

The ladies paused by the chapel door and Auntie Susan adjusted Eve's veil. 'You look gorgeous and no, I didn't invite your Granny Ferrell so you won't get tomatoes thrown at you. Now go marry that man properly.'

Effin was waiting there in a black suit with a mistletoe-patterned tie.

'You look beautiful, radiant, Missus,' he said and crooked his arm for her to take. 'But a word of warning before we go in: if you hear wings, don't flinch because it upsets him.'

'Wings?'

Dum-dum-der-dum-dum-der-dum. The first bars of the wedding march started up and Eve's nerves spiked. They entered the chapel and she saw Jacques waiting for her, wearing a stunning black tailcoat suit, white shirt with a high collar – very Poldarky – and she gasped at how handsome he looked. She really had expected him to be dressed somewhere between Elvis and a giant Robin. The chapel was decorated in twinkly snowflake lights and was full of people she loved: elves, Violet's husband Pav with their little boy Kasper, Myfanwy and her fiancé Robbie, Cariad, Phoebe's family, friends, Welsh lads, Polish lads, Patrick – Auntie Susan's other half – and Davy alongside Jacques. And standing at the front was Nick, in full Father Christmas costume and looking more like the real thing than the real thing ever could.

She began to walk down the aisle, Phoebe sashaying behind her, channelling her inner Kardashian, and dear Violet trying not to stand on her train.

When she drew level with Jacques, he winked at her and her heart kicked. She really was a lucky bitch.

'Dearly beloved, we are gathered here ...' was as far as Nick reached before the pain shot through her and it took everything she had to hold on to that holly-berry smile.

Chapter 75

Jackie wasn't the huggy sort; her compassion showed in the throw she'd had warming on her radiator for when Palma came in and the chicken that was roasting in the oven to feed her. Jackie had picked her up from the hospital on the day of the fight; Palma would stay at hers overnight, until Tommy and Neil came back from London. Jackie made her sit in the oversized rocking chair in the conservatory and put a hot chocolate down on the table at the side of her.

'Thank you for doing this, Jackie,' said Palma. 'I'd have been all right at Tommy's by myself.'

'Like hell you would,' said Jackie, in a tone that didn't entertain such nonsense. 'He'd never have forgiven me for leaving you alone and I wouldn't have forgiven myself. The least I can do is feed you and we can watch the fight together. Our telly is bigger than his anyway. Seventy-inch, his is only sixty-five.'

Jackie gave a little smile and looked down in her cup for a moment, as if taking a cue on what to say from the swirl of cream on the top.

'I'm sorry about what happened to your daughter, love,' she said eventually. 'I know it's nothing like, really, but I lost a baby when Neil and I first started living together. At five months. It was hard. The baby wasn't planned but . . . it hurt us. Tommy doesn't know.' She coughed away the slightest of wobbles in her voice. 'It never leaves you, but eventually you find a place to put your memories so they don't rub your insides raw.' Then she jumped up as if to move away from a draught of cold sadness that was threatening to envelop her. She whipped the throw from the radiator and put it on Palma's lap. 'Anyway, put this over you. Keep you warm.'

Palma was moved by such a simple consideration and said thank you, because gushing would have embarrassed her; less was more with Jackie.

'They told me that Gracie has already saved the life of one neonatal baby so it wasn't all for nothing.' She'd half-drowned in a pool of grief on the first day, but when she'd heard that on the second, the news had placed some solid ground beneath her feet. She'd felt her lungs take their first deep breath since Gracie passed and she'd slept for longer that night than she had in weeks. 'I know I couldn't have kept her, Jackie. My head knows that, my heart just needs to catch up.'

'Tommy's a good lad. He'll look after you . . . oh, talk of the devil and he's sure to appear,' said Jackie, as her mobile phone started playing 'Eye of the Tiger'. She picked it up and began to speak into it. 'Yep . . . she's here . . . course I picked her up . . . She's sitting with me and we're going to watch you kick Frank Harsh's arse, so you better not let us down . . . yep, I will . . .' She handed the phone over to Palma.

Tommy's dear voice conjured up a picture of him so clearly that he could have been standing in front of her.

'Hello sweetheart, how are you? Sorry, I said I wouldn't ask that because it's stupid.'

Palma smiled. No one had the right words. The nurses had smiled a lot and softened their voices when they needed to check her caesarean wound and do their obs. Annie had rung and said that she had no words for her but she and Joe were there if she needed anything; Iris had sent a card with the simple message, 'God Bless'.

'I'm okay, Tom. Are you?'

'I can't wait to see you tomorrow. We'll be driving up as soon as we can.'

'I'll be watching you tonight,' said Palma.

'I've given Jackie a big box of chocolates for you to share whilst I'm on. Don't let her eat them all.'

'I heard that, Tommy Tanner,' Jackie cut in.

'I'm bringing the belt back home for Gracie,' said Tommy.

'You do that,' said Palma. She'd told him to put all his grief in his boxing gloves and he promised her that he would.

'I love you, Palms,' he said, tenderly, emotion thick in his voice. 'I don't know, one minute I was helping you up from the ground in the park, the next you became my everything. How did that happen, eh?' His words found her heart, warmed it, healed it a little. She'd mend with Tommy, she knew. They'd be all the stronger for what had happened. Gracie had bound them together and she would always be part of them both.

'I don't know how. I'm just glad it did.'

Someone shouted to him in the background.

'Go do it for Jackie and Neil – and me and Gracie, Tommy. Do it for all of us.'

'I will. And then I'm going to buy you the biggest diamond I can find, if you'll wear it,' he said.

'I'll wear it,' she said, 'I love you, too and I'm so proud of you, Tom,' and she handed the phone back to Jackie.

After wishing him luck, Jackie put her phone down and sighed. 'Oh, Palma, it must have been hard telling him to go when you needed him the most.'

Palma smiled at her. 'It wasn't, Jackie. He was there for me and now I'm here for him. I'm part of it all. I want him to live out his dream because it's become my dream too.'

Jackie curled her hand into a fist and presented it to Palma who bumped it with her own.

'Welcome to Team Tanner, love. Nice to have you on board,' she said.

Chapter 76

These were contractions, no doubt of that at all.

'You okay?' asked Jacques, bending to her as the congregation sang 'O Little Town of Bethlehem'.

'Yep,' she squeaked. How many verses did that hymn have? It felt as if they'd sung twelve already.

Great. Now liquid was tickling down her legs. Her waters had broken in the chapel and had it not been for the massive frock, Father Christmas, twelve elves, a dozen snowmen et al would have been witness to a pregnant lady waterfall.

The interminable hymn finished at last. Nick asked if anyone had any lawful impediment to this marriage. No one did, but Davy MacDuff coughed as if he might, and there were a few chuckles.

'Do you take this woman ...' began Nick with slow, Santaesque gravitas. *Oh, please hurry up,* thought Eve. He was speaking like an old 45 r.p.m. record being played at thirty-three and a third.

'Do you take this man to ...'

'Yes, yes,' said Eve, interrupting him and then bowing over as another spasm of pain washed through her.

'Darling?'

'I'm okay, Jacques. I'm just ... giving birth. Nick, please, carry on.'

Contractions were supposed to come on gradually, weren't they? These had threatened to split her in half from the off. Her Granny Ferrell had sent a curse for not being invited to the wedding, like Maleficent in *Sleeping Beauty*. It was the only explanation.

Above her head she heard a swoop and locked still as Effin had told her to. Stephen the snowy owl landed perfectly on the altar carrying a ring bag on one foot, which Nick couldn't unhook and Effin had to step forward and do it for him.

Eve tried to say her vows but her brain could only retain one word at a time. *Candles, think birthday candles,* she thought to herself. 'For – *puff* – richer – *puff* – for – *puff* – poorer – *puff* . . .' She ran out of mental candles.

'Auntie Eve, I think you might have wet yourself,' whispered Phoebe from her side.

Eve crunched over, straightened up again and insisted she was fine.

Jacques said his vows at top speed then pushed a beautiful eternity ring onto her finger.

'Inowpronounceyoumanandwifeyoumaykissthebride,' yelled Nick as Jacques picked up his wife, bump, waters and all and ran down the aisle.

*

'Thomas, crank that train up,' ordered Jacques.

'Oh my goodness,' Thomas said, in full headless chicken mode. 'Oh my, my.'

'Thomas, you useless *coc*, full accelerator,' screeched Effin, jumping on the back. 'I'll drive you to the hospital, Missus. It'll be quicker than waiting for an ambulance.'

The Nutcracker Express did what it loved to do best; it sped down the track at full pelt, throwing its passengers from one side to the other then screeched to a halt, depositing them at the gates with whiplash.

Effin ran as fast as he could to unlock them, threw the gate keys back at Thomas, then helped Jacques to load Eve into his vehicle.

Please do not let me give birth on a dust sheet in the back of a builder's van, prayed Eve inwardly as she grabbed onto both her husband's hand and the corner of a bag of cement at the peak of her next contraction.

Chapter 77

Jacques 'Junior' Glace was born in the back of Effin Williams's builder's van on a dust sheet, delivered by his father two traffic lights away from the hospital whilst his mother grabbed onto the corner of a bag of cement to offset the pain of her contractions. He totally ruined his mother's beautiful wedding gown but she would learn to forgive him for that.

Later that night, when Eve had been transferred to a hospital bed and into her big T-shirt nightie kindly dropped off by her Auntie Susan, she lay with her nine pounds nine ounce baby, drunk with milk, sleeping gently on one side of her and her grinning, Poldarky husband on the other.

'That didn't go as planned,' she said with a sigh.

'The modern-day equivalent of a stable and a manger, maybe?' suggested Jacques.

'Oh, it was worse, much worse. I don't think Mary had that amount of stitches either.'

'We missed the buffet. And I had crackers made especially. And the cake – goodness me. Tiramisu-flavoured. With loads of rum.'

'I hope everyone enjoyed it for us,' Eve smiled and looked down at her boy. When it came to a choice between a few sausage rolls or meeting this little – well, huge – guy who had had the cheek to steal the bride's thunder, it really was a no-brainer.

'Effin and the Welsh lads have reached home,' said Jacques, lifting his sleeping son's tiny hand and marvelling at it.

'Oh that's good. We won't have Angharad on the war-path then.'

Jacques sighed contentedly.

'I think that anything you and I do isn't destined to go to plan, but I don't really care.'

'Me neither.' Eve chuckled. 'I think we should consider ourselves married and not try for another renewal, though.'

'What a great idea.' His phone beeped and he pulled it out of his pocket, looked at the screen and smiled.

'Tommy Tanner won. Knockout in the sixth round.'

'Oh, that's brilliant,' said Eve.

'It certainly is. I had twenty pounds on him at five to one. Will you be up and okay to make Christmas dinner on Monday?' Jacques took Eve's hand and kissed the back of it.

'I think it's safe to say that I'll be tucking into hospital food and you'll be eating tiramisu-flavoured wedding cake.'

'No, I'm going up to your Auntie Susan's for turkey with all the trimmings,' said Jacques. 'Obviously I'll come up and visit you afterwards.'

'Thanks a lot. Very kind of you.' Eve feigned indignation.

'She's invited us up for New Year, too. You and our son.'

Our son. They both grinned.

Right on cue, the baby stirred, frowned at this strange world where there was no liquid to bounce around in but warmth and milk and people who stared at him with big curves on their faces.

Eve handed him to Jacques. The man who had rekindled the blown-out flame in her heart. The man who made every day feel like Christmas Day. Where would she have been now had she not met him?

Jacques marvelled at the little boy in the cradle of his large hands. He was the most perfect thing he had ever seen in his life, give or take the sight of Eve walking down the aisle towards him with her green eyes shining. He would never tell her that she had looked like a very happy, very beautiful, very rotund snowwoman.

'I suppose I'll have to grow up now and be sensible,' sighed Jacques.

'Don't you bloody dare,' said his wife.

Daily Trumpet, 24 December

Last night the world of boxing saw Tommy 'TNT' Tanner hold on to his British Welterweight title as he knocked out Londoner Frank Harsh with a crunching left hook in the sixth round in London's O2 arena.

In an emotional speech delivered from the ring, TNT paid tribute to his girlfriend, who watched the fight from home. Their newborn daughter Gracie died three days previously of a rare condition. There was hardly a dry eye in the arena as Tommy said, 'On Wednesday my daughter lost her fight so I was determined to win mine in memory of her.'

The Following Summer

'Well here we all are – together again,' said Di, tilting her head back and letting the sun shine down on her face. Beside her, two red-haired little boys sat in their double buggy, kicking their sturdy legs contentedly and staring at the women lounging on the grass around them as if trying to work out the connection between them. 'Doesn't time fly when you're enjoying yourself?'

'You're cheerful, Di,' said Cheryl, distributing some paper plates in readiness for the sandwich sharing. 'Dare we ask?'

'All good with me,' replied Di. 'Husband back under the thumb where he belongs, Mum and Dad ready to babysit at the drop of a hat, all bits and bobs in full working order and regularly tested. In fact, I'm sure they put an extra stitch in. It's all much better than it was before, if you know what I mean, ladies.'

Fil cackled and set everyone else off.

'You've got your figure back, Di,' said Cheryl, who was plumper than she'd ever been in her life.

'You'll get yours back soon,' Di returned.

Cheryl huffed. 'I don't want mine back, I want Fil's.'

Fil reached for a tupperware box full of egg mayo sandwiches.

'I'm eating like a horse,' she said. 'You won't want my figure in a couple of months.'

'Wanna bet?' said Cheryl.

Palma was standing rocking Massimo. 'What are you feeding this monster, Annie? He's enormous. Enormous.' She gently pinched the baby's full cheeks and he giggled. She had been dreading seeing Annie's and Joe's baby for the first time, but she needn't have worried. There was no outpouring of stagnant grief, only a rush of gladness that two of her favourite people on the planet had been so blessed.

'How's the morning sickness, Palma?' asked Di.

'All done and dusted,' said Palma, restored to her pink-haired magnificence and glowing. 'I tell you, that first day when you realise you've made it through without having to lean over the toilet bowl.' She patted the small growing mound of her stomach. *Let's have our babies when we're young*, said Tommy. *Let's have it all.* They had moved to a bigger house with a conservatory and builders were starting on an Arctic cabin in the garden at the weekend. Tommy wanted her to have her dream too – and he'd gladly share it with her.

'Everything going okay with you, Palma?' Cheryl gave her a hopeful smile.

'So far so good. There's no reason to suggest anything could be wrong but they're keeping a good eye on me just in case. It feels so different to last time.'

Three children now had been given the letters written

by Palma to open when they were older and Palma and Tommy had taken a great deal of comfort from that. And Jackie had been right, the grief had lost its hard edges, the pain had eventually given way to something deep and thankful for the gift of her daughter. Palma wouldn't have missed having Gracie for the world, experiencing that connection, feeling life grow inside her.

'I have my first meeting at the Christmas Pudding Club on Wednesday. Phase two,' Palma went on.

'They won't be as nice as us,' sniffed Di.

'Obviously,' Palma smiled.

'How's the cracker business, Annie?' asked Cheryl.

'Thriving. Thanks to Palma. She's a marvel.'

'Who would ever have thought I'd find my true vocation in the land of crackers?' said Palma, directing the question to Massimo's toothless grinning face.

'And being a boxer's wife,' added Fil. Ayo was asleep in a nest of her lotus-positioned, endless legs.

'Fiancée, not wife yet.' Palma twinkled her diamond at Fil, who pretended to be blinded by it. Fil was pregnant again too. She'd told them that she didn't want to let all those maternity swimming costumes to go to waste.

The heat of the sun seemed to suddenly crank up by degrees and, as if annoyed by that, one of Di's twins scrunched up his face and started to cry.

'Oh, come here Jacob, you mardy bugger,' said Di, unclipping him, lifting him onto her knee and then expertly popping out a boob. Jacob latched on and sucked contentedly.

'I used to have sleep. I've forgotten what the thing is,' she said, looking down at her son. He stared back at her with big blue trusting eyes and she felt something sweet spread inside her, like warmed syrup. She'd loved many people in her life, but this love threw every other sort into shade. It was chuffing terrifying. 'I mean, why do we have 'em? They land like bombs in your life, they change it all. They're heartbreaks in romper suits. I can't look at anything on the TV where kids get hurt. It's like I've had a layer of my skin ripped off and I'm super-sensitive to everything now.'

There was a round of empathetic nods.

'We'll do everything wrong and beat ourselves up and there will be a supermum at school that does everything right. Manages to get her kids to enjoy broccoli and sprouts,' Di went on.

'We will worry about them their whole lives. My mum still rings me from Nigeria. "Ophilia, don't forget the clocks go forward in Britain tonight." "Ophilia, are you eating properly?" Ophilia this, Ophilia that. She even rings to make sure I have put the correct colour bin out. And one day I'm going to turn into her and say the same things to Ayo. And already I know I'm going to drive her mad. But the crazy thing is I finally get it. I can see into my mother's soul.'

'That's like a poem, Fil,' gasped Raychel as she considered Fil's words. Then Di ruined a beautiful moment.

'One of these might grow up to be a serial killer.'

'Di!' Cheryl and Raychel exclaimed together.

'Just saying.'

'Or invent a cure for cancer,' said Fil. 'Or become prime minister.'

'I'm already thinking about mine passing his driving test. I won't sleep when he gets a car,' said Palma with a chuckle. 'And he's not even born.'

'Someone's going to break their hearts,' said Cheryl, with a heavy sigh. 'And we'll have to stand back and let them learn lessons that hurt them. Then they'll leave us with an empty nest.'

'Like we left our parents,' said Annie, in an attempt to redress some balance before they all ran to the nearest doctor demanding Prozac. 'My mum helped me grow a fine pair of strong wings and I flew.' She'd flown straight into Joe Pandoro and they'd made a life out of love, fancy paper and mottos. If Annie did half as well at being a mum as hers had, she'd consider it a result to be proud of.

'But in the meantime we have a few years where we are the centre of their universe,' put in Raychel. 'Believe me, when they seek out your hand for the first time, you'll cry big, fat, happy tears. And then there's the Mothers' Day cards with a daffodil made out of an egg box and the first nativity when they're shepherds with a tea towel on their heads or you're up half the night making a halo out of a wire coat hanger and some tinsel. Precious, precious days. Loads of them. Strap yourselves in for the ride, ladies. We've got ups and downs and round the bends to come.'

'Crackers, that's what it all is, excuse the pun, Annie,' said Di, and Annie smiled because it was like a line stolen from the Gill Johnson book of corn.

'All we can do is our best for them, sprinkle their wings with flying dust, and hope when they take off, they head for the sun,' said Eve, remembering the words that Effin had written on his Happy New Baby card. He'd also said she'd feel that her heart was beating on the outside of her now, and she knew exactly what he meant. A new dimension had been created in her, one that made her as vulnerable as it did powerful, as fearful as it did exhilarated.

'What the hell have we signed up for?' said Cheryl, looking down at her sleeping daughter and knowing that if anyone hurt her, she could easily put them in hospital.

Massimo held out his pudgy arms to Annie and made her spirit soar with a joy so pure it almost hurt. This: the most beautiful, scary and crackers life force of all, complete with tears and laughter, uncertainties and egg-box daffodils – *Motherhood* – was what they'd signed up for.

PUBLIC OUTRAGE AT 'PERFECT' DAILY TRUMPETS

There were a record number of the *Daily Trumpets* produced between 24 December and 2 June with absolutely no errors in them. Sales have reportedly dropped by 37 per cent in the six months sales period. Reader Maureen Baxter from Wath said, 'If we wanted this sort of service, we would be reading another newspaper. The editor wants sacking.'

Editor Alan Robertson has been suspended on full pay whilst an internal review takes place. It is thought he will undergo training and rejoin the team in due course.

Acknowledgements

This book was inside me for years – it *had* to come out. It was like a meeting place for characters from a few other books and they would not lie still. It's a standalone, but if you have read *The Yorkshire Pudding Club, A Summer Fling, White Wedding, The Teashop on the Corner, Here Come the Girls, Afternoon Tea at the Sunflower Café, Sunshine Over Wildflower Cottage, The Queen of Wishful Thinking, Same Time Next Week* and *A Winter Flame* – where you first meet Eve and Jacques – you'll recognise a few crossover characters. I also have a short eBook called *The Barn on Half Moon Hill* should you want to read more about Cariad and Franco and Eve and the lagoon-opening event mentioned in this book. All the money it raises goes to my friend Claire Throssell, whose two children died in a fire started by her ex-husband. If you Google her and read her story, you'll realise why I wrote it for her – from one mother to another.

I have a whole host of thank yous for this book. My wonderful publishers Simon & Schuster and everyone in the team, my magnificent agent Lizzy Kremer who has my back at every turn, the brilliant ED PR who are as essential as Lulu Guinness handbags are in my life. And my copyeditor Sally Partington who I love working with, though I drive her bonkers.

I was brought up in a household that loved boxing. It was one of the things I loved to watch with my dad, and I've managed to find a Other Half who is a proper aficionado, so writing about the sport was always going to happen one day. The character Tommy Tanner is loosely based on Josh Wale, who was the British Bantamweight champion from 2017 to 2018 and a top Barnsley lad. He gave me loads of details about his boxing world for this book, and like Tommy, helps young local kids channel their emotions into positive rather than negative pursuits and to learn discipline through boxing training. He leads by example and shows that through hard work and determination they too can make something of themselves.

Thanks to Zoe Kilner for her sonography advice; her input was invaluable, as was the help given to me by midwife Sue Greenwood. It's important you talk to people in the know to get your research right.

Effin Williams was never meant to grow to this fame. But so many of you love him – and I have grown to love him too. It is always a joy to work with Owen Williams, who translates for me and has become the voice and spirit of Effin. My, how we have laughed over some of those translations.

And thank you to the lovely Geine and Tony Pressendo at www.simplycrackers.co.uk who gave me a crash course in the cracker-selling world. I learned everything from how to get my 'snap' right to the best boxes to use so you don't get your crackers crushed (ouch!). Also, I have found a new outlet for my jokes, because I'll always be a joke writer at heart. I'm indebted to them for being kind enough to help me and now I use their kits so I can roll my own every Christmas. I was so sorry to leave the cracker world behind that I brought it back in *Same Time Next Week*.

Thank you to my website designer, Stu, who is a marvel. I'm his best customer. He doesn't know this, I've put those words in his mouth.

And thank you to the smashing folk at Thirsk Falconry Centre (www.falconrycentre.co.uk) who have become my friends since I first wrote to them and said 'Can I have a crash course in flying your birds please?' I love them and their birds and if you haven't ever been there, you should go because I guarantee it will smash any expectations you have out of the water. It's one of the best experiences you can have with your clothes on.

Thank you to Pete, my beloved Other Half, my best friend – I'm not sure where I would be without him. And my ever-patient friends who put up with me saying I can't do X or Y because I have to edit, even though it's a Saturday night.

The subject of donations is very close to my heart, including blood donations. My father gave blood all his life and in the end he needed blood himself to keep going. And a transfusion saved my own life. Give blood if you can. It is needed and you get free tea and biscuits.

Originally this book was going to be called *The Christmas Pudding Club* because it was a title that harked back to my first book *The Yorkshire Pudding Club*, written from my pregnancy diaries. Now those little babies of mine are fully-grown adults and I have no idea where the years have gone. Motherhood is indeed a fairground ride that makes the biggest roller coasters look like flat lines, but I have loved it. It has thrilled me, scared me, worried me, turned me into a soppy mess and a tigress at times. My apron strings are loosening but they will never quite detach (that won't be allowed). So for my sons, Terence and George, a line that sums it up simply.

My hands have held some precious things in their time, but nothing that could ever hope to equal you.

Love Mum xx

Cracker Jokes

Just as a cracker has to have a no-nonsense snap, the joke has to have a totally nonsense punchline. The punchline isn't always obvious, you may have think about it... and then comes that delicious groan. These are some of my favourites.

What did the drummer call his two daughters?
Anna one, Anna two . . .

Why do bees stay in their hives in winter?
Swarm

What do you call a whale with no pants on?
Free Willy

Why didn't the rabbit join the navy?
Because he wanted to sign up for the hare force

Why was there a baguette in a cage in the local zoo?
Because it was bred in captivity

What's a librarian's favourite vegetable?
Quiet peas

Why did Picasso paint his wife in watercolours?
Because she was no oil painting

Why did the prawn start walking like a crab after taking his medicine?
Side effects

Why don't wasps stay in hotels?
Because they prefer Bee and Bees

Why did the right angle go to the beach?
Because it was ninety degrees

Why didn't the turkey have a pudding after his Christmas dinner?
Because he was stuffed

Which train station do crabs use in London?
Kings Crustacean

What do you call a blue chameleon on a pink cushion?
A rubbish chameleon

What's the difference between a korma and a vindaloo?
Two toilet rolls

What do you call a man who has never told his wife a lie?
A bachelor

What did the horse say when he stepped out of the fridge?
Brrrr

How do you make a slow person fast?
Don't feed him

What do you call a husband who buys you an iron for Christmas?
An ambulance

What's the fastest chocolate in the world?
A Ferrari Rocher

What do you do if the lights are too bright in a Chinese restaurant?
Dim sum

What do you call a goat that doesn't want a job?
Billy Idol

Where's the best place to go to learn how to say hello properly?
Hi school

What sort of owl is best at doing the dishes?
A teet owl

Where's the most fun place in the universe?
The Milky Way-hey!

Who is the patron saint of football?
St Off

Why were the elephants thrown out of the swimming pool?
Because they kept deliberately dropping their trunks

What's got 8 legs and sits on glass?
A black window spider

Why are old people like ancient plaster?
Because their main purpose in life is to keep dropping off

Why couldn't the sheepdog tell the difference between white and black sheep?
Because he was collie-blind

Why shouldn't you buy spiders from shops?
Because they're cheaper on the web

How do you recognise a mother-in-law clock?
It's got a really miserable face

What's the most magical dog in the world?
A labracadabrador

What do you call someone who gets into trouble for something he didn't do?
A plagiarist

Why do birds tweet at dawn?
Because they prefer it to Facebook

What's a pirate's favourite lesson?
Arrrrt

What goes 'ouch ouch ouch ouch ouch ouch ouch ouch'?
An octopus whose trainers are too tight

What's got two grey legs and two brown legs?
An elephant with diarrhoea

When do people say Noel at Christmas?
When they're asked 'is it nice to spend it with all your relatives?'

Why did the Christmas star go to the psychiatrist?
Because he was paranoid he was being followed

What's the difference between a small Christmas bird and a Christmas tree seller?
One is a robin redbreast and the other is a robin git

What sort of music do balloons hate?
Pop music

Why did the man finish with the opera singer?
Because she was all mi mi mi mi mi mi mi

Why do children have middle names?
So they know when they're in really big trouble

How do you stop a skunk from smelling?
Put a peg on his nose

What's green and not heavy?
Light green

Why do mermaids wear seashells?
Because B shells are too small and D shells are too big

What sort of romantic novels do monkeys read?
Mills and Baboons

Why should you never trust staircases?
Because they are always up to something

Why do football stadiums get hot after a match?
Because all the fans leave

Why aren't fish good at sitting exams?
Because they'll never get above sea-level

And the corniest of all . . .

Why did the invisible woman finish with the invisible man?
Because he was nothing to look at

Enjoyed this book? Pre-order Milly's newest novel, *Same Time Next Week*, now!

©2024 David Charles Photography

For news, appearance dates and information about Milly Johnson's other books, visit her at **millyjohnson.co.uk**